The Accidental Honeymoon

A Woke Up Married Rom Com

Wildflower Lane
Book 1

Vivian Wood

Author's Copyright

Acknowledgments

Cover art by Najla Qamber Designs.
Editing by Theresa from Fairy Plotmother.
Proofreading by Angela Schmollinger.

Chapter One

Calla

Wow. This house is *fancy*.

The gray Victorian looms before me, its wraparound porch beckoning like open arms. I did a little internet stalking of this couple before I came. Typical research, just to make sure that the couple requesting a wedding cake aren't serial killers or anything. Now that I'm arriving at their house, though, I realize that being a social media power couple must pay better than I thought.

I take a deep breath, calming my nerves, and then steady the tray of sample cakes balanced precariously in my hands. *This is it, Calla. Your big break into fine event cakes. Don't screw it up.*

I'm so focused on not dropping my precious cargo that I miss a step on the porch stairs. The world tilts sideways as I stumble. My stomach lurches. Panic floods my veins. My heart leaps into my throat. But seconds before disaster can strike, strong hands catch me, stopping both me and the tray from dashing to the ground.

"Whoa there," a deep voice chuckles, "don't fall for me."

I look up into cool blue eyes, blinking as I take in the face of my savior. He has russet brown hair that's just a bit too long, dazzling aqua eyes, a chestnut beard, and a wide, warm grin.

When I open my mouth but am unable to produce any meaningful sounds, he introduces himself. "Sorry. I'm Jay Rustin. I'm the groom."

My face flushes as I realize I'm pressed against the very handsome, very well-known, very soon-to-be-married Jay. *Great first impression, Calla.*

"I-I'm so sorry," I stammer, quickly putting space between us. "Thanks for the save. These cake samples are irreplaceable."

Jay grins, his perfect teeth gleaming. "Happy to help. But I must say, I expected a little more enthusiasm about me catching you. Most women would probably die for a chance to trip directly into my arms."

Is he... flirting with me? No, impossible. He's getting married in three days. This must be how he talks to everyone.

The last thing I want is for a bride to think I'm trying to steal her man, even if that man does happen to look like Prince Charming. This is my first shot at a big wedding. If I do well with this last-minute booking, I can expect more business to follow.

I roll my eyes and fire back with a measured quip, "Well, clearly I'm not most women. I'd rather dazzle you with my baking prowess than perform an acrobatic freefall. Though, believe me, tripping is practically my specialty."

I climb the stairs carefully, watching my feet the whole time. I curse the pair of high heeled black pumps that I am wearing. I am a diehard Converse wearer, but today I decided to borrow pumps and put on a dress and cardigan despite the below-freezing temps. Clearly, I should stick to my navy-colored Chucks and leave the heels for women who are able to walk in them.

"After you, cake master," Jay says, offering the door with an air of unspoken irony.

Holy cow. As I step inside, I can't help but marvel at the picture-perfect interior. Beige walls, gray furniture, warm ivory accents in exactly the right places. Everything looks expensive and well-designed like it's straight out of a home decor magazine. Is this really how the other half lives?

Focus, Calla. You're here on business, not to gawk at how the rich and famous decorate their homes. Still, as Jay leads me through a gorgeous, incredibly comfortable-looking living room and into a kitchen straight out of Architect's Digest, I can't help but wonder what it must be like to live here.

Really nice, is all I can come up with. God, the kitchen is gorgeous. It's got an enormous marble-topped island, bright yellow cabinets, and numerous fragile glass light fixtures hanging overhead that cast a warm glow throughout the room.

I steal a glance as Jay casually checks his watch while shedding his jacket. He probably has a schedule jam-packed with more "important" pursuits.

He wrinkles his nose . "Blake should be here any minute. She's fashionably late by design. You know, to keep us mere mortals guessing." There's no overt punchline. It's delivered flatly, leaving ambiguity as to whether it's meant to be humorous.

"Is this her house, too?"

His lips twitch with humor. "No. In fact, Blake hates this house. She wants us to move into something more modern. I agreed to talk about it a year from now."

"She hates it?" Looking around with wide eyes, I whistle. "That's sad. I'd be pretty pleased if this place was mine."

"I find it cozy." He raises both his hands in a *who knows* gesture. "Blake wants to build a new place. We'll see what happens."

Nodding, I set my tray down carefully on the immaculate kitchen island. "So," I begin with a wry tilt to my tone, "shall we kick off these cake tastings? Starting with the vanilla bean, if that's not too pedestrian for you?"

Jay leans against the counter, his casual posture at odds with the formal surroundings. "Absolutely. Though I have to warn you, I'm a tough critic. It takes a lot to impress me."

I raise an eyebrow, rising to the challenge. "Is that so? Well, prepare to have your taste buds blown away, Mr. Rustin. I didn't expand from cupcakes to wedding cakes to serve you mediocrity on a silver platter."

He gives me a sheepish smile. "That was a fib. I actually know next to nothing about cakes. Do you mind if I take some pictures, though? This wedding is all about squeezing out content to keep the fans interested."

"Of course!" I agree, my words coming out in a rush. "I'm doing this whole wedding for exposure, so take as many photos as you'd like. Just give me a heads up if I'm embarrassing myself."

He smiles as he pulls out his phone. "Will do."

As I begin arranging the samples, I can feel Jay's eyes on me. *Stop it, Calla. He's not checking you out. He's probably just making sure you don't break anything expensive.*

I clear my throat, pushing away the unwelcome thoughts. "This commission means a lot to me. It's my first big wedding cake, and I want everything to be perfect."

Jay is laser-focused on taking pictures of each square of cake. Without looking up, he says, "I'm sure it will be. From what I've heard about You Butter Believe It, you're the best in the city of Greater."

Greater is the small suburb of Atlanta, Georgia that I just moved to a few months ago. It's by far the nicest place I've ever lived, with its mix of shops and restaurants surrounded by concentric rings of idyllic yards with stately Victorian homes.

So far, I *love* it.

Jay's unexpected kindness catches me off guard, though. I duck my head, focusing on cutting perfect slices of each flavor. "That's... thank you. I just hope I can live up to the hype."

"That's what I'm counting on."

"Speaking of hype, how did you end up choosing my bakery? Greater's not exactly short on cake shops. There's Slice Slice Baby, Bake My Breath Away, If It Bakes You Happy..." I pause. "God, what is wrong with all of the bakeries in this town? Our names are all such eye-rolling song title puns."

"I'm sure yours is the best, though." Jay's eyes twinkle mischievously. "Would you believe me if I said it was destiny?"

I snort, unable to help myself. "Not unless destiny smells like buttercream and has a terrible pun for a name."

He chuckles, a warm sound that sends an unexpected flutter through my chest. "Fair enough. Truth is, I don't really eat sweets. But I remember seeing your shop in the town square. Blake and I were having a... discussion after she fired the new cake baker. We were walking through the square and I thought... why not go with You Butter Believe It? Plus, you picked up when I called."

"How romantic," I tease. "If stress and last-minute decisions count as romance."

"It was something, all right," he mutters under his breath.

I finish setting up then check the time. We've been waiting here for fifteen minutes. Ideally, both partners would taste all the cakes while I explained the flavor combinations. However, their wedding is in three days. If I don't get started on their cake soon, it could be disastrous.

"When should we expect Blake?" I check my watch.

He heaves an exaggerated sigh. "That's like asking me to predict the future. There is no way of knowing. She likes to keep people on their toes."

His tone is thick with sarcasm even as he admits it.

That's not great. And he looks so resigned as he says it. *Yikes on trikes.*

"All right," I announce, gesturing to the array of mini cakes. "We can get started, if you're down with that. Let's focus on the vanilla bean first. It's a flavor so classic that it borders on cliché—"

"Actually," Jay interrupts, flashing me a smirk. "There is one flavor I'm particularly interested in. Do you make Berry Gentilly Lace cake?"

"No..." I blink, caught off guard. "Should I have?"

"I don't know. It's the only cake that I really crave, though."

"I... haven't heard of it. But I can definitely look into it! What is it?"

As I make a mental note to research the recipe later, Jay's face lights up.

"It's incredible. I had it when I went to a wedding in New Orleans. It's an almond cake with fresh berries and a whipped mascarpone cream frosting. It's the perfect balance of sweet and tart, as light and fluffy as a cloud." He puts his fingers to his mouth and makes a chef's kiss gesture. "Perfection."

"Sounds like I need to do some research." I make a note on my phone that just says *Berry Gentilly Lace????* I'm only half convinced that the handsome groom is just making things up to mess with me.

"I like that you seem game for the challenge." His lips twitch.

Okay, now I'm like ninety percent certain that Jay is messing with me. I mumble, "Uh huh..."

He flaps a hand at me. "Since you seem to like outside the box thinking... what do you think about chartreuse for wedding decor? Blake hates it, but come on. It's exciting, right?"

"I'm going to have to agree with Blake." I chuckle, delighted. If all my wedding client meetings are like this one, I'm in for a world of fun. "Choose it if you want your guests to feel like they're inside a highlighter."

"That's exactly what I want. I want my wedding to be memorable," Jay says dramatically. "Memorable, outrageous, and worth gold on Instagram."

As we chat, I can't help but notice how easy it is to talk to Jay. He's nothing like I expected a wealthy lifestyle guru to be. He's funny, down-to-earth, and... well, pretty darn cute.

A traitorous thought sneaks in: I wonder if he has any equally charming (and single) brothers? Because I love this guy's charisma. Too bad he's taken.

I quickly shove that idea aside. *Focus, Calla. You're here to bake a cake, not daydream about your client's family tree.*

Suddenly, the kitchen door bursts open with a bang so loud I nearly drop the sample I'm holding. A statuesque blonde in a skin-tight leopard print dress storms in, her eyes narrowing as they flit between Jay and me.

"What's going on here?" she demands, her voice shrill.

Jay's easy smile fades. "Blake, honey, this is Calla. She's our new cake baker."

Blake's perfectly sculpted eyebrows shoot up. "New? What happened to the last one?"

"You fired her, remember?" Jay says gently. "And the one before that."

"I didn't mean for her to take everything so personally!"

Jay frowns. "You told her that she should quit her job because the cake sample she offered was so terrible."

"I was joking." Blake sighs. "She should learn to toughen up."

I feel my cheeks flush as I realize I'm the third baker they've gone through. Great. No pressure or anything. Their wedding is in hours, not weeks.

Blake's gaze locks onto me, scrutinizing. She seems to be making some calculations, though I don't understand what she's measuring. "Well, let's see what you've got then."

I straighten my spine, determined to stay professional. "Of course. I've prepared a variety of flavors for you to sample—"

"I want something that changes color," Blake interrupts. "And edible glitter. Lots of it."

I blink, caught off guard. "I'm sorry. Did you say changes color?"

"Yes, obviously," Blake snaps. She looks down her perfect nose at me. "It needs to be Instagram-worthy. Can you do that or not?"

A cake that can change color? I'm not even sure that such technology exists. I open my mouth to respond, but Jay beats me to it.

"Blake, let's start with tasting the flavors Calla's prepared. We can discuss design elements after." He nudges a cake square toward her and offers her a fork with a sweet smile.

Jeez. I wish I had someone to soft-pedal bad news to me like that. Blake huffs but doesn't argue.

As I present each sample, she nitpicks every detail. Too sweet, too bland, too ordinary. With each criticism, I feel my confidence wavering.

Jay, sensing my discomfort, sneaks a bite of frosting and gives me an encouraging wink. "Delicious," he murmurs.

I can't help but smile, grateful for his support. But as I turn back to Blake, I catch her glaring at our interaction, her jaw clenched tight.

Oh boy, I think. This is going to be a long afternoon.

When I've introduced all but two flavors, Blake's attention seems to wander. She pushes away a slice of cake and puts her fork down with incredible finality, as if she is about to make an announcement. But to my surprise, she instead whirls on Jay. Her eyes are gleaming with a manic intensity.

"Darling," she says, her tone the same as if she were coaxing a skittish horse out of a barn stall. "We should talk social media strategy. How many of your Alto & Ash followers will be watching the live stream?"

I freeze. That certainly wasn't the question I was expecting. And what's this about a live stream? For a wedding?

Jay looks uncomfortable. "I haven't really thought about it."

"We need to maximize engagement!" Blake cuts him off, her voice rising with excitement. "Something jaw-dropping needs to happen every five minutes. Maybe we could have the cake explode glitter at regular intervals?"

I can't help but snort, then quickly try to cover it with a cough. Jay and Blake look at me as if I am somehow intruding on a private conversation. I wish like hell that they'd talk about social media strategy after I leave. My time is money, although not as much as I would guess Jay and Blake's time is worth.

"Sorry, frosting fumes," I mutter. I fan the air, making a face.

Jay catches my eye, a hint of amusement in his expression. "Blake, I'm not sure that's a realistic plan."

"Don't you want this to be the wedding of the century?" Blake demands. "It's like you don't even care about viewership!"

I clear my throat, desperate to steer the conversation back to a more neutral topic. "Speaking of the wedding, I hear it's the talk of Greater. You must be so excited. Only three days away!"

Blake's attention snaps back to me. Her eyes narrow. "What's your point?"

"Well," I say, thinking fast. "Since it's such a big event, why don't we do something really special? I have an idea that might work. Both for the taste and the, uh, visual impact you're looking for." I can feel Jay's curious gaze on me as I continue. "What if we did a multi-tiered cake with different flavors in each layer? And then for the guests, we could do all-white cupcakes. Each will have a surprise flavor inside. It would be like a fun game for your followers. Guessing what's inside! Very Instagrammable."

Blake's expression shifts from skeptical to intrigued. "Hmm. That could work...."

I hold my breath, hoping she'll take the bait. *Please let this work*, I silently plead. I'm not sure my sanity can handle many more color-changing, glitter-exploding demands.

Jay's eyes light up. He turns to me with a grin. "That's brilliant, Calla."

Before I can think of a response, Blake's icy voice cuts through the air. "Listen, you two," she hisses, her perfectly manicured nails digging into Jay's arm. "On my wedding day, I want everyone's focus and attention to be on *me*. It's my day to shine. You two are there to make sure of that. I need you to commit. If you can't do that, Clara, I think that we need to find another baker."

There is a long beat where Jay and I are silent. I catch his eye, but he just shakes his head at me. His mouth presses into a thin line of displeasure as he turns to his bride-to-be. "Blake, that's enough," he says firmly, his easy-going demeanor evaporating. "This baker is here as a favor to us. We're getting married in three days!! You already fired two bakers. There are no others to be had." He pauses, taking a deep breath to calm himself. "If you fire Calla, the wedding's off. Period."

My jaw drops. Did he just...? I sneak a glance at Blake, whose face has gone from porcelain white to tomato red in seconds flat.

"You wouldn't dare," she sputters, but there's a flicker of uncertainty in her eyes. "We are the IT couple of Greater. Your fans love us together."

"Oh?" Jay crosses his arms, his stance unwavering. "Try me."

The tension in the room is so thick I could frost a cake with it. I want to sink into the wood floor. But that's not happening, so I'm stuck here, frozen.

Blake's gaze darts between Jay and me, her lips pressed into a thin line. Finally, she lets out a huff that could rival a steam engine. "Fine," she snaps, snatching up her designer handbag. "I don't care which cake we choose. But if this ruins my wedding day, I'll make sure you'll both regret it."

With that, she storms out of the room. I hear her high heels clacking through the living room and then the door slamming closed behind her.

I let out a breath I didn't realize I was holding. Blake is frenetic and there seems to be no good way of letting her energy out. "Well, that was... intense," I say, trying to lighten the mood.

Jay runs a hand through his hair, looking sheepish. "I'm so sorry about that, Calla. Blake can be... a lot sometimes. She's not all bad. Obviously, or I wouldn't be marrying her."

Sometimes? I think. *Seems like always.* But I keep that thought to myself.

"It's okay," I assure him, even though my nerves are still jangling. "These things happen in the wedding business."

This is a lie. I don't have any experience with crazy Bridezillas. But it seems to reassure Jay all the same.

His expression softens. "Still, I want to make it up to you. I promise I'll make sure your cake gets tons of attention at the wedding. I'll even film a short video about how much I loved it for Alto & Ash's social media."

My heart does a little flip at his thoughtfulness. "That's really kind of you, Jay. Thank you."

As he walks me to the door, I can't help but wonder what it would be like if things were different. If he wasn't engaged to a social media-obsessed Bridezilla. If we had met under different circumstances.

But I push those thoughts aside. After all, I'm just the baker. Nothing more.

Chapter Two

Calla

The wedding venue is a whirlwind of tulle and chiffon, a pastel explosion of high society Southern matrons and their beleaguered, dark suited husbands. I clutch my cake setup pieces like a bomb squad technician, heart pounding with a mix of excitement and sheer, unadulterated terror.

This is the big leagues. I'm just a small-town baker playing dress-up.

"Excuse me. Oh, sorry. Coming through!" I weave through the throng with the precision of a matador, my mind laser-focused on the task ahead. No time to gawk at the ice sculpture of a swan (gaudy), or the twelve-piece string orchestra (overkill). I have a cake to set up, and it has to be perfect.

The Greater Attic, where the wedding is being held, is an old movie theater that has been converted to a music venue and event space that can hold a few hundred people. In what used to be the concession area, the venue's catering staff have cleared a space for my cakes and cupcakes right beside a mountain of gifts that looks like it could trigger an avalanche. I set down my boxes of pastries and take a deep breath.

This is it. I'm in the eye of the storm. I can hear the guests arriving in droves. But I'm in a separate room from the main venue area. A few wedding guests do pop their heads in and make a beeline for the bar. But for the most part, I'm left alone to do my work.

My hands move with practiced ease as I unpack the tiers. Each one is a delicate confection of sugar and dreams and magic. I check my internal list: Fondant smooth? Check. Edges crisp? Check. Hand-painted roses intact? Miraculously, check. I stack the layers with the care of a mother bird building a nest, then step back to admire my work.

It's a thing of beauty, even in this over-the-top setting. The cake is tall and elegant, a lovely fondant-covered monument to caloric excess. Tiny edible pearls cascade down the sides like a sugary waterfall. I can almost hear the angels singing.

But there's no time for gawking at the scenery. I want to set up my cupcakes now, before the wedding ceremony begins. I spend the next ten minutes in intense concentration, setting up various cake plates and covering the rest of the table with a waterfall of white-frosted mystery cupcakes.

That done, I let out a sigh of relief and wander to the doorway, my eyes roving over the lavish wedding decorations. The reception hall is a cavernous space, all crystal chandeliers, gilt-trimmed walls, and soft red velvet movie seats. The stage looks like a wedding planner threw up all over it. White wisteria cascades down the wall, white rose petals are scattered across the floor, white string lights in Mason jars hang from the ceiling, a white wicker arch is set as the backdrop for the nuptials. No expense has been spared. No Pinterest wedding board has been unplumbed.

The thought makes me smirk, but only a little. This is exactly the kind of event that could put my bakery on the map.

One well-placed Instagram post, one glowing review from the right person, and You Butter Believe It could go from a struggling startup to the new must-have brand. I imagine the orders pouring in, the stress of making every batch on my own easing just enough for me to breathe. And maybe, just maybe, I'd finally be able to hire some help. I picture myself in a bigger kitchen. You know, one with enough counter space to roll out fondant without knocking over a tower of mixing bowls.

A girl can hope.

Walking back to my dessert display, I take out my phone and snap a few pictures, angling for the best light. The cake gleams like a diamond in a Tiffany's display case. I hover over the Instagram app, debating whether to post now or wait until the reception is in full swing. The thought of something going wrong before the photos go live makes my stomach twist.

I stuff the phone back in my bag and chew on a finger-nail. I glance at the cake, then the side door. It's freezing outside, but the side door has been propped open to allow some of the heat from the growing pool of guests to escape. An icy breeze flutters the edge of the tablecloths. My mind races with the worst-case scenarios.

A gust of wind topples the cake. A drunk groomsman stumbles into the table. A rogue pigeon gets in and attacks the cake topper.

My brain works overtime to pump out scenarios. Why won't it just focus?

I shake off the thoughts and take a deep breath. The cake is fine. The whole display is perfect. And this event is the kind of opportunity I've dreamed about for years. I just have to trust that my work will speak for itself.

In the main room, the string quartet shifts from a languid prelude into something more purposeful. I tiptoe to the doorway to watch as a hush falls over the crowd. The problem is, I can't see anything from way back here. I silently creep toward the back of the room, standing half-hidden behind a column, and watch as the guests take their seats.

My heart does a little tap dance in my chest. This is it. The moment of truth. If the cake survives the next twenty minutes, I'm golden.

A woman in a fascinator the size of a peacock takes the last open seat, and I bite my lip, chewing on the anticipation. The anxiety. I'm not even invested in this wedding, but the tension is contagious.

I crane my neck to see the altar. The bride and groom are already in position, looking like a pair of human dolls set atop a ridiculously expensive cake. The bride is a vision in white taffeta, her dark slick of red lipstick subdued into a pout. The groom, Jay, looks like he just stepped out of a men's fashion spread. Tall, dark, and annoyingly handsome in his tailored suit.

They are perfect together. Athletic, tanned, refined. Some small voice in the back of my head whispers, *I'll bet they don't last a year.*

It's just jealousy, though.

The bride is clutching her bouquet like it's a life preserver, her knuckles white against the gaudy spray of orchids. Jay stands with his hands in his pockets, the picture of nonchalance. If I didn't know better, I'd think he was bored at his own wedding.

The officiant begins to speak in a low drone. I can't quite make out what he's saying. Something about the sanctity of marriage and the joining of souls, I imagine. I tune him out and zero in on the bride and groom. There's a crackling energy buzzing around them, like the air before a thunderstorm.

Blake steals a glance at Jay, then at the crowd, then back to Jay. She's skittish, a deer caught in the headlights. She's poised to bolt at any moment. And Jay? Jay just looks... calm. Too calm.

Jay says something to Blake, too quiet for the audience to hear, and a spark of anger flashes in her eyes. She turns her head away from him with her nose in the air, and I think she might storm off. But she doesn't. She just stands there, frozen, a bride on strike.

The tension is unbearable. I feel like I'm watching a soap opera, the kind my YiaYia used to binge, where every episode ends on a cliffhanger. *Will they? Won't they? Tune in tomorrow to find out!*

But this is real life, and tomorrow is right now. The officiant looks at the bride, then at Jay, then at the crowd. His uncertainty makes it all the more delicious. I hate myself a little for enjoying this, but I can't look away.

"Do you take Jay to be your lawfully wedded husband?" the officiant asks her, his voice tentative.

All eyes are on the bride, but mine drift to Jay. He's still infuriatingly relaxed, like he's waiting in line for a latte. How can he be so cool about this? Maybe he really doesn't care. Maybe he's just going through the motions, playing his part in the farce.

The bride opens her mouth, closes it, then looks out at

the sea of faces. I follow her gaze and spot a photographer at the ready, lens poised like a sniper's rifle. He's not even trying to be discreet. This whole thing is a spectacle, and everyone watching knows it. It's the kind of drama that makes for juicy blog posts and social media fodder.

"I—" she starts, then falters. The room seems to lean in, hungry for her next word.

My hands are clammy, my pulse a jackhammer in my ears. I'm not sure who I'm rooting for. Them? Me? The cake?

And then, nothing. The silence stretches like taffy, taut and sticky, as the ceremony teeters on the edge of something. But the bride doesn't say another word, and the officiant shuffles his notes like he's not sure what to do next. Everyone waits. So do I.

The bride's face morphs, her red lips twisting into something sharp and brittle. *Oh no.* I know that look. It's the expression of someone teetering on the edge, about to take a swan dive into the deep end of bad decisions.

Blake takes a step back from the altar. The movement is small, but it ripples through the crowd like a stone tossed into a pond. She looks at the groom, then at the officiant, then at the doors. My breath catches.

She's going to run.

And then... she *does.*

Blake hikes up her dress and bolts off the stage, a white blur of taffeta and terror. She disappears for a moment. But when she reappears, she's still dead set on escaping.

The venue is stunned into silence, as if someone has hit the mute button on a very expensive remote control. All eyes track her as she sprints for the exit, wobbling on her impractical heels.

My mouth hangs open. I can't believe it. This kind of

thing only happens in movies where the jilted lover finds true happiness in the next scene. But here she is, the runaway bride, and here we are, the dumbstruck audience.

She makes a beeline for the back door of the venue. The doors open with a creak of protest. Then a moment later, they slam shut behind her, like a jail cell slamming shut.

For a moment, no one moves. No one speaks. It's as if the whole room is holding its breath. We're all waiting for the director to yell "Cut!"

A rising tide of murmurs breaks the spell. Guests turn to each other, murmurs and whispers spreading like a brushfire. I catch snippets of conversation: "Can you believe?" and "I thought they were solid!" and "What about the cake?"

What about the cake? I want to shout. *Eat it, for God's sake.*

I sink back against the column, my legs suddenly jelly. The tension that's been winding me up all day unspools in a rush. Now I'm left slightly lightheaded and feeling hollow.

This was supposed to be a sure thing, a slam dunk. Now it's a question mark. Worse, it's big, fat, frosting-covered X.

I scan the room and find the groom still at the altar. He hasn't moved an inch. His hands are out of his pockets now, hanging uselessly at his sides. He looks down the empty aisle, then up at the ceiling, then closes his eyes and exhales.

It's not quite a sigh. It's the slow, measured breath of someone trying to keep it together.

A pang of something, maybe sympathy, tweaks my chest.

The knot of people nearest the altar starts to loosen, and someone calls out to the groom. He opens his eyes and nods, but his expression is distant, like he's watching all this from another room. He steps down from the stage with the grace of a man walking on glass, each step looking like it pains him to take .

The guests are on their feet now, forming clusters of speculation and allegiance. I overhear more speculation. Debates about what just happened, and the occasional attempt to laugh off the awkwardness.

Jay stands in the center of a growing maelstrom, a lone palm tree in a hurricane. He straightens his tie, then loosens it, then straightens it again. The gestures are small, almost imperceptible, but they speak volumes. He's trying to maintain his cool, his composure, but the cracks are starting to show.

"Thank you all for coming," he says, his voice cutting through the din. It has the effect of a teacher clapping their hands in a noisy classroom. Conversations taper off, heads turn. "Please enjoy the refreshments."

I linger by the door, watching as the guests shrug and disperse. Someone makes a beeline for the champagne; another checks their watch and sighs. No meal will be served. Certainly no cake will be eaten.

My eyes find the cake, still perfect and untouched. I imagine a hundred different scenarios where it gets saved, where someone takes a slice and posts a picture with a hashtag. All that exposure, all that potential, now slipping through my fingers like super-fine sugar.

I start packing the cupcakes back into their boxes. If nothing else, I can sell them at a steep discount in my little shop across the town square. Cursed Wedding Cupcakes, $1! I can see myself writing out the signage already.

It takes a while to re-pack the cupcakes, carefully refolding the cardboard cupcake holders and layering the sweet desserts in between. By the time I'm done, Jay stands alone, looking out over the room. There are only a few event workers left cleaning up. If any friends or family comforted Jay immediately after the disastrous event, I missed it while I was in the Cupcake Zone.

His hands are stuffed in his pockets now, his head tilted slightly downward. He's the picture of quiet defeat.

I should go. There's nothing for me here now and staying just makes it worse. But I can't tear myself away. Some morbid curiosity, or maybe a sense of kinship, keeps me rooted in place.

He did everything right. That's what gets me. He played his part, said his lines. He was supposed to be wed by now. But instead, he is at loose ends.

I take a step toward the exit, then stop. I can't just leave him like this. Not after everything. My professional instincts kick in, reminding me that this isn't just about him. My career is tied to this disaster, too.

But it's more than that. It's empathy, or something close to it. I turn back. Jay is making his way toward the side door that leads out into the alley between the buildings. When he pushes open the rickety metal door, the burst of sunlight he unleashes momentarily blinds me. I squint and start to follow, my Converse whispering against the marble floor.

What am I doing? He's not my friend. He's a client. Was, he *was* a client. And it's not like I can save the wedding. Still, I follow him anyway.

As I trail after Jay, I think about the fact that I am almost definitely going to need to ask him for some Instagram exposure. Damn.

This day has really not turned out like I thought it would.

Chapter Three

Jay

Empty tables and a cavernous silence fill the Tin Shed Pub. It's a stark contrast to the earlier mayhem. I planned to have the wedding reception's afterparty here. Now, I am surrounded by platters of French bread, plates of fine cheeses, tiny cups of Brunswick stew, miniature burgers, and Shepherd's pie bites. Bennett watches me out of the corner of his eye as he wraps the platters in plastic wrap.

"You sure you're okay?" he asks, for maybe the fourth time.

As one of my best friends, Bennett had the pleasure of seeing Blake dump me in front of everyone earlier tonight. Now, he's keeping me company in the restaurant he owns while I brood. So he probably knows as well as anybody that I'm not really *okay*.

Cutting my eyes at him, I grimace. "I could use another drink. This IPA is just not hitting the spot."

"Mi casa es su casa," he says. "Have whatever you want. There are forty beer taps at the bar and every kind of liquor you could ever want."

"Thanks."

He hefts a stack of platters and heads into the back with them. I hop up from my barstool and go behind the bar, rooting around until I find the perfect thing. "Ahhh, tequila. My sweet, sweet friend. You'll do."

Grabbing a shot glass, I settle myself back at the bar. Bennett comes back twice for more platters, shuttling them to what I assume is a big refrigerator in the kitchen. Then he disappears into the back hallway. He's always busy; I can't remember the last time I saw him at rest. He's always cutting orange wedges, stacking menus, or passionately waving his hands as he dives into the history of beer through the ages.

Bennett doesn't date. Instead, he runs this bar like a precision instrument, constantly fiddling with things and making changes so small that they're almost unnoticeable. He may have it right: it's much easier to pour yourself into your business than it is to feel the way I feel right now.

The cap spins idly between my fingers before I shrug and pour a healthy shot. The burn as it slides down my throat is a welcome distraction from the ache in my chest. Blake's dramatic exit replays in my head, a silent movie on an endless loop, mocking me.

How did I get here?

Where did I go wrong?

Pondering that, I help myself to another shot. The creak of the door pulls me from my thoughts. For a split second, hope flickers. Then, just as abruptly, it dies, because it's the sweet cake baker, Calla, poking her head inside.

"Well, if it isn't my cake angel," I say, my voice rough. The joke surprises me. I guess when I'm feeling blue, it's easier to let her see my sarcastic side. "Come to frost my wounded ego?"

She steps inside, shutting the door against the cold January night air. "Just coming to see if you're all right," she says.

Her tone carries the faintest edge pity. I frown. I don't want it. I stare at her, belligerent thoughts forming. She doesn't deserve them, obviously. But the last thing I need right now is someone being *tender* and *charitable* toward me.

The idea of it makes me queasy.

"If you're wondering how I knew where to find you..." Calla slides onto the stool next to me, dropping her over-sized tote on the bar. She's still wearing her blush pink dress and sneakers. "I followed you from the venue."

I snort and gesture to the cake box on the counter. "If you're looking for the top layer, I have it right here. It's still intact if you want to rescue it. I was planning to destroy it later."

"No thanks. What would I do with it, anyway?" Her eyes narrow as she studies me. "If you don't mind me saying, Jay, you look like hell."

I raise my shot glass in a mock toast. "I didn't realize that you were the called-off wedding police."

"I'm not." Calla wrinkles her nose. "Why are you alone right now? Don't you have family and friends to keep you company?"

"I sent them away." I down the shot, the tequila smoothing the edges of everything. "Anyway, your timing is impeccable. I was just drowning my sorrows."

Her head tilts. Her eyes rake over me like she's trying to piece together a puzzle with half its pieces missing.

"I can come back," she says softly, but she doesn't move.

I wave her off. "Stay. Misery loves company." I pour

another shot and push the bottle her way. "Want some? It's top shelf. Probably. It's whatever Bennett keeps in stock, which is undoubtedly some amazing stuff."

"I don't think so. I don't drink while I work." Calla's expression pinches.

I bleat out a laugh. "You're not working. In case you didn't notice, the wedding is off. The guests have gone home."

Her face softens in a way that I can't stand right now. "Yeah. I'm really sorry about that, Jay."

It's cool. It's not like I'm not drinking so I don't cry or anything. Scrubbing a hand through my hair, I sigh. "Why are you still here, Calla? The wedding's over. If you're not here to keep me company, and you're not working...."

She fidgets, looking down at the bar. "I was hoping for some exposure. Photos of the cake, a mention in the press. 'Local baker creates masterpiece for Rustin wedding.' Something to help the bakery."

"Ah. I'm sorry. We'll still post something on Insta and TikTok. It's not the same, I know. But it's all I can do now. Blake vanished without a word."

"Can I ask you something?"

I lean on an elbow. "I live to answer your mildly intrusive questions." I frown. "That came out sounding more sarcastic than I meant it. What I meant to say is, go ahead. I'm not going anywhere."

Calla stares at me for several beats. This close, I notice that her eyes are an intriguing shade of hazel. She leans forward on the bar, closer to me. "Did you really not see this coming?"

I shrug, the motion heavy with resignation. "Blake loves a good spectacle. I figured she'd wait until the honeymoon to pull something like this, though. Make it a reality show intervention or some crap." I rub my temples, the tequila doing little to dull the pounding in my head. Putting my head down, I mutter, "Why did I even propose? I knew what I was getting into."

Calla doesn't say anything. For a second, I wonder if she's left. I don't have the energy to check. Then she speaks, her voice softer than usual. "People do stupid things for love."

I laugh, but it comes out quiet, almost gentle. "Love. Yeah. Something like that." I look at her again. This time, I see that she's watching me with an expression I can't quite read. "I'm touched that you're sad for me, Calla."

"I'm not sad *for* you," she says, sitting up straighter. "I'm sad the wedding didn't happen. I needed the exposure."

She stands up, and I think she's going to make excuses and leave. But then, to my surprise, she sits back down, moving slowly, like she's testing the water.

"One shot," she declares. "For research."

My eyebrows shoot up. "Research?"

"That's what I say when I am doing something sketchy." Her eyes twinkle.

I chuckle. Standing up, I fish another shot glass from behind the bar. Then I slide the clean glass her way.

"It's an acquired taste. Like poison." I pour the shot and watch as she picks up the glass, sniffing it cautiously.

"This smells awful. To your health," she says.

Before I can stop her, she throws it back in one go. Her face contorts through a series of expressions: shock, disgust, and a little confusion. Then she makes a strangled noise and slams the glass down.

I burst out laughing. "Oh my god, that was priceless. You looked like you were giving your first blowjob."

Her eyes widen at the same time as her cheeks flush a deep, mortified red. Her mouth opens and then snaps shut. She's *speechless*. It's... adorable.

The wicked grin that breaks out over my face is irrepressible.

"I mean, not that I'd know what that looks like. But I can imagine." I lean in closer, watching her squirm. "You going to be okay? Need me to pat your back? Get you some water?"

"You're an ass," she mutters, glaring at me. But it's half-hearted, and we both know it.

"Probably," I admit, still smiling. "But you're the one who walked in here. So what does that make you?"

"That was truly vile. The worst thing I've ever tasted."

The chaos of a few hours ago, Blake in her ridiculous peacock dress, the hurried preparations. It feels like a lifetime ago, the memory bleeding away.

"You know," I say slowly, an idea forming in my tequila-soaked brain. "We could still make something of the day. We could at least make this wedding disaster memorable."

She looks back at me, suspicious. "How?"

I grab the tequila bottle and stand, swaying slightly. "Come on. I promise it'll be more fun than sitting here wallowing."

Calla hesitates, her eyes flicking between the bottle and my face. "I really should get home."

"You should. But will you?" I extend a hand to her. "Keep me company, Calla."

She stares at me for a moment, then takes my hand. I pull her to her feet, grinning.

"You're insane," she says. But there's a note of curiosity, maybe even one of excitement, in her voice.

"Probably." I lead her toward the door. "But you're coming along for the ride."

For the first time in hours, I feel a flicker of something other than despair. Maybe hope. Or maybe it's just the tequila. Either way, I'll take it.

I lead Calla into the back of the restaurant. It's deserted. Bennett has gone into his office or run out to get something. Either way, I pull her toward the walk-in refrigerator.

"Where are you taking me?" She wrinkles her nose, distrustful.

"You'll see in a second." I pull open the walk-in. The wedding cake is sitting there on a wheeled cart, swathed delicately in cling wrap. It was brought here by Bennett, who offered to keep it in the restaurant's fridge for guests to enjoy during the reception.

Only now that the reception is called off, there is no need for a huge five tier wedding cake. I'm not getting married today.

With some difficulty, I pull the cart out of the walk-in, showing Calla what I've rustled up. "Voilà!"

"Okayyyy...?" she says, eying me. "The wedding cake. Why are you showing me the wedding cake?"

"Like Marie Antoinette said. The people are starving. Let them eat cake!"

My announcement makes her blink several times. "Where are you planning to serve cake?"

I shrug. "Wherever there are people. We have a cart. We can go anywhere we want. Let's start outside."

Calla takes a deep breath and says, "If you want to...."

"I do," I say quickly, cutting off whatever else she was going to say. "Help me get this out front."

I shrug off my tux jacket and convince Calla to help me wheel the massive cake out onto the street. At first, she hesitates, probably imagining it toppling over and creating a sugary avalanche. But my enthusiasm wins her over.

The night air is wintry. The streets are quieter now too, but there's still a trickle of people moving through the town square. I peel the cling wrap off, letting her use a chef's knife and a stack of bar napkins to make little cake bundles. Together, we start slicing the cake and offering pieces to anyone who'll take them. College students, people leaving restaurants, a pottery class that has just let out.

I hand out samples for a while before I realize that I have a smoking gun left unused.

"Hold on," I say, pulling out my phone. Angling it towards us, I catch Calla instinctively ducking, but I keep her in the frame anyway. "Hey everyone, it's Jay. So, the wedding didn't quite go as planned, but we've got a ton of cake here. Come get a slice! Oh, and prepare to have your taste buds blown away by the one, the only, Calla!"

I turn the camera to her. She freezes, awkwardly waving. "Hi?" is all she manages to say.

I turn the camera back to me and encourage my fans to come down to the Greater town square, where we will give out cake until we succumb to hypothermia.

"Seriously?" Calla whispers harshly as I hit the upload button. "I look like a deer in headlights."

"You look adorable," I say. Even I can hear the warmth in my voice. Maybe I had too much tequila, but I don't really care. "Trust me, this will be good for you. For the bakery."

She doesn't look convinced, but it's too late now. The video is live.

"See? My followers are already liking and commenting at a furious pace." I show her the screen, and a few familiar names from the community pop up. One person writes, "On our way!"

I see Calla tense with a mix of fear and excitement.

"We're turning this into a party," I say, grinning.

As we continue handing out cake, I film little snippets, each one more ridiculous than the last. I make exaggerated yummy noises, interview random people about the cake, and even try to start a chant of "We love Calla!" which mercifully doesn't catch on.

Through it all, Calla laughs, her reservations melting away. There's something liberating about it all.

Not caring for a moment, just letting the chaos unfold.

A young couple walks by. I practically tackle them with my enthusiasm. "Have some cake! It's free, and it's amazing!"

They take a slice each, and the girl asks if this is the cake from the video. I nod. "Sure is!"

The girl squeals, taking a selfie with me and the cake. I make sure to mention You Butter Believe It again, catching Calla's soft smile out of the corner of my eye.

"Okay," she says, grabbing the knife. "If you're going to make me a star, it's time for you to enjoy some cake. I *insist*." She cuts a huge piece and holds it out to me. "Berry Gentilly Lace, just like you wanted."

My eyes light up. I take the plate with almost reverent care. "You really made a whole tier in this flavor? I thought you were just humoring me."

"I aim to please," she says, her voice lighter now. "And I would like to point out that I actually made the base layer Gentilly Lace, so the cake is more this flavor than any other. Go on, try it."

I take a bite. My initial reaction is *damn, Calla can bake*. I already sort of knew that, but this taste of heaven confirms it. My eyes roll back and I give an exaggerated moan. "Calla, this is... I have no words. It's perfection."

I stuff more into my mouth, grinning as she laughs at how ridiculous I look. Cake isn't my thing, but this cake is heavenly.

"I'm in love," I declare, mouth full of cake, words all but indecipherable. "In love with this cake."

"Don't talk with your mouth full." Her words are belied by her grin.

I swallow and wipe my mouth with the back of my hand. "Sometimes it feels good to be bad," I tease.

Before Calla can respond, a group of my fans arrives, drawn by the allure of free cake and social media fame. They cluster around us. I find myself playing the gracious host, dishing out slices and taking more selfies. I pull Calla into a few shots, ignoring her half-hearted protests. She puts on her best unimpressed face, but I can see the hint of a smile she's trying to hide.

The crowd thins eventually. I notice that Calla is shivering. I drape my coat over her shoulders without thinking. "I think that's enough charity," I say. "Thanks for keeping me company tonight, though."

"No problem," she says softly, her eyes meeting mine. "Tonight was actually fun."

"Yeah, it was," I reply.

The street is quiet as I wheel the decimated cake back into the Tin Shed Pub. I try to judge her mood so I can figure out if she's up for more. "So, what's next for you?"

She exhales, her expression thoughtful. "Back to reality, I guess."

"Reality can wait," I say, almost pleading. "Stay a little longer."

She hesitates. For some reason, I find myself holding my breath. When she nods, relief washes over me.

"Maybe just for a bit."

"I'll take it." I grin at her mischievously. "How about another shot?"

The night stretches on. And for a while, reality does wait.

Chapter Four

Calla

My first semi-conscious thought is that my head feels like a piñata, post-party. Shifting in place, I groan. I'm not in my warm, soft bed. I'm lying on something way too hard.

I am tempted to just roll over and try to go back to sleep. But something flashes brightly, very close to my face. Even though my eyes are clenched shut, the after effects of the flash mark an agonizingly bright square in the darkness.

I open my eyes a slit to try to understand what could be flashing.

Whatever it is, it needs to stop. Right. Now.

I'm halfway blinded by another flash. "Oh, I think she's awake," giggles a feminine voice.

My vision begins to clear enough for me to make out two figures a few feet away. There's a white picket fence between us, which is pretty confusing. Did I fall asleep in a yard somehow? The taller of the two figures, this one vaguely male in shape, leans in for a better look.

"We'd better jet. She doesn't look happy."

As I push myself up, the two scuttle away. Only I'm too

overwhelmed by nausea to notice. My head pounds. The taste in my mouth is distinctly fermented tequila, which makes me doubly nauseous.

Unpleasantly, I become aware of several very important facts all at once.

One, the place I've been napping? It's the Greater town square gazebo.

Two, it's freezing cold outside. I'm shivering and shaking, my teeth chattering.

Three, I'm very much not alone.

Jay lies next to me, his dark hair a disheveled mess, his chiseled features softened by sleep. We're wrapped in a single blanket. A terrifying thought strikes me. I peek underneath the fabric, catching an eyeful of velvety skin, a dusting of body hair, and abs.

That's when I make the final discovery.

Me and Jay?

We're naked.

Together.

Oh.

My.

GOD.

My kneejerk reaction is to sit up straight and snatch the thick wool blanket to my chest. The entire world tilts. For a second, I'm lost.

But in the back of my mind, I'm already asking the pertinent questions. Like, how the hell did we get here? The last thing I remember is a round of tequila shots at Tin Shed Pub.

Or was it two rounds?

"Calla?" Jay's voice is a gravelly whisper. He rubs his eyes and squints at me. "What the hell?"

"I have no idea." My voice sounds squeaky with panic. I

scan the square, taking in the historic brick buildings and the grassy area in the center. It's eerily quiet for early on a Saturday morning. Too quiet.

A figure jogs toward us, and my heart stops. It's a young woman holding a smartphone and grinning like an idiot.

"Congratulations!" she squeals. "Can I get a picture with the newlyweds?"

Jay and I exchange looks of pure confusion.

"Newlyweds?" I ask. My voice literally could not get any shriller. If I look anything like I sound, I've turned into an agitated squirrel, asking braindead questions.

"Uh, *yeah*." The girl rolls her eyes. "You guys were so cute last night! I can't believe you're still in the square. True love, right?"

She shoves her phone in our faces. The screen shows a series of photos: me in a wedding dress made of toilet paper, Jay in his rumpled tuxedo. We appear to be dancing on top of the bar at Tin Shed Pub. Then Mr. Lim, the owner of our beloved local coffee shop, is holding a bible. The next photo shows us deeply, passionately kissing.

As in, it looks like we are trying to wrestle each other or possibly climb inside of each other's clothes.

The blush that comes to my cheeks is bright maroon, I'm sure.

The video after that shows us singing karaoke, belting out Savage Garden's "Truly Madly Deeply". Actually, singing is the wrong word. We're *butchering* the damn song. Jay's doing a falsetto, his voice cracking every few seconds, and I can't seem to hold my shit together for long enough to stop giggling.

While our onscreen selves continue scream-singing, I scrunch up my face. "Turn it off, please," I ask nicely.

The fan turns her phone back to face her and grins at

the screen. "Dunno why you sound so bummed out," she says. "This is *beyond*."

Shaking my head, I turn back to Jay. I'm freezing and ready to get my butt inside. Before I can say anything, he mutters something I almost don't hear.

"We got married?" Jay says, more to himself than to anyone else. He looks at his hand, and my eyes follow. A simple gold band adorns his finger. He holds it up, inspecting it like it's a foreign object. "Damn. These were supposed to belong to me and Blake."

I look at my own left hand. I somehow hadn't noticed the weight of it, but a diamond the size of a small planet glares back at me. "Oh, no. Jay, this is expensive. We have to—"

"Relax," he says, with an air of finality. He doesn't look relaxed, though. "We'll figure it out."

I start to pull the ring off, but it's stuck. *Damn*. Of course it's stuck. Nothing about this makes any sense. Why would we get married?

"Remember now?" The girl is nearly bouncing. "You said you'd only do it if it didn't cost anything. Azi did it for free. It was the cutest thing ever."

I feel like I'm going to throw up. Not from the hangover. Okay, maybe from the hangover. Tequila is seriously nasty stuff. But it's the sheer absurdity of the situation that gets me.

"We were joking," I say, exasperated. As if that will somehow undo everything. "We didn't mean it—"

Jay cuts me off. "Can we see those pictures again?"

The girl shrugs and hands him her phone. He scrolls through the images. I peek over his shoulder, cringing at each new revelation. There's a horrifyingly adorable quality to them, like something out of a rom-com montage. Except this is real life, and I'm living it.

Jay lets out a low whistle. "We look pretty happy for a joke."

I want to die. "This is going to ruin me. Jay, my bakery cannot stand a public scandal."

"We'll get it annulled. Seriously. No one has to know."

I snatch the phone from him and shove it back to the girl. "Delete those."

She pouts. "But—"

"Please," I say, desperation seeping into my voice. "We're in enough trouble as it is."

"I got most of these from your Insta, Jay. Deleting them won't do anything."

She has certainly got us there. While I'm making the same face as a deer caught in headlights, she starts tapping her phone screen. "One more for memories!"

Before we can protest, she makes a peace sign and pokes out her tongue. She takes a quick photo with us in the background, then beams.

"C-*ute*! Listen, I left a gym bag with clothes by the gazebo. Thought you might need it. Thanks for everything, Jay!"

Jay's phone buzzes, and he fishes it out from underneath his body. "Thanks," he says to the girl, but he's already distracted by the caller ID. The girl waves and jogs off, leaving us in a stunned silence.

"Hello?" Jay says into the phone. He winces, holding it a bit away from his ear. "Yeah, Mike. No, everything's fine."

I can hear the angry squawk of the person on the other end, though I can't make out the words. Jay's expression shifts from concerned to something more resigned.

"We'll talk about it later," he says, cutting the guy off. "I've got a situation here. Yeah. Sure. Thanks."

He hangs up and looks at me. "That was one of my sponsors. He called to be sure that the honeymoon package is still going to be used. I guess I called last night to leave him a voicemail about how love stinks."

I want to scream. "How did we even— I mean— What—?"

Try as I might, I can't seem to formulate the right words to voice my frustrations. Jay rubs his hand against my upper arm, soothing me. It's funny, because it sort of works.

"Freaking out isn't going to help. Let's just take a breath and figure this out logically."

"We're not Vulcans, Jay. We're humans who make incredibly stupid decisions when drunk, apparently."

He runs a hand through his hair. For a moment, I swear he looks as lost as I feel. It's strange, because every second I have known Jay, he always seemed to have a good grasp of what is going on. Now that I'm seeing him adrift from reality, it looks odd.

"Let's get dressed. We'll think better with clothes on," I say gently.

We try to stand up at the same time, both clutching the blanket. Jay notices me struggling, and with a shrug, he drops his corner. He's seemingly unbothered by his nakedness, and looks like a Greek statue come to life. He pads over to the gym bag as I sneak a glance at his physique and immediately regret it. My cheeks burn hotter than the rising sun.

It may be freezing cold outside, but Jay's erect cock juts proudly, swinging with every step he takes. It's glorious, massively long and thick, giving a new meaning to *morning glory*. I have never been both so mortified and so unable to stop staring at anything in my whole damn life.

If Jay notices my struggle, he is kind enough not to say anything. He tosses me a set of clothes from the gym bag: a men's XXL T-shirt and a pair of basketball shorts. I slip them on under the blanket, grateful for the absurdly large sizes. They make me feel like a child playing dress-up, which is oddly comforting given the current nightmare.

I wrap the blanket around myself. Even bundled in the clothes, it's still below freezing in Georgia and I'm shivering so hard I can't think properly. Out of the corner of my eye, I spot the first early morning runner.

Yeah, it's time to get the heck out of Dodge.

Jay pulls on bright pink basketball shorts and a tie-dyed hoodie. The hoodie looks comically small on him, making me snort. He looks intently at his wrist. He pulls the cloth away from his skin, working the hoodie's sleeve up to his elbow.

"Whoa. Fresh ink," he says. A small calla lily is tattooed on his forearm, covered by a sheer bandage.

Oh. I get a flashback to last night. I have a vague memory of getting something painful etched into my flesh.

"Oh my god," I whisper. I check my own wrist and nearly scream.

A tiny jay bird is perched there. Its beak is open, as if singing.

"Added bonus," he says, though there's no real humor in his voice. "A bird and a flower. Huh."

I close my eyes, shaking my head. "No. A Jay bird and a Calla lily. I remember laughing really hard about that."

Jay whistles. "We were wasted. Well, at least they're tasteful."

I'm beyond words. This isn't just a bad dream; it's a full-blown calamity. How could we have been so... so stupid?!

"Come on," Jay says, motioning for me to follow. "Let's go before more people show up."

I hesitate. "Where?"

"My place. We need to lie low until we can sort this out."

"I think I should just go home. I live above my shop." I point to You Butter Believe It, way at the end of the town square. I'm thinking that if anyone else sees us together like this, the gossip will spread faster than a buttercream frosting on a too-warm cupcake.

"Calla. Let's just go to my house. I promise we'll fix this. But we need a plan. And clothes that weren't scrounged out of a teenaged girl's gym bag."

A small crowd has started to gather at the edge of the square. I recognize a few faces: bakery customers, curious townies. Whispers ripple through them.

Personally? I feel the weight of a thousand judgmental eyes.

"Let's go," I whisper hoarsely, my heart sinking. "Quickly."

We make our way down the steps of the gazebo. Jay puts a hand on my shoulder.

"You know," he says. I brace for something awful. But he shocks me with, "We could just stay married. Save ourselves the shame of getting our quickie marriage annulled so soon."

I stop in my tracks and stare at him, waiting for the punchline. He's grinning, but there's a tiredness in his eyes. He might be loopy.

"Are you insane?" I say. "Or did you hit your head while we were drunk?"

"It'd be easier than dealing with the fallout." He shrugs, raising both hands.

I want to slap him. I want to laugh. I want to cry. Instead, I just shake my head and start walking again.

"Come on," I mutter. "We'll go to your house."

The crowd parts as we cross the square. I can almost hear the rumor mill grinding to life. My mind races with thoughts of damage control, of how to explain this to my family, to the town, to myself.

One thing is clear: this is far from over.

Chapter Five

Jay

"When I said I wanted something else to wear, I didn't mean *slightly different* gym clothes," Calla complains from my office.

I'm in the kitchen, shirtless, trying to decipher the French press instructions through a hangover haze. Calla trudges in, and I nearly burn myself on the kettle. She's wearing one of my softest white T-shirts and a pair of soft gray sweatpants, both absurdly large on her petite, curvy frame. Her hair is a tousled mass of dark brown, to match perfectly with those piercing hazel eyes of hers. She looks vaguely like a kid playing dress-up in her dad's clothes.

Or she would, except that I can see the hard nub of her nipples poking out of my T-shirt. She shifts and now I can see not only the outline of her breasts, but I'm fairly certain that I see the faint hint of areola...e. However you say that word.

Hot *damn*.

I swallow and blink. Calla is *hot*. Not in the girl-next-door kind of way that I found her attractive before now.

She's a fucking *siren*. And she's calling to me as she sits at my kitchen counter.

"I look ridiculous," she says, crossing her arms and glaring at me.

I chuckle, then wince as the sound ricochets in my skull. "You make them look good. It's a new fashion statement."

She snorts, an unladylike sound that I find oddly endearing. "I'm changing as soon as I get back to my house."

I pour us each a cup of coffee, black and steaming, and slide hers across the marble countertop. She eyes it warily, then takes a tentative sip. Her shoulders relax just a fraction.

"Why did we think this was a good idea?" she asks. She is pointedly not looking at me.

"The tequila thought for us," I say, rubbing my temples. "Look, Calla, I'm as shocked as you are. But maybe this isn't the disaster it seems."

Her eyes snap to mine, sharp and disbelieving.

"You think it's not a disaster that your wedding cake baker is now your wife? Do you not think that the whole-ass internet will have a field day with this news? I can see it now." She waves her palms in the air to emphasize her point. "'Jay Rustin rebounds with girl he met only hours before'. Yeah, that'll really help your brand."

I flinch, not at her words, but at the truth in them. My brand. The business. Everything I've built is precariously balanced on public perception. She's right. This could topple it all.

"That's why we need a plan. Come on, Java Monkey is just a couple of blocks away. We can walk."

She looks down at her bare feet, then at my shoe collection neatly lined up by the door. "Got any shoes that would fit a kid?"

* * *

The morning air is crisp. I can see my breath as I walk.

Calla shuffles beside me in a borrowed pair of sandals, her steps cautious. It isn't icy here, but in Georgia, you never know where black ice will spring up. She holds the waistband of the sweatpants with one hand and has the other stuffed into a pocket of the oversized fleece I leant her. She looks impish; I half expect her to produce a slingshot and start aiming at weathervanes.

We turn the corner onto Greater Street. Now the town square is truly coming to life with early risers and dog walkers. The sight of the Java Monkey's glowing neon sign makes my stomach growl, though the thought of food still turns my stomach.

We step inside, the bell tinkling overhead. A cheerful barista greets me with a smile that's way too bright for this early hour. Calla orders pancakes and a frilly latte. I order a veggie scramble and another black coffee. Once I've paid for our meal, I turn to see that Calla has taken a seat by the window. She's staring out at the square, her expression unreadable.

Sliding into the chair across from her, I set down her coffee. "Food's coming. You can change after."

She nods, sipping her latte. I try to take her cue and enjoy a bit of coffee in silence. When the food arrives, Calla eyes my plate with a mixture of disbelief and amusement.

"Are you on a diet or just allergic to joy?" she quips, taking a generous sip of her sugary, whipped-cream-topped latte.

"Who, me?" I lean back in my chair, letting a smug grin spread across my face. "This body doesn't maintain itself on pastries and lattes, you know. Discipline is the name of the game."

She raises an eyebrow, clearly unconvinced. "Discipline, huh? You make it sound like you're training for the Olympics. It's just breakfast." She gestures to her own plate, piled high with pancakes. "Food is meant to be enjoyed."

I shrug and take a measured bite of my egg whites. "Everyone has their vices. I just choose to enjoy mine in moderation. Besides, someone has to balance out all the hedonism in this marriage."

Calla makes a noise that is somewhere between a laugh and a giggle. It's a genuine, warm sound that catches me off guard. "Hedonism? Please. I'm the most boring person you know. I'm rigid in every way except my diet."

"Maybe that's why you married me," I suggest with a wink. "So you can loosen up and enjoy life a little more."

She sticks out her tongue and smirks. "Or maybe you married me for my superior taste in breakfast foods. You know, because you secretly want to convert."

"Have you seen my abs? Don't lie, I know that you have."

Her face turns the pink color of a bouquet of carnations. "Maybe. But that isn't all that life's about. You have to live a little."

Our banter feels easy, almost natural. For a moment, I let myself imagine that this could be real. That we could actually make a go of it. That Calla could be my sweet, devoted little wifey. Would that be so ludicrous?

This thought makes me think of Blake. The woman who was supposed to be my wife. I wince as I picture her face; it's like a hot knife slid right into my belly.

What is she doing right now? Is she alone, or with another man? Because I just realized that I don't know anything about Blake. Maybe I was just blind the whole time, dazzled by the flash of her camera.

I quickly shove that thought aside. There will be time to mourn my relationship with a twelve pack of beer and my best friend Ryan to keep me company. Now is just not the right time.

Calla finishes her coffee and leans back, stretching her arms. "You know," she says, thoughtfully, "if we were really married, this would be a pretty decent start to our mornings. Minus the hangovers, of course."

I study her, wondering if she's starting to see the same thing I am. The tiny spark of possibility amidst the absurdity. "Yeah," I say slowly. "It wouldn't be the worst thing."

The conversation shifts, pulling me back to reality. I tell her about the missed calls and texts from my sponsors, all demanding to know what my plan is. Some of them are already threatening to pull out, which is a disaster for my business.

Calla frowns. "My sister Cora is an attorney who might help us get an annulment."

I shake my head. "It's not just about us; there are other factors to consider. This affects a lot of people, not just you and me."

She leans back, crossing her arms. "So, what, you need a focus group to decide if you want an annulment? It's just hitting the undo button on last night's bad decisions."

"I see it more like damage control for our accidental foray into drunk matrimony. If we just rush into an annulment, it could make things look worse. Like we're trying to hide something."

Her eyebrows shoot up. "Jay, it was a stupid, drunken mistake. People will understand that."

"Will they? The internet loves a scandal. And a quick

annulment? There's nothing juicier. An annulment is like admitting guilt. If we take our time, it'll seem less like a cover-up and more like... I don't know, like we're being responsible."

"Responsible," she repeats, testing the word on her tongue. "I have a business to run too, you know. You were a client. If people find out that I married you, even though you were jilted at the altar, it could be bad for me. My clients need to trust that I can keep my personal life separate from my work"

"But if we handle this the right way, it could blow over without ruining either of us. We just need to be smart about it."

She sighs, clearly unconvinced but not entirely dismissive. "So what's your brilliant plan, then?"

"We don't rush into anything. We see how things unfold and make decisions based on that. In the meantime, we can frame this as a temporary situation."

"Temporary." She studies me for a long moment, weighing my words. "Only until we have thought everything through. Right?"

"Exactly. I promise, you'll get back to your normal life before you know it."

As we finish eating, I catch her looking at me thoughtfully. I grin and say, "See something you like, wifey?"

She rolls her eyes but can't suppress a smile. "I was just thinking," she starts, hesitant. "You're actually more charming in person than in your videos."

I raise an eyebrow. "Oh? So you've been watching my videos? Doing some research on your future ex-husband?"

She blushes and looks momentarily flustered. "I had to know what I was getting into," she defends herself. "You're quite the character."

I laugh. "Well, well. I'm on my honeymoon with my stalker. This just keeps getting better."

She turns an even deeper shade of red but bites her lip, trying to hold back a laugh. "Don't flatter yourself. I only watched a few."

"Sure, sure. You know, I think I'm going to enjoy this. Teasing you, I mean. For as long as we're still married."

She shakes her head, but there's a twinkle in her eye. "You'd better not get too used to it. This whole thing is temporary, remember?"

"I know," I say, more seriously. "But that doesn't mean we can't make the best of it while it lasts."

Calla rolls her eyes. But I can't help but notice that she's blushing at the same time.

I just hope that she's thinking about making the best of our situation too.

Chapter Six

Jay

After breakfast, I walk Calla to her apartment. It's simple enough because her apartment is above her bakery on the other side of the town square.

"So this is you," I say too loudly. I stare at the peeling lavender door of Calla's upstairs apartment. A neon "You Butter Believe It" sign glows pink in the bakery window below.

She leads me around the side of the building, jingling her keys. "Don't sound so disappointed, Mr. Been-My-Husband-For-Five-Minutes."

I lean against the brick of the building. "Not disappointed. Just noticing."

"Of course." She grins. "I'll catch you later."

"Count on it, Mrs. Rustin."

Two perfect pink circles form on Calla's cheeks. She arches a brow. "That's Ms. Nikolakis to you."

My chuckle sounds foreign even to me. There hasn't been much laughing this morning. Not since Blake left me standing at the altar with two thousand orchids and zero fiancées.

I give her a mock salute and she turns toward the door, shaking her head. Calla's brand of sarcasm feels like lightly pressing on a bruise. It's a little painful, but proof that I'm still alive.

She disappears upstairs without so much as a goodbye. I walk home past Java Monkey and the couple blocks home. My gaze is downward, and my thoughts are a churning mess. When I hit my yard, my agent startles me.

"Rustin!"

Grady's polished oxfords tap impatiently as he waits on my porch steps. His navy suit screams "midlife crisis meeting spreadsheet". As opposed to my wrinkled Atlanta Braves jersey, which whispers "I might have gotten married last night."

"Hey. Uhh... I wasn't expecting you."

"No?" He blocks my key in the lock. "We need to talk about the elephant hiding in your Instagram comment section."

"Ah. So the news is out, huh?" I slump against the gray Victorian's siding. "Blake ran off and left yours truly standing at the altar."

He whips out his phone like a deranged magician. "#BachelorJay has three hundred thousand tweets."

The morning mist settles in my lungs. "Great. Can't wait to sell protein bars with 'abandonment issues flavor.'"

Grady steps into my personal space. "Your honeymoon tour starts in three days. Twenty sponsored stops. Five hundred grand tied to couple's content." His index finger jabs my sternum. "I talked to your accountant Darius. He says every cent of that money is already allocated. Crew paid. Insurance benefit checks scheduled. You cancel? We're talking layoffs. Restructuring. Possibly selling this very charming house you're not inviting me into."

I grit my teeth. "Come in, then. Let's discuss our options."

We head inside. I walk straight into the kitchen and grab two bottles of coconut water. It's supposed to be magic for hangovers. When I go back in the living room, I offer one to Grady. He looks at the perspiring bottle like I'm offering him a ticking bomb.

"No thanks." Grady flops onto the distressed leather sofa that took six weeks to source from Marrakech. "So. Contracts. Want me to start drafting cancellation notices for Mount Gem? Tell Claxon's Fruitcake Committee that you have a tummy ache?"

"No. I was thinking that we could renegotiate. Turn couple's retreat content into... solo empowerment quests. Or maybe a lonely hearts anti-honeymoon trip."

"No way is that going to work." He squints, eyeing me. "Unless you want to pivot full alpha male. Grow the full beard back. Film yourself chopping wood shirtless while ranting about gold diggers. Sponsor testosterone supplements."

I ponder that for a full three seconds before shaking my head. That's not who I am. I don't want to push away women that like my platform.

"I can't do that."

The silence in the room is so perfect you could hear a feather floating to the ground. "You need Blake. Period."

"Blake doesn't want me, if that wasn't already perfectly clear." The fridge hums louder than my eighth grade clarinet recital. "Not calling her."

"Cool. Should I text Wren her severance package now? Or should we wait until after her six month anniversary with Alto & Ash next week?"

I glare at him. Grady isn't my favorite person, mostly

because I don't like his constant cynicism and complete distrust of everyone he meets. But he's magic at signing contracts with clients. This interaction is exactly the type of thing that makes me itch to fire him.

"We are not firing my sister," I say. Opening my coconut water, I suck a quarter of it down, not taking my eyes off my agent.

Grady spreads his hands wide.

"I'm just trying to make sure that you understand. Her salary pays for Anna's health plan." He ticks off fingers. "James' 401k match. Your Whole Foods addiction. Without the honeymoon sponsorships..." His shrug could level cities.

"I thought you were here to help. Telling me to fire my staff is not what I would consider as helping."

"Who said I was here to help? I'm here to make you see that you need Blake."

"Am I going crazy? I thought I just said no to that idea. No to Blake."

"Since your runaway bride turned our revenue stream into Niagara freaking Falls." He pulls a crumpled spreadsheet from his back pocket. Red ink bleeds through the folds. "Let's just see here. Your first stop on the honeymoon road trip is supposed to be Mount Gem. Mount Gem's liability clause? You miss opening day, you owe them double the sponsorship fee. Extreme Ropes Course will want their deposit back plus twenty percent. Even the damn Waffle House Museum has language in their contract that penalizes you for skipping them."

"Enough!" I grab the paper from him, balling it up. The paper crumples easier than my dignity. "I'll handle it."

Grady catches my wrist before I can massacre another column. "Handle it how? Unless you've got a backup wife hiding in the panic room..."

The laugh leaves me like the breath leaves my lungs after a punch. "Oh sure, let me check Hinge really quick. 'Recently ghosted, need stand-in spouse for monetized road trip! Must look good in athleisure!'"

His grip tightens. "Blake answers on the first ring. Ask me how I know."

Cold spreads through my veins. I pin him with my gaze. "You called her?"

"She called me. Ten times since the altar dash." His thumb hovers over his call log. "She says she's sorry. Says she'll explain."

My mouth twists as a bitter taste spreads across my tongue.

"No. I knew that going through with the wedding was a mistake. I had this feeling in the pit of my stomach that something would go wrong." I pause, shaking my head. "You know what I thought when I saw Blake run away from me at the altar? I thought, yeah. Makes sense. I'd run too."

Grady looks surprised. "You knew she was going to run out?"

"No. But when Blake was gone, I felt like a heavy weight was lifted off my chest. I felt relieved, Grady."

Grady looks at me like I just called his mother a filthy name.

"Let me tell you something, kid. Your Instagrammable life's held together with credit lines and influencer collabs. Cancel the sponsorships, and next month you're auctioning off Blake's stupid porcelain unicorn collection to pay property taxes."

"That's not true. I own this house outright. Things are not as precarious as you're making them seem."

"Oh no? What do you have to fall back on? Have you got some family money that I'm not aware of or something?"

Swallowing, I stare him down. As a matter of fact, I do have a trust fund. But that's not any of Grady's business. And besides, I've been completely financially independent since college.

A cold trickle slides down my spine. I lean forward and my thumb finds the chip in the black quartz coffee table where Blake tried to "open champagne like a Parisian" last New Year's.

At last, I reply to Grady's question with a weak, "The apartment complex at the end of the block. That's solid equity. Passive income."

He gives me a tired look. "Refi the house, sell the rentals, or start filming budget reels in your childhood treehouse. Or, you can get your head out of your ass and call Blake. Those are your choices, Jay."

His words are tough to hear.

"But Alto & Ash has three million followers!" I protest.

Grady mimes pressing a gun to his temple. "Face it. You're one algorithm change away from being that guy who hawks waist trainers between bar trivia nights."

"There's got to be a third option."

"Option three involves chloroform and a Vegas chapel, but kidnapping laws cramp my style." Grady straightens his cuffs. "Call Blake and grovel. That, or find a replacement wife by Monday. Those are your lifelines."

"Right." My chuckle tastes like battery acid. "I'll check Wife Depot. Aisle seven, between lightbulbs and light treason."

He doesn't smile. He just slides his phone across the counter, the contact list open to BLAKE (ICE QUEEN) in all caps. "Fire me last if you want, but Anna's insurance portal locks in three weeks. James's husband..." His throat works. "They're prepping for another round of chemo up at Emory."

"I'll fix it." The lie slips out smoother than my morning matcha. "New plan. Better plan. I'll come up with a clever way around it. You'll see."

For a heartbeat, Grady pauses. "Don't make me the villain here, Jay. I'm trying to save your ass."

"Okay." The word sounds defeated coming from my mouth.

Grady says goodbye. Soon, the front door clicks shut.

What the hell am I supposed to do? I'm between a rock and hard place. God, if I told Grady that I didn't marry Blake yesterday but accidentally married Calla, his head would probably explode.

Calla's sultry laughter rings through my skull. It sounds throaty and unpracticed, the opposite of Blake's performative giggles. I screw my face up.

What if...

I pull out my phone and text Ryan without thinking. "Hypothetically, how illegal is staying pretend married to a complete stranger for brand sponsorships?"

Three dots pulse.

"Illegal? No way. Immoral? Depends. Is this stranger hot?"

A notification pops up. @BlakeDoesItBetter just posted a poolside selfie titled #LivingMyBestLife. Diamond anklet glinting. It's the piece of jewelry that she insisted I gift her for our engagement party.

That's the moment that breaks me. I hurl the phone and it skids under the $4000 leather sofa Blake chose because it elevated the room's feng shui.

So my task is...

Find another bride.

Save the company.

Become the kind of man who asks near-strangers to fake matrimony for content clicks.

This is a fucking nightmare.

Chapter Seven

Calla

Despite the very-distracting fact that I somehow got married last night, I'm not thinking about it right now.

No, I'm thinking how Jay's house is not what I expected from watching his videos. I've been here already, of course. But now I'm getting the chance to look around.

I say this, because it's literally picture perfect. It's easy to imagine curling up on the sofa with a blanket and a good book. The kitchen is immaculate and infinitely Instagram-worthy. And Jay's office is truly a work of art, with dark wood paneling, sleek brass fixtures, and a large desk of dark wood that's undoubtedly an antique.

For a man who runs a lifestyle brand, I imagined Jay would have a flashier, more ostentatious home. Instead, it's intimate, expensive, and cozy. The kind of place you'd find in a home décor magazine, sure, but understated. Tasteful.

We sit at his reclaimed wood dining table, the kind with a distressed finish that probably cost a small fortune. He runs a hand through his hair, which only makes it look more artfully tousled. "The sponsors are my biggest worry," he explains. "I spent years wooing them. I can't lose them now."

"Back up. What is a sponsor? I mean, I know the word, but not in this context."

Jay sucks in a breath and then blows it out. "A lot of my posts feature sponsored content. Like a sporting goods company that wants me to feature their gear when I post from a hiking trail. Or a tailor wants me to post about having my wedding tux fitted there. That kind of thing."

"Right. That makes sense."

"In this case, I have three months' worth of tourist traps and off-the-wall places to visit. Each one has several sponsored content posts lined up." He traces lines in the kitchen island. "My agent lined them all up months ago."

"Your agent?" My eyebrows fly up. "I thought you were a one-man operation."

He laughs. "Far from it. My company, Alto & Ash, employs twelve full-time employees. Not only do I have camera and sound people, but I have an agent, a lawyer, a PR firm... There are a lot of moving parts."

I breathe out, trying to grab reality and hold on for everything I'm worth. This whole situation is surreal. Yesterday, I was just a cake baker, rushing to get Jay's order completed. Now, I'm in Jay's house. And I have a new last name.

I'm *technically* Mrs. Jay Rustin. Thinking about it nearly gives me a panic attack, so I shove that thought aside, not giving it room to dominate my thoughts. Instead, I focus on what Jay is telling me.

"What are your options?" I ask. I'm genuinely curious. But selfishly, I also might be a little concerned. After all, if Jay tanks after marrying me, it could reflect on me and my business.

"My agent hasn't been here yet to remind me of what I already know. I have close to half a million dollars in sponsored content that is supposed to play out as my 'Honeymoon Road Trip'. If I cancel any of the posts, it'll cost me serious money. So... yeah, I don't know what my options are, really."

"Whoa! Five hundred thousand dollars?" I swallow. "That's some serious cash."

"My agent has been working his ass off to ink these deals. He's panicking right now." He squints. "He dropped by earlier and was extremely displeased with the whole situation."

"It sounds like Blake just screwed you both over."

"Not just the two of us. Everyone in the company will be affected. I'll have to fire people. Basically, if I don't go on this road trip, I'm going to have a week to replace the honeymoon trip's sponsored content. It took my agent four months to set those dates up."

"Oh." I purse my lips. "Well, let's game everything out. Let's talk about all your options. Surely you have more than just begging Blake to still go on your honeymoon with you."

"Ugh. That's never going to happen. I had a bad feeling about Blake going into the wedding. Then she ditched me at the altar and I woke up married to you!" His shoulders slump. "But how can I play this off as a 'Solo Honeymoon'? Sponsors want real newlyweds, not a solo vlogger."

I put my fork down. My face suddenly feels flushed. "So... you're saying you can't do it alone?"

"I could. It just won't have the same impact. The whole point was to show a genuine, relatable experience. If I go by myself, it looks sad. Pathetic, even."

I study him. He's handsome in that rugged, everyman

way, but there's a fragility to his eyes that I hadn't noticed before.

He's scared. This is more than just a business venture for him. It's his life.

"Jay, I'm sure we can annul this quickly and you can find another way to—"

Before I can finish, the front door bursts open and a whirlwind of energy and noise sweeps into the room. Jay's team, I assume. A man in his late twenties, dressed in a too-tight blazer, is juggling a stack of papers and a tablet. Behind him, a petite woman with neon pink hair brandishes a selfie stick like it's a magic wand.

"James! Lana!" Jay says, standing. "I thought we were meeting later."

James, the blazer, gives Jay a look that says, *Are you kidding?*

"I'm your business manager. You have business that apparently needs managing." James thrusts the tablet into Jay's hands. "The sponsors are freaking out."

Lana isn't paying attention. She's circling the table, angling her selfie stick to capture different shots of Jay and me.

"This is so cute. We should do several posts about the surprise wedding. You have footage, right?"

"Lana," Jay says, a warning in his tone. She pouts but lowers the selfie stick. Jay looks at me apologetically. "Sorry. Lana just loves her job."

I feel like I'm watching a reality show, one of those behind-the-scenes episodes where the cast and crew bicker about creative differences. Except this is real, and I'm in it.

"Are you going on the honeymoon together?" Lana asks.

"What?" Jay looks at her sharply. "What gave you that idea?"

Mortified, I slide off the stool and smooth my skirt. "Uhhh... I should go. It sounds like you have a lot to work out."

Jay looks at me, then at his team. "Calla, wait. We haven't finished talking."

I hesitate. Do I want to wait? This isn't my world. These aren't my people. But something in his pleading, desperate tone makes me pause.

"Just give me a minute," he says. "Please?"

Wordlessly, I sit back down. But my eyes are sharp and they take in the scene. My body stays tense, ready to spring up and flee at any moment. Jay and James are huddled together, whispering fiercely. Lana slides into a seat across from me. She taps away on her phone, probably updating a thousand different social media accounts.

"Calla," Jay says, walking back to the table. James hangs back, arms crossed. His face is a mask of disapproval.

Jay hesitates, then runs a hand through his hair. "Can we talk? Just us. Privately."

"Fine," I say, pushing myself to my feet. "But make it quick."

He leads me down a hallway into the laundry room. It's cramped, with a stackable washer-dryer unit and shelves overflowing with neatly folded linens. The door closes with a soft click.

Suddenly, we're in our own little world.

"I've got a proposition for you."

More ominous words have never been uttered. Here it comes. The real pitch. I brace myself.

"What?" I ask, crossing my arms. Jay flashes me with a smile.

"We stay married for the duration of the honeymoon

trip and a short period after. *Then* we get the marriage annulled."

I stare at him, waiting for the punchline. When it doesn't come, I say, "You're joking."

"I'm serious. This way, the sponsors see a real couple visiting the weird tourist stops that they are paying me to promote. We fulfill the contract... and then we go our separate ways."

Schooling my expression, I give him a look. "How long?"

"Well." His smile widens. I see now that Jay uses his smile to hide his discomfort. Interesting. He spreads his hands wide. "I'd need you for four months. I know that seems like a long time—"

"Absolutely not." I shake my head. "There is no way. I have a business to run! I can't just take off for a few months. And what about my family? My sisters? What would I tell them?"

He leans against the washer and crosses his arms over his chest. "I thought about that. What if I make sure word spreads about your business? Boost your profile, feature your baking skills. You'll get more exposure than you ever could on your own. And I'll help you hire someone to fill in while you're gone."

I bite my lip. The exposure *would* be huge. Still.... "How will we explain deciding to split up?" I frown, trying to picture it. All I'm getting right now is a very blurry, distorted image.

Jay uncrosses his arms and takes a step toward me. He puts a gentle hand on my arm. "I'll take full responsibility. We'll tell everyone it was an elaborate, humorous stunt. My fans will eat it up. I promise. And...." He raises a finger.

"You can tell your sisters that the marriage is fake *if* you can trust them to keep it to themselves."

I focus on a bottle of fabric softener on the shelf instead of the man in front of me. His hand on my arm is making my resistance soften ever so slightly.

This is insane. Completely, utterly insane. No sensible person would agree to what he's proposing. But is it any more insane than waking up married to a stranger in the first place?

"Come on, gorgeous," Jay says softly. I glance at him just in time to see him get down on one knee. He takes my hand. A jolt of electricity shoots up my arm. "Will you stay fake married to me?"

"I... uh...." My mind is a whirlwind. Part of me wants to laugh at the absurdity. Another part of me is screaming to *run for the hills*. A chuckle escapes me. "Are you always this persuasive?"

He stands but doesn't release my hand. "Only with beautiful bakers who accidentally become my wife."

I roll my eyes, but a small smile tugs at the corner of my lips. "Flattery isn't going to get you anywhere, you know."

"It's worth a shot." He shrugs, that easy confidence returning.

There's a moment of silence, but it's not uncomfortable. I think about the money that I could make, the exposure that this venture would net me, and the ridiculousness of the whole situation. Can I really do this? Can I pretend to be his wife for a few months and come out unscathed?

Yes? That's my answer. Yes with a question mark at the end.

"Fine," I say. Jay's eyes light up and I forestall him with a finger. "Do me a favor. Let's agree, here and now, that we won't end up falling in love with each other. I have a bakery to run. You? Yesterday, you were set to marry another woman."

"Don't remind me!" He clutches his chest, playing the part of a tragic hero. "I'll try really hard not to be swept off my feet. It does help that I just got dumped and happen to think love is for suckers."

"That's reassuring," I say, though a tiny part of me feels a pang of something at his declaration. Disappointment, maybe? It's too faint for me to tell.

Jay extends his hand and gives me a devilish smile. "Deal?"

My lips twitch with humor. "You've got yourself a deal."

I take his hand and we shake. It's awkward, like neither of us is sure how long to hold on. The handshake morphs into a hesitant hug. I'm hyper-aware of his body against mine. His warmth, his scent. We pull away and for a moment, we just look at each other.

"Okay," I say awkwardly. "Well, I should get home. The cupcakes won't frost themselves."

I turn to leave. As I open the door, he says, "Calla."

I pause, not turning back, waiting. My heartbeat sounds like a bass drum in my ears.

"Thank you," Jay murmurs.

I step outside into his house, nerves jangling. But for the moment, I have the feeling that everything might just be okay.

Chapter Eight

Calla

You know what no one warns you about? Hangovers getting worse as the day goes on. I don't have much experience with heavy drinking. But you'd think people would talk about this part more.

My apartment is on the town square, above my bakery shop You Butter Believe It. It is accessed through its own door at the back of the building, though you can get into the bakery that way too.

I drop my keys twice as I try to jam them in the lock. "Seriously?"

Finally, I get the door open and head up the dark, rickety staircase.

I burst into my apartment with enough energy that the door slams against the wall. The resulting bang makes my already throbbing head threaten to explode. The sound echoes in my skull like a bad punk rock concert.

Okay, I haven't actually been to a punk rock concert. But I have been to the Red Masque, a dingy goth club, and danced my ass off. I think that counts for something.

I wince, rubbing my temples. *Aspirin. I need all the aspirin.*

This has been the craziest twenty-four hours of my entire life. I still can't believe it.

Married.

To Jay Rustin.

And now a honeymoon? Is this whole thing a colossal mistake? Did I make a mistake just because I have a wretched hangover?

I dump my purse on the kitchen counter and rummage through the cabinets, knocking over a tower of Tupperware and a bag of quinoa. When I finally find the bottle, I dry-swallow a handful of pills. Here's hoping they'll work some kind of immediate, miraculous magic. I don't have time for a hangover. I don't have time for any of this.

On the walk home from Jay's place, my mind bounced back to the night before, and Jay's charming smile as he slid the ring on my finger. It was supposed to be a joke, the kind of silly, drunken dare that gets laughed off the next morning. But here we are, with a marriage license and viral wedding photos.

Guess the joke's on me.

I groan and pull up the biggest of my three suitcases from the hall closet. What does one pack for a fake honeymoon?

I hold up a bikini, examining its bright orange ruffles. It's an unflattering color, but it was on clearance. And it actually fits my body like a dream. As someone who is bigger than a size six, I always jump at the chance to find something that actually fits.

And a bikini that is flattering is the holy grail!

I'm still considering the garment when the door bursts open. I nearly jump out of my skin.

"Calla!" My sister Cora storms in, all five feet of her bristling with righteous fury. She holds up her phone. Even from across the room, I can see the familiar image of me and Jay at the chapel, my mouth open in a surprised O, his in a confident, almost cocky grin. She grimaces. "Explain this. Now."

I sink onto the edge of my bed, bikini still in hand. "Cora. I was about to call you."

"You were not. You're packing, apparently. Now tell me what is going on!"

She crosses her arms and taps her foot. I've never been able to lie to my big sister. The problem is that I know she's not going to like the truth.

I take a deep breath and launch into the story: how Jay got dumped at his wedding, how we ended up drinking way too much tequila, how the whole thing was supposed to be a funny, temporary distraction from his real-life drama. Or at least, that was my logic when I was drunk as a skunk. I tell her about Jay's proposal to turn our accidental marriage into a publicity stunt, about the fake honeymoon and his promise that it will boost my business.

As I talk, Cora's expression shifts from anger to something like disbelief. "You can't stay married to him! You barely know him!!" She waves her hands to emphasize her point.

My neck heats. Pinching my mouth, I shoot her a glare. "I know him enough."

"Really? What'd his middle name? How about his favorite color? What was his high school superlative?"

"I... I don't know that stuff just yet. But that doesn't mean I don't know who he is. We just get each other." I smile, trying to bolster my weak-ass explanation.

"Calllllaaaaa...." Cora rolls her eyes back in her head.

"You're being impatient, trying to make a square peg fit in your round hole. You'll meet someone in your own time. You don't need to go to extremes to make some dudebro pay attention to you."

I gasp. "I am not!"

"So you're saying that you don't have a secret plan that involves the two of you ending up together?" She gives me a hard stare.

"What? No!" I protest, maybe a little too loudly. "This is all for business. You know how important exposure is."

Cora makes an exasperated sound. "You have a history of making these grand gestures for complete losers who don't see you the same way. You know you do."

I blush. It's too hard to hold my sister's accusing gaze, so I start shoving clothes into my suitcase with more force than necessary. "This is different!"

"Babe," Cora says, her tone softening. She grabs my hand and sits on my bed, pinning me with her hazel gaze. "Don't pick this guy. The man just got jilted at the altar. He's not looking for love. At best, he's looking for a rebound."

"I'm not looking for love either! I'm looking for Instagram followers... for my cakes!" I pause, holding a push-up bra in one hand, then I toss it into the suitcase. "This is just a business arrangement."

"You need a push-up bra for a business arrangement? I don't think so."

"I can't believe how judgy you are! Especially about a situation that you don't understand." I fling a handful of clothes into my suitcase, taking my frustration out on it like a five-year-old would.

"Calla... Look at me."

I do, but I can't shape my face in any way but a pout.

She tucks a strand of my dark hair behind my ear and touches my face. "I love you. I'm worried about you. You always make these grand gestures for guys that don't even look your way. I want to make sure that you aren't doing that again."

"Well, you can put your mind at ease knowing that I'm perfectly fine. Rest assured; my heart is safe. There are zero feelings between Jay and me." I pull away from her and start sorting through a pile of dresses. "The sequin dress? For a potential sponsored post. The sexy lingerie? In case we visit a luxury hotel partnership."

Cora rolls her eyes so hard I think she might strain something. "Calla. I'm serious."

I stop and look at her. My big sister always has her life together. She never takes a risk she can't calculate the outcome of. She can't understand this. "Grand gestures are the right thing sometimes, Cora. Look at Mom and Dad! Dad won Mom over with a 25-step love letter scavenger hunt culminating in writing 'Will you marry me?' in fireworks. When it's the right person, they will love your antics, not run the other direction."

"Mom and Dad were unbelievably lucky. But for every success story, there are probably a hundred bad luck stories. I just want you to be practical."

I take a deep breath and let it out slowly. "Thank you. Really. But it's all under control. Jay and I agreed and shook hands. It's basically a business venture. Feelings won't ever enter the picture."

Cora stands and smooths her skirt. "Just be careful, okay?"

"I will," I say, and I mean it. At least, I think I mean it.

Cora checks her watch. "I'm sorry to say that I've got to run. I have to finish drafting these stupid briefs before I can sleep. Text me tomorrow and we'll set up a sister brunch."

"Totally. Love you!" I am aware that I'm being suspiciously bright as I say my goodbyes.

Cora leaves. Suddenly, the apartment is too quiet. I look at the mess of clothes on my bed and start to pack with more care.

A part of me knows Cora is right. Another part of me is already explaining all the ways that she's wrong.

I'm immune to Jay's charm, I tell myself. And it's just a makeshift solution to a temporary problem.

Chapter Nine

Calla

It's funny. I agreed to be Jay's fake wife only yesterday. And yet today, I'm dragging my feet as Jay leads me across the Greater town square. Saying I will be his wife is one thing.

Actually doing the things I promised? It seems like an *obligation*. And forcing myself to smile and seem happy the entire time is just exhausting.

You can do this. You can pretend to be Mrs. Jay Rustin, I tell myself. *Hell, you already married him. What's the worst that can happen?*

I keep up a stream of chatter to bolster myself as Jay and I walk down the sidewalk at dusk. Jay is looking at his phone and muttering to himself. He is dressed like a giant groundhog. Apparently, everyone who attends this event will be.

I shudder. I don't like anthropomorphized creatures. And this pub crawl is going to be packed with them. As we approach the square, I can hear distant shouts.

Swallowing convulsively, I try to steel myself. Jay notices and puts his arm around my shoulders, pulling me closer than I'd like. The scent of his cologne is something woodsy and undoubtedly expensive. It fills my nose, making me acutely aware of his presence.

"Are you ready to start our fake honeymoon?" he asks.

"Uhh... yup." That's the best I can come up with.

"You're making a face like I'm leading you to your execution. Cheer up! We're going to have fun," he assures me.

I shoot him a look. He has the kind of confidence only the truly delusional possess.

"Define 'fun,'" I say. But Jay has already turned his attention elsewhere. We pass through the big intersection that dumps us out into the packed Greater town square. Festive lights hang around all of the shop doors, twinkling madly. There are comical wood cutouts of groundhogs on window displays, and a giant inflatable groundhog hiding his eyes from the sunlight. The crowd is already loud. They're all dressed in various levels of groundhog-themed ridiculousness.

One woman in a full fur suit waves a paw at us, making me flinch. She may intend to be cute, but the fur glued to her face is pretty startling.

Before I can say anything to Jay, someone on the far side of the town square shouts something that I can't make out. Everyone lets out a cheer, making me even more confused.

Jay whoops like a college freshman and grabs my hand. "The crawl has begun!"

I adjust the furry ears on my head and glare at him. "These things itch," I complain.

He looks down at me, his blue eyes sparkling with something I can only describe as mischief. "I think you look cute. Almost as cute as my whiskers."

He strokes the drawn-on lines with a mock-vanity that would make a peacock blush.

I snort. "You look like a deranged cat."

"A dashingly deranged cat," he corrects, then grins. "You know, you look hot as a groundhog. I've never been so attracted to furries before."

My cheeks heat as I gently hit him on the arm. "Shut up."

"Relaaaaax," Jay purrs.

I look away, focusing on the historic brick buildings that line the square. Greater is beautiful in a quaint, small-town way. The kind of place where everyone knows your business. Which, of course, is why I'm here, playing along.

As a small business owner, my reputation depends on being reliable, professional, and community-minded. The last thing I need is a rumor that Calla Nikolakis refused to support a local charity event.

"Come on, Calla," Jay says, elbowing me. "This is for a good cause. Put a smile on your face."

I know he's right. The Tin Shed Pub donates a portion of the crawl's proceeds to the animal shelter. As a business owner in this community, I should be all in. But spending an entire evening with Jay Rustin, even in the context of a fake marriage, feels like playing with fire.

"We're only doing this until the first stop," I remind him. "I have to work in the morning."

"Whatever you say, crawl wife." There's a teasing lilt to his words that makes me want to either punch him or kiss him. Probably punch.

The crowd starts to move. We shuffle along with them. Someone hands Jay a plastic cup of something brown and frothy. He takes a swig, coughs, and then offers it to me.

"Want some courage juice?" Jay wiggles the cup enticingly. I shake my head. "Suit yourself."

He drains the rest in one gulp. His exaggerated sigh of satisfaction is so absurd, I almost laugh.

We're almost to the first bar when Jay pulls out his phone. He holds up the camera, and I can see our reflection on the screen. My groundhog ears are lopsided, my expression a mix of resignation and horror. His stupid whiskers are already smudged, and he's grinning like an idiot.

"Just documenting the fun. Say hi to my followers."

"Hi, followers," I deadpan.

That's not enough for Jay. He nudges me with his shoulder, causing me to almost lose my balance. "Come on, Calla. Where's your spirit?"

"Groundhog Day isn't even a real holiday!" I protest. I force a smile at his phone and wave. "Hope you're all enjoying the crawl as much as we are."

Jay laughs, deep and melodic. It makes my fake smile falter. He kills the video and pockets his phone. "See? That wasn't so hard."

I don't respond because I don't have a clue what I am supposed to say.

We reach the first bar, which is the Tin Shed Pub. The crowd surges inside. Jay looks down at me, his handsome face serious for once. "You can bail if you want," he says. "I'll understand."

I hesitate. If I leave now, I'll watch reruns of my favorite TV shows for a few hours before falling asleep. My fluffy duck jammies are calling me. But something in his eyes stops me. A flicker of... what? Vulnerability? Hope?

Maybe he's not as put-together as he pretends to be.

"One drink," I say.

His face lights up like a kid on Christmas morning and

he picks me up, spinning me around like I weigh nothing. I laugh and he grins. "You won't be sorry."

I put up my hands. "Just promise you'll keep the tequila far away from me."

Maybe I am playing with fire. But for now, the warmth feels nice.

At the Tin Shed Pub's 'Punxsutawney Phil's Prediction Station,' we take turns pulling a lever that supposedly predicts the future.

"Six more weeks of winter," Jay reads from the screen. "Looks like we're stuck in this for a while longer." He waggles his eyebrows.

"Stuck?" I say, crossing my arms. "I thought you were having fun."

"Look, this is the start of our honeymoon agreement." He shrugs, a playful glint in his eye. "Maybe I'm worried you'll start enjoying being Mrs. Rustin a little too much."

"Your ego has to be so oversized if you really think that," I retort. "This is all strictly professional, Mr. Instagram."

He laughs. I can't help but smile. The banter is starting to feel less awkward and more akin to slipping into a well-worn pair of shoes. When the crowd begins to move, I go along with it. Jay doesn't say anything as he heads outside into the cold for the next stop on our crawl. But I can see him sizing me up, doing some kind of calculations.

What is he thinking about?

We move onto the next stop. As we walk, I notice that our crowd has thinned. People leaving early, I suppose. Like I should be doing right now... if only I weren't having fun.

Manuel's Saloon is the oldest bar in Greater, with a historic landmark plaque to prove it. The place has a rugged charm, like an old cowboy who's aged into a kindly grandfather. The walls are lined with vintage beer signs and assorted bric-a-brac. The tables are a mismatched collection of wood and metal. Everything I look at is scarred with the patina of decades of use.

Jay and I find seats at the back, where a makeshift stage has been set up for trivia night. The owner, Manuel, has a booming voice as he takes the microphone.

"Settle down, here," he calls, his rural Georgia accent as thick and slow as molasses. "Y'all hush up so I can read the card."

The crowd quiets. Manuel launches into the rules: teams will answer questions related to groundhogs, Groundhog Day, and the movie Groundhog Day. Wrong answers mean taking a drink. Right answers earn points. Eventually, prizes will be had.

Seems simple enough.

Jay leans in close. His breath is warm on my ear. "I hope you're ready to drink. I'm terrible at trivia."

I wrinkle my nose and smirk. "Don't worry. I've got this."

The first round starts as a waitress delivers a tray of drinks to our table. Jay picks one up, examining the amber liquid like a jeweler with a loupe. He runs the glass under his nose and then does a double take. "What is this, apple juice?"

I take a whiff of mine. "Smells fruity. Could be dangerous."

"Let's hope we don't have to find out." Jay rests his hand on my knee casually and all my thoughts are erased; I can only think about the warmth of his fingers against the denim of my jeans.

The emcee reads the first question: "What is the scientific name for a groundhog?"

Jay looks at me, wide-eyed and clueless. I blink. "What was the question?"

"I thought you were good at this!" he says. "He asked what the groundhog's scientific name—"

I press the buzzer and call the answer out. "Marmota monax."

"Correct!" the emcee says. "Also known as a woodchuck. How much wood would a woodchuck chuck if a woodchuck could chuck wood?"

The crowd groans at the bad joke. Jay on the other hand is just staring at me, dumbfounded. "How did you know that?"

I shrug. "I have no idea. The answers just embed themselves in my brain, lying dormant until the moment the question is read aloud."

"You're super smart, huh?" He looks at me admiringly. "That's another very attractive trait. Score one for me, I guess."

To hide my blush, I take a sip of my drink and sputter when it turns out to be a Buttery Nipple. Gross!

The next few questions fly by. We learn that groundhogs are part of the squirrel family, that the first Groundhog Day was celebrated in 1887, and that Bill Murray's character relives the same day for an estimated 10,000 years. Jay guesses at most of the answers. He's consistently, almost impressively, wrong.

I save us each time, much to his growing amazement and my smug satisfaction.

"Which U.S. President was born on Groundhog Day?" the emcee asks.

Jay presses the buzzer before I can stop him. "Lincoln!" he declares with the confidence of a man who's just sunk a game-winning three-pointer.

"Incorrect," the emcee says. "Lincoln was born on February 12th. Take a drink."

I laugh as Jay mutters something about historical trick questions. He lifts his shot glass, and I clink mine against his. "To your stunning intellect," I say.

He downs his in one gulp, then makes a face like he's just bitten into a lemon. "That stuff is lethal."

I sip mine, letting the disgusting brew trickle down my throat slowly. "It's not so bad if you're used to it."

"Are you drunk?" Jay wipes his mouth with the back of his hand. "You're full of surprises tonight."

I shrug, sliding my shot glass to him with a laugh.

The emcee moves on to the next question: "In the movie, what song plays every morning when the alarm clock goes off?"

I press the buzzer. "I Got You Babe" by Sonny and Cher."

"Correct! Sounds like someone here has a groundhog obsession."

Jay calls out, "She's a ringer. I demand a recount."

The final question of the night: "According to folklore, if the groundhog sees his shadow, what does it mean?"

Jay slams the buzzer. "Six more weeks of winter!" he yells.

"Correct!" the emcee says. "Looks like we have some real groundhog experts here. Let me bestow the prize... a VHS copy of Groundhog Day!!"

"Oh god," I groan. Jay grabs me and lifts me off my feet, cheering. My cheeks hurt from grinning. "I can't believe we won."

"Are you kidding? You demolished the competition." He sets me down, letting his hands rest at my waist. "Thanks for hanging in for so long."

I beam up at him, my heart beating so loud that I'm certain he can hear it. "I had fun," I admit. "Can I keep the VHS?"

A laugh bursts from Jay's lips. "Yes. I don't have a VCR. I don't even know anybody who does."

"More for me, then. Maybe I'm just lucky."

"You're lucky, all right." He squeezes me before reluctantly turning me loose. "Should I walk you home?"

"You don't have to. I can see my apartment from here." I check the time on my phone, sighing. "But I do need to get to bed. I'm supposed to work the early shift before we head to the first stop on our so-called *honeymoon*."

"Are you sure you won't stay at my house tonight?"

Looking at Jay, I know that there is no way that I can be in a room with him and just sleep. The chemistry between us is combustible. And the last thing I want to do is set fire to our new agreement.

We might be married, but only on paper. I'd do best to remember that.

"I need to stay at my place tonight. I have to get up at three-thirty anyway."

Jay nods and sticks his elbow out expectantly. "What kind of husband would I be if I didn't at least offer to walk you home?"

Shaking my head, I take his elbow and let him walk me out of Manuel's Saloon. It's a quick walk to my apartment, even for two not-completely-sober newlyweds. We make it in no time, even though I don't want the night to end.

When we get to my door, I turn, sighing.

Jay steps closer. My breath catches as I tilt my head back and look at him.

"I had a really good time tonight, Calla."

I nod. "Same."

My mind is a whirl of thoughts and feelings I don't want to examine too closely. The night was supposed to be a chore, an obligation. But it's turned into something else.

Something dangerously enjoyable.

Jay's hand rises to my cheek. His touch sends a jolt through me, like static from the dry winter air. I can't help but step into his touch. He leans in, his forehead nearly touching mine. I can feel the heat of his breath on my lips.

My eyes close. My heart thuds a quick drumbeat against my ribs. I tilt my head up, waiting. Mostly, I'm wondering if I should stop this... I don't really want to.

We pause, suspended in the moment, and time stretches like taffy. One beat. Two. Three.

Then, as if on cue, we both pull back, laughing nervously.

"Method acting!" Jay says, rubbing the back of his neck. "For our fake marriage."

As if I needed that part explained.

"We're really getting into character. It just goes to show how devoted we are to fooling your sponsors."

"My sponsors. Right," he says. I'm pretty sure he had forgotten them entirely.

The silence that follows is heavy with everything we're not saying. I know there's a spark between us. Tonight made that undeniable. But it's a spark we can't afford to ignite.

This is supposed to be a temporary arrangement, a convenient fiction. Adding real feelings to the mix would complicate everything.

I open my door. The warm air rushes out from the doorway. I stand halfway in and halfway out of the door, awkwardly. "Good night," I say. "See you tomorrow."

"Yup." Jay thrusts his hands in his pockets and smiles at

me while I close the door. With a final wave, he turns to go. I close the door, resting my palm against the flat surface.

Cora might have warned me of my habit of making grand gestures for guys I like. But sometimes? Grand gestures are worth it. Even if it's just for Jay, a man who is technically my husband, but will never be more than a friend.

Worth. It.

Chapter Ten

Calla

I'm *dying*. Maybe not literally, but I only slept for a few hours. And because I was tipsy when I finally crashed, those hours were not good sleep.

But I put on a brave face this morning because I don't want to seem like an old lady who needs her routine. Which, let's be real, is exactly what I am.

In any event, Mount Gemstone is exactly as I remember it from that one YMCA summer camp I went to as a kid. It's quaint, colorful verging on tacky, and utterly charming in its kitschy, Wild West glory. The ticket booth at the entrance looks like it was plucked straight from an old cowboy movie, complete with peeling paint and crooked signs. I half expect a mustachioed sheriff to pop out and demand to see our gold.

What I don't expect is the sheer size of Jay's crew. We've barely stepped out of his SUV when a small army of photographers, assistants, and one very harried-looking publicist descends upon us. Jay waves them off with the practiced nonchalance of a man who's used to being swarmed, but I can see the tension in his shoulders.

This is supposed to be a low-key shoot, yet nothing about it feels low-key. Especially not me. I've been mind-numbingly nervous since dawn this morning.

The parking lot is mostly empty, a vast expanse of cracked asphalt and faded lines. On weekends, this place is probably packed with families and school groups. But today is a late Monday morning, so it has the forlorn air of an abandoned amusement park.

We start the long walk to the entrance with Jay's crew trailing behind us like a procession of ducklings. He stuffs his hands in his pockets and slows his stride to match mine. I glance at him out of the corner of my eye, trying to read his expression. He looks calm, but there's a tightness in his jaw that gives him away.

Jay is as unsettled to have me at his side as I am to be there. Knowing he is also anxious makes me feel less like I'm about to puke, though.

The ticket booth attendant greets us with a grin as wide as the Stetson she's wearing. "Howdy, partners! Y'all here to strike it rich?"

Jay flashes his trademark grin, the one that's sold a million yoga mats and protein shakes. "Just here for some nostalgia."

The woman hands us two tickets and tips her hat. "Enjoy your day at Mount Gemstone, folks."

We pass through the turnstiles. The park opens up before us in a riot of pastel colors and faux-frontier buildings. It's beautiful in a gaudy, over-the-top way; sort of like a wedding cake decorated by a drunk cowboy.

The sounds of a makeshift frontier town fill the air. There's the clatter of a wooden rollercoaster, the tinny notes of a player piano, and the sizzle of frying funnel cakes. I can almost enjoy it. If I close my eyes, I am almost transported back to childhood summers at this park, when life was simpler.

Almost.

I look up at Jay, wondering how he remembers it. For me, that camp was a brief escape from the chaos of home. For him, this whole park is probably layered with happy memories, the kind that can build a person's foundation.

Part of me wants to open his head and crawl inside so I can know what he sees when he looks up at the Ferris wheel. His expression is unreadable, which only makes my curiosity run deeper.

As we walk toward the main street, Jay takes my hand. I stiffen, but he squeezes it gently and leans in. "Look at the cameras," he whispers, nodding toward two guys with high-end equipment. One of them gives a thumbs-up; the other adjusts a lens.

I force a smile. Jay grins wider, like we're sharing a delicious secret. What it is, I don't know.

The park is more ramshackle than I remember. The once-vibrant building facades are now faded and chipped. There's a grungy charm to it, reminding me of a beloved toy that's been played with a little too roughly.

We stroll down the main street, hand in hand. I can almost pretend we're a real couple, here for a day of innocent fun. Almost.

Is this what our fake relationship is going to be like?

The Silver Dollar Saloon beckons with the scent of beer and fried food. A neon sign buzzes lazily, casting a pallid glow over the entrance. My stomach growls. But Jay pulls me onward. "We'll come back," he promises. "Maybe."

I work up a smile. "I'm game for anything."

Jay raises an eyebrow at me. "I'll keep that in mind for later when we get to the hotel room."

I know I'm blushing a deep crimson. I could kill him. But one of the camera guys laughs, making me think that Jay's words are playing perfectly to his audience. So I work to keep myself from scowling at him.

Appearances are everything.

We walk by Wild Bill's Saddle Shop & Gifts next. The windows are crammed with paintings of horses, all done in the same gaudy, airbrushed style. I point at one that features a rearing stallion with a rainbow behind it. "That would look amazing in the living room."

Jay laughs. "Only if you help me pick out the frame. Do you like the one with the horseshoes or the lasso around the border?"

"Both!" I declare.

Character actors in fringed vests and calico dresses wander the street, staying just enough in character to be charming, not obnoxious. One tall man in a ten-gallon hat tips it at us and says, "Howdy, lovebirds!"

I blush while Jay waves.

We pass Miss Penny's Sweets. I spy a display of giant circular lollipops. Barrels overflowing with salt water taffy threaten to spill out the door. The sugar rush just from walking by is almost enough to make me dizzy.

I turn to say something to Jay. What? I'm not sure.

"My tattoo is itchy," is what comes out. Technically, it's true. The healing tattoo on my wrist does, in fact, itch. I show him my wrist.

Jay looks at it for a second. "That looks a little dry. Have you been putting lotion on it?"

"Am I supposed to?" I scrunch my face up.

"Yeah. You don't want your skin to dry out." He flashes me a grin. "Come here."

He takes my hand and walks me back to Wild Bill's. We

head in, passing the racks of Mount Gemstone cowboy hats and souvenir painted "I Survived Mount Gemstone" rocks. Jay seems to know where he's going, so I try to act like I don't feel intensely weird about his hand holding mine.

"Ah! That's what we need." He comes to a stop way in the back of the shop, before a small wall of suntan lotion, antacids, and small plastic bandages. He plucks a small tube of intense skin barrier repair lotion. He waves it at me. "Let me see your wrist."

"I can do it…" I say.

Jay pins me with a glance. "Give me your hand, *wife*."

Ah. I can't see the camera, but I know that it can't be far away if Jay is calling me his wife. Keeping my face blank, I bare my wrist. He squirts a little lotion onto my skin. As he smooths it over my wrist, I can feel my cheeks heat.

Why in the *fuck* am I blushing? I'm not even sure. This isn't exactly sexual. He does make eye contact with me the entire time, though.

When he finishes, he pulls my sleeve down and tucks the tube of lotion in my pocket. "There you go."

"Thanks." The word feels clunky rolling off my tongue.

He looks over my shoulder to Wren. "Will you pay for the lotion? We need to get moving."

Wren nods, brandishing a credit card. "On it."

Before I can say anything, Jay grabs my hand again. "Come on. We have to ride the rides!"

He's like an overgrown kid, eyes sparkling with excitement. I let him pull me along and he weaves us through the park's twists and turns like he does this all the time. The cameras are still on us. But for a moment? I forget to care.

Jay drags me to the Haunted Train Ride first. The exterior is all gothic spires and cobwebs. A giant, grinning skull perches atop the entrance like a macabre cherry.

"Oh god." I wrinkle my nose. I don't like anything scary, even things that are more tacky than terrifying. Why would I pay money for someone to make me feel frightened?

"We have to," Jay insists. "It's tradition."

I don't bother complaining that it may be his tradition, but it isn't mine. Instead, I let him pull me into the short line. A wooden sign creaks in the breeze, proclaiming a wait time of five minutes. The paint is so faded it looks like it's been gnawed on by termites.

We board a rickety train car, the kind that runs on a track set into the floor. It lurches forward with a groan. My heartbeat immediately picks up as we plunge into darkness. I brace myself for the first jump scare. I'm clutching the side of the car so hard my fingers hurt, and my knuckles must be white.

I've only been on this train once. I tried it when I went to camp here, fifteen or so years ago, and was so scared that I never tried it again. I'm expecting much of the same experience.

But Jay slides his arm around my shoulders and tugs me close. I focus on his nearness, his warmth, his muscular thigh pressed against mine. Leaning into the embrace, I pretend I'm just acting scared.

Jay squeezes my shoulders. *I can do this,* I think. It's not that bad when I'm not alone.

Then the ride ends up being... underwhelming, if I'm honest. Animatronic skeletons creak and sway like retirees at a zombie-themed bingo night. Ghostly figures on wires descend from the ceiling, moving with all the urgency of a Monday morning commute. The whole thing is more corny than scary. It reminds me of a haunted house that my elderly next door neighbors put together every year when I was a kid.

Well-meaning, but completely toothless. Just the way I like it.

I see the red glow of a camera and remember why we're here. "Aaaaaah!" I scream, as unconvincingly as a bad soap opera actress.

A vampire pops out of a coffin, but its cape catches on a nail. The fabric tears with a pitiful rip. The next thing I know, the vampire's head lolls to one side. Its eyes are half-closed in eternal, animatronic boredom. Jay loses it, his laughter echoing through the ride like deranged hyena calls. He's *hyperventilating*.

"Shhh," I whisper, squeezing his knee. But I'm giggling too. The sheer ridiculousness of it all is contagious.

We round a corner. We can't even manage to feign surprise when a ghost on a stick slowly wobbles into view.

"Boo," it says, in a voice as flat as week-old soda. "Boo... boo... boo..." It's stuck on a loop. The monotone "boos" stack up like a pile of unwanted Christmas presents.

I burst out laughing again, the sound explosive as my whoops echo in the confined space. Jay wipes a tear from his eye and points at the ghost. "I might die of fright," he howls.

The train car jerks to a stop at the end. We clamber out of the vehicle and are momentarily blinded by sunlight as we exit the ride. I'm still laughing, dragging in gulps of air. It feels strange but good. Stretching a muscle I'd forgotten I had.

Jay looks at me and his eyes are crinkled with genuine amusement. "That was worth the ten-dollar park entrance fee."

"It was pretty fun," I admit.

We step back into the park. I can see the crew setting up for the next shot. The spell breaks.

Oh... yeah. Suddenly, I remember why we're here and what we're doing.

"On to the next ride?" I ask, trying to sound enthusiastic.

Jay nods. "Yep. Let's go."

We wander through the park. Jay and I are walking closer now, our shoulders almost brushing.

We make it on to two more rides before Jay yells to the crew following us. "I think we're done for the day. You can go ahead and call it. We'll see you tomorrow." He looks at me. "I figured we could do the hotel tonight by ourselves."

"You're the boss," I say with a faux salute.

The crew calls it a wrap, packing up their stuff. I feel a mix of relief and something like disappointment. Jay and I have been playing our parts so well that it's starting to feel... I don't know, natural?

We walk through the park toward the parking lot. I glance back at the Ferris wheel, its neon lights flickering in the early evening haze. "I wish we'd had time for the Ferris wheel. It was my favorite ride as a kid."

Jay stops and looks at me. "I'm not in a hurry. We can still ride it if you want."

I hesitate, but only for a second. "Really?"

"Yeah," he says, shrugging. "Why not? We're not pressed for time. We can't check in to the hotel until five anyway."

We get in line. I feel a very slight twinge of guilt. This extends our time together, our make-believe. *But it's just a ride,* I tell myself. *Just one more scene.*

The line moves quickly. Soon we're squeezed into a tiny, rickety bucket seat. The attendant pulls a bar down over our laps and the seat sways back and forth gently as we start our slow ascent. Jay puts his arm around my shoulders. I stiffen, then relax into him.

It feels... comfortable.

I'm at a loss for what to talk about, but Jay doesn't seem to have the same problem. He chats about the park, about how the day went, about his plans for the week. His voice is smooth and easy. If there was pressure on me to act a certain way, it's gone the second he opens his mouth. I start to enjoy the moment, the way the park looks from up high, the way his arm feels around me.

Why Jay feels the need to embrace me, I don't know. It's not like there are cameras on us. But I don't exactly protest. It feels *nice*.

When there is a moment of silence, I speak up. "I remember coming here as a kid. My parents loved the Ferris wheel. They were high school sweethearts, you know. In it for the long haul, compatible in all ways. Friends before anything else."

"Oh yeah?"

"That's the only way to truly be happy, I figure. Just find your person, date for a hundred years, and marry when you're ready to have kids."

Jay laughs, then stops when he sees my face. "Oh. You're serious?" He shakes his head. "I've never been in a partnership like that. Not even with Blake. I don't even think it's possible at my age. I'm thirty-three. Looking forward, if I were to date for a hundred years, I'll be dead by the time I would even think about proposing marriage."

"I guess so." I frown and consider my next words carefully. "Is stability something you look for in a partner?"

He thinks for a moment, his eyes tracking the horizon. "I'm more interested in someone willing to climb mountains and travel to far-flung destinations with me. An activity partner."

I raise a brow but don't say anything. Of course he wants a thrill-seeker, someone who can match his pace.

Someone, I'm guessing, like Blake. I can't be that person. But it doesn't matter. This is all pretend, a temporary arrangement. We're just faking it.

Still, I can't help but feel slightly deflated. No one likes hearing that they're not someone's type.

The wheel reaches the top and pauses. The park sprawls out beneath us, a glittering patchwork of lights and shadows. Jay shifts. I think he's going to say something profound, but instead he pulls out his cell phone.

"One last shot for the fans," he says, starting to record. He turns the camera on us, and I put on my best "adoring wife" smile. Then, without warning, he leans in and kisses me.

He catches me dead in the center of my mouth. I'm startled, my body going rigid. The kiss is soft, his lips gentle against mine. I know this is for the camera, for his brand. But it feels awfully... real.

My heart hammers in my chest. Putting my hand onto his chest, I tentatively deepen the kiss, letting myself get lost in it for just a moment.

It's not hurting anybody for me to enjoy being kissed by Jay. And by God, the man knows how to kiss. Shivers of pleasure course through my veins. I press my thighs together.

Yeah, it's been a long time since I remember anybody kissing me like that. Jay did on our wedding night, I guess, but it's all a blur. Right here and now, it seems like Jay wants to tilt my head back, cup my jaw, and devour me whole.

He stops recording, but for some reason we keep kissing. The world around us dissolves into a haze of colors and sounds. When we finally pull away, I see a flicker of something in his eyes. It might be confusion, maybe. Or hesitation? Hard to say.

"We should..." I start, but my voice trails off.

"Yeah," he says, clearing his throat. "We should go."

As the wheel starts its descent, we sit in silence, the weight of what just happened pressing down on us. I don't know what to say. For once, neither does he.

When we reach the bottom, we make our way to the parking lot, our steps slow and measured. The day has taken on a surreal quality, like a dream that's starting to fade upon waking.

The Ferris wheel vanishes into the distance, its neon lights spinning like a tiny star in the darkening sky.

Chapter Eleven

Jay

If Mount Gemstone was a slightly wobbly Wild West fantasy, then the lobby of the Wagon Wheel Inn is a full-blown Wild West fever dream.

It's *deranged.* Wagon wheels hang crookedly on the walls, everywhere I look. And there's a massive, slightly terrifying statue of a rearing mustang smack in the center of the room. I can practically hear the theme music to an old Western playing in the back of my head.

Calla stands next to me, her nose wrinkling slightly as she takes it all in. She doesn't say a word, but I can almost hear her internal monologue: *What the hell am I doing here?*

I grin, letting the absurdity of it all wash over me. "This place has character," I say, aiming for optimism.

My voice echoes in the cavernous room and bounces off the tacky decor. Her gaze flicks to me, pinning me in place. I can't read her thoughts but I would guess that she is wondering if I've led her into an insane asylum or not.

We approach the front desk, where a woman wearing a fringed leather vest and a cowboy hat beams at us like she's been waiting all day for this moment. "Howdy, folks!

Welcome to the Wagon Wheel Inn. Do you have a reservation?"

I step forward. "Should be under Rustin. We've got the honeymoon suite." The words come out smoothly. But even as I say them, a small, absurd part of me wants to laugh.

Honeymoon suite. Yeah, right.

Beside me, Calla stiffens, but she doesn't say a word. I glance at her out of the corner of my eye, wondering what's going through her mind. Again, my best guess is that it's probably a mix of dread and regret. Maybe a little resignation.

I'm trying not to let it show, but this situation's got me on edge too. Fake marriages don't exactly come with an instruction manual. Especially not when you just shared a fairly spectacular kiss with your supposed wife and it left you all riled up.

The desk clerk's nails, bright red and tipped with rhinestones, click against the keyboard.

"Ah, here y'all are," she chirps. "Congratulations to the both of you!"

She hands me a keycard and slides a gift basket across the counter. It's full of cheesy Wild West trinkets: a mini cactus, a bottle of sarsaparilla, and a pair of ceramic shot glasses shaped like cowboy boots. "Enjoy your stay!" she croons. "Don't forget to check out the nightly square dance at the dining hall!"

Calla looks like she's about to object. Square dancing?! But I'm already steering her toward the elevators. She pulls her arm free from mine as soon as we're out of earshot. "This is crazy."

I press the elevator button and turn to face her. Her arms are crossed, her expression wary. I'm not sure what she's worried about. Me? The hotel. It doesn't matter at this point.

"Let's just go to see our room. We have to film a little content to satisfy the sponsor. But they only paid for three pictures of the newlyweds canoodling. We don't have to leave the hotel room if we don't want to."

The elevator dings and the doors slide open. Calla hesitates, then steps inside. I follow her, and we stand in awkward silence as the elevator hums to life. I can feel the tension rolling off her in waves, and I know I need to say something to break it.

"I'm just tired," Calla finally says. "I didn't get much sleep last night, remember?"

Ah. Now that she brings it up, I do seem to recall us staying up into the wee hours last night.

"Right." The elevator doors open before I have to figure out what to say next. We step into a hallway that's just as over-the-top as the lobby. Lasso-shaped light fixtures hang from the ceiling. The walls are lined with paintings of cowboys and Native Americans that look like they came straight out of a discount art store.

When we reach the door marked "Honeymoon Suite," I swipe the keycard and push the door open. The sight that greets us is... a lot. A massive heart-shaped bed with a wagon wheel headboard dominates the room, covered in a quilt that's an eye-searing mix of turquoise and coral. A stuffed bison head hangs on the wall, its glassy eyes glaring down at us like we've just invaded its territory.

I run a hand through my hair. "It's... something," I say, trying not to laugh.

Calla lets out a short, sharp bark of laughter. It's unexpected. For a moment, I see something shift in her expression. "It's hideous," she announces, shaking her head.

I grin. "Memorable, though. You've got to give it that."

She rolls her eyes but doesn't argue. Instead, she moves toward the window and pulls back the curtains, revealing a view of the hotel's indoor pool. It's shaped like a giant horseshoe, complete with a bronze statue of a bucking bronco in the center.

"Should we just bite the bullet and go check out the pool? It's empty right now," I venture.

Calla shakes her head but she is smiling. "If it will make you happy, I'll follow you anywhere. Well, anywhere I can get on a tank of gas, at least."

"Wow. That's a lot of trust. I'll try to live up to it." He grins. "Get your bathing suit on."

* * *

We stumble back into the room, dripping wet and laughing like idiots. Calla's hair is a tangled mess. The towel slung over my shoulder is doing nothing to soak up the water running down my back. That hot tub session turned into a splash war real fast, leaving us soaked but somehow grinning like kids.

Plus, Calla in a bikini is an absolute stunner. The entire time we were getting comfortable in the hot tub, I had to desperately try not to stare at her breasts. It was as tense as disarming a missile.

"I can't believe you," she says, still catching her breath. "You're like a giant, clumsy puppy."

I rake a hand through my wet hair, flicking droplets onto the walls. "Admit it, you had fun."

Her lips quirk up, even though she's trying to play it cool. "It was exquisite," she says.

We stand there for a second, the laughter dying down as

the silence stretches. My gaze flicks to the heart-shaped bed in the center of the room. Calla notices me noticing. She shifts on her feet, crossing her arms.

"So," I say, breaking the awkward pause. "How do you want to do this?"

She raises an eyebrow. "Do what?"

"Sleep. Er, the sleeping arrangements."

She bites her lower lip, thinking. "I can take the floor. There are plenty of blankets and pillows."

I shake my head. "Don't be ridiculous. We can share the bed. It's big enough."

"Is it?" she shoots back. Her tone is teasing, but her expression mildly wary.

"We're adults. We can put a pillow barrier down the middle if that makes you feel better."

She studies me, clearly weighing her options. I can tell she's torn. But eventually, she sighs. "Fine. But no cuddling."

I laugh at that. "I'll try to resist your gravitational pull."

We grab dry clothes. Calla disappears into the bathroom while I change as quickly as possible. I slide onto my side of the bed, propping myself up on an elbow. I've traded my usual polished look for a pair of plaid pajama bottoms, which feels weirdly casual in front of her.

Calla emerges, clutching a pillow like it's a shield. She walks to the bed slowly, almost like she's approaching a wild animal, and eases herself onto the heart-shaped mattress. She places the pillow down in the middle like a fortress wall.

That's when I see that she's wearing a silky black teddy. God damn, she is hotter than molten fire. My jaw drops and it takes me a solid three seconds to roll my tongue back in my mouth.

For the most part, I've only dated Instagram girlies like

Blake. She was a fitness freak like me and stick-skinny to boot. But Calla makes a very persuasive argument for a fuller figure being the sexiest of the body types. Big tits, nipped-in waist, and a shapely ass that looks amazing wrapped in black silk. One glance at her and I can physically feel my preference shifting to... well... *her*.

"So, uh...." Calla sits down on the bed, pulling another pillow in front of her body. I hate that pillow. I want to look at my fill. We don't always get what we want, though.

"Ready for bed?" I ask.

Her eyes are on my torso. She realizes that I see her looking at me and her cheeks color. "Yep. Totally ready."

She stares at me for another beat and then lies down, turning onto her side and facing away from me. I lie back, staring at the dimly lit ceiling for a moment before settling in. The sheets rustle, then silence again. I can hear the sound of her steady breathing.

"Calla," I say softly. She doesn't respond, but I know she's listening. "Goodnight."

Her silence stretches for a moment before she replies. Her voice is quiet. "Goodnight, Jay."

I heave a sigh and turn onto my side, trying to count sheep.

Chapter Twelve

Jay

Punching my pillow, I clench my teeth. All I can think about is how stunning Calla looks and how we're supposed to just sleep now.

Who in the world thought that having just one room was a good idea?

I can hear her breathing, slow and steady. She's probably asleep now. Lucky girl.

I, on the other hand, am a mess. I'm all wound up from the kiss we shared on the Ferris wheel earlier. That, plus seeing her in that ridiculously sexy teddy, has made sleep an impossibility. All the blood has left my brain and rushed to my dick, which is throbbing like a second heartbeat.

I toss and turn, trying not to disturb her. After what feels like an eternity, I realize there's only one way I'm going to get any relief. I need to take care of this, or I'll be up all night thinking about her.

About the way Calla's lips felt against mine. About her soft body so close to me in bed.

I get up as quietly as I can and tiptoe to the bathroom. The last thing I want is for her to wake up and see me like this. I'm a walking cliché, the horny dude who can't keep his dick in line. But I'm desperate.

The bathroom is a shrine to kitschy romance, with rose-patterned wallpaper and a massive glass shower. I turn the water on and let it heat up, hoping the sound doesn't wake her. My cock is still painfully erect as I strip off my pajamas and step into the shower. The hot water cascades over me. I take a deep breath, letting the steam fill my lungs.

I soap up my body. My cock is demanding attention, and I don't try to resist for long. I close my eyes and imagine Calla in her teddy, her hands running over my chest, her lips teasing mine. I groan and start to stroke, slowly at first, then with more urgency.

In my mind, she's on her knees, taking me into her mouth with a hunger that matches mine. I bite my lip, trying to keep quiet, but the pleasure is too intense. I imagine what her perfect pussy would feel like, how it would grip me.

In two minutes, I'm already dangerously close to the edge. That suits me just fine. The sooner that I come, the sooner I can crawl back in bed beside her and... well, probably still be horny.

The bathroom door opens. My eyes snap open in horror. Calla pokes her head in, her hair tousled and her eyes sleepy. She sees me jerking off and goes maroon, her mouth opening and closing like a fish out of water.

"I— I thought I heard you calling me," she stammers. "Are you... uh... okay?"

Was I calling her? Maybe. I'm not even sure at this point. My cock is still hard, even with her standing there. I'm proud of my body and not opposed to anyone looking as much as they want. But I've just been caught holding my dick while moaning her name.

Right now, there's a degree of mortification that even I feel.

"Calla," I say, my voice rough. "I was thinking about you. Maybe I did call your name." I take a breath, then plunge ahead, figuring I'm already as deep in as I can get. "Not to be crude, but if you want to join…"

To my amazement, she doesn't run. She bites her lip and just stares, considering. Then, after what feels like an eternity, she steps into the bathroom and closes the door behind her.

My heart is pounding so hard I can hear it in my ears.

Is this really about to happen?

The steam swirls around us and creates an almost dreamlike haze. A thousand thoughts race through my mind, each more frantic than the last. What will this mean for us? Will it ruin everything or make it all more real?

All I know for sure is that I'll die if she backs away now. Before I can second-guess myself, I crook a finger. Beckoning her closer. Daring her to take the next step.

Calla hesitates for a split second, her hand lingering on the doorknob. I prepare myself for the crushing disappointment of her walking away. But then she lets go and moves deeper into the bathroom, her bare feet silent on the tiled floor. My breath hitches.

She's all in? God, so am I.

I step out of the shower, water dripping from my body, and seize her, my lips crashing against hers with a desperate hunger. Her skin is cool against my wet, heated flesh. I can taste the remnants of her lip balm, sweet and intoxicating. My hands travel down her sides, feeling the slippery silk of her teddy. I tug it down over her hips. It pools around her ankles. Then she stands before me, vulnerable and breathtaking.

"You're so beautiful," I murmur. My voice sounds so strange, tense and thick with longing. I cup her breasts, feeling their weight, their softness. Her lips part and she lets out a small, needy whimper. Her nipples are hard against my palms. I brush them with my thumbs, eliciting a gasp from her.

There's no time to savor her like I want to. The train has left the station, and we're hurtling forward at breakneck speed. I kiss her again, more urgently, and she responds with a fierce passion that takes me by surprise. I back her into the shower. The hot water cascades over us, turning her hair into a dark, glistening mess.

Calla's hand slides down my torso. Her touch sends electric shocks through my body. She wraps her fingers around my cock. I suck in a breath, my entire being focused on that single point of contact.

"Fuck," I mutter, my forehead resting against hers. "Don't be gentle. I want to feel your touch."

She strokes me with a deliberate, unhurried rhythm. Meanwhile we kiss wildly, our tongues battling for dominance. The water creates a slick, slippery surface for my hands to wander over. Her body glistens like she's been coated in oil. Her breasts, her ass... the shadowed crease between her thighs calls to me. I want it *all*. I want to take her right here, right now, but I force myself to let her set the pace.

Easy boy. No need to act like you've never been to the damn rodeo before.

Under her sure strokes, I can barely stay still. The tension in my body is unbearable as I start to thrust against her wet fingers. Each movement sends a jolt of pleasure through me, making my knees weak.

Calla's eyes are locked on mine. I see a mix of desire and

admiration as she whispers that my body is amazing. Her words nearly push me over the edge. I grit my teeth, trying to hold on just a little longer.

"Don't judge me too harshly," I manage to say, my voice strained. "I'm so close to coming already."

She looks up at me with a teasing smile, her lips curving seductively. "Let go," she commands, her voice soft but unwavering. That smile... *fuck*, it's my undoing.

I go wild, fucking her hand with a desperate intensity. My hips drive forward with a mind of their own. Our mouths collide in a frantic kiss. I can feel her slick, hot body pressed against mine, every curve and contour fitting together like we were made for this. The sensation is overwhelming. My skin is hypersensitive from the water and her touch.

My orgasm crashes over me like a tidal wave. The pleasure is so intense that it borders on pain. It's the best, longest release of my damn life, each spasm wringing me out completely. I groan deep in my throat. My body convulses as it empties itself. It just keeps going and going, an unending stream of ecstasy that leaves me dizzy and breathless.

When I finally finish, she continues to stroke me, milking every last drop until I'm too sensitive to bear it. I grab her hand, pulling it away gently, and kiss her with all the gratitude and affection I can muster. My legs are like jelly, but I manage to stand as I push her back against the glass wall, pinning her there with my weight.

She tries to speak, pushing against my chest weakly. "It's okay, you don't have to—"

"Shhh. You're crazy if you think I'm not doing exactly what I need to be doing right now."

Her eyes widen slightly and her cheeks go a bewitching

shade of hot pink. She darts her tongue over her lips, wetting them. Excited, I growl, determined to give her the same pleasure she's just given me. I kiss her lips, her gorgeous breasts, savoring the taste of her skin. Everywhere my lips fall, her body is so soft and sweet.

I part her thighs. She opens them for me, her body trembling with anticipation. For a moment, it feels like we're in another world, a place where only our desires exist.

When I touch the slit between her legs, she moans loudly. "God, Jay. That feels so good."

I have the feverish thought that this is exactly what the Honeymoon Suite should be used for.

I use my hand to lift her leg, then slide my fingers into her, feeling the hot, wet clutch of her body. I kiss her lips, her cheeks, her neck. I savor the taste of her skin as I whisper in her ear.

"I love hearing you lose control, Calla."

Her breathing is ragged, her chest heaving. She lets out a series of small, helpless whimpers. She kisses me back with a desperate hunger, like she's been starving for this, for me. *It's been a while since my little wife has been touched like this*, I muse. The thought sends a possessive thrill through me.

She tries to close her thighs, to trap my hand and intensify the pressure, but I'm not done teasing her yet. I trace my hand up to find her clit, swollen and aching. I rub it slowly, deliberately, my wet fingers shaping the tender bud with gentle precision.

The look on her face is rapturous. I want to take a picture of her just like this to be able to remember just how amazing I feel right now. She closes her eyes and bites her lip, her face a mask of pure need. "Please," she whispers, her voice cracking with longing. "Please, touch me more. Make me come, Jay."

Her plea sends a jolt of arousal through me. I have to fight the urge to take her right now, to bury myself in her and make her scream my name.

"Patience, honey. Patience."

I keep my pace agonizingly slow. I want to draw out her pleasure, to make this last. Her hands clutch at my shoulders, her nails digging into my skin. She starts to writhe against me, her body moving with a will of its own.

I imagine what it would be like to do this every night, to come home to her and undress her slowly, to take her into the shower and blow her mind. The thought is almost too much to bear. I push it away, focusing on the here and now, on the way her body responds to my touch.

She's so close, teetering on the edge. I can feel her trying to hold back, to prolong the exquisite torture. Calla presses her lips together and lets out a groan.

"Jay..." she whispers. "Fuck!"

"That's what I like to hear, little wife," I murmur. "Let me hear how badly you need me to play with your clit."

Her lips part. A high, keening moan escapes her. Her body arches, every muscle tensing. Her orgasm is barreling down on her and she fights against the overwhelming sensation of it. I rub her a little harder, a little faster. I watch with pleasure as her hips start to buck against my hand, seeking more, demanding it.

"Let go," I whisper. "Isn't that what you said to me? Let go."

She screams, her body arching. I keep rubbing her clit, playing her like a violin.

"Good girl. Give me everything you have, Calla. I'm starving for it."

Her convulsions are intense. I can feel the flutter of her pussy clenching against my fingers. I don't let up, continuing to rub her clit as the orgasm stretches on. Her moans echo in the steamy bathroom.

When I think she's finished, I begin to slow. But her body tenses. Suddenly she comes again, the second wave crashing over her with even more force.

"God *damn.*" It's a revelation for me; I've never been with a girl who could have multiple orgasms, much less two in a row like this.

A surge of pride swells within me. How have I lived so long without knowing this incredible feeling of giving such profound pleasure?

I watch her face. Her eyes are screwed shut, her mouth open in a silent cry. She's absolutely stunning in her raw, unguarded ecstasy. Holy hell, I love this. I love seeing her like this, knowing that I'm the one making her feel so good. Thoughts of what this means for us flit through my mind, but I push them aside. Right now, all that matters is this moment and the way we're connecting physically.

I kiss her softly, tenderly, and she responds with a weary sweetness.

"Jay... that was incredible."

"I want to do it again. Give me another one, wife."

There's a new familiarity in the way we touch. She giggles.

"You're awfully greedy."

"Maybe I just like feeling you come on my fingers. I would touch you all night if you'd let me."

Calla kisses me tenderly. "I think you really would."

She has to pull my hand away to stop me from going for round three. We kiss, both laughing. As her spasms subside,

I rise slowly, my body protesting from the hot water and the intensity of the encounter.

"What now?" I whisper.

She gets up, rises on her tiptoes to kiss me, then takes my hand. "I think we should just go to bed."

"No talking about what just happened?"

Her lips twitch with humor. Instead of answering, she leans close and turns off the tap behind me.

Guess I got my answer.

We step out of the shower, dripping and flushed, and both grab towels from the rack. The warmth of the fabric against my skin does little to calm the storm inside me. I watch her as she dabs at her hair, her body still glistening, her movements slow and deliberate. There's a new softness in her eyes. A vulnerability that tugs at something deep within me.

I wrap my towel around my waist and take her in my arms, pulling her close. The dampness of her skin seeps through the towel. I kiss her forehead, her cheek, her lips.

Each kiss is a promise, a confession. We're treading dangerous waters, and we both know it.

"Jay—" she starts. But I silence her with another kiss, this one lingering, filled with all the things I'm too afraid to say out loud. She was right to suggest not talking. I don't want to talk anymore.

Talking will make this real. I'm not ready for reality to intrude just yet.

Calla pushes against my chest and gently separates us. I sigh and grab the heap of our clothes from the bathroom. There is a moment of awkward silence as we both pull our sleeping garments back on.

We make our way to the bed. She lies down first, her body stretching out like a cat. I can't help but admire the way she moves, the easy grace of her. I lie down beside her, propping myself up on one elbow, and trace a finger along her collarbone.

She meets my gaze. Her lips twist and for a second, I swear she's about to ask me if I want to fuck again. The answer on my lips is *absolutely, yes.*

"This doesn't have to change anything," Calla says quietly. "You know?" I can hear the doubt in her voice. She's trying to protect herself. To protect us both.

"Calla," I say. I want to say the right thing, but I don't know what that is. I settle on, "I know."

But do I really? Can we go back to the way things were? Have we crossed a line that can never be uncrossed?

Chapter Thirteen

Calla

Can you start a new batch of eclairs? I text Erica, the young woman I left in charge of my bakery. *I'll be in late tonight to bake and frost cupcakes for tomorrow.*

Less than a minute later, Erica sends a thumbs up. She's not the most communicative texter, but I put that down to her age. She only just graduated from Greater High. Content that my bakery will make it another day, I put my phone away.

Jay is driving the car this morning. I am in the passenger seat, trying my hardest to seem like last night was no big deal. Like, yes! I have incredible, life-changingly good sex almost every day! What of it?

He hasn't brought the topic up either. Instead, he keeps nervously promising me that today is going to be *amazing*. Honestly, after last night, my standards for things that are *amazing* might have changed. Maybe I'll like whatever he's got planned.

The drive from the Wagon Wheel Inn to our next stop

on our road trip takes less than twenty minutes. As we approach the town limits, a giant, peeling billboard proclaims, "Welcome to Claxon: Home of the World's Most Fun Leftover Fruitcake Festival!" My jaw drops as I read it.

"Most fun?? It's got to be the only one in the world!" I exclaim.

Jay slows the car. I can practically hear him grinning. "Welcome to the town where fruit goes to retire!"

"More like where dignity comes to die," I mutter.

There are a lot of people here. People who apparently think that fun and fruitcake can comfortably be used in the same sentence. Those people are wrong, just so we are on the record.

Jay pulls onto Main Street. I cast a skeptical eye over the kitschy decorations lining the street. Every lamppost is adorned with tinsel and little brown and green blobs; I can only assume that they're fruitcake ornaments. It's like a bad Christmas movie set; except it's the beginning of February. We missed the Christmas mark by six weeks.

Jay parks the car and I take a moment to smooth my skirt and adjust my hair in the visor mirror. Have to look good for all the Claxon locals, I guess. We step out into the chill of the winter day. Almost immediately, I regret my choice of attire. A-line skirts and sleek tops are my uniform, but today I wish I'd opted for two more sweaters under my heavy coat. At least my Converse are comfortable.

We make our way toward the town square, where a makeshift stage has been erected. A banner flaps lazily in the icy breeze, announcing the "25th Annual Fruitcake Toss." The crowd is a mix of locals and curious tourists, all huddling close to the heat lamps that dot the street. I spot a woman wearing a fruitcake-themed bikini top.

My soul cringes in sympathy. She really must be freezing her tits off.

"Is this for real?" I ask Jay.

When I look at him, he's scanning the crowd with the enthusiasm of a Labrador at a dog park. "It's tradition," he says, as if that explains anything. "Small towns have a way of making the ridiculous seem charming."

"Charming," I repeat, dubious. "We live in a small town. This? This is just bonkers."

"You must be Jay and Blake!" A man in a gaudy, fruit-laden hat approaches us. He's beaming. "You're here to film yourselves participating in the fruitcake toss, right?"

Jay scowls, his hand slipping around my waist. "Jay and Calla."

"Oh. I'm sorry, there must have been a mix up in our public relations department. No matter. Welcome to Claxon! I'm Mayor Abernathy."

I open my mouth to say something. I'm not sure what.

"Nice to meet you." Jay cuts in with a broad smile. "We're here to observe this time. Maybe we'll participate next year."

Next year? I shoot him a questioning look. We're not supposed to be making long-term plans for fruitcake festivals.

The mayor's smile doesn't falter, though his hat wobbles precariously. "Well, make sure to try some of the fruitcake punch. It's a local favorite." He hands Jay a flyer. Before I can say anything, he's turned to greet another hapless couple.

"O-kay...," I say. We give him a wide berth as we continue down the jam-packed street. Out of curiosity, I tug the flyer from Jay's hand. It's covered in cartoonish fruitcake graphics that seem to be competing with one another for the title of 'most garish'. It's a list of the events today and the corresponding times. I fold it and stuff it in my pocket.

"Hey, I just realized that there's no camera crew today." I raise my brows and rub my hands together for warmth. My tattooed wrist, freshly anointed with lotion, tingles faintly. "What gives?"

"The company van had a flat tire." Jay flaps a hand. "It'll be back on the road soon enough."

"So it's just us today, huh?"

Jay smirks. "Yup. Just you and me. That won't be a problem, will it?"

The way he's looking at me makes my cheeks flush. But I can't give him the satisfaction of knowing that he made me look away, so I keep full eye contact.

"I can't imagine it will be," I reply as sweetly as possible. "I didn't get that much sleep last night, so—"

Jay trips over his feet, looking like a startled baby bunny. "Uh, yeah. Same."

I clear my throat. I didn't realize that things could be this awkward between Jay and me. But here we are, not talking about the elephant in the room.

Jay points to a building that people are streaming in and out of. "Maybe we should head in there. The Fruitcake Bakery should be... safe."

I nod and let him usher me along as I let that word sink in. Safe? Safe? What am I supposed to read into that? We hurry inside while I ponder the meaning of the word.

The Fruitcake Bakery is a shrine to bad taste in every sense of the word. Shelves groan under the weight of neon-colored fruitcakes, each more hideous than the last. A glass display case at the counter showcases slices in a dizzying array of flavors. It seems to dare anyone to take a bite.

Jay and I step further inside, and I take in the décor: a Christmas tree made entirely of stacked fruitcake rounds. The tree twinkles with tinsel and ornament shards. It's like a holiday hallucination coming to life.

"Can you believe this place? It's like walking into a time capsule from the 1950s." Jay looks as happy as a kid on his birthday. He seems to take joy in these weird, horrible, kitschy places.

His attitude is kind of admirable, if you can get past how tiring it can be. Places that I would never in a million years deign to go? Jay dives into them headfirst and smiles while he does it! He is either secretly a serial killer... or he's just a counterbalance against my practical, *occasionally* terrible, attitude.

I make a noncommittal noise and focus on the menu board above the counter. It lists flavors in a curly, hand-painted script. Each name is more absurd than the last: Tropical Temptation, Berry Suspicious, Citrus Surprise, Nuts About Bacon, Pickle Me Fancy.

They all sound inedible.

A woman in a flour-dusted apron steps out from the kitchen. She scans the crowd, but most of the tourists are clearly still looking around. Her eyes lock on me. "What can I get for you folks?"

Jay leans on the counter with the casual grace of a man who's never had to rush for anything in his life. "We're here for the samples."

The woman beams. "Help yourselves!" She gestures to a platter laden with bite-sized pieces of fruitcake. Each one is stuck with a toothpick and labeled with a flavor tag.

I hang back as Jay grabs a handful. He stuffs a few in his mouth before passing me one. "You have to try this one. It's actually pretty good."

I take a piece of Berry Suspicious and reluctantly nibble the corner. He's right. The fruitcake is moist. The spices are heavy but nicely balanced. It tastes like a bite of autumn. Overall, I'm disarmed by how not terrible it is.

"See?" Jay says. He pops another piece into his mouth. "Told you." I just shrug. He pulls out his phone and puts his arm around me. "Come on. Act like you like me," he jokes.

You're not the worst guy in the world. And you gave me multiple orgasms last night. That is very much the problem in this scenario.

Instead of saying that, I smile for the camera and kiss Jay's cheek.

We work our way through the platter, commenting on each flavor like judges on a reality cooking show. Some have a nice tartness; others are overly sweet but bearable. Some flavors are so insane that it's comical. The pickle cake is the actual worst. It's the only one that makes me gag and I spit it out.

Jay insists on bringing an entire Pickle Me Fancy cake home with us.

"As long as I don't have to eat it," I shrug. "I just hope you give anyone that tries it fair warning."

"Where would the fun be in that?" Jay asks.

When he looks at me with the biggest grin on his face, I'm pretty sure he is the devil incarnate. I suppose I should be happy that his devilry is not directed at *me*.

When we walk out of the store, a small crowd has gathered around the doorway. Someone waves, and Jay returns it with the easy familiarity of a politician on the campaign trail.

I forget, sometimes, that he's a minor celebrity. Or maybe I just try to forget.

"So," Jay says, breaking into my thoughts as we step out

onto the slushy sidewalk. "Do you really think love is all about being best friends?"

I frown. Where is this coming from? "That's what the studies say. Friendship is the foundation of a lasting relationship."

"Studies." He blows a raspberry. "I think love is more about excitement. Spontaneity. Keeping things fresh."

"Sure, in the beginning. But that fades. You need something deeper to sustain you. Ten, twenty, thirty years on? You can only white-water raft or go to Fiji so many times. By the time you're getting up there in years, you have to have friendship to lean on."

He stops. "So, you're saying our whirlwind fruitcake romance isn't the epitome of true love?"

His tone is light and playful. He's not searching for any real truths. He's just making conversation to pass the time. That's more than fine by me. He opens his mouth to continue our banter, but he is cut off when a voice calls out Jay's name.

I turn my head to see Jay's camera crew approaching. I guess the blown tire didn't hold them down for long. My stomach tightens. I was sort of enjoying not being on camera constantly. But now his crew is ready to capture every moment on film. There's no use being bitter about it so I just paste on a smile.

Jay jogs over to them, then turns back. "Calla," he says, beckoning me. "We need a few shots together. Let's do this quickly."

I step in, and a member of the crew directs us to various poses. Each one is more intimate than the last: Jay holding me from behind, our hands intertwined around the fruitcake, our still brand-new tattoos stinging. Me standing on tiptoes, pretending to kiss his nose. The whole thing feels like play-acting. Yet there's an undercurrent of awkwardness that makes me uneasy.

"That should do it," says the crew member after what feels like an eternity. "We can just follow you two around for the next hour to get the B-roll we'll need."

Jay turns to the crew. "Can I see what shots we have so far?" he asks, but it's not a question. His demeanor has shifted in an instant. Gone is the laid-back jokester. In his place is a man of purpose, focused and precise.

I watch, wide-eyed, as he tells the crew what kind of shots they should be looking for next. His directions are clear and confident. This is a side of him I haven't seen before. Honestly? It's... impressive.

Jay's not just coasting on his abundant charisma. He actually knows what he's doing.

In the crush of crew members, I spot a petite woman. She has long reddish hair, big pink glasses that frame her blue eyes, and freckles upon freckles. I recognize her as Jay's younger sister. She often appears in his social media posts. Jay likes to tease her for being nerdy.

Wren is standing a few paces away, scrolling through her phone. I take a deep breath and walk over to her.

"Hey, Wren," I say, summoning my most genuine smile. I don't know if she's in on the ruse or not, so I say, "We haven't properly met. I'm, uh, your new sister. "

Wren pushes a heavy set of glasses up her nose. Her shy smile doesn't scream *I'm complicit in your scheme*. She steps forward, offering me her hand. "Calla, right? I'm so pleased to meet you."

Her voice is almost too soft for me to pick it up. She seems sweet and a little nerdy.

Yeah, this is awkward. "Would you like to join me for lunch while Jay finishes up?"

She looks up, surprised, then glances toward her brother. "Sure," she says, tucking her phone into her bag. "I'd love to."

We find a small café just off the town square, its interior a hodgepodge of vintage furniture and eclectic art. A space heater buzzes noisily in the corner, doing little to combat the day's chill. We take a seat by the window, keeping our coats on, and a server hands us menus before wandering off.

"My apologies. I sort of just figured out that you're Jay's sister." I glance at Wren over the menu. "I know who you are, but I don't really have any details to fill in the sketch."

Wren pushes her glasses up her nose and gives a dry laugh. "Same, I guess. What do you want to know?"

I narrow my eyes, considering her question. "Have you always lived in Greater?"

The server returns with our drinks, and we pause to take sips. Mine is a sweet tea, heavy on the sugar; Wren has a lemonade.

"Born and raised," she says. "My parents actually live in Celtic Hills. Jay went to Emory, so I went to Emory too. I copied him for years." She laughs. "Now I live on the same street as he does."

"Wildflower Lane?"

She bobs her head. "Yeah. I live in apartment building way at the end. Jay owns the building." Wren shrugs. "It's a decent place to live while I try to figure out what I'm going to be when I grow up. I guess I'm still copying Jay a little."

"How old are you?"

"Twenty-two. My birthday is in a couple of months."

The waitress returns and we both order. A bowl of white beans and cornbread for me, a roast beef sandwich for Wren.

"Well, let me tell you," I say when the waitress is gone.

"I didn't have my life figured out right away. I'm twenty-eight, but I didn't get my little bakery until six months ago. Before that, I was baking from home when I lived on College Avenue. There were always sheet pans of cookies cooling on every surface in my little studio apartment."

"That sounds nice! I do love a good sugar cookie when I'm trying to clean my living room slash bedroom."

"You would have been obsessed with my old place, then. It was so small! The rental agent kept saying it was quaint and cozy." I laugh, rolling my eyes.

"Hey, if it had heat and AC, that's all you really need." Wren smiles.

Silence fills the space between us. I grasp for a new topic. Then I realize what I really want to ask. Wren probably has all the dirt on Jay. "So," I say, trying to sound casual. "Did you hate Blake and are glad the wedding was called off?"

"God." She laughs. "I'm so glad. Don't tell Jay, but I thought Blake was a self-important snob."

Hearing Wren say that is like a balm to my soul. It's not that I'm feeling competitive with Blake. It's more like she is just a gorgeous, skinny, Instagram-perfect wife. And being placed side-by-side just makes me feel... *less than*.

I give Wren a secretive smile. "Good. I was hoping that you would say that. I haven't met your mom, but I hope that she wasn't on Team Blake either."

"You probably won't meet Mom until she and Dad are back from their trip. They weren't at Jay and Blake's wedding. They... aren't exactly the warmest people." Wren leans back in her chair, stretching her arms behind her head. "Our parents are busy people, very career-focused. We had a nice upbringing. But it was Jay and me against the world most of the time. We were inseparable."

That explains a lot. "Sounds like you two had a solid childhood."

"We did," she says, though there's a wistfulness in her tone. "We were lucky. Jay made sure I was never lonely, even when our parents were off doing their thing."

I take another sip of tea, letting her words sink in. This is the background I needed, the context to understand why Jay is the way he is. He's someone who's had to create his own support system.

Wren continues, "When Jay started the company, I wasn't sure what I wanted to do. He offered me a job, and it just made sense. Working with him is like an extension of our childhood."

I tilt my head, curious. "And the company... it's doing well?"

She laughs, a short, bright burst. "You could say that. We all worked hard, but Jay was the driving force. He's built something pretty amazing."

I remember what Wren said earlier about Jay taking care of them. "It sounds like he's more than just a boss. Like he's a mentor."

"Exactly," she says, nodding. "He's taught me so much, and not just about the business. He's always been there for me, for all of us."

Our food arrives. My stomach audibly growls, making Wren giggle. We dig in, eating in silence for a few minutes.

Wren finishes half of her sandwich and sits back. She eyes me with a newfound curiosity. "You know, you're not what I expected."

I freeze. "Oh? And what did you expect?"

She shrugs, but there's a slyness to it. "Someone more... I don't know. Someone different."

I laugh, though it comes out more nervous than I intend. "Different how?"

Wren breaks the silence. "I'm just saying, you seem more grounded. More real."

"Thanks," I say, though I'm not sure it's a compliment. If she thinks I'm real, does that mean she sees through the ruse?

"Anyway," Wren says, her tone lightening. "It's obvious that you care about him."

I blink. "What?"

"Jay. The way you look at him. Like he's a prime cut of beef. Blake never looked at him like that, you know."

I feel the blood rush to my cheeks. "I— We're just—"

Wren waves a hand, dismissing my stammering. "It's okay. I get it. My brother is a handsome dude. And it's obvious that he worships you, too."

My eyes widen with shock. What is she talking about??

Before I can protest, Wren's eyes flick past me. She sits up straighter. I turn to see Jay walking toward us. He's got this relaxed stride that belies the intensity I know lurks beneath the surface.

"How's it going?" he asks. He takes an empty chair from a nearby table and spins it around to sit down. "What'd I miss?"

I look to Wren, wondering if she'll spill everything. My not-so-sneaky interrogation. Her observations about me. Her thoughts about Jay liking me. Instead, Wren just smiles, her eyes sparkling with mischief. "Nothing important," she says.

I let out a breath I didn't know I was holding. Jay looks from Wren to me, then back to Wren. It's as if trying to decipher a code. "O-kay," he says, "Be cryptic. The real question is, do y'all have room for dessert?"

"You're having dessert?" Wren asks.

He looks at me meaningfully. "I sure hope so."

My cheeks glow so red that I'm not sure they'll ever cool down again.

Today was supposed to be a simple exercise in playing our parts. We were just doing our best to make the whole marriage look convincing.

Chapter Fourteen

Calla

"Ready for our next adventure?" Jay asks. He's in the driver's seat, taking us toward our next sponsored stop.

I squint. Instead of answering, I say, "Aren't you worn out? This has probably been the longest week of my entire life. You conveniently forgot to mention that."

He grins and hands me a brochure. The words "Ultimate Ropes Course" leap off the page and strangle my courage. I can feel the blood drain from my face.

"I'm looking forward to it. I've never done a ropes course before," Jay goes on.

"Heights are my archnemesis," I squeak, hoping he'll show mercy. "You can't really expect me to go along for the ride when I think we both know it's basically a death trap."

Jay gives me a funny look. "But you were okay with the Ferris wheel?"

"Okay. I amend my phrasing. I hate being really high up without a floor under my feet. Thus, Ferris wheel, totally cool. Ropes course? Not so much."

"Well, I guess I can manage on my own." He shrugs, all

nonchalance and playfulness. "But I think my fans will be disappointed. Not to mention that Blake was jazzed about coming here."

Blake? Oh, fuck no. She had her chance and threw it away. My competitive spirit ignites faster than the fire on a flambéed dessert.

"On second thought... maybe I will do fine." The lie comes out of my mouth weird.

Jay narrows his eyes at me, sensing my awkwardness. "Are you sure?"

I swallow. All I can imagine is me falling off some terrifyingly high ledge and going splat. I feel *green.* "Absolutely," I bluff. "It'll be... fun."

If he has any reservations about that statement being true, he wisely keeps them to himself.

We arrive at the course, a towering labyrinth of ropes and platforms that looks like it was designed by a sadistic Boy Scout. I swallow hard. Jay surveys the course with the casual interest of a man inspecting his lawn after a light rain. I, on the other hand, probably look like I'm about to hurl.

He reaches out to me, cupping my elbow. "You're sure you're okay?" he asks. Genuine concern softens his chiseled features.

"Fine," I lie. "Totally fine. I want to do... that."

He pulls me into a side hug. "I'll be with you the entire way," he promises. "We'll both crush it."

I lean into his warmth, savoring the contact for a few seconds longer than necessary. It's easy to suck in a deep breath of his natural scent mixed with his cologne. This feeling of not being alone?

Not having the clinging thought that the person I am trying to impress is laughing at me is *huge.* I've had that several times before, with guys I wanted to date.

The feeling is nice. I could get used to it.

We grab harnesses and try to get into them. I must look like a complete fool trying to put mine on. The harness has twelve straps made of nylon webbing in different colors, and as I wrestle with them, it only becomes less clear what color goes where.

Jay gets his on with little difficulty and then tries to help with mine. "Here, you've got this strap backward," he says. With a certainty that could only belong to a handsome white man, he detangles my harness. "Okay, now step into this loop."

I let him manipulate my body for half a minute while I give him the stink eye. "Aren't you supposed to be a newbie?"

He shrugs. "It's intuitive."

"It's a bunch of different colored ropes in a pile. What am I not picking up on?"

"Dunno. Maybe it's just all the rock climbing I've done."

"That would make sense." I wonder if Blake rock climbed with him. Probably. That's probably why he wanted to marry her. Me, he married by complete mistake.

His hands pull at the front of my harness, making sure it's snug against my breasts. "You sure you want to do this?"

"I'm not going to let a little thing like mortal terror stop me," I say, attempting bravado.

The truth is, I don't want to look weak in front of him. And he brought up Blake as a comparison. I feel awkward when we are measured with the same stick. How can I not be in competition with the woman he was supposed to marry?

The harness cinches me in like a wasp's thorax. It's definitely not made for comfort. But I have to admit, my butt looks pretty fabulous. I catch Jay sneaking a glance at my ass. I give him a mock glare. He just grins and shrugs.

"Ready?" he asks.

No. Not even a little. But I nod, because some batshit part of me is actually looking forward to this.

"As ready as I'll get."

The trees swallow us as we ascend, their leafy canopies creating a dappled green tunnel. My legs are already trembling as we rise. As we tackle the first obstacle, Jay moves with the grace of a panther. His balance is impeccable, thanks, I assume, to his power yoga and morning runs. I, on the other hand, am a teetering stack of dishes, ready to crash at any moment.

He catches me as I stumble for the fifth time. While I like having his hands on my body, I actually loathe how terrible I am at this. Why did I think this was a good idea again?

"Just take it slow. You'll get the hang of it." His voice is annoyingly calm and makes me feel like punching him.

I shoot him a look that could curdle milk. "Easy for you to say, Mr. Fitness. You actually look hotter when you're doing something physically demanding."

He gives a surprised laugh. "Calla, you need to forget about how you look. Ropes courses don't flatter anyone. Just focus on having fun."

I want to argue, to tell him that looking ridiculous is the least of my concerns. But he's right. I need to remove my main fear: the fear of falling.

So I take a deep breath, close my eyes, lean my head back, and step backwards, knowing I will tumble down.

The fall is immediate and terrifying. I plunge into a

void that yanks a scream from my lungs. Then the safety harness catches me, yanking my whole body to stop me from falling. I swing like a pendulum. My heartbeat slams against my ribcage.

After a second, I open my eyes to see Jay letting go as well. His body arcs through the air with the abandon of a kid on a playground. He whoops. I can't help but giggle.

"I just wanted to see how it felt to fall," I say, raising my hands in a shrug. "Not terrible."

"You did that on purpose?" Jay looks at me and I think I catch admiration in his eyes. "That's smart."

Ropes course employees reel us in like two floundering fish. My legs are jelly. My hands are raw from gripping the ropes. But a strange exhilaration buzzes through me now.

I can do this. It's not that bad.

"The first challenge," Jay announces. He points to an angled trestle bridge that looks like it was stolen from a pirate ship. "Piece of cake."

I glare at the so-called piece of cake. It's a wobbly mess of planks and ropes, suspended at a precarious angle. My stomach does a somersault.

We clip in and start across. I take tiny, shuffling steps, my knees knocking together like castanets. Jay prances ahead, light on his feet, a caffeinated mountain goat in human form.

"You're doing great!" he calls back. He's already three quarters of the way across.

"Shut up," I mutter. A small part of me is proud that I've made it this far, though.

I take another step, then another, my confidence growing ever so slightly. I'm going to make it. I'm really going to—

The bridge wobbles beneath me. I breathe out and

refuse to look down at the ground thirty feet below me. I focus on my next step, forcing myself to keep moving forward. My knuckles blanch as I grip the ropes for dear life, but I don't stop.

Finally, I reach the platform at the end. I unclip and lean down, my legs shaking with exertion. "Oh god. I did it."

Jay comes over and gently moves me further away from the edge. I straighten and suddenly I'm in his arms. He grins. "You did great, Lily."

"Lily?" I say, tilting my head and scrunching up my nose.

He pulls up his shirtsleeve to show off the tattoo that he got the night we got married. "I think I can give you a nickname if I want. Don't you think I've earned the right?"

"And what do I call you? Bird?" I lean against his chest, a small smile breaking out across my face.

He smirks. "I wish you would, Lily."

I roll my eyes, the corners of my mouth twitching despite myself. "Yeah, yeah. What's next, Tarzan?"

The partner balance beam stretches out before us like a tightrope in a circus. I eye it with the suspicion of a cat confronting a cucumber. It seems completely unnatural.

Jay steps up first, extending a hand to me. I take it. We both teeter recklessly as I join him on the beam.

"Remember, it's all about balance," he says, as if imparting ancient wisdom. I resist the urge to smack him, but only because I am currently trying not to tip us both over.

"See? We're getting better."

I almost believe him. "That's good. Because if we put all of today's footage online, we probably wouldn't ever get laid."

He turns to me, an eyebrow arching. "We're married.

We shouldn't have to look outside the marriage for hot sex. We have everything we need right here already."

The suggestion hangs in the air. My mind races ahead of me, picturing scenarios I have no business imagining. Like, for instance, our little shower encounter.

Jay stripped off his clothes.

Jay stripping off my clothes.

The look of sublime passion on Jay's face when he slides into my tight pussy and fucks so hard, so deep, that we both start to—

"Whoa—" I lose my balance and topple sideways again. The harness bites into my skin as I begin to fall.

But Jay is right there this time. He steadies me. "Are you okay?"

God, I definitely lost my balance because I was thinking about being fucked. "I'm fine," I mumble. "Let's just finish."

We start moving again, slower this time. It's quiet for a moment as we both concentrate.

"Have you ever wondered if we've already had sex?" he asks, as casual as if he's inquiring about the weather.

"*What??*" I balk. "No! Why, do you think we have?"

"I mean, maybe. I woke up with whipped cream in places whipped cream shouldn't be."

My cheeks burn. "You did not!"

"All I'm saying is that it's possible that we did the dirty on our wedding night. And I for one hold that possibility close to my heart."

I'm speechless, a thousand thoughts colliding in my head like bumper cars. He can't be serious. Or can he? The idea that he's even considered this makes my heart do weird, uncomfortable things.

I knew, on some level, that he thinks about me in a sexual way. I mean... that was what he was doing when I barged into the bathroom and found him... uh... touching himself.

But now I have to face the possibility that maybe it wasn't just that one time.

Maybe he thinks about fucking me a lot.

Maybe as much as I think about fucking him.

Tongue-tied, I put my head down and finish the obstacle. We reach the end of the beam and unclip, my hands shaking not just from the exertion. This whole time, I've thought that he only married me because he was drunk. But now, I'm not so sure. Maybe he married me because he thought I was hot. The way he teases me, his easy charm. It feels different, like he actually *sees* me.

And that thought is almost as unsettling as dangling in midair.

The grand finale looms before us: a tandem zipline stretching through a valley of treetops. My heart is already in my throat and we haven't even strapped in yet. Jay takes the lead, as usual, his confidence an unshakeable foundation.

He beckons me over as if he hasn't just thrown me for a loop. I shuffle like a condemned woman walking to the gallows.

"Come here," he says, his voice warm and inviting. He pulls me into his chest, his arms wrapping around me from behind. My entire body tenses, then melts, then tenses again as I realize how close we are. How... intimate.

"It's for safety," he adds, though I can hear the grin in his voice. "And maybe a little something else."

Shameless flirting. What the hell am I supposed to do with this? My mind is a whirlwind. My thoughts are a confused tangle of anxiety. I can't decide if I want to push him away or pull him closer. I'd be lying if I said I wasn't desperate for another taste of his lips.

The staff member waves at us. "Y'all are good to go."

Jay and I take a collective breath. That answers that, I guess.

"Three, two, one—" The lady yanks the lever and we're off like a shot.

The initial drop is a gut-wrenching freefall. I scream so loudly I surprise myself. The wind tears at my hair, my clothes, my skin as we shoot through the trees like a two-human cannonball. I expect terror, but what I get is a rush of pure, unfiltered joy.

Jay holds me close, making me feel invincible.

"This is so going on Insta!" I shout. My words are muffled by the trees whizzing by me.

Jay's laughter mixes with the wind. I can *feel* him grinning against the back of my head. For a moment, I forget everything.

The accidental marriage, the awkwardness, the worry. All that exists is the here and now, the exhilaration of flight, and the man holding me tight against his body.

Too soon, we see the end of the line approaching. Our speed slows. The landing platform rises to meet us. My feet touch down first, wobbly and unsure.

Jay steadies me with a hand on my shoulder. I turn to thank him, to say something. I'm really not sure what. But before I can figure it out, he pulls me in and kisses me.

It's not a tentative, testing-the-waters kiss. It's a full-on, bending-me-backward, making-a-scene passionate kiss. My hands fly to his chest, then his shoulders. My eyes flutter closed. I kiss him back, putting all my feelings into it, because why not? We're still riding the high of the zipline.

The kiss feels like the natural conclusion.

He cups my jaw. His fingers tangle in my hair. His tongue slides against mine, promising wicked things.

When he finally breaks the kiss, I'm breathless. My lips are tingling, my head is swimming. Jay looks at me with an intensity that makes my knees weak. "I could get used to that," he whispers against my lips. "My little wife."

My brain scrambles to process what just happened. God, I think that means he likes me. He really likes me. And the craziest part is, I think I like him too. I *really* like him.

We unclip from the zipline harnesses and make our way down a winding path to the ground. The silence between us is thick with unspoken words, with possibilities. I'm afraid to give voice to the feeling between us. The worst thing in the world would be for Jay to tell me that I misinterpreted his words.

My little wife. I doubt very much that I took it out of context.

Once we are safely back down on solid earth, Jay runs a hand through his hair, a gesture I've come to recognize as his tell. He's thinking. Maybe even overthinking. "I just got out of a relationship, for heaven's sake. Three days ago I was almost married to someone else."

I stop walking and turn to fully face him. His eyes are somewhere far away, his mind clearly wrestling with something.

"Jay—" I start, but he cuts me off.

"It's just... you're not what I expected, Calla."

My heart does a little flip, hopeful and terrified all at once. "What did you expect?"

He meets my gaze. For a moment, he's stripped down. The humor that he hides behind is gone, the carefree thrill seeker vanished. He looks sort of puzzled.

That's funny. I'm also puzzled. I've got a lot of questions about our relationship. More with every day, it seems.

"Someone a little easier to deal with," Jay says at last. "But a lot less interesting, I suppose."

I don't know what to say to that. Should I be flattered or insulted? He's giving me compliments wrapped in confessions, all tied up with the ribbon of our complicated situationship.

"This is already messy." He sighs, seeming frustrated. "Maybe we could make it... I don't know, a little simpler? Friends with benefits who are also married?"

My breath catches. Is he serious? Part of me is tempted. Sorely tempted. But another part knows this would only complicate things further. I open my mouth to tell him that but no sound comes out.

"Think about it. No pressure either way."

Jay starts walking down the path leading us back to the adventure park's entrance. I follow a few steps behind him, still reeling from his revelations. The rush from the zipline lingers in the air between us, a spark neither of us wants to acknowledge yet can't quite extinguish.

Chapter Fifteen

Calla

There is a break in our "honeymoon" after the three appearances, just enough time for me to "move in" with my "husband with benefits" and to check if my store had burned down yet. Our next sponsored appearance isn't for another three days.

Originally, I planned to spend the downtime baking cupcakes and potentially reacquainting myself with my vibrator, like *a lot*. But Jay had other plans, so I'm here.

At Jay's house.

Yup.

I stand on Jay's doorstep with three enormous suitcases. I've packed as if I were moving for real. In truth, having all my things here will make the charade more believable. So why am I having trouble ringing Jay's doorbell?

The door swings open, unbidden. Jay's face lights up. "Finally!"

"It took me a while to pack. But I was always going to show up here. I like to keep my commitments."

He steps aside to let me in, then reaches for the nearest suitcase. "Here, let me."

I hesitate for a moment, then let him take it. He lifts it with ease. I can't help but notice the way his muscles flex under his shirt. *Focus, Calla. Fix your mind on anything that isn't a replay of Jay asking you to be friends with benefits.* I've gone through that particular moment enough for today.

Jay sets each of my suitcases down in the living room, then looks back at me with an expression I can't quite read. Indecision? I rush to fill the awkward void.

"So, where am I going to sleep? The guest room? The couch?" I hate the second idea, but I try not to let it show.

He crosses his arms over his chest. "Calla, if we're going to make this believable, my wife should sleep in my bed."

Heat rushes to my face. I'm sure I look like an over-ripe human tomato. "Your bed? You mean with you in it?"

"Unless you had something else in mind?" Jay shrugs, his nonchalance driving me insane. How can he be so cool about all this? "It's a big bed. Besides, it's just sleeping. Right?"

"Just sleeping," I echo. My voice sounds strangled. This man is surely going to be the death of me.

He pushes off the wall and walks toward me. He stops just close enough that I have to tilt my head back to look up at him. "Relax. You can sleep wherever you want. I'm just saying what would make the most sense."

He touches my shoulder in a way that could be a caress... or could be nothing more than reassurance from a friend.

I swallow hard, my mind racing with possibilities. "Noted."

He drops his hand and steps back. Suddenly, I can breathe again.

"You shouldn't sleep on the couch, though. And there isn't a bed set up in the guest room. The downstairs is more of a museum than a living space. It's all for show. You should see how I live upstairs."

"I guess I will." I glance around the posh living room. It does have a staged quality, like something out of a glossy magazine. "You said that someone decorated this place. For Instagram, I'm assuming?"

He laughs. "If I'm honest, my ex-fiancée decorated it. Blake was 'getting my place ready for her to move in.' It's her taste, not mine. Why would I choose that?" He points to a painting of rugged mountains and a stream with an enormous jumping fish. "Where is that supposed to be, huh? Colorado? Alaska? Montana? Also, not for nothing, but I hate fishing. It's fucking boring."

My mind instantly conjures the photos I'd googled the morning after the cake tasting. Jay and Blake, the picture-perfect couple, smiling at some gala or other. She'd been wearing a very expensive dress and a diamond the size of a golf ball. He's been posing in a tuxedo, looking every bit the successful influencer.

To find out that the relationship wasn't as rosy as Instagram made it seem fills my chest with a strange feeling. Well, that and the fact that Blake bailed on the their wedding. I feel... hope? I can't figure out why I feel this way, so I ask, "So you don't even like it?"

He shrugs. "It's not even remotely my style. None of this is. This is less a house and more a very expensive set for playacting."

I put my hands on my hips. "It won't do for you to live in a place you don't love."

He raises an eyebrow. "No?"

"No," I say, more firmly. "This is your house! You should at least be comfortable when you're home for long enough to enjoy it."

He seems to consider this, then nods. "You're right. So, what do you suggest?"

I look around the living room. Now that we're talking about it, the sterile perfection of it all does jump out at me. It practically screams in my face. "First, we need to de-Blake it."

A slow grin spreads across his face. "De-Blake it? I like the sound of that."

"Which pieces are hers?" I ask.

"Pretty much everything," he says, watching me circle the room. "She had... expensive taste."

I start by lifting a framed print of abstract art off its hook and setting it on the floor. Then I move to a glass sculpture on a side table, something that looks like a mutant chandelier, and tuck it under my arm. I heft them both, and Jay wordlessly opens the door to his office.

The next twenty minutes are much the same: I move through each room, identify the most egregious examples of Blake's décor choices, and then put them into Jay's office. Jay helps me move several pieces of furniture.

By the time we're almost done, the place is so sparsely decorated that you could mistake it for being recently robbed. I lean the final picture against the wall and wave my hands over everything I've tagged as got-to-go. "So, if you didn't buy any of this, what would you choose?"

He thinks for a moment. "Something more functional. More lived-in."

I nod, mentally rearranging the room. "We'll need a new couch. You know, something you can actually sink into. Maybe a coffee table with some character. And real bookshelves."

I take down the last piece of art and survey the now-bare walls. The room looks empty, but also full of potential. "This is a good start."

Jay walks over to a high-backed chair and runs a hand along its fabric. "You've got a good eye. Maybe you should do this professionally."

"Decorating?" I scoff. "I can barely dress myself."

"Well, you're good at figuring out what doesn't fit, then." He snaps his fingers like a light bulb goes on in his head. "I know a furniture company that sponsors me. We can pick out some pieces online."

"Sure," I say, though I wonder how much input I should actually give. This is his space, after all.

We move to the kitchen and he opens a laptop on the kitchen counter. The website he pulls up is filled with sleek, modern furniture. It's nothing like the warm, eclectic mix I grew up with.

"What do you think of this?" he asks, pointing to a sectional sofa.

"It's nice," I say, noncommittal. "Looks uncomfortable, though."

He studies it, then nods. "Yeah, you're right. What about this one?"

We go through the catalog, discussing pieces that catch our eyes. To my surprise, he takes my opinions seriously. I suggest a reading chair with an ottoman. Jay adds it to the cart without hesitation. We spend the next hour clicking through pages, commenting on fabrics and finishes. It's almost... fun.

Okay, it is fun. I could never spend this much money on my own home. But Jay doesn't even notice. A little voice in the back of my head wonders exactly how much Jay makes per year. With his large staff, I'd guess that it's somewhere in the millions.

At one point, he leans in closer to point at a rug. I catch a whiff of his cologne and my heart does a stupid little flutter.

God, I'm so thirsty. It's humiliating. I force myself to focus on the screen.

"We've got a good mix. I think it'll feel more like a home now," he says, oblivious to my torment.

I nod. "It'll take a few weeks for everything to arrive. I hope we didn't blow your budget."

"Nah. I get a healthy discount. It's been a while since I made a video for this site, so they'll be excited to hear from me again." Jay closes the laptop and looks at me. "In the meantime, we'll make do. Thanks for your help."

"Don't thank me yet," I say. "You might hate it."

"I doubt that," he says. "I like everything you do."

I can't tell if he means the furniture or something else. Blushing, I stand, stretching my arms above my head. "I should get some sleep. Where do we do that?"

"Sure, yeah. Come on." Jay leads me up the stairs, insisting in carrying my suitcases. "Prepare thyself."

Instantly, I'm struck by the contrast between the pristine, photo-ready downstairs and the cluttered chaos of the upper floor. Plastic packing crates are stacked haphazardly in the hallway. I see no furniture as we squeeze past a large, undecorated bathroom. It's pretty apparent that no woman has ever had any say over this part of the house.

"Huh," I say. Downstairs is sparse; upstairs is *bare. It reminds me of a frat house up here!*

"Welcome to Casa del Chaos," Jay says with a slightly embarrassed grin. "Downstairs is for the 'gram. Upstairs is where dreams of organization go to die."

I can't help but laugh. "So, your house is like a mullet? Business in the front, party in the back?"

He chuckles. For a moment, it feels like we're just two friends ribbing each other. That is, until we reach his bedroom.

It's the only room upstairs that looks lived-in, with a large bed and a nightstand. The bed is an unmade heap of linens. A pile of clothes sits in the corner. My heart starts to race as I remember his suggestion that I sleep here.

We stand in the doorway, neither of us making the first move. "I guess this is it," I say, my voice smaller than I'd like.

Jay rubs the back of his neck, looking uncharacteristically unsure. "You can have the bed. I'll take the floor."

I frown, trying to sound casual despite the heat creeping up my neck. When we first negotiated sleeping arrangements, my answer was definitely more along the lines of, "we can share a bed as long as pillows separate us."

But now that I know what Jay has to offer in the bedroom, I want nothing between us. Not pillows, not blankets, not pajamas. I'm horny, even if I have a hard time just coming out and saying it to Jay.

So I manage a confident, "Married people usually share a bed. We can manage, I'm sure."

He lets my suitcases slide to the ground and takes a step toward me. There's an intensity in his eyes right now. My breath catches as he comes closer. "Calla, we need to make this look real. If we're awkward around each other, no one's going to buy it."

"So... what are you suggesting?" I play dumb.

He takes another step, towering over me. Now he's close enough that I can feel the heat radiating from him. "We should practice. You know, to make it more convincing."

"Practice?" I ask. I know exactly what he means, though. He wants to feel the same kind of heat that we felt at the

Wagon Wheel. And I'm so starving for him that I'm practically on fire.

"Practice kissing." There's a dangerous glint in his eye. "Think of it as method acting, but with more tongue."

I roll my eyes, trying to play it cool. But my pulse quickens. I have to act as nonchalant as Jay. "Ah yes. Because nothing says 'true love' like rehearsed smooching."

He raises a hand to my cheek and cups my jaw. There's a fire burning behind his eyes. A blaze that can only be quenched by touching me. But his touch is surprisingly gentle. His thumb brushes against the skin over my pulse in a way that sends sparks down my spine. He doesn't pull back. Jay never admits defeat.

He just waits, impatient yet steady, until I relax. I let out a deep breath and he moves in.

"We can start slow," he murmurs. His lips are just inches from mine. "Build up to something believable."

I should pull away. I should tell him this is a terrible idea. But instead, I close my eyes and wait.

His lips brush against mine, soft and tentative. My hands find his chest. I'm surprised at how fast his heart is beating. We kiss like teenagers, unsure and exploring at first, but wildly hungry for more.

I'm greedy. I want to kiss Jay for hours. It's all I can think about.

Just when I think he's going to pull back and leave me wanting, he deepens the kiss. A heat builds in me spreading from my core to my breasts, from my lips to the tips of my fingers. I press against him, opening my mouth to let him in. Our tongues meet in a slow, deliberate dance.

This is dangerous. This is stupid. This is amazing. I never want it to end.

When he finally breaks the kiss, I'm left panting, feeling

ravaged yet incomplete. I search his face frantically as I try to summon the guts to tell him that I need *more*.

When he speaks, his voice is rough as gravel. "I meant what I said about being friends with benefits."

My mind is a whirl. My body is already screaming *yes* while my rational side tries to regain control.

"Did you?" I ask. I need to hear it again.

"Fuck yes," he says. "I was waiting for you to bring it up. But since you haven't—"

Before I can second-guess myself, I pull him back to me and crush my lips against his. He kisses me with a hunger that sets me on fire. His hands roam my back, my hips. I'm lost in him, drowning.

We stumble toward the bed. Jay lifts me, his movements rushed and impatient. My body aligns with his as he sets me down gently on the mattress. His eyes search mine, asking for permission without saying a word.

This is it. This is where we cross the line.

"Jay," I say, my voice trembling with need and fear.

"Yeah?" he answers, his breath hot on my neck.

"Let's make it convincing."

He captures my lips again. I moan against his mouth. All I can think is a hasty, *this is going to change everything*.

But then I'm too busy to think at all.

Chapter Sixteen

Calla

Our lips crash together with a fervor that sends electric jolts through my body. Jay's hands are everywhere, tracing the curves of my shoulders, the arch of my back, and then down to my hips. He pulls me closer, as if trying to fuse our bodies into one. I fumble with the buttons of his shirt, too eager to wait. His hands find the hem of my blouse and yank it over my head. The cool air on my skin is a shocking contrast to the heat radiating from us.

His fingers expertly unfasten my bra and he throws it aside like it's an obstacle in his path. His eyes darken with lust as he takes in my bare chest. A wicked smile plays on his lips. He dives in, hungrily kissing and sucking each breast. His hands knead them with a rough tenderness that makes me moan his name. Every touch sends waves of pleasure coursing through me. I can feel my resistance melting like wax.

He groans. "Fuck, you're so hot."

I grip his shoulders. "I want you, Jay. I need you inside me."

"My cock is so hard just thinking about your wet pussy,"

he growls. The raw need in his voice sends a shiver down my spine.

I slide my hands up his chest, feeling the tension in his muscles. Slowly, teasingly, I pull his shirt over his head. He seizes the moment to kiss my neck, each brush of his lips spark that makes me gasp and clutch at him. I yank at his belt and then his pants, pushing them down as he kicks them off.

Just as he tries to push down my panties, I twist away, laughing, turning it into a playful wrestling match. He grabs my waist. I wriggle free, then he catches my wrist. He turns it over, peering at my tattoo

"I love my namesake etched into your skin, Calla. I like knowing that it's there forever."

I give a throaty laugh as he pulls me back into his chest. We breathe heavily then tumble across the bed. Our hands explore as our lips steal quick, passionate kisses.

Jay's eyes are wild with desire as he lets me pin him down, my hands on his wrists. His skin is feverish to the touch. The pretend-battle really turned him on. I can feel his hardness pressing against me. He could easily flip me over and take control. But he surrenders, letting me 'win'. I sit up, straddling him, and grind my hips against his in slow, torturous movements, feeling the power surge through me. His hard length presses against my center, sending a jolt of desire straight through me. I move my hips in slow, deliberate circles, dry humping him with just enough pressure to drive us both mad. My hands run over his chest, tracing the lines of his abs and the contours of his pecs, committing every detail to memory.

"Jay," I whisper, leaning down so my lips are just a breath away from his. "My pussy is already wet and ready for you." I pause, letting the words hang in the air, watching his reaction.

His eyes close for a moment, his jaw tightening as he struggles to keep control. When he opens them again, they're burning with an intensity that makes my heart race.

"Where do you want to be touched first?" I ask, my voice a seductive purr.

Instead of answering, he lets out a low growl. His hands shoot up to my waist. For a split second, I think he's going to pull me down and thrust up into me, taking what I've offered.

But he surprises me by flipping me over in a swift, fluid movement. He hovers above me, his breath hot on my face. I brace myself for the onslaught of kisses.

He starts with my lips, capturing them in a passionate, lingering kiss that leaves me dizzy. Then he trails down to my neck, planting soft, tantalizing pecks that make me gasp and clutch at his shoulders. My skin tingles with anticipation as his lips move lower, kissing my collarbone, then each breast in turn. I arch my back, offering myself to him. He takes his time, sucking and nibbling with a mix of tenderness and roughness that's almost too much to bear.

My hands tangle in his hair as he kisses down my ribs and across my stomach, each touch setting my nerves on fire. I can feel my panties growing damp, my body aching for him. He bites the waistband, then tears the fragile fabric with a swift yank. The cool air on my most intimate parts is a shocking contrast to the heat of his breath as he kisses his way around my inner thighs, my slit, everywhere but my slick channel and aching clit.

I whimper with need, lifting my hips to meet his mouth, but he holds me down, torturing me with his teasing.

He edges me with excruciating precision, each kiss and

lick a calculated move in his game of control. My body is a live wire, every nerve ending sparking with a mix of pleasure and pain. I whimper, my hands clutching the sheets, my hips rising to meet his mouth in a desperate plea for more. Just when I think I can't take the teasing any longer, he slides two thick fingers into my pussy, stretching me, filling me. His lips close around my clit with a possessive suck.

A bolt of electricity shoots through me. I come undone, the orgasm crashing over me like a tidal wave. I call out his name, my voice raw and unrestrained. My hips buck and rock against his hand and mouth. The pleasure is so intense that it borders on agony, every muscle in my body tensing and releasing in a rhythm I can't control.

My vision blurs. My mind is a hazy swirl of sensations. I feel my wetness coating his fingers, his hand, and dripping down to the bed. He doesn't relent, flicking his tongue at my clit in a relentless pace. His fingers curl inside me, hitting that perfect spot again and again, catching me in the after-shocks. Each one a mini-explosion that sends me spiraling deeper into bliss.

As my orgasm wanes, I expect him to pause, to give me a moment to catch my breath. But he doesn't stop licking my clit or flexing his fingers inside my passage. The overstimulation makes me squirm, my body twitching with sensitivity. I try to pull away, but he's unyielding.

"It's too intense," I manage to gasp, my voice trembling.

He looks up at me, his eyes dark and determined. "I'm going to make you come again," he says, his voice a low, seductive promise. "I want you to let me, little wife."

His husky whisper makes my pussy quiver and a fresh wave of wetness floods his hand.

The thought of another orgasm is both terrifying and

tantalizing. I'm not sure I can handle another one so soon after the first. But the idea of his mouth and hands working me to another peak is too tempting to resist.

"Yes," I breathe, "but be gentle."

He grins wickedly and returns to his task with a devotion that makes my heart race. He doggedly sucks my clit, his tongue and lips creating a maddening friction. A third finger pushes into my tight pussy, stretching me further. I gasp at the intrusion. It's uncomfortable at first. But he moves with such skill that the discomfort quickly melts into a building pleasure.

I bite my lip, trying to stifle the cries that threaten to escape as his fingers work their magic. The sensations build and build, a tight coil of pleasure in my core that's ready to explode. I grind against his face, my movements growing more frantic, more desperate. "Please, Jay. Make me come. I *need* it."

He doesn't say a word. His focus is unbroken as he maintains the perfect rhythm. His tongue swirls around my clit, his fingers pump and twist inside me. My body takes over, moving of its own accord. The pressure is unbearable, the pleasure is excruciating. I feel myself teetering on the edge. With a final, helpless thrust of my hips, the orgasm rips through me, violent and all-consuming.

I scream his name, my hands flying to his head to hold him in place as I ride the waves of ecstasy. My entire body convulses. Each spasm sends another jolt of pleasure through me. It feels like it will never end, like I'm caught in an endless loop of bliss. My vision whites out. My hearing dims. Time loses meaning as I float in this state of pure sensation.

When I finally come back to myself, I'm panting and drenched in sweat. My limbs are heavy and useless. He's still between my legs, his breath warm on my over-sensitive skin, his fingers resting inside me. He's been so patient, so thorough. I can tell he's proud of what he's accomplished.

I would be too, in his position.

He doesn't ever fully stop. His touches are gentle but unceasing, keeping me in a state of heightened arousal. I'm pretty sure that he's about to go for round three. The thought makes my heart race with a mix of panic and desire. I imagine another prolonged session, the intensity of it all.

I know I can't take much more.

"Jay," I whisper. I reach down and gently pull him away. He looks up with questioning eyes, his lips and face glistening with my juices. I tug him up to meet my lips.

Has there ever been anything hotter than tasting myself on his tongue?

When I pull back, my chest is heaving. "I've never had multiple orgasms with another person before. Only with my vibrator."

He wipes his mouth with the back of his hand and grins. He was deadly serious before. Now a playful light returns to his eyes. "So I'm as good as your toys?" There's a note of genuine curiosity in his teasing as if my answer really matters to him.

He has to already know that he's a fucking sex god.

I kiss him again, slowly, letting him feel how much I mean it. "You're so much better."

I see the pride and relief in his face. This isn't just about physical pleasure for him; it seems like it's about trust and intimacy.

We lie tangled in each other, our breathing slowly returning to normal. His hands caress my back and sides. Not with the urgency of before, but with a tender affection.

I stroke his hair and trace the lines of his jaw. I'm committing these softer moments to memory.

Storing them away for later, when I'm alone again.

"Jay," I say, breaking the silence. He looks at me, his blue eyes soft and warm. "Thank you."

He cocks his head. A small, confused smile is on his lips. "For what?"

"For being patient. For making me feel this good." I pause, choosing my words carefully. "I've never been with anyone who cared so much about my pleasure."

"It's...." He searches for a word. "Exquisite."

My cheeks heat. "I wouldn't go that far."

"Really? I would. I just watched you come. It was fucking amazing." He brushes a strand of hair from my face and kisses my forehead. "I want this to be good for both of us, Lily. We're in this together, remember?"

His words ground me, reminding me of our peculiar arrangement. We're supposed to be playing a part, but every touch, every kiss, feels disarmingly real. How did we get here so quickly?

I let him savor the moment of stillness, then slowly reach for a crumpled dress shirt on the floor. He watches me with a mix of curiosity and hunger. I straddle his hips and lean forward, tying his hands together with the shirt. The fabric twists and knots easily. I make sure it's tight enough to hold but not to hurt.

His chest rises and falls quickly, anticipation evident in every breath.

I run a finger down the center of his chest, tracing a line to his navel.

"What do you want, Jay?" I let my lips hover close to his, just out of reach. I'm enjoying the power I have over him.

"Do you want me to ride your cock? Or would you prefer if I sucked your dick?"

He closes his eyes for a moment, as if the choice is too deliciously painful to contemplate. "Wife... I'm going to need more latitude to move the first time my cock enters your pussy. Now if you want to untie me—"

I shake my head slowly, letting a wicked smile spread across my face. "Not yet."

I shift my weight, grinding my wetness against the hard length that strains against his boxers. His body tenses, and a low growl escapes his throat. I capture his lips in a deep, probing kiss, tasting the remnants of my own flavor on him.

I take back what I said before. This is actually hotter than anything I've ever experienced. Being on top of him, grinding against his cock, tasting a hint of my own pleasure when I kiss him. It might be heaven.

He strains against the makeshift bonds. I break the kiss and look into his eyes, which are dark with lust. "You like this, don't you?" I whisper. "Being at my mercy?"

He doesn't answer. But the way he tries to thrust up into me tells me all I need to know. I kiss him again, more fiercely this time. His mouth opens to mine, our tongues wrestling for dominance. My hands explore his chest, his shoulders, feeling the tension in his muscles as he fights against his desire to take control.

I sit back, breaking our kiss, and run my hands down his stomach. The way his abs contract at my touch is breathtaking.

"Your cock is so hard." I grind my hips in a slow, torturous circle. "I can feel how badly you want me. Are you imagining how it would feel to fuck me right now?"

His breathing is ragged now, his eyes half-lidded with need. "Calla," he pleads.

"Shh," I cut him off before he can voice his complaints. I place a finger on his lips. "Let me enjoy this. You had your turn."

I kiss my way down his throat, each peck sending a shiver through his body. I take my time, moving to his collarbone, then to his pecs where I flick my tongue over his nipples. He gasps and bites his lip, tilting his head back in surrender.

I continue my descent, kissing each ridge of his abs, savoring the taste of his sweat and skin. When I reach his waistband, I pause and look up at him.

His eyes are closed, his face a mask of concentration.

Emboldened, I hook my fingers into the waistband of his boxers. Moving ever so slowly, I peel them down, freeing his cock. It springs up with an eager bounce, looking even more impressive than I'd remembered. Thick and veiny, it's a testament to how excited he is. I straddle him again, intentionally letting it rest against my soaking-wet slit. Not penetrating. Just teasing. His hips thrust upward, but I put my hands on his chest and hold him down. The tension between us builds as I kiss him. It's a coiled spring ready to explode.

Our bodies move together, grinding, creating a friction that's almost unbearable. I move down from his lips to tease him, letting my tongue flick and swirl around the head of his cock, tasting the pre-cum that's already leaking out. His whole body tenses with each of my delicate touches. He mutters curses under his breath as I take my time. Every little movement I make sends a jolt through him. I can see the strain in his face as he tries to hold back.

Finally, I look up at him and say, "Show me how you want it, husband."

Jay's eyes snap open, dark and hungry. I can see the

conflict in them. He wants to seize control, but he also loves being at my mercy. He tilts his hips up slightly, guiding me with his body as I take him into my mouth. His hands, still tied, flex and clench as he fights the urge to grab my head and force me down.

"Go slow, wife. If you go too fast, I won't last. I'm too fucking excited."

His raw need sends a thrill through me. I love that he's this worked up, that he wants me this badly. I start with a gentle suction, my lips and tongue working in unison as I take him deeper. Then I pull back. His hips twitch and he lets out a strangled moan.

"I want to last for you, Lily," he says, his voice cracking. "I want this to go on longer than a minute. I'm trying to resist."

His honesty is disarming. It makes me want to blow his fucking mind.

I close my mouth around him again and start to bob my head, setting a slow, deliberate rhythm. Each stroke takes him a little deeper. I can feel his cock throbbing with each pass.

He groans in pleasure, his body responding uncontrollably to my movements. "Fuck, Calla. Your mouth... it feels so good. I've been fantasizing about this for so damn long."

His words spur me on. I take him as deep as I can, stretching my lips to accommodate his girth. I move up slowly, letting my tongue trace the underside of his cock, then plunge down again.

"You're such a good little wife," he whispers. "You know just how to suck my cock, baby."

I feel a rush of heat at his praise. I quicken my pace, taking him deeper and faster, my hand joining in to twist and stroke in sync with my mouth. His breathing becomes erratic, and he starts to thrust his hips in time with my movements.

I can taste him more intensely now, the saltiness of his skin mixed with the musky flavor of his arousal. His cock is hard as steel. I can feel every vein and contour as it slides in and out of my mouth. He moans louder, his body tensing as he nears the edge.

"Fuck, Calla," he growls. "I'm going to fill your fucking throat with cum. You'd better be ready to take all of it."

Who had any idea that Jay would talk so dirty? His cock twitches. He's on the brink. I cup his balls, gently rolling them in my hand. That's all it takes to push him over the edge.

His whole body convulses as he lets out a guttural moan. Hot spurts of cum shoot into my mouth, each one a burst of his essence. It's salty and earthy, the pure taste of him. His orgasm seems to go on forever. Each wave is as intense as the last. I do my best to hold every drop, my cheeks bulging with his release.

I glance up to see his face. His eyes are squeezed shut; his mouth open in a silent cry. His hands are white-knuckled around the makeshift bonds. I can feel the heat radiating off him, see the sweat sheening his skin. His chest heaves with each ragged breath and his cock pulses with the last dregs of his climax. I wait until he opens his eyes to let his cum slide down my throat in one large gulp. Then I lick my lips and take him back into my mouth, cleaning him with gentle strokes of my tongue. He flinches at the sensitivity, but doesn't pull away. He's letting me love him in my own way, watching me as I finish my task with a reverent care.

"That was amazing," he whispers. "I love the way you

touch me." His eyes meet mine. I can see the gratitude and adoration in them.

I crawl up his body. Our skin sticks together as I kiss him softly. He tastes like me, like us, a heady mix of sweat and sex. His kiss is soft, almost tender, a stark contrast to the raw passion we just shared.

I reach above his head and start to untie the dress shirt. I work slowly, not in any hurry to release him from this moment, but the fabric eventually loosens and he rubs his wrists. Then he stretches his arms to me.

We kiss again, deeper this time. Our lips and tongues move in a languid dance. There's no rush, no urgent need to take things further. It's a kiss that speaks of contentment. His hands find my waist, then my back, pulling me closer as if he doesn't want to let go.

I break the kiss and rest my head on his chest, listening to the steady thump of his heart. He strokes my hair, my back, his touch soothing and affectionate. He shifts. I roll to the side, expecting him to get up, but instead he turns to face me. He traces lines on my arm, my shoulder, then my cheek. "You're incredible." I can see the sincerity in his eyes.

I touch his face, running my fingers through his stubble. "You're not so bad yourself," I say, trying to keep the mood light. But I know he can see the deeper meaning in my eyes. This is more than just physical.

There's a connection growing between us. One that I'm not sure I'm ready for.

He leans in and kisses me again, softly, then pulls me into his arms. We lie there, tangled together, our breathing slowing to a calm, rhythmic pace. The post-sex haze envelops us, making everything feel distant and dreamlike. His hand strokes my hair as I nestle my head against his chest.

"I can't wait until next time," he murmurs. "Until I get to bury my cock deep inside you."

I shiver at the thought and a tingle of anticipation runs through me.

"You mean you'll tie me up and have your way with me?" I giggle, imagining the roles reversed.

He chuckles softly. "Maybe. But I promise you one thing. You'll have at least three orgasms. I can't just stop at two."

I want to protest, to tell him that it's not about the numbers. It's the connection that matters. But I'm falling into the trance of sleep, so I just let his promises wash over me.

He pulls the blankets over our bodies. The warmth makes my eyes grow even heavier. We lie still, holding each other. The silence is filled with the unspoken understanding of what we've just shared.

Chapter Seventeen

Jay

Java Monkey on a Saturday afternoon is chaos incarnate. The small coffee shop buzzes like a beehive, all energy and noise. The scent of espresso and sugar is thick in the air.

Calla's sisters sit in a corner with their heads together. Their expressions teeter between concern and curiosity. I take a deep breath and jog to catch up with Calla, who's trying her best to slip past them unnoticed. "Calla, wait up!" I call out.

She turns, crossing her arms in that defensive stance she takes when she's bracing for battle.

"You're not going to ditch me, are you?" I ask. I try to keep my tone casual.

"I can handle my sisters." Her voice is firm. "You don't have to chaperone us."

"I want to." I cut her mood off with the grin I know she finds irritatingly charming. "Besides, I've got to make a good impression on the in-laws."

Her sigh tells me she knows she lost this round. "Fine. But if Cora kills you, it's on you."

We continues to weave through the crowded shop. I can feel the tension radiating off her. She's nervous about this. I don't blame her. Meeting the family is never easy, but especially not under these circumstances.

The accidental marriage. The fake smiles. The pretense.

Yeah, it's a mess. But I've learned that messes can be managed. You just have to lean into the chaos. That's what I'm here to do.

Lean in.

"Calla! Jay!" The one with cotton-candy hair, who I assume is Calla's younger sister, waves us over. Her enthusiasm is palpable. It cuts through the noise like a spotlight. "Oh my gosh, you brought him!"

The other sister is dark-haired, slim, and dressed like she's ready to dominate a courtroom. This must be Cora, the attorney. She is staring a hole through the center of my chest.

That's probably not a good sign.

Calla's muttered "kill me now" makes me chuckle as we approach the table. She isn't happy either, it seems, but exchanges hugs with her sisters.

Iris dives right in to hug me next, but Cora merely offers me a cool smile. "You came along. How... nice."

"Cora, chill out." Iris beams. "Sit down! Tell us everything! How did this even happen?"

Before Calla can answer, the owner, Azi, swoops in like a caffeinated hawk. His wild silver hair and twitchy energy make him seem like he's fueled entirely by espresso shots.

"Congratulations!" he declares. He waves a handful of pink tissue paper. "Are you moving out from the apartment above your shop?"

I jump in before Calla can say anything. "Thank you, Azi. We're still figuring that out."

She snaps her head to me. Her eyes are wide.

I give her a reassuring smile. Then I turn back to Azi, who's already stuffing tissue paper into a vase like it's the most important task of his life. "There's plenty of time. I've never met two people who were crazier about each other. It was a pleasure to be your wedding officiant."

Cora leans forward. "Azi, this is our first time meeting Jay. Can you believe it?"

"No?" He stills, looking between Calla and me. "I think you should have some space."

"You're a darling," Cora purrs. "I love your Valentine's Day decorations."

Azi sets down a plate of heart-shaped sugar cookies before us and beams. "Thank you! I'll just be behind the bar if you need anything."

"Actually." Cora sits back with a sigh, eyeing the pieces of pink tissue paper. "They don't look great, but they do look like Azi put a lot of thought into them."

"So, about you two," Iris prompts, still beaming.

"Yes, let's talk about that. What exactly is your plan?" Cora certainly has a way of cutting through the bullshit.

"Well—" I start.

Calla immediately cuts me off with a hand to my arm. "Cora, cool your jets. You're not facing off with Jay in family court. You're meeting your brother-in-law."

Cora's eyes flash and her nostrils flare. "I am just trying to protect you, Calla. That's all I'm ever doing."

Calla looks at her sister for a moment, then smiles and slides her hand across the table. Cora looks pinched as she squeezes her hand. "You're the best big sister anyone could ask for. But I think I've got the situation handled."

I do a moment's math. "Am I the situation?"

"That's right." Calla leans into me, letting go of Cora. "A very cute situation."

"Cute? Can't I at least be handsome?"

Iris speaks up. "I think you're dreamy, if it helps."

Everyone but Cora laughs at that. I nod my head. "Thanks, Iris."

Iris blushes and looks pleased. Cora continues to seem bewildered. Calla squeezes my hand. "Show them what you've been working on, *husband*."

"Oh, right." I clear my throat. My tone shifts to dramatic. "Kalimera... uh... sas?"

Iris bursts into laughter. "That means 'Good morning, you all,' but close enough!" She giggles. "You're adorable."

Cora raises an eyebrow at me and her expression softens slightly. "You're brave. I'll give you that."

"Some say brave. Some say stupid." I lean back with a grin. "I guess the jury is still out."

Calla's thrilled expression makes my stomach do flip-flops. She makes me feel like a hero. First, she gave me everything I could have asked for and more in bed last night. Then I score major points just by repeating a phrase in Greek.

I'm already too comfortable with her. So comfortable, that I'm not quite sure when the lie ends and the truth begins. I feel like every day, the line blurs a little more.

"So, Jay," Iris says, going into full interrogation mode. She leans forward like she's interviewing me for a reality show, her enthusiasm bubbling over. "What's it like being married to our Calla? She's a bit of a control freak, isn't she?"

"Iris!" Calla hisses. Her cheeks flush. She looks like she wants to melt into the floor.

I laugh. The sound comes easily. "I haven't really come up against that, yet. I imagine it's right around the corner, though."

Iris laughs so hard she snorts. Calla pinches the bridge of her nose, trying not to join in. Even Cora, who seems like a tough nut to crack, allows a small, reluctant smile to creep across her face.

Victory.

"So, what are your intentions, Jay?" Cora asks, once she's schooled her rogue smile back into a courtroom ready frown.

I meet her gaze head-on. Cora doesn't blink. I respect that. She's the gatekeeper. The enforcer. I get it.

"Well." I keep a straight face. "I figured marrying your sister was the fastest way to get the secret family baklava recipe."

Calla snorts, trying to stifle her laughter. The tension around the table cracks like an egg. For a brief moment, we're all just people sharing a joke.

But Cora isn't done. "I'm serious here. Calla's not some... some *project* for you to take on in order to boost your brand, or whatever it is you do."

I nod and shift in my seat to face her fully. "I understand where you're coming from. You're protective of your sisters. You should be. But I promise you, Cora, this isn't a game to me. Calla's important. I'll do everything I can to take care of her."

The sincerity in my voice surprises even me. It's not a line or an act and Cora seems to sense that. Though her eyes remain skeptical, she doesn't press further.

Iris, ever the peacemaker, claps her hands. "Okay, okay. No more grilling. Let's just be happy for them."

The conversation lightens up after that. We share the

ridiculous details of the "proposal." Even Cora seems less worried, despite herself.

Outside, Iris gives Calla a big hug, whispering something to her that I can't hear, but that makes her smile.

Cora approaches, then pauses, looking between us like she's weighing her next words. "Take care of her." Her voice softens as she speaks directly to me. "That girl deserves the world. If you aren't prepared to give it to her, you should let her down easy. And do it sooner rather than later."

Whoa. How much does Cora know?

Unsure, I nod. "Thanks. I plan to."

As they walk away, I glance at Calla. She's watching them. Her expression is unreadable.

"Well." She exhales a long breath once they round the corner. "That could have been worse."

"Your sisters are great." I keep my tone light. "I especially liked the part where Cora basically threatened to murder me."

Calla laughs. A real one this time. Her shoulders relax for the first time all day. "She knows that our marriage is fake. She's just protective. Besides, you'll live."

"Hope so." I step closer, letting my tone drop a notch. "Because I'm starting to really enjoy this whole 'pretend marriage' thing."

Her eyes flick to mine. The air between us shifts. Tension. Heat. Whatever you want to call it, it's there. Undeniable.

"Jay..." she starts. Her voice is uncertain.

But I'm already leaning in. My hand brushes her waist as I close the distance. When our lips meet, it's soft at first. Tentative, like we're both testing the waters. Then it deepens. It's a rush of something neither of us can deny anymore.

When we finally pull back, she looks at me. Her cheeks are flushed. Her breathing is shallow. "This is a bad idea." Her whisper cuts through the tension. "It's dangerous."

I smile. I brush a strand of hair from her face. "Life's more fun when it's a little dangerous."

Chapter Eighteen

Jay

I push open the glass door of You Butter Believe It. The scent of freshly baked bread and sugar hits me like a baseball bat to the face. Calla is behind the counter, decorating a cookie with her lips screwed up in a crooked line of concentration. When she looks up to see me, those lips burst into a smile. "Jay! I thought you were sending your crew."

"I decided to give them the day off." I shrug like it's no big deal. "Figured I could handle it solo. Plus, it's more fun this way."

Calla's eyes sparkle with excitement. "More fun, huh? Well, I'm all for fun. What do you want to film?"

I set my camera bag on the counter and pull out my handheld. "I was thinking a Valentine's Day cupcake-making class. You show me how it's done. I pretend not to ruin everything."

She laughs. The sound is like tinkling glass. "Pretend, huh? This should be good."

We move to the kitchen. Calla starts pulling out ingredients while I set up my camera and do a quick intro. I explain that we're at the famous You Butter Believe It with the talented Calla Rustin. She waves and bites her lip, looking adorably nervous.

"Okay, Calla," I tell her once we're ready. "Teach me your ways."

She dives in, explaining every step with the enthusiasm of a kid showing off their favorite toy while I try to keep up.

With just the cracking of eggs and measuring of flour, it's already clear that I'm out of my depth. When it comes time to mix the batter, I put the bowl in place and turn on the mixer, full speed. A mushroom cloud of cocoa powder explodes into the air.

"I'm making it rain chocolate!" I shout.

Calla bursts out laughing and accidentally steps on a stray egg yolk. She goes flying. The bowl of sprinkles she was holding goes flying too, and the sprinkles rain down like edible confetti.

"Look, Jay! A rainbow!" she gasps from the floor, laughing so hard she can barely breathe.

I help her up. We salvage what we can of the batter and put a batch in the oven, but the kitchen looks like a war zone. I turn off the camera and lean against the counter. "Calla, can I ask you something?"

"Sure." She wipes chocolate from her cheek.

"Do you think people only hang out with me because of my online fame?"

The question arose this morning when I was scrolling through the comments on the last few posts. The posts heavily featured Calla, so there were definitely some haters in the posts saying that Calla only wants me because she knows that dating me will equal fame.

The comments stuck with me. Because in Calla's case, they're entirely true.

Calla tilts her head. "I think... that people are drawn to you because you're interesting and cool. The fame is just a bonus. Who wouldn't want to hang out with you?"

I raise an eyebrow. "Are you hitting on me, Mrs. Rustin?"

She laughs and shakes her head. "You wish, *Mr.* Nikolakis."

She puts the second batch in the oven, and pulls out the first, setting it on a rack to cool. I turn the camera back on and aim it at the cupcakes. "Calla, these look amazing. I didn't think we'd actually make something edible."

"You have so little faith." She smirks. "But you're right. I did most of the work."

I grab a bowl and start making frosting with a spatula. Calla watches, bemused. "You know, for someone with millions of followers, you'd think at least one would've taught you how to make buttercream properly."

I shrug. "I'm a fast learner. Watch this." I take a glob of frosting and fling it at her. It hits her apron with a splat.

"Jay!" she scolds me, but she's smiling. "This is serious business." She starts frosting the cupcakes, her mood sobering. "I'm really glad you came. The bakery... it's been tough. The profit margin on cupcakes and cookies is so slim."

"Is that why you're getting into wedding cakes?"

"Sort of. But also, I just love weddings."

She turns to the camera and explains how to make rosettes with a piping bag. I watch her. She's genuine. Relatable.

When she finishes, I announce, "You're a great baking influencer, Calla. That's a thing I just made up. Still, you're teaching me a lot today."

She laughs. "Influencer, huh? Maybe I'll steal some of your followers."

"Having tasted your cake, I don't know why you aren't rolling in money. You're the most talented baker I know."

"Flattery will get you everywhere." She says it lightly, but I can tell she's pleased.

"Your cupcakes are so good, they should be illegal. I might have to call the dessert police."

She blushes and thanks me. I make some more buttercream and offer her a taste on a spoon. She takes it and grins, dabbing a bit on my nose playfully. I laugh and grab a frosting filled piping bag. "Time for the grand finale. I'm going to write 'You're Sweet' on this cupcake." I squeeze the bag. The frosting comes out in a wobbly line. I try to control it, but it's like trying to write with a broken pen.

"I think it says 'You're Sweat'," Calla giggles when I show her the end result.

"Well, you do make me sweaty." I wink.

She blushes furiously and takes the cupcake from me. She scrapes the frosting off with her finger and holds it up. "Sugary treats are my love language," she says, then feeds it to me.

I take it into my mouth, savoring the sweetness, then lean in. She doesn't pull away. Our lips meet, soft and tentative at first. Then more urgent. We kiss, forgetting the camera. Forgetting the cupcakes. Forgetting everything.

When we finally break apart, she laughs. "How's that for a sweet ending?"

The resulting video goes viral. Not for the baking tips. But for what fans dub "The Great British Cake-Off: Disaster Edition."

It's also our first real memory as a couple. Laughter. Frosting-covered faces. A surprising sense of closeness.

And blackmail material on each other for life.

Chapter Nineteen

Calla

Our footsteps echo against the stone walls as we approach the entrance to the cave. Jay's hands are stuffed casually in his pockets. He tilts his head toward me with a lopsided grin. "I'm telling you; it's going to be amazing. Like a nature documentary, but with more banjos."

I raise an eyebrow. I try to imagine what a "Redneck Wildlife Safari" could possibly entail. "I'm sure it'll be... something. Do you think we need helmets?"

He laughs, the sound bouncing off the cavern's walls. "You're such a pessimist. Where's your sense of adventure?"

"Safely stored away with my common sense." I can't help but smile. His enthusiasm is infectious, even if I'm still wary of this quirky adventure.

We step into the dimly lit cave. I squint, trying to make out shapes in the darkness. Suddenly, a burst of colorful lights illuminates the walls. The scene that appears stops me in my tracks.

Raccoons in trucker hats and flannel shirts are posed

around a miniature campsite. Their beady eyes reflect the light like tiny, sinister lasers.

"Oh my god." My voice is barely above a whisper as a mix of surprise and amusement bubbles up. "They're like... hillbilly animatronics."

Jay chuckles. He nudges me forward. "See? I told you it'd be great."

I take a tentative step closer, examining the raccoons with a growing sense of wonder. One is holding a tiny banjo. Another is digging through a cooler. It's all so ridiculous and over-the-top that I can't help but be charmed.

"They look so real," I half-speak to myself. "Like they're about to start moving or something."

"State-of-the-art craftsmanship." I can hear the grin in his voice. "Probably cost a fortune."

I shudder. It's not from the cold but from the eerily lifelike nature of the scene. "I think their eyes are following us."

Jay leans in. His shoulder brushes mine. "Maybe they're just curious about the newlyweds."

A tingle runs down my spine, and I pull back and cross my arms, trying to regain my composure. "Well, they can mind their own business. We're on the clock."

"Relax, Calla. This is supposed to be fun." He pauses for a beat, then his voice turns teasing. "I'm sure that fox in overalls over there is a big fan of your work."

I glance to where he's pointing. A fox in a Confederate cap and overalls is perched on a rock. Its glassy eyes are uncomfortably intense.

I stifle a laugh. "Yeah, he looks like my target demographic."

Jay steps in front of me and starts walking backward. He adopts an exaggerated Southern drawl. "Y'all, this here's the finest weddin' baker in the land. She'll make yer big day as sweet as a possum pie."

I can't suppress my grin. "You're ridiculous."

He continues his mock narration, weaving a tale of raccoon romances and shotgun weddings as we make our way through the cave. I try to focus on his words, on the absurdity of the whole situation, but the lifelike animals and their frozen expressions keep pulling my attention. I'm convinced they're more than just decorations. At any moment, one will blink or twitch.

We reach the end of the first tunnel and I let out a breath I didn't realize I was holding. "Okay, I'll admit, that was kind of cute. In a terrifying, animatronic sort of way."

Jay's mischievous grin softens. "See? You're having fun."

I want to argue. I want to remind him that this isn't a real honeymoon, that we're just playing a part. But he's right. Despite myself, I am having fun.

"Don't get too cocky." My words lack any bite. "We still have the rest of the safari to survive."

He extends a hand. For a moment, I hesitate. My practical side screams at me to pull back. *He's just doing this for show, right?* But the warmth of his fingers against mine quiets that voice.

"Onward, then." He leads me deeper into the cave.

As we arrive in another cavern, the new scene comes into focus. It reveals woodland animals with garish, fluorescent mullets striking exaggerated celebrity-style poses. A beaver with a guitar grins with oversized front teeth. A squirrel with pouty lips vamps in a red dress. An owl with oversized glasses peers down from a tree with a knowing smirk.

Jay stops in his tracks and I nearly run into him. "No

way." His voice is almost reverent. "It's a celebrity who's who of the animal kingdom."

I peek around him, taking in the absurdity. "Are those... pun names?"

He points at each one. "Justin Beaver, Squirrel Johansson, Woodchuck Norris... This is brilliant."

I roll my eyes, though a tiny part of me agrees. It's so over-the-top that it circles back around to clever. "I think 'brilliant' might be a stretch."

He turns around and starts walking backward, his face lit up with childlike glee. "Come on, you have to appreciate the craftsmanship. Look at Hedgehugh Jackman. They even got the sideburns right."

I glance over. Sure enough, the hedgehog's spiky hair is styled into perfect little mutton chops. My lips twitch, threatening to form a smile. I force them into a straight line. "It's definitely... something."

Jay doesn't let my lack of enthusiasm deter him. "And there's Meryl Streepowl. You can see the wisdom in her eyes. And Brad Chipmunk... just look at those cheekbones!"

I follow his gaze, taking in each ridiculous creature. The names and faces are so on-the-nose that it's impossible not to recognize them. A deer with a soulful expression that can only be Forest Whitdeer. An otter with a punk rock sneer that screams Otter Lavigne. Every diorama is a parody, each one more ludicrous than the last.

"Do you think they had a focus group for this? Like, sat a bunch of people down and asked, 'Which animal best embodies the essence of Leonardo DiCapriowl?'"

Jay laughs. "I hope so. I like to think there was a big debate over whether to make him a raccoon or an owl."

"The owl was definitely the right choice."

He raises an eyebrow. "Are you saying you approve?"

"I'm saying I can see the logic behind it." I try to sound nonchalant. "Owls have that wise, enduring quality. It's a natural fit."

Jay's narration becomes more animated as we walk slowly from scene to scene. "Here we see Lynx Hemsworth in his natural habitat, flexing for the camera. And over there, Reese Witherpaws, clutching her tiny golden acorn." He's like a kid at Christmas. I'm starting to feel a warmth in my chest that I'm not entirely comfortable with. It's nice, this side of him. Unpretentious. Real.

"And who could forget Emma Stoat?" His tone is filled with exaggerated awe. "Her range is incredible. She can play any role, from a weasel to a ferret." I let out a snort and quickly cover my mouth with my hand. He eyes me triumphantly. "Did you just laugh?"

"No." I try to deny it, but it's too late. The smile has taken over my face, and I can't fight it anymore.

He stops and puts a hand on his chest as if wounded. "Calla Rustin, laughing at something so lowbrow? I must be dreaming."

"Don't get used to it," I chide, but my voice is playful. The tension in my shoulders has melted away, and for the first time today, I feel... happy.

We reach the end of the celebrity animal gauntlet. I take one last look over my shoulder. "Is that... Cardi Bee?" I ask, spotting a bee with oversized sunglasses and a microphone we'd somehow missed.

Jay follows my gaze and bursts out laughing. "Now that's just too much."

I shake my head, still smiling. "Yeah. *That's* what's too much."

We stand there for a moment. The ridiculousness washes over us, filling the space with something light and unspoken. I realize I'm not in a hurry to move on. I'm actually enjoying this pause, this breath of silliness in the middle of our contrived honeymoon.

"Ready for the next chapter?" Jay's voice is soft as he holds out his hand.

I look at his hand, then at his face. The cameras are far enough away that they can't catch the details, but close enough that we still need to play our parts. At least, that's what I tell myself as I take his hand in mine. "Let's do it."

We round a corner, leaving the neon mullets behind. "You're going to love this," Jay promises. His tone is conspiratorial.

I follow his gaze to a new diorama and my jaw drops in disbelief. It's a scene straight out of Victorian England, but with squirrels. They're dressed in tiny waistcoats and bonnets and posed around a miniature parlor holding teacups and saucers. One even has a monocle.

Jay nudges me gently. "Check out Lord Squirrelington and Lady Acorn. Pure class."

My laugh starts as a small chuckle, then grows into something fuller, more genuine. The scene is just so over-the-top, so ridiculously detailed. "This is amazing. They look like characters from a squirrel Dickens novel."

"Great Expectations." Jay adopts a posh British accent. "Or perhaps A Tale of Two Nutters."

I wipe a tear from the corner of my eye. "You missed your calling as a pun writer."

He shrugs modestly. "I dabble."

We stand there for a moment, just taking it in. The squirrels are frozen mid-gesture. Their tiny hands and elongated faces are filled with an exaggerated sense of propriety. It's like a snapshot of a rodent soap opera.

"I wonder how long it took them to sew those outfits."

My voice drops, more thoughtful now. "There's a lot of craftsmanship here."

Jay's shoulder brushes mine. "You sound almost impressed."

"I am." I nod, conceding the point. "It's like a labor of love. You can tell they really cared about getting it right."

"It's nice to see you appreciating the work that goes into something." I can feel his eyes searching mine. "Even if it is a bunch of stuffed animals."

I turn back to the diorama, not sure how to respond. He's right, of course. I do appreciate the effort, the attention to detail. It reminds me of the care I put into planning a wedding. How every little piece has to fit together perfectly.

"Calla." Jay's voice softens, and I brace myself for whatever serious thing he's about to say. "If we were squirrels, which one do you think you'd be?"

I blink, momentarily caught off guard, but quickly scan the scene with new purpose. "There," I say. "I'd be the one in the corner, making a checklist for the weekly nut inventory."

He laughs warmly. "Of course you would. And I'd be the one throwing a nutty party and inviting the whole forest."

I imagine that for a moment. Jay as a carefree squirrel, dancing on a tree branch, while I sit below with my clipboard, trying to keep everything in order. It's a silly thought, but it makes me smile.

"You know," I point out, "squirrels have a pretty tough life. They're always preparing for winter, always storing up nuts and hoping they don't starve."

Jay tilts his head, considering this. "Yeah, but they also get to run around in the trees and have nutty adventures. It's all about balance."

"Balance." The word lingers in my mind. He's always talking about that. Balancing work and life, balancing the needs of his brand with his personal desires. It's something I've never been good at. For me, it's always been about control, about making sure everything is just so.

We fall silent again, but it's not uncomfortable. I understand him a little better, I think. Or maybe I'm just letting myself see what's been there all along.

"Ready to move on?" His voice breaks the quiet.

I take one last look at the Victorian squirrel scene. Their tiny, intricate costumes and absurdly dignified expressions feel like a reminder of the care and humor that life can hold, even in the strangest places. "Yeah." My voice is lighter as I squeeze his hand. "Let's see what else they've got."

We wander through the rest of the dioramas, giggling and joking the whole time. At the end of the cave tour, Jay and I start walking back toward the cave entrance. He's still holding my hand, and I let him. It makes me feel like a schoolgirl. He glances at me, a smile tugging at his lips.

"I really enjoyed seeing you relax and have fun." His tone is casual but sincere.

Part of me is flattered. The other part is wary. Letting my guard down like this is dangerous. If I start to like him, really like him, what's to stop me from falling for him? And then what? Eventually, we'll get divorced. This whole thing is temporary. Isn't it better to keep some distance between us?

"I had a good time." I choose my words carefully. "It was nice to do something silly."

We walk in silence for a few moments. The gears in my mind grind, trying to make sense of the conflicting emotions swirling inside me. I glance at Jay, who's looking straight ahead, his expression unreadable. Does he feel the same tension, the same pull?

We reach the gift shop, a small, brightly lit area near the cave entrance. Shelves are lined with souvenirs. Keychains, T-shirts, and an array of stuffed animals, all with the same wide-eyed, lifelike expressions as the dioramas. Jay lets go of my hand and starts browsing one of the shelves. I take a moment to collect myself and push down the rising tide of feelings that threaten to overwhelm me. *Distance,* I remind myself. *I need to keep some distance.*

Something on the shelves catches my attention. It's a small stuffed chipmunk with huge, soulful eyes. Its tiny hands are clasped together as if they were in prayer. There's something endearingly pathetic about it, like a character from a children's book who's just lost its acorn.

I pick it up gently, cradling it in my hands. "If I had a familiar, it would be this squirrel." I show it to Jay. "Look at those eyes. It's like it's saying, 'Why me?'"

Jay laughs. The sound is genuine and hearty, and it makes my heart ache. "It's perfect. I can totally see the resemblance."

I scoff, but I'm smiling. "I'm serious. This thing is adorable. I need to take a selfie with it."

"Go for it." He steps back, giving me room.

I pull out my phone and angle it so the chipmunk and I are both in frame. I mimic its wide-eyed, forlorn expression, and snap a few pictures. "These are going to be priceless." I hold up my phone to show him.

His breath brushes against my neck as he looks over my shoulder, sending a shiver down my spine. "You're a natural."

I turn to put the chipmunk back on the shelf, but Jay stops me. "You should keep it."

I raise an eyebrow. "The whole point of a familiar is that it's symbolic. I don't actually need to own it."

He shrugs. "Consider it a memento. Something to remind you of today."

"Today's not over yet." My words are light, but I know what he means.

"Still." His tone is insistent. "I want you to have it."

I hesitate, looking at the chipmunk's imploring eyes. It's cute in a hopeless sort of way. I do feel a strange kinship with it. Maybe it's the way it looks so out of its depth, like it's trying to survive in a world that's too big and too fast.

"Okay." My voice softens. "But I'm not taking it as a gift. I'll pay you back."

Jay shakes his head, but his smile stays. "Whatever you say, Calla." He takes the chipmunk from me and walks to the register.

He's making this so hard. Hard to keep my distance. Hard to stick to the plan. *Hard to remember why I was so mistrustful in the first place.*

Jay returns with the chipmunk in a small gift bag and hands it to me. I take it carefully, as if it's something fragile and precious.

"Thank you." My voice carries more weight than I intend. Not just for the chipmunk, but for everything.

"Ready to go?"

I nod. We leave the gift shop and emerge from the cave. The cool air meets the warmth of the outside world, creating a brief, swirling breeze. I clutch the gift bag to my chest, feeling the chipmunk's eyes on me. A silent reminder of the day we've had.

As we step into the sunlight, I take one last look at Jay. My heart flutters, and a question lingers in my mind. *How much longer can I keep my heart safe from him?*

Chapter Twenty

Calla

Today, we're visiting someplace that I happen to be really excited about. I skip to the car, making Jay raise his eyebrows. "Waffle House?" he asks. "That's what it takes to get your engine revving?"

"Umm *yeah*. Waffle House went from a little diner in our very own Avondale Estates neighborhood to a franchise with thousands of locations throughout the country. It's a cultural *touchstone*. Eggs, bacon, waffles... what more could a person ask for? So yes, I am really excited to go to a museum devoted to Waffle House."

He laughs. "Wow! So much passion over some waffles."

"That's the understatement of the century. Waffle House is everywhere. It's open every single day of the year, every hour of the day, offering a hot meal at an affordable price to patrons from all walks of life. Waffle House doesn't discriminate about who they hire or who they seat at the restaurants. They just want to serve good food." I stop to draw in a much-needed breath. "Welcome to my TED talk. I am delighted that we're going to a museum about an institution I can really get behind."

"Love the excitement. Save some for when the camera is on, okay?"

I scrunch my nose up and nod. When I was a kid, Waffle House was a special treat usually reserved for Sundays after my father forced my whole family to sit through church. In my mind, Waffle House occupies a prized space that's normally reserved for my favorite cake recipes and Oprah Winfrey quotes.

When we get out of the car in the museum's parking lot, I already have a grin plastered on my face. The Waffle House Museum is a two-room shrine to all things greasy and glorious. Yellow-tiled and chrome-bright, it has the nostalgic sheen of a 1950s diner set piece.

Jay holds open the door for me. A bell jingles as we step inside. The smell of syrup and coffee hits me like a warm hug.

Something in my brain chemistry reacts to the faux-diner setup with glowing positivity. I feel like I've just had a big hit of an illicit substance. I suck in a breath and reach my hands toward the sky.

"Can you believe this place?" Jay says, his eyes sparkling with genuine delight. It's infectious, that sparkle. Dangerous.

"It's amazing," I say with an exaggerated shrug. "I'm not living out my dreams right now or anything."

"Noted." Jay's expression is one of amusement. "Shall we?"

A woman in a Waffle House apron greets us and hands us a sample waffle on a paper plate. "Enjoy, y'all!"

We walk around the diner. There are informational displays scattered about, and small clusters of museum visitors talking to employees.

I grab the waffle from Jay's hand and tear off a chuck. I

pop it into my mouth, mmming as the buttery, carby flavor hits my taste buds. "So good," I moan, offering Jay the plate. "You have to try it."

He takes the smallest piece of waffle imaginable and pops it in his mouth. He nods. "It's good."

"That's all you have to say?" I ask. "Good lord."

"We've been through this. I'm just not a big dessert-for-breakfast fan."

"You're crazy. This is not just breakfast."

I focus on the exhibits: old menus, vintage uniforms, a timeline of Waffle House milestones. It's charming, in a low-rent kind of way. Like a yard sale curated by someone's grandmother.

One display catches my eye: a laminated list of "short order slang." I read it aloud, testing the words on my tongue. "Scattered, smothered, and covered. Top it. Wind the clock." I arch a brow at Jay. "Do I sound cool?"

"The coolest," he assures me. "You thinking of a career change?"

"Just getting into character," I say. I clear my throat and adopt my best short-order cook voice. " I'll take a Wind the Clock with a Double Bubble, lasso the hog, and, uh, Chicken in the Coop, on the fly!" I throw in a dramatic flourish, waving an imaginary spatula.

He laughs, the sound warm and rich. "You're ridiculous."

"You love it," I say, smirking. For some reason, my cheeks flush. I'm having too much fun vibing with my fake husband.

Before I can dig deeper into this roleplay, a woman in a Waffle House apron approaches us with a clipboard. "Y'all want to try your hand at makin' a waffle? We got a station set up in the back."

"I defer to the Waffle House fan girl. What do you think?" Jay asks me, but I'm already rushing to follow the woman. Jay pulls out his phone and starts filming. I shoot him a sour look. He's always after content, even when I am genuinely having a moment over here.

The station is a small kitchenette with a waffle iron and a griddle. The woman hands us each an apron and gives us a quick rundown on how to pour the batter in the griddle and close it, flipping the whole thing in the process.

Jay ties his apron with a flourish, but fumbles making the first waffle.

"Whoa!" I step in, gently touching his hand to correct him. "You need more batter."

With my help, he pours the second waffle with more success. He catches my eye and grins. I stick my tongue out at him. He grabs me by the waist and hauls me against his body. "If this is what it takes to make you playful, I'll get a waffle maker at home," he promises. "I love seeing your devilish side."

I blush scarlet when I realize that he's filming this. He dips me back and ravishes me with a kiss that goes on too long. By the end, I'm breathing hard. "You're a beast," I tell him.

"Only for you," he says. "I'm well-behaved for every other girl in the world."

I enjoy clinging to his chest for another moment before reluctantly letting go. Today, I'm excited. And Jay is only amplifying my good mood.

We've always had chemistry but today is like we have achieved nuclear fission.

We make a decent-looking waffle and cut it in half. I haphazardly drizzle my half with syrup, and a little spills onto my hand. Before I can reach for a napkin, Jay takes my hand in his.

The world slows. Our eyes lock. I see something raw and unguarded in his eyes. He lifts my hand. For a heart-stopping moment I think he's going to kiss it.

Instead, he pops my fingers into his mouth, his eyes never leaving mine.

A soft sigh leaves me, unbidden. I know *just* what Jay can do with that mouth of his.

He sucks the syrup off my hand, leaving me winded. "All clean."

I swallow hard. "Thanks."

Jay has the audacity to wink at me. It only makes me more tongue-tied.

We finish our waffles and tour the remainder of the room. There are charts showing how many eggs, strips of bacon, and waffles have been served since the restaurant's inception in 1955. I point at the next display and gasp. "This is crazy! It says that each Waffle House has an extensive disaster management plan. In times of emergency, every Waffle House has an on-site generator so that operations can continue without the power grid. There are emergency "jump teams" of staff and supplies that can be brought into areas affected by natural disasters." I scan the rest of the display and gasp again. "Listen to this. The ability of a Waffle House to remain open after a natural disaster is called the Waffle House Index. It's used by FEMA as a measure of disaster recovery."

I turn, open-mouthed, to find that Jay isn't really paying attention. I hit him gently on the arm. His head snaps up. "What? Did I miss something?"

"I'm trying to tell you how important Waffle House is to America. Pay attention!"

"I am!" he protests. He pulls his phone out and starts to film. "Say it again, wife. Why is Waffle House so important?"

I roll my eyes but repeat the information for his followers, hoping that a few will absorb the gist. Probably not, but who knows.

His phone beeps and as he glances at it, I use the distraction to take a deep breath. I'm being too intense about today. I know it.

"You have to see this," Jay says, showing me the screen. It's one of the selfies of us he posted to his Instagram. The comments are a mix of swooning and envious. Every single one is centered on how much chemistry we have.

"Looks like your fans approve," I say, my cheeks burning.

He shrugs, but there's a mischievous glint in his eye. "They're usually pretty spot-on." He pauses, then adds, "So, what do you think? About us?"

I don't answer. I can't. The truth is, I don't know what to think. He's nothing like I imagined. That scares me more than if he were exactly as I expected.

He saves me from having to respond. "My suggestion would be practice."

"What does that mean?" I slide him a skeptical look.

"You know what they say... practice makes perfect... And I want to spend some time making sure that we've got every detail right." He smirks.

I smile and shake my head. It's hard to take him seriously. But if he insists on practicing... I'm more than willing to put in the effort.

Chapter Twenty-One

Jay

Calla shouts, "I thought you said we needed more practice!" as she follows me down the packed street. I pause and wait for her to catch up, then take her hand. "This is practice," I say.

She gives me the stink eye. "I thought that by practice you meant..."

I tease, "...spending hours in bed together?"

"Yes! I mean, not just that, but... yeah," she laughs.

I pick up her hand and place a kiss on her wrist. "I promise to take you straight home after this and chain you to the bed post. Will that please you?"

Calla shrugs, looking slightly foolish. "Whatever."

"This is good practice, too. Faking a relationship around my friends is more of a challenge," I add.

She smiles and replies, "As you wish." Holding her hand, I start to look around at the parade goers.

I like to describe The Great Couch Potato Parade as Mardi Gras for the terminally lazy. Floats shaped like couches, remotes, and oversized snacks trundle through the square, showering the crowd with free samples of chips and soda. It's a celebration of sloth, a festival for the indolent, and it's my favorite day of the year.

Normally I'm pro-exercise, don't get me wrong. But all of my favorite people participate in the festivities. Every year since college, we've pulled out all the stops to make the parade one of the most fun events in Greater.

Today, I put all my health-nut tendencies to the side, and exchange them for terrible habits. I drink sugary soda, I eat meats wrapped in other meats, I pretend that cholesterol isn't going to one day clog my arteries and attempt to murder me.

Calla and I are standing at the corner of Greater and Church with Ryan, Bennett, Wren, Ellie, and Iris. We're a motley crew. Each of us clutches oversized foam fingers and inflatable recliners like true parade enthusiasts.

A float shaped like a gigantic TV remote rolls by. Ryan lets out a whoop. "This is the best thing ever!"

Calla nudges me and points to the next float coming down the street. It's shaped like a huge bowl of popcorn. People on the float are tossing handfuls of the stuff into the crowd. I duck as a kernel whizzes past my ear.

"Catch some for me!" Calla shouts. She holds her inflatable recliner costume up like a shield.

I grab a few pieces off the ground and stuff them in my mouth. "Delicious."

She wrinkles her nose in mock disgust. "You're unhinged."

"Don't judge me, Lily. Anything goes today."

"Unhinged!" she declares.

I pick her up and attempt to throw her over my shoulder, letting her squeals of ohmygodputmedownrightthisminuteJayRustin sail right past me. The recliner she's wearing is bulky but I slap my full hand right on the meat of her ass. It makes a delightful sound that wouldn't be out of place in a porno.

But today is a family event, so instead of taking the logical next steps, I let her roll off my body and free herself.

She huffs indignantly, but I can tell that she's trying not to laugh. "You're the worst."

"But the best husband," I add with a wink. "You can't forget that!"

Wren blows a whistle and waves her hand in the air. "Guys! Look!"

For a minute there, I'd forgotten that other people exist. No big deal. Not a sign that I might secretly have feelings for my fake wife. Definitely not that.

We all turn to see a float shaped like a giant recliner. It's covered in plush fabric and there's a big-screen TV mounted on the back. A man in a bathrobe and slippers lounges on the chair, holding a remote and sipping what looks like hot cocoa. The whole thing slowly tilts back. The crowd goes wild.

"That is some next-level laziness." Ryan sounds almost reverent.

Calla leans in close to me. "Imagine the craftsmanship that went into that." Her breath brushes my ear.

"Yeah. It's... impressive." I focus on the float as it tilts back even farther. The crowd's cheers grow louder. I can't help but laugh at the absurdity of it all.

Calla grabs my hand and squeezes. "I'm glad we came."

"Me too." I mean it. I wink at her, then turn my head, craning to see the next float in the parade. Out of the corner of my eye, I see something I wasn't expecting.

.   .   .

Ryan and Wren stand off to the side, looking like a married couple entering their fortieth year of constant bickering. Wren picks at her nails and looks agitated. Ryan stares off into the distance. It's obvious that they've just had words.

"Hey, you two!" I call out. "Why the long faces?"

Ryan shrugs. "Just taking a breather."

I look at Wren. She won't meet my eyes. "Wren, what's up? Why are you being so weird?"

She looks up sharply. "Maybe I'm just tired, Jay. Or maybe it's something else. Maybe you should mind your own business."

I'm stunned. Wren has never talked to me like this. She's my little sister. I'm supposed to know what's going on with her. "Wren, I—"

"Forget it." She walks away. "You two both suck."

I look at Ryan. He just shakes his head. "Don't look at me, dude."

The parade's cheerful chaos swirls around us. I feel like I've been punched in the gut.

"She didn't mean it." Calla puts a hand on my arm. "Whatever it is, she'll come around."

"I just don't get why she's angry at me."

"Sometimes it's easier to be mad at someone else than to deal with what's really bothering you. And maybe it's not about you at all."

I see the concern in her hazel eyes. She's probably right. She usually is. "Thanks."

"Anytime."

After the floats, there are costumed groups to contend with. The Snuggie Squad marches by first. A phalanx of people in matching Snuggies marches by holding remote controls and oversized popcorn buckets. They wave lazily. The crowd responds with half-hearted cheer.

Next come the Sleeping Beauties. They're dressed in pajamas and sleep masks, with intentionally messy bedheads. They carry pillows and blankets. Some of them yawn and stretch as they walk.

Calla tugs on my hand. "I'm hungry."

"Oh, that's a great idea." I give her a mischievous smile. "The food booths here are amazing. Come on."

Calla and I stroll through the gaps in the parade. We weave between clusters of people in costume, eventually catching up with Ryan, Bennett, and Wren. They're standing in line for a food truck.

Ryan is poking fun at Wren for something. She fidgets with her glasses, looking anywhere but at him. I brace myself for another explosion, but she just mutters something and shrugs. Ryan lets it drop.

"Hey, remember the time Jay tried to start a food truck?" Bennett's eyes light up with mischief as he catches sight of me.

I groan. "Oh, come on. Not this again."

Calla looks at me, curious. "You had a food truck?"

Ryan laughs. "'Had' is a strong word. He rented one for a week, thinking he could make a killing selling goji berry smoothies."

"Goji berries are good for you." I sound defensive.

Bennett smirks. "But they taste terrible. That's okay, though, because in order to find out how bad they taste, someone would have had to actually buy one from you. You sold this many." He makes a zero with his hand and holds it up to his face.

"They weren't that terrible. Just verrrry sour. I figured I could just skip adding sweetener and I'd be fine."

Bennett grins and jabs his thumb at me. "This guy, am I right?"

I can see Calla trying to picture me as a failed food truck entrepreneur. She's probably wondering why I never mentioned it. The truth is, it's one of those stories that's more painful than funny. At least for me.

"So, what happened?" Calla tilts her head.

Ryan grins. "One guy tried a sample and spat it out. It was all downhill from there."

Calla laughs softly. It's sympathetic. I can tell she's holding back, trying to gauge how I feel about the whole thing. It's weirdly comforting.

We order some snacks. Nachos, corndogs, and something called a "deep-fried couch cushion" that turns out to be a massive, pillow-like piece of dough filled with cheese and bacon. We find a spot on the grass and sit down, forming a loose circle.

As the banter continues, I notice that Calla is fitting right in. She rolls with the punches, even throwing a few jabs of her own. When Ryan and Bennett gang up on me, she doesn't pile on. Instead, she watches. She's learning our dynamics and our history.

"Remember when Jay tried to run a marathon without training?" Ryan's grin says he's winding up for a punchline.

"Oh god." I cover my face with my hands. "Please, no."

Bennett takes over. "He made it to mile five and called us to pick him up. He was crying like a baby."

"I was not crying." I sit up straighter. "I was sweating from my eyes."

Calla looks at me, then at Ryan and Bennett. "You guys are really mean to my husband." Her voice has a playful edge. "I hope you realize that."

Ryan waves it off. "It's all in good fun. Jay knows we would walk through fire for him."

"Would you?" Calla raises an eyebrow. "Because it

sounds like jealousy to me. Maybe you're just envious of his goji berry empire and his marathon medals."

There's a moment of silence as Ryan and Bennett try to figure out if she's serious. I hold my breath, wondering the same thing.

Bennett laughs. "She's got us figured out."

We inhale our treats and Calla insists on seconds. As we make our second pass through the food booth offerings, I'm struck by something. Calla is in the middle of describing a funny anecdote to me. I'm not listening to her, not precisely. Instead, I'm thinking about how easy it is to talk to her. There's a rhythm to our banter, a natural flow that feels... good. She's not as guarded as she usually is. She's goofy and funny and sweet. I like this side of her

We stop at a booth called Marshmallow Mound, which is selling sweet potato pie loaded with torched marshmallows. I hesitate. "This might be overkill," I say as I eye the gooey mess.

"Come on." She nudges me. "You're not eating the whole thing anyway. Just two bites."

"Two bites?"

"It's a technique." She gives me a mock-serious look. "Two amazing bites of each thing. That way, you get the full experience without turning into a stuffed potato."

I raise an eyebrow. "Stuffed potato, huh?"

"Trust me. I'm a professional."

I hand over my money and grab a serving. When we head to find a seat, there are an insane number of people trying to squish into the tables set up for food booth customers. Ryan and Bennett are sitting at the very end of a table occupied by a group of people dressed in colorful inflatable hippo costumes. Wren is nowhere to be seen.

Ryan seems deep in conversation with Bennett, so I lead

Calla to a table way on the other side. A group of people are just leaving and I snag a seat. Calla sits beside me, digging in with an enthusiasm that's honestly kind of adorable. She takes her two bites, closing her eyes like she's savoring some deep, existential truth.

I take my two bites. The pie is warm, gooey perfection. "Okay, I get it now. The two-bite thing is genius."

"I know. It really is."

The moment stretches into silence. It's not awkward, though. Just... quiet. Comfortable. I find myself watching her, the way her face softens when she's relaxed. She's stunning. Not in an overdone, magazine-cover way, but in a way that feels real.

I nudge her with my elbow. "You're not what I expected." The words come out before I can stop them. "You're real, Calla. My ex... she was all about appearances. But you? You're something else entirely."

She toys with the small gold cross around her neck. "Oh yeah?"

"Absolutely." I smile. It's not my usual ridiculous grin. It's softer. "You're full of surprises. You know that?"

She brushes it off with a faint smile. "I'll take that as a compliment."

"Good." We start walking again. The silence between us doesn't feel like something missing, but like something shared. For once, I don't try to push it away. For the first time in a long time, I let the moment linger.

Stranger things have happened.

Chapter Twenty-Two

Calla

I rub my eyes, still groggy, when Jay's voice cuts through the quiet. "How do you feel about hiking?"

"Uhm..." I blink at him, then glance around, realizing I'm still in his bed. "I feel like it's walking. But more vertical."

He grins. "Well, the weather is supposed to be suddenly nice. Sixty-five degrees and sunny."

I frown. "What the hell. It's February."

"Yep. Pretty unusual, even for Georgia. It hasn't rained for a while, so any hiking trails should be clear and dry. Add a few days of sixty-degree weather to that, and you've got perfect hiking conditions."

I scrunch my nose. "If you say so."

"I do! You. Me. Right now. I know a good beginner trail with a great view from the top. What do you say?"

My mouth twists. I'm trying this new positive outlook thing. Just experimenting with it, seeing if being upbeat always feels as good as it did at the Waffle House Museum.

So far, it's been... okay. Baby steps, you know?

But Jay is putting my new perspective to the test before my feet even touch the floor this morning.

"It'll be fun," he presses. "You'll get some fresh air. Clear your head. Trust me."

Trust him. That's the crux of all this, isn't it? I bite my lip and weigh my options. "I don't have the right gear."

I hope this will be the out I need, but Jay waves a dismissive hand. "I've got plenty. Sponsors send me more stuff than I can use. Come on. I'll show you."

"Give me twenty minutes. I need to get dressed and brush my teeth." I can't think of anything good right now. So I just focus on not thinking anything bad.

What is that, a quarter of a baby step?

When I am dressed and relatively clean, I force myself to go find Jay. He is in the kitchen, pouring a cup of coffee for me. I open my mouth to ask where I can get sugar, but he beats me to the punch and pulls a bottle from the fridge. "I got this special for you. Can't have you telling people that I deprived you of your morning brew."

He tosses it to me. It's marshmallow-flavored coffee creamer. A smile spreads across my face without me realizing it. "For me?" I open it and pour a healthy slug into my coffee mug. "Thanks, Jay. I'm touched."

The fact that he put something marshmallow-flavored in his refrigerator full of kombucha and carrot sticks means that he thought about what *I* would like. He wants to make *me* comfortable.

Jay brushes it off like it's nothing. "Drink up. We should get moving."

He leads me to a small storage room that looks like a sporting goods store exploded. Shelves and bins overflow with jackets, boots, and backpacks. All kinds of gear are in here, everything shiny and new, like it's waiting to be photographed for a catalog.

He rummages through a pile and pulls out several pairs of hiking boots. "What size are you?"

"Eight." I'm still in shock at the sheer volume of stuff.

He tosses me a pair of boots and I catch them awkwardly. "Try those on. Here are some thick socks too. They should help the boots fit."

I sit on a nearby bench and slip my feet into the rugged, leather monstrosities. They're surprisingly comfortable.

"Why do you have so much stuff?" I ask. The curiosity is genuine.

He shrugs. "Perks of the job. Companies want me to use their products in my videos. It's all about brand alignment."

I stand and take a tentative step. Then another. The boots feel solid, like they could conquer a small mountain, or at least a steep hill. "Don't you ever feel... I don't know, weighed down by all this?"

Jay looks at me. For a moment, I see something in his eyes. A flicker of uncertainty. Maybe even longing. But it's gone as quickly as it appeared. His confident demeanor returns. "It comes with the territory. Here." He hands me a jacket. "You'll need this too. The weather can change fast up there."

I take the jacket. It's a sleek, high-tech thing that looks like it could survive a hurricane. "Thanks."

I mean it. This stuff isn't cheap. Neither is his time.

"No problem." There's a softness in his voice that makes me think he understands my hesitation. "Calla, this will be great. We'll take it slow. I promise."

I nod and clutch the jacket to my chest. "Okay. Let's do this."

The trailhead is more crowded than I'd expected for a

Sunday morning. Young families with strollers, retirees with walking sticks, and an alarming number of people in neon spandex mill about. Everyone is stretching and hydrating. I tug at the collar of my borrowed jacket. Already, I feel out of place and overheated.

"Don't worry," Jay whispers. "The rest of these newbies follow the marked trail. We're going to branch off after a bit. That way we can hear each other talk without a bunch of Joe-shmoes hot on our heels."

"It's funny that you think I'll be able to talk and hike at the same time."

He wiggles his eyebrows. "I keep telling you. We'll go at a snail's pace if you want. Honest."

Jay looks perfectly at ease, like he's stepped out of one of his own promotional videos. He wears a fitted fleece and cargo pants. Adjusting the straps on his backpack, he glances at me. "Ready?" he asks, as if this is the most natural thing in the world.

"Sure." That answer is more of my 'new outlook' bullshit. It's a lie. I already dread the first incline.

We set off at a moderate pace. The trail winds through a forest of towering pines. Their needles form a soft, springy carpet underfoot. Birdsong competes with the rustle of leaves. The air has a crisp, clean quality that makes me uncomfortably aware of my city-dulled senses.

All this pretty nature, and I have to hoof it like I'm fucking Sisyphus rolling a boulder up an eternal mountain.

I focus on putting one foot in front of the other. The stretch and pull of muscles I'd forgotten I had keeps my mind busy. Sweat beads on my forehead. I wipe it away with the back of my hand and curse silently. This is Jay's element, not mine. Every step feels like a lifetime.

Seriously, are we there yet?

Still, I can't deny the beauty of it. Sunlight filters through the canopy in golden shafts, dappling the trail with shifting patterns of light and shadow. A small creek babbles alongside us. Its water is clear and cold as glass.

I steal glances at Jay as we climb. He moves with the easy grace of someone born into the woods. There's a serenity to him here that I find disarming.

"Blake would have hated this."

My serenity suddenly sails out the window at the mention of her name.

"What?"

"This. Hiking. She refused to go with me. According to her, anyone that would go for a hike instead of just tackling the stair climber at the gym was crazy."

For several seconds, I'm silent, my mind churning.

"Why did you propose to her?" I finally ask. "I still don't really understand. You don't believe in long-term commitments. Why would you decide that you should tie yourself down to someone who doesn't like the things that you like?"

Jay stops and turns. His expression is unreadable. "Who says I don't believe in them?"

"You did. Indirectly at least. I can't stop wondering why you were prepared to marry Blake."

"I proposed to her because I loved her. Or I thought I did." He takes a deep breath and looks up at the swaying treetops. "The farther away I get from that disaster of a wedding, the more I realize that I was more swept up in the narrative I was telling my fans than anything else. I try to remember how I felt for Blake and...." He goes quiet for a minute. "It just feels fake compared to—"Jay stops midsentence, clapping his mouth closed.

I tilt my head. "Compared to what?"

He turns and looks at me for a few seconds. His blue

eyes probe me, studying my face as if looking for hidden answers. But I have none; I was asking *him*.

"Could we get to the top before we get too tired to finish?" he asks. "I promise that it's not much further."

There's a strange jitteriness to his words that makes me reach out and stroke his arm. "Of course."

Jay takes off like he's a rabbit who's just heard a fox rustling nearby. It is not lost on me that he promised we would take it slow. I trudge behind him, slowly falling behind, feeling upset in a way I have no right to feel.

Then he looks back and realizes his mistake. "Oh. Uh... Sorry, Calla." He doubles back, falling in step with me. Nothing is said. It's just companionable silence and hard climbing for the next few minutes. He is as good as his word and stays with me the entire time.

Just when I think my heart is going to give out, we crest the top of the ridge.

For a moment, there is no sound but gasping for breath. I lean against a tree and pant. Jay looks like he just finished a casual stroll while I try not to die. "You okay?" he asks.

I shake my head, unzipping my jacket and pulling my shirt away from my skin. He rubs my back in slow circles and offers me water that he magically pulls out of his pack. I take the water and lean into his touch.

Up here, it's just me, Jay, and the trees. Who's going to tell?

At length, I stand up straight and look around. "Did you say something about an amazing view?"

"I did." Jay's teeth flash as he smiles. He holds out his hand and I take it. "Come on, Lily."

We climb the last few steps to a small, lightly wooded plateau. The view punches the breath right out of me the second I see it. The trail was a steep ascent, but this... this is like standing on the edge of the world.

The valley below is a living, breathing thing. I can see a patchwork of bright green farmland squares nestled amongst the sloping hills. Each side of the valley starts off with a subtle rise only to angle and jut sharply upward toward the top. It's breathtaking. The stream I noticed before snakes into a river that weaves a sinuous ribbon flashing sapphire here and there between emerald hills.

"Wow," I say. I'm pretty sure that my brain has been short-circuited. That's the most eloquent thing I can muster.

Jay's face is alight with a boyish excitement. "Pretty amazing, right?"

I nod, unable to tear my eyes away from the panorama. A cool breeze tugs at my hair, and I pull the borrowed jacket tighter around me and zip it back up. For a moment, I forget everything. The fake marriage, the looming career crisis, my ingrained mistrust of men. All that exists is this view, this moment, and the surprising sense of accomplishment that fills me.

Jay sets down his backpack and unzips it, pulling out a small checkered blanket. He opens it with a flourish. "I thought we could have lunch up here," he says, spreading the blanket on the ground. "Best seat in the house."

I hesitate. Not because I don't want to, but because the idea of sitting still and enjoying something feels so foreign right now. Like an indulgence I haven't earned.

But my legs are wobbly from the hike. The thought of standing for a second longer than is strictly needed is enough to convince me. "Sure," I say, sinking gratefully onto the blanket.

Jay joins me, sitting cross-legged. He starts unpacking containers from his backpack. The scent of fresh fruit and sandwiches mingles with the piney air. My stomach growls. He hands me a sandwich and I inspect it closely. "Let me guess. Gluten-free, vegan, low-carb?"

Jay laughs. It's the easy, unguarded laugh that I've come to like more than I should. "It's just a turkey sandwich, Calla. I'm not that much of a health nut."

I take a bite, and it's delicious. Real turkey, not the processed kind, with crisp lettuce, Swiss cheese, and a smear of mustard. Jay must have prepared these sandwiches while I was getting ready this morning. That warms my heart.

We eat in companionable silence. No one rushes to fill the space. No one needs to.

I watch a hawk circle lazily on a thermal. There's a serenity up here that I can't quite reconcile with my usual, frantic life. Should I move to this mountaintop?

Jay finishes his sandwich and leans back on his hands, stretching out his torso. "So, how are we doing?"

I look at him, confused. "Doing what?"

"Connecting," he says, a sly grin playing on his lips. "You know. Getting along."

I roll my eyes but can't help smiling. "I think we're making progress. The hike was a good idea."

"Told you it'd be fun."

"Don't push it," I say. But there's no bite to my words. I'm too relaxed, too content. This is dangerous territory.

He sits up and reaches for a container of strawberries, offering me one. I take it. Our fingers brush. A spark of static, or maybe something more, jolts through me.

It's time for us to connect in another way.

Chapter Twenty-Three

Jay

Desire surges through me as I push aside the Tupperware from our lunch. Our bodies collide with an almost explosive force as I lay her back on the blanket. She lets out a mischievous giggle. "This is the closest I've come to public sex," she says with a wink.

I trail kisses along her neck, savoring the faint taste of salt from our hike. "If you're as loud as you usually are," I murmur, "we might get caught."

She looks at me with a mixture of fear and excitement in her eyes. "That's a risk I'm willing to take."

"Are you sure?" I run a hand slowly up her thigh, feeling the heat radiate through her leggings. "We could always wait until we're somewhere more private."

"Don't you dare." She pulls my head down to meet her lips again. The kiss is urgent, needy, as if we're trying to consume each other. My hands explore her body, tracing the curves that I've come to know so well. Her fingers dig into my back, pulling me closer, demanding more.

I glance around quickly. We left the crowded trailhead and veered off onto a less-used trail, so the hiking trail behind us is deserted. The thought that someone could appear at any moment adds a thrilling edge to our encounter. I like this side of her, the one that's willing to take chances, to live in the moment. It makes me wonder what other surprises she's hiding.

"Remember," I say. I pull back just enough to look into her eyes. "You might want to save some energy for the walk back down."

She laughs softly. It's a mix of exasperation and longing. "I think I'll manage." She bites her lower lip seductively.

I force myself to take it slow and savor every second, even though every cell in my body is screaming to fuck her right now. Our lips meet in a series of deep, languid kisses, each one stoking the fire that's already blazing between us. My hands trace the contours of her body with a deliberate slowness. She squirms beneath my touch. Her breath comes in short, eager gasps.

Just when I think I can't hold back any longer, she takes control. She flips us with a surprising strength and straddles me. Her hips grind against mine in a rhythm that makes my head spin. I can feel her heat through the thin fabric of our clothes. It's going to be nearly impossible to take it slow when she's all but begging me to fuck her with every movement, every desperate kiss.

She leans down. Her hair creates a curtain around us as she bites my lower lip. "I've been waiting for this for a long time, Jay."

The pain mixes with pleasure, sending a jolt straight through me. I grab her hips, holding her steady as I thrust upward, meeting her grind with a force that makes her moan. "I'm going to make sure that patience is rewarded."

The sound of her groans is almost enough to push me

over the edge, but I grit my teeth and hold on, wanting this to last.

With a quick, fluid motion, I roll her over and take control back. I hover above her, taking a moment to drink in the sight of her flushed cheeks and parted lips. My hands move to her shirt, lifting it slowly, teasingly, until her sports bra is exposed. I kiss her breasts through the fabric, feeling her nipples harden against my lips. She arches her back, pressing herself into me.

"Take it easy," I say.

"I don't want it easy. I want it hard," she breathes.

Fuck. Hearing that makes me want her so badly that my hands shake. The anticipation is killing me. Yet I am determined to take my time.

I peel Calla's leggings off with agonizing slowness. Leaving her in just her bra and panties. The sight of her nearly naked makes my mouth dry. She's a vision. Every inch of her radiates an irresistible allure. She reaches for me, pulling at my clothes with a frantic urgency. I let her strip them off, piece by piece, until I'm down to my boxer briefs.

The cool mountain air prickles our skin, but the heat between us is enough to keep us warm. I press my body against hers, feeling the softness of her curves, the rapid beating of her heart. Her hands roam over my back, my arms. She pulls me closer, never close enough.

I run my hands slowly down her sides. Her skin is like silk, warm and inviting. I take one of her nipples in my mouth, swirling my tongue around it, then gently biting. She gasps and arches her back, pushing her chest closer to me, silently begging for more. I switch to the other breast, giving it the same reverent attention. My hands are never idle as they caress her hips and thighs.

I run my lips down her throat and collarbone, making

her breath stutter. My lips trail down her stomach, each kiss a promise of what's to come. Her breathing quickens. Her entire body tenses.

I stop at the waistband of her panties. My breath is hot against her skin. I look up to see her eyes closed, her lips parted in a silent plea, then hook my fingers around the fabric and pause, letting the moment stretch, making her wait.

She opens her eyes and looks down at me. "Jay," she whispers, her voice hoarse with need. "Please, baby. I need you to touch me."

"When you ask so nicely..." I give her a wicked smile and slowly, ever so slowly, pull her panties down, exposing her completely. The sight of her naked and vulnerable sends a surge of lust through me. I keep my movements measured, deliberate. I want to savor every second of this.

I kiss her inner thighs, taking my time, feeling her squirm with each touch. She's so wet, so ready, but I'm not done teasing her yet. I let my breath wash over her core, close enough to make her think I'm going to dive in. I place several light kisses up and down her wet slit. I want nothing more than to open my mouth and suck her pretty clit. But I hold back, kissing my way back up her body.

"God," she says, almost whimpering, as I reach her lips. "Jay, you're killing me."

I kiss her deeply, letting her taste her own arousal on my mouth. Her hands clutch at me, trying to pull me in, but I resist, keeping just enough distance to drive her crazy. "Not yet." I murmur against her lips. "I want this to last."

I touch her pussy, still teasing, still drawing this out. She bites my lower lip. Her kiss trails down to my neck, where she leaves a series of hungry, urgent pecks.

My fingers trace her slit, now dripping wet and radiating heat. I slide two thick fingers into her hungry pussy, feeling her warmth and tightness envelop me. I finger fuck her hard, relishing the sounds she makes. Each moan, each gasp is a note of desire that makes my cock twitch. Her hips lift to meet my hand with every thrust, her body moving in a desperate, needy rhythm.

I watch her face, the way her eyes flutter closed, the way her mouth forms a perfect O when she lets out a particularly loud moan. It's almost too much to bear, knowing that I'm the one making her feel this way, that I have this kind of power over her. I find her clit and circle my fingers around it, applying just enough pressure to make her squirm.

She rocks her hips, needing more.

"Greedy girl." I chuckle, giving her what she wants, increasing the speed and intensity of my movements. "You're such a good girl." She arches her back and gasps. "I can't wait to watch you come on my fingers." I groan, getting more aroused by the second. "It turns me on so much to see you unravel like this."

Her breathing becomes ragged, her body tensing as she nears the edge. "Come for me." My voice is a low, commanding growl. "I want to feel you come, little wife."

She comes suddenly, her eyes rolling back in her head, her pussy convulsing under my touch. Her entire body shakes with the force of her orgasm. She cries out, the sound echoing off the mountains around us.

I keep my fingers moving, prolonging her pleasure. I feel her wetness coat my hand as she rides the waves of her orgasm. I take in every detail of her, the way her chest heaves with each breath, the flush that spreads across her cheeks and down her neck, the dazed, blissful expression on her face. It's a sight that will be forever burned into my memory.

I hope her face is the last thing that flashes through my mind before I fucking die.

I kiss her deeply as she slowly descends from her orgasmic high, her body still trembling with aftershocks. She pulls me closer, her nails lightly scratching my back. I can feel her heartbeat calm. "Make me come again," she whispers into my ear. "Please, Jay. You know just how I like to be touched."

The words send a jolt of electricity straight through me. I move my hand down between her legs, ready to give her what she wants, but she stops me. "Wait." Her eyes lock onto mine with a burning intensity. "I want your cock deep inside my pussy. I want you to come with your cock buried deep inside my pussy."

Her words are like gasoline on a fire. I'm ready to tear off what's left of my clothes and take her right here, but then a thought cools my fervor.

"Calla." My voice is strained with desire and thick with need. "I can't. I didn't bring a condom."

She hesitates for a moment, biting her lip, then says, "I'm on birth control. I trust you. I want you."

Fuck, I want her too. Every part of me is screaming to just dive in, to lose myself in her. The trust she's placing in me makes this even more intense. It's not just physical; there's something deeper at play, something that scares me and excites me in equal measure.

"I want you so bad that I don't know what to do with myself." My forehead rests against hers. "But I still need to ask. Are you sure?"

"Yes," she breathes, her hands sliding down to my hips, trying to pull me closer. "Please, Jay."

That's the last coherent thought I have for some time. I kiss her neck, her collarbone. I press my boxers-bound cock against her belly, grinding slowly, and let out a deep, guttural groan. She's quick to tug at my waistband. I help her by lifting my hips. She slides them down. I kick them off with one swift motion.

I don't feel the cold. All I can focus on is Calla. Her warmth, her touch, her scent. She wraps her legs around me. Her heels dig into my lower back, pulling me in. My hard cock presses against her slit. She's so wet that I can feel her dampness coating me.

I take a moment to look at her. Her eyes are half-closed, her lips slightly parted. She's absolutely stunning like this, vulnerable yet so incredibly strong. I lean down and kiss her softly, then more passionately, trying to pour all my feelings into that one kiss. "Calla. You're amazing."

She doesn't respond with words. Instead, she takes my hand and guides it to her breast. She runs her fingers down my arm, my chest, and finally to my cock. She grips it firmly, guiding me to her entrance. The contact makes me shudder. I have to summon all my willpower not to thrust into her immediately.

"I need you. *Now*. Fuck me, Jay. Show me how you feel about me."

Her words spur me. *Damn right. I'm about to make you forget that there's anybody in the fucking world except for me.*

I position my cock at her entrance, feeling the slick heat of her pussy as I push in, each inch a slow, torturous delight. Her body grips me so tightly, like a velvet vise, hot and wet and everything I have dreamed about since the moment I woke up spooning her in the gazebo. She gasps at the invasion. Her nails dig into my shoulders. I pause, giving her a moment to adjust, savoring the way her muscles flutter around me.

"Oh god, Jay." Her voice trembles. "Your cock is so *big*. It feels... it feels amazing. You're stretching my pussy out."

Her words send a jolt of pride and lust through me. I start to move, pulling out slowly before thrusting back in with a steady rhythm. The friction is exquisite, each stroke sending waves of pleasure through my body. I can feel the pent-up desire, the frustration of wanting her and not being able to have her, all coming to a head.

She meets my thrusts with her hips, creating a perfect, synchronized dance of our bodies. Her breasts bounce with each movement. Her face is a picture of raw, unfiltered ecstasy. I lean down to kiss her, but we're both too breathless, too consumed by the moment to do more than let our lips brush together.

The sounds of our sex fill the air. Her moans. My grunts. The wet, raw slapping of our bodies. It's primal, almost animalistic. It drives me wild. I'm so close already, but I want this to last. I desperately need to stretch out every second of it.

"Fuck, Calla," I groan, trying to pace myself. "You feel so good. Too good."

She wraps her legs tighter around my waist, pulling me deeper. I can't help but quicken my pace. The tension in my body builds to an almost unbearable level. I know I won't be able to hold back much longer.

"We need to slow down." I manage to say this, though every fiber of my being is screaming to just let go. "I don't want to come yet."

Calla makes a frustrated sound. "What if I want you to finish?"

I peer down at her. "Are you really ready for this to be over? It feels like we just started."

She bites her lip and shakes her head, her eyes glazed

with lust. We both take a moment to catch our breath. I pull out of her. The sudden coolness is a shock to my overheated skin. She's left a wet, glistening trail on my cock. The sight of it makes me throb with need.

"I'm going to make you come. But we have to take our time."

"Jay." She rakes her nails lightly over my pecs. "I'm yours. Take me where you want to go. I'll follow."

I kiss her, grateful. I've never been with anyone like Calla before. I've never had this kind of connection with another human being.

I love the feel of her body against mine, but I know I need to change things up if I want her to come again before I do. I slide down her body, kissing her skin as I go, and position myself between her legs. The scent of her arousal is intoxicating. I take a slow, deliberate lick along her slit, savoring her taste.

"So good," I mumble. "If I could, I would burn your taste and scent into my brain."

I don't hear what she says, because I'm focused on her clit, flicking it with my tongue before sucking it hard. Her hands fly to my hair, tugging and guiding me as her hips start to rock.

Her moans grow louder, more urgent. I can feel her getting closer with each stroke of my tongue. Just when she's on the brink, I pull back and blow gently on her swollen clit. She lets out a frustrated whine that makes me chuckle. I love this power, this control. "Be a patient little wife."

I kiss her inner thighs, nibbling softly, then trail my lips back up her body. Her skin is a mix of cool and hot, flushed with desire. I take one of her nipples into my mouth and bite just hard enough to make her gasp. She squirms beneath me, her hands roaming my back, my arms, anywhere she can reach to pull me back down to her.

"Jay, please," she begs. "I can't take it."

I move back up to her lips, kissing her deeply, letting her taste herself on my tongue. She bites my lower lip and I growl. The sound vibrates through both of us. "I want you so bad." Her eyes burn into mine. "Finish what you started. Make me come!"

I can't resist her. I don't want to. I position my cock at her entrance again, feeling the slick heat of her pussy inviting me in. I push in slowly, every inch a sweet agony, until I'm buried deep inside her. She wraps her legs around me, pulling me even closer. I can feel her heartbeat against my chest.

I pull her close and bunch the blanket under her hips, tilting them up to meet mine as I start to fuck her slowly, letting the anticipation build. I've been careful to leave enough room between our bodies for my hand to find her clit. I find it and circle the bud gently as I fuck her with a mix of tenderness and urgency.

She gasps and her eyes lock onto mine. "Don't hold back, baby. I want to feel all of you."

Her words are like gasoline on a fire, unleashing the full force of my desire. I thrust harder. Deeper. Each stroke is a declaration. She bites her lip and throws her head back, exposing her throat like a submissive lover. Her nails rake down my back in a mix of pain and pleasure that sends a shiver through me.

She pulls my hand away from her clit and places it on her breast. "I'm going to come on your cock. Don't you dare stop. Fuck me like the savage I know you are."

I thought that coming from a cock was a myth, but she knows her body better than I do. The realization that I'm enough, that my cock can bring her to the brink on its own, fills me with a primal pride.

Freed from any remaining concern, I let go completely, ramming into her pussy as hard as I want. She meets each thrust with equal force, her hips rising to collide with mine. Her moans grow louder. More urgent. I feel the tension in her body coiling tight like a spring.

"Oh god. Oh god. Jay...."

The pressure in me builds to an almost unbearable level. I'm so close, teetering on the edge, and I just hope that I can hang on long enough to make Calla come first. Every thrust is a battle against my own impending release.

"Fuck, Calla. Fuck!"

"Jay! Don't stop. That's the spot. Just like that."

Her encouragement is both a blessing and a curse. It spurs me on, but it also brings me dangerously close to the point of no return. I grit my teeth, focusing on her, on the way her body moves, on the sounds she makes. Each detail is a distraction, a way to pull myself back from the brink.

"Come for me, honey. *Please.*"

Her eyes squeeze shut and her mouth opens in a silent scream. Her pussy flutters around me, the first signs of her orgasm. It's almost too much to bear, and I have to summon every ounce of willpower not to explode right then. Somewhere in the back of my mind, I know I have to make this the best sex she's ever had.

I only manage to fuck her for half a minute more before her pulsing, wet, hot pussy sends me over the edge with a force that feels like it's tearing me apart. My orgasm barrels down on me, an unstoppable wave of pleasure that crushes me.

"I fucking love you," I grunt. I'm out of my mind, completely caught up in the moment. "Calla...."

My cock pulses, each throb releasing heavy jets of cum, painting her pussy walls with my seed. She grips me tightly, her body milking me for every last drop. Her nails dig into my back, leaving trails of burning pain that only heightens the pleasure coursing through me. Every muscle in my body tenses, then releases in a series of shuddering spasms.

She kisses me with intense tenderness as we ride the waves of our orgasms together. Our bodies are locked in a perfect union. Time seems to stretch and bend, each second an eternity of exquisite sensation. I can feel her heart pounding in her chest and it mirrors the frantic beat of my own. The heat of our exertion creates a steamy cocoon around us. The world outside fades into nothingness.

Slowly, the explosive rush begins to subside, leaving a warm, afterglow in its wake. I collapse onto her, pinning her down as we both struggle to catch our breath. Her skin is slick with sweat. Her hair is a tangled mess. She looks absolutely beautiful.

I brush a stray strand from her face and kiss her forehead. The tender gesture feels almost out of place after the ferocity of what we just experienced.

I roll onto my side and take Calla with me. We lie together, facing each other with our bodies entwined. "Did you..." Calla starts, then stops. "Did you tell me that you love me?"

Sucking in a breath, I scan her face. "Did I?"

She ducks her head, deflating. "Maybe not. I must've heard you wrong."

My heart is suddenly beating so loudly that I'm sure she'll hear it. All the moisture is gone from my mouth. And my stomach won't stop doing flips.

I'm not sure if I said I loved her. I certainly didn't mean to. But that doesn't make it untrue.

I do love her. How could I not?

"You didn't hear me wrong."

Calla's eyes snap to my face. "What?"

"I do love you, Calla. I'd be a fool not to fall for you."

Her eyes shine with tears. She doesn't say anything for a moment. But then she exhales, and kisses me ever so gently on the lips. "I love you too, baby," she whispers.

Chapter Twenty-Four

Jay

The warmth of the café washes over me as I hold the door to Java Monkey for Calla, chasing away the chill of the morning air.

Unfortunately, it doesn't chase away the tension that's been clinging to us since the hike.

Calla and I haven't talked about anything deep since that moment when we confessed our feelings for each other while we were naked and vulnerable.

Since then? It's been markedly awkward between us.

Mr. Lim waves from behind the counter, his ever-watchful eyes sparkling with mischief. "Jay! Calla! Ready to spread some Valentine's Day love?"

I nod back, offering a tight smile. Calla flashes him a wave, her expression soft but guarded. We make our way to the back of the café, where a box overflowing with decorations waits for us. She glances at me, her teeth tugging at her bottom lip. I wonder what is going on behind those eyes.

"So," I say, breaking the silence before it swallows us. "We should probably figure out a game plan."

Calla nods. Her relief at having a task to do is almost

palpable. "I'll start with the windows. You can handle the tables."

I grab a handful of decorations and set to work. Calla moves to the windows. She stretches up on her tiptoes to tape heart-shaped doilies to the glass. Her movements are deliberate, almost hypnotic.

She's tied one of my T-shirts up at the waist and is wearing it over a paint-spattered pair of pants. Her outfit is perfectly innocuous. Work clothes, my grandmother would have called them. But there is something sexy about Calla wearing one of my shirts in public.

It calls to the possessive part of me. If I'm honest, her butt looks amazing in those slightly too tight pants, too.

I catch myself staring. I shake my head and focus on the table in front of me. Fiddling with a centerpiece that looks too sparse for the over-the-top theme is better than being distracted by my wife. She can't catch me drooling over her.

Not when things are so... *undefined* between us.

"Jay?" Calla waves a hand, trying to get my attention. "Are you with me? I was saying that we need to make the place look extra romantic if we're going to have a Valentine's Day photoshoot."

I glance up. "Yeah. Don't worry, I've got experience with this kind of thing."

"Decorating for Valentine's Day?" She raises an eyebrow.

"Set design." I smirk. "Less is more."

Calla snorts, the sound surprising both of us. "You can't have too much when it comes to Valentine's. It's supposed to be over-the-top."

"There's a fine line between charming and gaudy."

"Gaudy can be charming," Calla shoots back. A smile tugs at the corners of her mouth.

I can't help but match it. "As long as it's not gauche," I tease. "That would be unbearable."

She sticks her tongue out at me and I grin wider.

The silence that follows feels different. It feels less like a storm cloud and more like a quiet breeze. She moves from the windows to the tables, inspecting the centerpieces I've put together. A single red rose sits in a glass vial, a lone heart cutout standing at attention paired with it.

"Too sparse. Your whole display needs more love."

Our fingers brush as she hands me the ribbon. I glance at her, amused. "I thought you said I was in charge of the tables."

"You are." She crosses her arms, her tone teasing. "I'm just providing suggestions."

"Your sister Iris warned me that you were a control freak." I tie the ribbon and doily around the rose.

"I'm not a control freak. I just have high standards." Her expression stiffens, just for a moment.

Looking to placate her, I hold up the finished centerpiece. "How's that?"

She smiles softly. "It'll do."

Her attempt at nonchalance makes me chuckle.

We finish decorating the place pretty quickly. It's a tiny shop, so by the time we're done, Java Monkey is decorated with what I would call a decidedly maximalist style.

Not that I really object to Calla's taste. From what I've seen so far, I like it. After all, she had the good taste to say she loves me.

The barista arrives with two steaming mugs of cocoa. I take a seat, wrapping my hands around the mug. Calla finishes up tying a bow *just so*, then does the same.

"We used to spend hours here," I say, gesturing around the café to take in the mismatched furniture, the eclectic art, the stacks of well-loved board games. All of it feels like home. "Ryan and me, and the rest of the crew. This place is like a second home."

Calla looks toward the camera that's perched on a tripod near the counter. She waves, addressing the lens. "It's true. Java Monkey has been a fixture in the community for years. I remember coming here the week it opened. I was, what, twelve? It's changed a lot, but it still has the same spirit."

"It's a community center as much as it is a place of business."

She scrunches her face. "Well, not as much as the actual community center two blocks away. But yeah, I have tons of great stories that feature Java Monkey. It's local institution."

I lift my mug to the camera in salute. "Please come here and spend all your money. Make sure that this place is still here when our kids are growing up."

Calla inhales hot chocolate and has a terrible, loud coughing fit. I stop the camera and hand her a pile of napkins. The barista grabs her a glass of water.

After the fit subsides, Calla looks at me with wide eyes. "Our kids?" She wipes her eyes with a napkin. "That's a big step. We just admitted that we have feelings for each other. Maybe we should let that sink in for a while before we start picking out baby names."

"Are you saying that you don't want a family?"

"...no. I want a huge family, just like mine. But I'm not in any hurry. My mom had Iris when she was 45. I've got time."

"So... you want to have this conversation, but not right now?"

"Not yet." She waves her hand at the customers in the shop. "Besides, this is not the place for serious talks."

I shrug. "Suit yourself. Can I tell you one thing, though?"

Calla hesitates, then nods. "Anything."

"Good." My face splits into a grin. "We would have adorable kids. Can you imagine? Your dark hair, my bone structure. They'd all be gorgeous."

"You are unbelievable." She shakes her head. "Truly, completely insane."

As she speaks, the front door opens and a bunch of parents come in with their young kids. The kids shriek noisily as they excitedly try to order. The parents do not make eye contact with the rest of the customers. I would guess that they're too tired to put up a fight.

While they're still ordering, I sneak over to sit beside Calla and slip my arm around her. "I guess kids are just another thing we will have to talk about *privately*," I whisper in her ear.

She hits my arm in a playful manner. "You are such a flirt."

As soon as the parents head into the other room to sit with their kids, I pick up the camera and aim it at Calla. "So, Calla, how would you rate our decorating so far?"

She places a hand on her chin, striking a thoughtful pose. "I'd say we're at a solid seven. Could use more hearts."

I laugh, the sound breaking through the tension I didn't realize was still there. It's nice that there is always this warm banter when we're done bickering.

"I thought we were aiming for a ten."

"There's still time. Still lots of time." She pins me in place with her eyes.

Yeah, we're going to have the talk about feelings soon.

Chapter Twenty-Five

Calla

"I'm wearing the entirely wrong shoes for this," I mutter.

The field is a swamp of enthusiasm, mud, and poor decisions waiting to be made. People in bright orange jackets wave the slow-moving line of cars to open parking spots. When it's finally our turn, Jay parks his SUV as I peer out the window into the sunlight. It's bright and unseasonably warm today. Great weather for a demolition derby. Or so I assume; this is the first one I've ever been to.

We step out into the mire. My Converse soak through immediately.

"Perfect." I cringe, but soldier on. This isn't my first time trashing my Converse.

"Calla, are you sure you're up for this?" Jay's handsome face is etched with something that might be concern. Maybe it's just the sunlight playing tricks, though.

"Are you kidding? This is like a slice of home," I announce. "Seriously, it reminds me of my mom and dad. You haven't met my parents yet, but they're very... entertaining."

Yet? I say that as if Jay will meet them any day now. In reality, I'm just praying that video of me drunkenly marrying Jay never makes it to Facebook. That's where my parents hang out.

We trudge over to the main event. In the center of the bracket of stands, a large field of mud stands at the ready. All around it is pure chaos. The 'Smash 'n' Bash Extravaganza' is in full swing, featuring men with beer guts and trucker caps, women in cutoff denim jackets, and more muddy cowboy boots than I can count.

The air smells of wet grass and cheap lager. I take a deep breath.

Jay looks skeptical, but willing to be convinced. "I thought you hated this kind of thing."

"I have a complicated relationship with redneck culture," I say, shrugging. "On one hand, ew. On the other, I am from Georgia. Some part of me can't help but love it."

Jay's film crew appears and starts trailing us, hoping to capture every awkward step in a mud puddle and every sidelong glance between us. I can't help but think about how they'll edit this later. They'll cut and splice until we look like a perfect, happy couple.

We slosh our way toward the makeshift stadium. Thousands of fans are already filling the bleachers. An announcer's voice crackles over the PA system, hyping the crowd for the first round of vehicular mayhem.

"Can we stop for a snack?" I ask.

"I offered you some trail mix in the car!" Jay looks at me like I'd just kicked his shins.

"I want real food." I feel my cheeks burning. "I can buy my own popcorn if that's the issue."

He pulls out his wallet and eyes me. "I just want you to live past forty."

"And I want to enjoy the time I have on this planet." I hold out my hand, scrunching my fingers. "Gimme, please."

His lips twitch with humor as he hands me a stack of twenties. We line up at the concession stand. It's a rickety setup of folding tables and mismatched coolers stocked with cans of soda and plastic-wrapped hot dogs. Jay buys a bottle of water. I ask for a Coke and a hot dog.

He takes a swig of his water, his eyes flicking to me and then away. "Calla," he starts.

I already know what he's going to say. Or at least, I hope I do. I don't think I can take him apologizing. "Yeah?" I reply, paying close attention to my hot dog.

He hesitates, running a hand through his perfectly tousled hair. "About last night—"

The PA system roars to life, drowning him out. I flinch at the sudden volume. Jay just sighs and looks toward the track. A convoy of battered sedans and pickup trucks are lining up for the first event. The crowd surges with anticipation.

Yup, this is happening all right.

I stand on my tiptoes to reach Jay's ear. "We should find our seats," I yell over the din.

He nods and starts to lead me up the slippery bleacher steps. A couple of times he pauses, making sure I am following him closely.

It's nice to be thought of.

We find our seats. I plop down with a squelch and survey the track below. The field is a lake of mud. The vehicles are already fishtailing and colliding in a glorious, slow-motion ballet of destruction. I can't help but smile.

"This is your thing, huh?" Jay asks.

I flush as I realize he's been watching me, not the

carnage. "I can appreciate a good smash-up," I say, deflecting. "It's therapeutic."

He laughs. "Maybe I should take notes."

The tension between us is a live wire, sparking and dangerous. I know this can't last. This will-they-or-won't-they, this tentative friendship, this whatever-it-is. But for now, I let the noise and the mud and the sheer ridiculousness of the moment wash over me and drown out the thoughts I'm not ready to face.

The first event is over pretty quickly, with a minimum of destruction. All the cars competing just kind of clanked to a stop, leaving only one that may ever drive anywhere ever again. The announcer declares the winner, and the crowd erupts.

Jay leans in close again. "Calla, I just want you to know—"

I turn to him, our faces inches apart. "I know," I say, cutting him off. "Let's just enjoy the show."

"You know?" He sounds as if he isn't sure.

Yeah, I've been given the 'it's not you it's me' line a few times. And the 'I'm just not in the place for a relationship' line? Heard that one, too. "I'm good," I say.

He sits back. For a moment, I think he looks relieved. The film crew zooms in, capturing our silence, our unresolved everything.

Is this the worst or what?

Twenty minutes later, we're walking around, scoping out booths selling "You Might Be a Redneck If" T-shirts and camo belt buckles, and I find myself wishing for that awkwardness again.

"Calla, look!" Jay's pointing to a banner flapping in the breeze. It reads 'Couples Mud Run' in big, drippy letters. "We should totally do that."

"A mud run in February? Who thought that was a brilliant idea?"

"It'll be fun! It's nice enough outside. Cool, not cold." He looks over my shoulder at the track on the far end of the field.

I follow his gaze and my stomach does a little somersault. The track is a quagmire of obstacles: tire walls, balance beams, and pits that look like they could swallow a person whole. I'd paid no attention to it when we arrived but now I wonder if it was just self-preservation that made me miss it. "You're serious?"

"As a heart attack." He grins, the kind of smile that could melt glaciers. "Come on, Calla. I need to live out my redneck dreams. Think of it as team building. Plus, the cameras will love it."

Of course. The cameras. I glance over my shoulder at the film crew, who are busy capturing B-roll of the crowd. Jay notices, and his expression softens. "We can skip it if you really don't want to do the run. I just thought..."

He trails off, and I know he's trying. Trying to make this less weird, trying to make me less resistant.

I sigh. "Fine. But if I break an ankle, you're paying my medical bills."

Jay's face lights up. "You won't regret it," he says, taking my hand and pulling me toward the signup tent.

"Famous last words," I deadpan, but inside I feel a tiny spark of excitement.

That spark is snuffed out the second we hit the starting line. We're surrounded by couples who look far too enthusiastic about this whole endeavor. Jay strips off his shirt, casually revealing a torso that could be the centerpiece of a fitness magazine.

I try not to stare, but come on. The man is a Greek god.

"You might want to take off your top," he says casually. "It'll just get ruined."

I cross my arms over my chest. "I'm not wearing a sexy bra."

"Every bra you own is a sexy bra. Plus, I have an extra shirt in the car if you need it. It's going to weigh you down when we run through all that mud."

I uncross my arms, feeling petulant and ridiculous. With a sigh, I pull off my hoodie and top. The cool air hits my skin, but when I shiver it's not just from the cold. I fold the clothes and stack them atop my purse, handing it over to the camera crew for safekeeping.

Jay looks me over. He's not leering, just... appreciating. "You look great," he says.

"I look out of place." I look around at all the women in their bikini tops and sports bras. Not one single gray underwire bra in the group.

"I'd rather be wherever you're going." He grins at me.

Why, oh why, does my heart do a somersault in response?

Before I can respond, a whistle blows and we're off.

The first obstacle is a mud pit. Everyone leaps in like a pack of deranged lemmings. The mud is thick and cloying. My feet instantly feel like they're encased in concrete. I take one step and faceplant, the muck slurping hungrily at my body.

Strong hands pull me up. Jay is laughing. I'm embarrassed and I want to be angry, but his laughter is infectious. I wipe mud from my face, smearing it worse, and start to giggle.

"We're going to crush this," he says, though it's obvious we're dead last already.

"I like the optimism."

We trudge through the next set of obstacles: a slippery balance beam that I crawl across on all fours, a wall of used tires, a frame made of cargo netting. On the last one, Jay reaches down and lifts me up with shocking ease. Each time he touches me, little electric shocks through my body remind me of our private mountain sex. Of his hands, and his mouth, and—

I slip in the mud. *Focus, Calla.*

We reach another mud pit, and I hesitate. I don't know how shallow it is. I don't know if there are creatures lurking at the bottom, ready to snatch at my feet. Jay notices my pause and takes my hand.

"Together," he says. "Come on!"

I'm not the type of person to just blindly take a leap. But Jay is doing it. Somehow, I am certain that he wouldn't jump into a snake-infested mud pit.

I close my eyes, nod tightly, and squeeze his hand as I jump.

The mud explodes all around us and we land in a tangle of limbs. I expect it to be cold, but it's warm from the sun. We struggle to our feet, laughing.

For a moment it feels like we're an actual team. Like we're figuring this out together, even if it's just for now.

A shout goes up from the crowd. We turn to see a tiny, wiry woman barreling toward us. She looks like she was born in a trailer park and raised on a diet of scrap metal and moonshine. She's a force of nature, and she's holding a makeshift flag.

"Move it, lovebirds!" she yells. We sidestep just in time as she streaks past, mud flying in her wake. She crosses the finish line, and the crowd goes wild, hooting and hollering.

Jay and I look at each other, panting. He shrugs. I start to laugh. A deep, uncontrollable laugh that wipes away all the tension of the last twenty-four hours. He joins in.

"We can still make it to the finish line. Team Last Place!" I suggest.

We make our way to the finish line, hand in hand. At the end of the race, many of our competitors stand waiting for us. They're watching us until we cross the line and then hollering bloody murder when we do.

When we pass over the checkered line, Jay cheers, picking me up and kissing me. I grin as that grizzled woman waves her flag victoriously. Jay high-fives her, still holding me up. "Nice run," he says and she cackles.

I retrieve my purse and try to wipe my hands clean before digging in, but it's no use. "Here," Jay says, handing me his shirt. I take it, grateful, and pat myself down as best I can.

"That was...actually kind of fun," I admit. "Disgusting, but fun."

"Told you. We make a good team."

We start to walk back to the parking lot, leaving a trail of muddy footprints. The film crew catches up. I realize I don't even mind them right now.

Let them film. Let them see.

Jay slows and turns to me. "Calla, about what I was trying to say earlier—"

I hold my breath.

"Thank you. For all of this. I know it's not easy."

I exhale and nod, appreciating the effort he's putting in without making it unbearably awkward.

"We're in it together, right?" It nearly sounds convincing.

"Yeah," he says. He offers me his hand and his eyes hold mine a moment longer than they need to. "Together."

We reach his SUV, and I pause before getting in. The mud run, the laughter, his hands on me. They've all stirred something I'm not ready to confront.

"Jay," I say. He looks at me expectantly. "I know this is just an arrangement, but...."

"But?" he prompts.

"But I appreciate that you're taking it seriously," I finish. *Yup. I chickened out.*

He nods. "I appreciate you, Calla."

I slide into the passenger seat, my heart a confused, muddy mess.

Chapter Twenty-Six

Calla

The bakery has sold out of cupcakes, by noon, almost every day in the last month. I need to increase the volume of cupcakes by enough to last the full day, but not to where we'd have leftover cupcakes.

So how many twenty-five pound drums of flour and sugar should I buy?

It's like one of those word problems from algebra. Except with this question, there are actually stakes. The flour and sugar actually cost me *money*.

I'm sitting in You Butter Believe It's kitchen, drinking a cup of coffee and going over an inventory list for my bakery. I tap a pen against my lips and write down a conservative number. Then I scratch it out and write a bigger number.

Hmm. If I don't order enough supplies, we'll keep running out of cupcakes. But if I over-order a few times, I will be in hot water financially. I can always put an order or two of supplies on my business credit card... but I need to be sure that I'll have the cash to pay it off when the bill comes due.

My phone buzzes on the counter. I mindlessly reach for

the phone, still running through my calculations. I was never a great math student, and that makes running my own small business challenging.

The phone buzzes again in my hand.

Incoming! Cora texts. *Mom saw your wedding video. She's in a mood.*

Oh, crap. This is exactly what I don't need. I'd hoped to go through the whole three-month period as a married woman without my parents ever finding out. Now that's out the window.

Like magic, my phone starts to ring. I glance at the screen. It's my mother. Bracing myself, I swipe to answer.

"Mom!" I say, adopting a cheerful tone. "I was just thinking about you."

"Calanthe Anastasia Diana Nikolakas!" My mother is a force of nature, like a Mediterranean hurricane. "Why didn't you tell us you were getting married?"

Double crap. She's serious if she's using my full name. I can almost see her with her hand on her hip, her dark curls bobbing with each indignant head shake.

Before I can respond, she plows ahead. "We had to find out from Facebook! Do you know how embarrassing that is for your father and me? I said to your dad, 'What do you think we've ever done to Calla that she would keep us out of her life like this?'"

"Daphne," my father cuts in. Stavros is ever the peacemaker. "Calla, sweetheart. We are happy for you. But surprised. Very surprised. We have whiplash over here."

I switch the phone to my other ear. I'm already exhausted. Now I have to make up a lie on the spot, which has me flustered. Well, it's not a lie per se. It's more of a massaging of the truth.

That doesn't make it any easier to say it out loud.

"Mom, Dad. The reason I didn't tell you is that we aren't sure that it will stick. We like each other, but we're not sure it's love."

"You're not sure?! How did you end up in this situation, *agapi mu*?" God. There it goes. My dad is breaking out the Greek terms of endearment. The next thing I know he's going to be doing a *zeibekiko* and smashing plates in celebration.

"Tequila, I think?" I slump against the counter, staring at the cup of coffee in front of me.

"Oh, sweetheart." My mom sounds concerned. "Have you talked to Cora about getting an annulment?"

"Not yet. We're playing it by ear. And I would really appreciate if you just supported me rather than asking me a million more questions."

There's a pause. I can almost hear them exchanging one of their long-married-couple looks. I bite my lip, waiting for the other shoe to drop.

"You need to bring him to dinner, Calanthe," Mom orders. "*Tonight*. If he's going to be part of the family, even temporarily, we need to meet him."

I groan inwardly. Dinners at my parents' house are a gauntlet under the best of circumstances. They're an hours-long affairs just with the family. Throwing Jay into the mix is a recipe for certain disaster.

"Mom, can it wait a few weeks?" My whole marriage might be over by then.

"Calla." Dad interrupts, his voice taking on a rare note of sternness. "Family is important. You know this. We will see you both for dinner. Your mother will roast a leg of lamb."

I sigh, defeated. "Fine. We'll be there."

"Good." Mom sounds mollified. "And Calla? We love you, even when you're being ridiculous."

"I love you too, Mom and Dad."

I hang up and stare at the phone for a long moment. This whole thing was supposed to be simple. A quick way to drum up business without any real complications. Now I've got my parents thinking I'm disrespecting our traditions. And Jay....

Well, Jay is a whole other complication.

* * *

Jay and I stand on the doorstep of my parents' house. The scent of oregano and roasted lamb wafts through the air. He adjusts his shirt collar, looking uncharacteristically anxious. I feel bad for him.

"Ready?" I ask. I know full well he's not.

He gives a half-hearted nod. I close my hand around his and ring the bell with the other.

The door flies open instantly, unleashing a wave of sound. My Greek relatives never do anything small. A "casual" family dinner means a spread that could feed a small army.

"Calanthe! Jay!" My mother is the first to reach us. She pulls me into a tight hug before giving Jay a once-over. "I told the family you got married. So, strap in. Unless you want to be the one to explain your decision to your grandmother?"

"Mom—" I start, but she's already waving us into the chaos of the living room. Every surface is covered with either food, children, or family photos of the whole clan. The noise level is somewhere between rock concert and jet engine.

As soon as we step inside, a phalanx of aunts and cousins descends on us. Well, on Jay, really. They peel him away from me, commenting on his looks and asking how a "nice boy like him" found their Calla. I hang back, letting them have their fun. It's not every day they get to interrogate a semi-celebrity.

"He's even taller in person," one cousin gushes.

"Those eyes! Are they real?" an aunt wonders.

Jay takes it all in stride. He seems nervous to me, but I think my family will be fooled by his confident smile. My grandmother swoops in to examine him. She's a tiny woman, but her presence is enormous.

"Sit. Sit!" she commands. She pushes Jay into a chair and thrusts a plate of spanakopita into his hands. "Eat up if you want to keep up with a strong Greek wife!"

I stifle a laugh as I watch him try to balance the plate. He fends off more questions. His cool facade is starting to crack, and I have to admit that it's kind of endearing.

"How did you two meet?" demands my uncle, the family's unofficial interrogator.

The room quiets. All eyes are on Jay.

"Uh, we met when Calla was doing a cake for my wedding," Jay says. He coughs into his hand and I see his neck flushing. The table murmurs with interest. "As you can see, things didn't go as planned."

"And you ran off with your cake baker?" one of my aunts gasps. She clutches her pearls.

"After my fiancée left me standing at the altar, I married Calla." He looks like he's sweating bullets, like a kid playing Operation.

"So fast! Was it the magic of fate or...?" She lets the question hang. Her suspicion is palpable.

"It was love at first sight," my mother cuts in. She beams. "Isn't that right, Calla?"

I want to strangle her but plaster on a smile. "Uhhh yep.

Once we knew that we could be together, we just—" I make a 'taking off' gesture while whistling. Why? I have no idea.

Jay, ever the quick study, jumps in. "I just couldn't resist Calla's charm."

I shoot him a look. I'm half amused, half exasperated. The younger cousins giggle.

I notice something I hadn't before. Jay's genuine excitement about other people. He's not just tolerating my family. Even though he's so clearly overwhelmed, he's engaging with them despite their loaded questions. Even enjoying responding.

That's something new that I hadn't noticed before. It makes my heart squeeze in my chest.

"So, when do we get grandchildren?" my grandmother booms. "Calanthe's not getting any younger!"

I choke on my drink. Jay lets out a nervous laugh. He glances at me to see how he should play this.

Before he can dig us into a deeper hole, my mother cuts in. "They'll have to go to Greek school. You know, classes at the Cathedral. Our kids went. Right, Calla?" she asks.

The family nods and breaks off into smaller groups, talking about Greek school.

Jay breathes out. I can't help but admire the way he's navigating this minefield. He's more adaptable than I gave him credit for.

A small part of me starts to wonder if we could actually pull this off. You know, be a real couple.

It's funny. Jay and I don't have to fake anything right now. We are just being our genuine selves. I can't decide if that's cute or absolutely terrifying.

"Come on," I say. I gently pull Jay away from the table. "You need a break."

We retreat to the kitchen. I hand him a glass of water

and he downs it in one gulp. He leans against the counter, eyes closed. "Your family is... intense."

"You have no idea." I roll my eyes. "And this is just the warm-up."

"I get it." He shrugs. "If my parents had feelings, I'm sure they would be grilling you, too."

I clear my throat. "We should get back."

We eat a lavish meal, each plate heaped high with lamb, roast potatoes, couscous salad, ripe tomato slices sprinkled with pepper, *lahnosalata*, lemon rice, and *briam*. Mom and my *yiayia* keep trying to refill Jay's plate.

I lean over and whisper in his ear. "Just say no. They are experts in making you feel like you're hurting their feelings by turning down more food, but I promise you're not. You have to be firm."

He doesn't take my advice and ends up with a third helping of lamb and cabbage salad. I laugh and he just shoots me a look.

Once we finally finish, the dining room calms down a bit. The initial frenzy gives way to the languid pace of a level ten food coma.

Just as I think we might escape unscathed, my father appears with a bottle of ouzo.

"Ouzo!" Jay says. "Now this is a part of Greek life that I already like."

My father pours two generous shots. He hands one to Jay.

"A toast," my father declares. "To family."

Jay hesitates for a split second. He clinks his glass against my father's. The ouzo goes down hard. Jay's face contorts in a mix of pain and surprise. He sputters and coughs.

"Smooth," he says, once he's done almost throwing up. I can't help but laugh.

A family member strikes up a traditional Greek song. Soon we're all on our feet, forming a circle. Jay looks to me, pleading. I grab his hand and pull him into the dance. He's clumsy, stepping on toes and nearly toppling over, but laughs it off.

Honestly, if he keeps this up, he'll win over my family with his effort. His smile is genuine. His eyes are bright. He fits in better than I ever expected.

For a moment, it all feels real. Too real.

As we leave, Jay is exhausted but grinning. "I've never met a family with so much... enthusiasm."

"Yeah, they're something." A strange mix of pride and dread swells in my chest.

He pauses and looks back at the house. "You're lucky, you know. To have all this."

I don't know what to say to that. Instead, I unlock the car. We slide into our seats. "Thanks for doing this." I speak finally. "I know it's a lot."

He shrugs. I can tell he's pleased. "Anything for my wife."

I roll my eyes. There's a warmth in my cheeks I can't deny as we drive away. He handled my family better than most of my real boyfriends have. Maybe even better than I do.

And that scares me. It makes this whole ridiculous situation feel possible. Like maybe our "fake" relationship could be something more. Even something worth fighting for.

Chapter Twenty-Seven

Calla

Jay fumbles with his keys. I lean against the doorframe, every muscle in my body screaming for mercy. When the door finally swings open, I almost collapse into the foyer.

Dinner with my parents went late, as it always does. I told Jay to be ready for three or four hours. We were there for nearly six.

The first two hours were spent eating. The last four were just a lot of my mom and my grandmother sitting on either side of Jay, showing him pictures of me as a kid. It was cute when it started, but an hour in, I was tired.

By now, I'm exhausted and starving.

"I could sleep for a hundred years." I mutter, kicking off my pumps. I dressed up for dinner, which I regretted after we had been there less than an hour. My feet throb with a vengeance. "Also, I'm somehow very hungry. We did go for dinner, right?"

"We did." Jay ushers me into the living room with an infuriatingly charming smile. He checks his watch and I think I know why.

It's almost ten p.m. Things here in Greater start to slow down at seven-thirty; by nine, most shops are closed. Getting a food delivery at this hour would be difficult.

"Make yourself comfortable on the couch. I'll see what we have to eat."

I hesitate for a moment, then shuffle over to the couch and sink into it. The cushions are ridiculously soft. I feel myself start to melt. *Just a quick rest*, I tell myself. *I'll just close my eyes.*

The sound of clattering pots and pans pulls me from the edge of unconsciousness. I sit up slowly, every bone in my body protesting. I glance toward the kitchen. I can hear Jay humming something melodic under his breath.

Curiosity gets the better of me. I drag myself off the couch and pad toward the kitchen. What I see stops me in my tracks.

Jay is wearing an apron.

It's a ridiculous thing, bright red with white polka dots, and it clashes horribly with the rest of his upscale, designer kitchen. He looks like a fashion doll someone's over-accessorized. But in a weird way, it kind of works for him.

He notices me and waves a wooden spoon in my direction. "I thought you were asleep."

"I was." I lean against the doorframe, my lips twitching with amusement. "What are you doing?"

"Cooking." He says this as if it's the most obvious thing in the world. "You're hungry, right?"

"Yes, but I thought you were going to microwave popcorn. I don't want to put you to any trouble."

"Okay, first of all, it's not any trouble for me to cook for you. Second, I could nibble on something. Third, though I rarely do it, cooking is very relaxing. I want to showcase my prowess."

I step closer, peering over his shoulder. He's got a mixing bowl full of something that looks suspiciously like ground poultry and a cutting board piled high with greens. "What is all this?"

"My special turkey meatloaf, black-eyed peas, and a green salad." He says this with a touch of pride. "It's the only culinary trick up my sleeve."

The smell is already making my mouth water. There's something disarming about seeing him like this, in an apron with his sleeves rolled up, hands messy with meat and spices. It feels so domestic.

"I appreciate it." I'm surprised by how much I mean it. The whole situation is surreal. But there's a strange comfort in the thought of a home-cooked meal.

Well, to be fair, my mom did have quite a spread at her house. But this is the second time in one day that someone else cooked for me.

I could get used to this.

He washes his hands and wipes them on the apron. Then he takes the meatloaf and slides it into the oven with a practiced ease.

"Low and slow." He says this more to himself than to me. He moves to the stove and stirs a pot of black-eyed peas. The aroma mingles with the scent of the meatloaf. "These just need to simmer."

I take a seat at the kitchen island, resting my chin in my hands. "Where did you learn to cook?"

Jay leans against the counter and crosses his arms over his chest. "My mom. She was a high-powered corporate raider so she wasn't around much. But when she was, she made sure we had time together in the kitchen."

There's a softness in his eyes when he talks about his mother. A tender vulnerability that tugs at something in me. I push the feeling away, filing it under "useful information."

"The house smells amazing." I don't know what else to say.

Jay grabs a glass of water. He raises it to me with a small, crooked smile. "Here's to not starving."

"Hear hear." I wink at him.

Jay laughs. It's a sound that I desperately want to hear more of.

"Hey, since you're cooking... I can start to unpack and organize upstairs. My fingers have been itching to tame that part of the house."

The thought of putting his house in order is oddly appealing. It's the kind of task that would let me switch my brain to autopilot. I need a breather from the thousand complications currently vying for my attention.

But I'm also dog tired. My physical exhaustion wars with my need to help Jay make his house a home.

He considers my offer, but shakes his head. "No," he says gently, and waves me toward the living room. "Come sit down. Relax."

He leads me back to the couch. I follow, too tired to argue. We sink into the cushions. For a moment, we just sit in silence. It's not an uncomfortable silence, which surprises me. I've grown so used to the constant hum of activity around Jay. His never-ending stream of notifications and updates seem like they are a part of him. I'd forgotten what a quiet moment can feel like.

I scoot closer and rest my head on his chest. His arm comes around me. I feel his steady breathing, the rise and fall of his chest beneath my cheek. It's a surprisingly grounding sensation.

For the first time today, I feel like maybe I'm doing something right.

"Tell me about your family?"

"My parents?" Jay's fingers trail idly along my shoulder as he talks. "They're... hands-off. They retired early a few years ago. Now they're on a world cruise, for eighteen months. I couldn't even tell you the last time I talked to either of them."

"That's..." I hesitate, searching for the right word. "Lonely?"

He shrugs. A small movement that I feel, more than see.

"Not really. I've got Wren. We've got Wildflower Lane. All my college friends moved here, too. We wanted to make sure we stuck together, so we all bought houses on the same block."

"That's sweet."

"I even bought the apartment building at the end of the block," he adds. "Wren's living there while she sorts things out."

"Really? You're a good brother."

He chuckles. His hand brushes a stray hair from my face. "But what I want is to be a good husband."

"Oh yeah?" I raise an eyebrow at him. "Prove it."

His hand slides down to the small of my back. "Challenge accepted."

I don't know who moves first, but suddenly, our lips meet. His kiss is warm and deliberate, like he's savoring every second.

I lose myself in the moment. The taste of him. The way his hands settle on my waist like they belong there. I move to straddle his lap and wind my arms around his neck.

His hands slide over my hips. "You smell amazing," he murmurs against my neck.

I laugh softly and tug at the hem of his shirt. "You're not so bad yourself."

Clothes fall away, piece by piece, each one discarded with a breathless laugh or a teasing remark. I run my hands over his shoulders, marveling at the strength in the muscles beneath my fingers.

"Are you real?" I ask. "Or did I just dream you up?"

He grins, flexing playfully. "Real as it gets."

His lips find mine again. The world fades away. Every kiss, every touch, is unhurried, deliberate, like we have all the time in the world. He worships me with his hands and his mouth.

"You're incredible." His breath is so warm on my skin that it makes me shiver.

Then Jay pulls away. For a moment I think it's over, that the spell has broken. But he kisses me, hard and full of promise. "Hold that thought for just a second."

Before I know it, Jay sprints into the kitchen. I hear him turn off the beans. Then the oven.

He's got a better memory than me. I would've left the food to cook until it was ash.

He returns, and before I can sit up, he scoops me into his arms. I let out a small yelp of surprise. "Put me down! You'll hurt yourself." But I'm laughing as I protest.

His hard muscles are so warm where our bodies meet. "I'm not that fragile." He starts up the stairs, carrying me with an easy strength. "And besides, I've barely begun to enjoy your body."

My heart skips at his words. He says them with such *certainty*. I should protest. I should set boundaries. But I don't want to. I want to enjoy Jay for every second that I still have him.

I wrap my arms around his neck and hold on tighter. The black-eyed peas can always keep until the morning.

Chapter Twenty-Eight

Jay

The morning light filters through the blinds and casts striped shadows across Calla's bare skin. I trace a finger along her curves, half expecting her to swat me away and pull the covers over her head. Instead, she stretches like a contented cat, then turns to face me, her hazel eyes soft and sleepy.

"Morning," I whisper.

She yawns, then smiles. "Morning."

I lean in and kiss her, slowly at first, testing the waters. Her lips are warm and pliant. The kiss deepens, and I feel that familiar spark ignite in my chest. One thing leads to another, as it always seems to with us.

That's a little bit of a lie. I knew that when we woke up, there was a good chance that we'd fuck again.

Soon we're tangled in the sheets. Calla throws her head back and moans. I grasp my cock and sink deep into her pussy. Our bodies move in a rhythm that's become almost second nature.

God *damn*, I love this. *Imagine if every morning were just like this one.*

After, we lie in a sweaty, satisfied heap. I play with a strand of her hair, twirling it around my finger.

Moments like this make me wonder if I'm in over my head. They make me think I might have actually fallen in love with her. The thought terrifies me, but holding it in is starting to feel unbearable.

Before I can decide, she speaks. "Can we have a No Photo Day today?"

I blink, pulled from my internal tug-of-war. "A what now?"

"A day without pictures. Without posting. Just us."

She's looking at me with something like hope. My traitorous heart does a stupid little flip at her expression.

I *need* to give her what she is expecting from me.

"Sure. Today we're just hanging out in Greater, anyway. Some down time sounds nice."

Her smile could power a small city. "Thank you. I just need a break from... everything."

I get it. The last few weeks—with the wedding, keeping my sponsors happy, and our not-so-simple arrangement—have been intense. A day to breathe sounds perfect.

She slides out of bed and starts gathering her clothes. I admire the way her body moves. When we first started this, she was so guarded, so unsure. Now... well, now she's Calla.

"I need to take care of some business," she says, getting dressed in last night's clothes. "I've been neglecting it."

"Neglecting?" I tease. "You mean prioritizing your husband?"

She rolls her eyes but laughs. "Something like that. I'll be back by lunch."

She comes over and kisses me on the forehead. It's such a tender, wifely gesture that I almost tell her right then.

Hey, you know how I blurted out that I love you? Well, I still love you.

With Calla gone, I try to tackle my inbox. Sponsorship proposals, collaboration offers and fan mail pile up like a digital avalanche. I start a pot of coffee and settle in at the kitchen table, opening my laptop with a sense of dread.

The first email is from a protein shake company. They want me to be the face of their new campaign. I flag it for later. The next is from an outdoor gear brand offering a proposed trip to Patagonia to sweeten the deal. I should be excited, but the thought of traveling without Calla makes my stomach sink.

I flag it and move on.

Halfway through my first cup of coffee, I give up. I'm too distracted. I close the laptop and lean back in my chair, staring at the ceiling. I miss her. She has only been gone a couple of hours, but I miss her.

That realization hits me harder than I expect. Have I ever missed someone like this before? With Blake, it was different. When she was away, I valued the space, the time to do my own thing. But with Calla away... the silence is *boring.*

Calla is so different than Blake. She's actually different from anyone I've ever been with. Where Blake was sleek and sophisticated, Calla is warm and real. Blake fit neatly into my life and into my brand. Calla doesn't. Or maybe she didn't fit into what I thought my brand would be.

Then something *changed.*

Calla is my opposite in so many ways, yet she makes my life more enjoyable. More genuine.

But this isn't genuine, is it? We have a little over a month left of our three-month agreement. That's all.

What happens when our time is up?

I run a hand through my hair. The weight of it all makes my shoulders tense with the uncertainty, the fear of losing something I didn't even know I wanted.

Someone I'm not sure I can *have*.

The front door opens. Calla walks in, her cheeks flushed from the morning chill.

"How'd it go?" I ask, standing.

She shrugs. "Caught up. Mostly."

I pull her into a warm hug, holding her for a second longer than normal. "What would you say to hanging out with my friends?"

"Uhh. Sure." She smiles. "We can do whatever you want. Just no phones."

* * *

Calla and I arrive at the Tin Shed Pub just as the afternoon sun peaks over the town square. The glass-fronted windows are dark. A "Closed" sign hangs crookedly on the door. Calla hesitates. I just push the door open with a flourish.

The interior is all wood and kitsch, with mismatched tables and chairs giving the place a homey, disheveled feel. A large, U-shaped bar dominates the right side of the room, and the smell of fried food and stale beer lingers in the air. It's empty, save for a small crowd in the back.

It strikes me that Calla and I haven't really been in here since the night of our wedding. Aww, how *romantic*.

"Jaybird!" Bennett calls out. He's my old college room-mate and owns this place. He waves a pint glass. "Amber?" he asks, referring to the beer, not a person.

I wave and shout, "Give me a few," then take Calla's hand and lead her to the table where my friends are sitting.

"These are the guys," I say, though she already knows.

I've introduced her to parts of my crew before at the Couch Potato Parade. Today is just going to be a chill, more intimate gathering.

Ryan, Bennett, Gabe, and Zach are all crammed around a table. Reece Carson, the only woman to join our friends group, is perched on Gabe's lap. Even Ellie, Ryan's younger sister, is here. She's stretched out on a bench, poking at her phone with the disinterest of someone who's just in it for the free food.

"Thought you bailed," Ryan says, standing to give me a bro hug. He's tall and blond, the very picture of confident masculinity. Calla once described him as "ridiculously handsome," which I pretended not to hear.

"Had to finish something up," I say, leaving out the part where Calla and I were just lying in bed, talking about nothing and everything. Or the part where I was busy answering emails while Calla baked. "Y'all remember Calla."

There's a chorus of hellos and welcomes. Calla waves, looking a bit overwhelmed but pleased.

"Make yourselves at home," Bennett calls from across the room. "I've got a spread coming out."

We squeeze into the tight seating arrangement. Calla ends up next to Reece, with me on her other side. I like this setup. It means I can keep an eye on her and make sure she's comfortable.

"So, Calla," Reece says. "How's married life treating you?"

"It's... an adventure," Calla says, smiling. "Jay is full of surprises. Did you guys know he cooks?"

"Let me guess." Ryan grins. "He made you turkey meatloaf. He must really think you're special."

"I would hope so," she replies. "He did put a ring on it."

"Very true. Well, if you're looking for embarrassing dirt on the guy," Zach says, waggling his eyebrows, "he's got a whole catalog of excruciatingly awkward college stories."

Calla's eyes light up. "Oh, do tell."

"Let's just say he had his moments," Bennett says, appearing with my pint. He sets it down on the table in front of me. "Some more tragic than others."

Ryan chuckles. "You wouldn't believe some of the things this guy got up to."

Zach stretches. "He once painted his body blue and gold during spirit week. Only he didn't remember to use washable paint. He was bright blue for a week."

"Ooh!" Reece laughs. "Remember when Jay had Professor Franz? Franz hated everyone, but he especially hated Jay. Made his life hell. Jay meant to send an email totally blasting him to "Friends Group" but sent it to him by mistake. Franz blew a gasket and made Jay spend a whole Saturday volunteering for a Shakespeare fest."

The table erupts in laughter. I just grin and bear it. These are my people. This is what we do. Besides, it's kind of nice to see Calla enjoying herself, even if it's at my expense.

"Franz was a pain in the ass." I sigh dramatically. "But he actually gave me an A."

"I need to hear more of these stories," Calla says, mock-seriously.

"There are no more stories," I lie. "All evidence has been destroyed. Anyone who tries to convince you otherwise can't be trusted."

"Hah!" Ellie laughs without looking up from her phone. "He's just lucky you didn't take more pictures."

Calla beams. "I'll have to hear all about this later."

Ellie shrugs. "Come find me."

Bennett returns, carrying a tray laden with various English pub foods: fish and chips, bangers and mash, meat pies. He sets it down with a flourish. The table dives in with the enthusiasm of a starving pack of wolves.

As we eat, the stories continue. Calla asks questions about me, and my friends are all too happy to provide answers. She learns about the time we road-tripped to New Orleans, my brief obsession with Ultimate Frisbee, and the ill-fated attempt to start a college radio show. Through it all, she looks genuinely delighted.

I start to see myself through her eyes. It's a strange, humbling experience.

I notice Wren flitting around the bar. I knew she was going to be here because we texted back and forth a little earlier. My little sister is not in her usual baggy attire. Instead, she wears a fitted blouse and apron, her hair tied back in a neat ponytail. She looks out of place, like a shy mouse playing dress-up.

"Since when does Wren waitress?" I ask Ryan, who's seated across from me.

He shrugs. "She picks up shifts here and there. You know, for extra cash."

"What, am I not paying her well enough?"

Ryan looks at me pointedly. "Do I look like Wren's keeper to you?"

"You're so witty." I pull a face. "Did someone force her to wear that outfit?"

"I have no idea what you're talking about. Doesn't she normally dress like that?"

He looks Wren up and down, his nose wrinkling slightly. He thinks he's doing a great job at hiding his disdain for my little sister, but he's not a very good actor.

"Where's Bennett? I want to find out more about the dress code here."

Wren approaches our table. She notices me, then looks at Ryan and hesitates. She still hates him for some inexplicable reason. Then again, he is kind of a dick to her. So I guess it's not totally out of the blue.

"Can I get anyone another drink?" she asks, pushing her glasses up the bridge of her nose.

Ryan leans back in his chair, stretching. "I could go for another pint. How about the rest of you?"

There's a chorus of agreements. Several people shout out orders and Wren starts scribbling notes. When she gets to Ryan, he grins. "Don't you already know my drink order by heart, you stalker?"

She blushes and stammers something unintelligible. He ruffles her hair and she jumps back as if burned and scurries off to the bar.

I scowl. What does he mean by calling her a stalker?

Calla nudges me with her elbow. "What's that look for?"

"Nothing," I say, too quickly.

She raises an eyebrow but lets it go. For now.

Wren comes back with the drinks, and the table grows louder and more boisterous. Zach proposes a toast. To what? I'm not sure. We all clink glasses. Calla sips her cider, then leans into me. "Are you mad?" she asks softly.

I'm confused. "Why would I be mad?"

"Because you're awfully quiet." She pauses. "I liked hearing about your embarrassing moments, by the way."

I laugh despite myself. "They were glorious."

She studies me for a moment, as if deciding whether to press further. "You were scowling at Ryan. Did he do something?"

I sigh. There's no point in hiding it from her. "I love

Ryan. He's my best friend. But he's a jerk to Wren. He torments her."

"Ah." Calla looks over at Ryan, who's deep in conversation with Reece. "And you don't think Wren can handle it?"

"I don't know. I just hope he keeps his eyes off her. I love him, but he's a total player. He dated Reece for a few months and was such a jackass that he almost drove her out of our friend group. It took them years of awkwardness just to be able to talk to each other again."

"Considering that they seem fine now, maybe it's not as bad as you think," Calla says. "And Ryan isn't dating Wren. They're just friends, right?"

"I don't know if I would say that Ryan and Wren are *friendly*. I'm more worried that Wren needs me to stand up for her. You know what? I'm going to say something to Ryan. He can't put his hands on her like that."

"Jay." She waits until I fully meet her eyes. "I don't think that's what's happening here. Wren is a big girl. She can handle herself."

Calla has this special ability to challenge me and make it seem like she's still on my side. I'm not sure how that's possible, but it is. I like that about her.

I take a deep breath and let it out slowly. "Yeah. You're right."

I look back at Wren, who's pretending to polish a glass while eavesdropping on the group. Calla would approve of her nosiness, I think.

The afternoon wears on, and the food diminishes to a collection of greasy platters. Just like at the parade, she fits in well. I don't know why I keep expecting she won't. Maybe I'm just really invested in the most important people in my life getting along. I try to relax, but I can't seem to let the Wren situation go. I would be a bad big brother if I didn't check in on my little sister.

"Excuse me," I say to Calla, standing. "I'll be right back."

I find Wren in the kitchen, stacking dirty dishes. "Hey," I say.

She jumps. "Jesus, Jay. We're going to have to put a bell on you."

"Very funny. Always with the jokes." I soften my tone. "Can we talk?"

"What's up?" She crosses her arms, waiting.

I rub the back of my neck, unsure how to start. "Is Ryan bullying you?"

"Yes." Wren's response is so quick that I'm taken aback by it. She holds her hand up to forestall my questions. "It's fine. It's more of the same. He's just being a dick. Nothing that crosses a line, though. Nothing inappropriate."

"Okay, because I saw him put his hands on you out there. That is extremely not cool."

"I told you, it's fine. We've always had this combative relationship." Wren shrugs. "I don't want you to stick your nose into it and make things weird for me. Just watch. Ryan will get a girlfriend again and be on his best behavior for a while."

"Yeah, until he dumps Ms. Perfect for having nail beds that are too short or not liking Faulkner enough. I would call him shallow, but I think he just gets bored easily."

"As much as I would love to chat about that douchebag some more...." My sister stacks a bus tub full of dishes and lifts it. "Some of us have to work for a living."

"Love you!" I call as she breezes through the swinging doors.

She merely says, "Yeah. You too," without looking back.

I rejoin the table, and Calla looks at me expectantly. I

just shrug. "We should get going," I tell her. "It's getting late."

She nods, and we make our goodbyes. Ryan pulls me into a hug. I pat his back, wondering if he has any idea about the storm I've just tried to quell.

Do I need to worry about my best friend bullying my little sister?

Outside, the air has cooled. Calla wraps her arms around herself. I put an arm over her shoulder, pulling her close. "You okay?" she asks.

"Yeah," I lie. "Just tired."

The sounds of the town on a weeknight absorb me as we cross the square. Calla stops and turns to me. "Are you going to feel bad when you have to tell them?"

"Tell them what?"

"That your marriage is fake."

I look back at the silhouettes of my friends through the distant window. The question makes my blood run cold. Not only do I not want my friends to think that I'm a liar... but I don't want Calla to leave.

I want her to be in my life. I want her to be my wife, for real this time.

"I don't know," I say, turning back to her. "We'll cross that bridge when we get to it."

She studies me. I wonder what she sees. A man torn between his friends and his wife? Between what's real and what's pretend?

"Come on," I say, gently steering her down the sidewalk. "Let's go home."

Chapter Twenty-Nine

Calla

Outside my shop window, the snow that's falling gently on the town square looks like powdered sugar, the kind I dust over our scones. It's piling up on the windowsill and creeping in when customers come through the front door. I can almost taste its cold sweetness.

Erica and I have been working like maniacs to finish all the bakery orders. Fruit-flavored macarons, chocolate and vanilla cupcakes, and the chocolate éclairs all need to be finished today.

My favorite, though, are the mini king cakes. It's Mardi Gras next week, so I've made individually-sized pastry wreaths, stuffed them with a sumptuous cream cheese filling, drizzled the tops with royal icing, and decorated them in purple, green, and gold sugar.

Yum. I put the finished trays of decorated king cakes aside. These are definitely going in the display window at the front of the shop.

"Calla, do you want me to start on the eclairs?" Erica asks. She's got a streak of pink frosting in her blonde hair.

I'm not saying it makes her look like a human cupcake, but I wouldn't want her around if I had a craving for sweets.

I glance at the clock. "You can take off. The roads are getting bad."

She hesitates. "Are you sure? We still have a ton to do."

"I'll finish the eclairs. Go on. I don't want your mom yelling at me again."

Erica shrugs, but I can see the relief in her eyes. She's a good kid. But she's also new to the driving game. I don't want her to hit a patch of Atlanta's infamous black ice and drive her car straight off the road.

"Thanks, Calla. See you Monday!"

I watch her bundle up and trot out into the storm with gritted teeth. She's going to slip, I just know it, and then her mom will really yell at me. But she somehow makes it to her car intact. *Whew!* I let out a breath I didn't realize I was holding.

The bakery is quiet now. Only the hum of the refrigerators and the occasional pop from the old radiator break the silence. I like it this way. Peaceful. I'm definitely in my happy place, creating sweet desserts that will make other people feel loved.

Humming, I pick up a piping bag and finish decorating the last donut. It's gaudier than the rest, a true testament to my love of tacky holiday sweets.

Why am I in such a good mood? I should be exhausted and stressed.

Maybe it's all the hot sex I've been having, I giggle to myself. Who even am I right now? This isn't me. At least, not the me I thought I was. I don't do giddy, romantic moods. But here I am, smiling like an idiot because of a guy.

A guy who's turning out to be way more than I ever expected.

I set the donuts aside and start on the eclairs. The dough is tricky and requires concentration. But I like the challenge. It keeps my hands busy.

Once I get the dough wrangled, I can let my mind wander. It's been wandering a lot lately, usually in the direction of Jay.

I used to think his life was perfect, the kind of perfection you see in beautiful lifestyle TikToks. Curated and catalog-friendly. But now that I've seen behind the curtain, I realize his life is just as messy as mine. Maybe messier.

But he has a way nicer house than anyone I know. So there's that.

The eclairs are finally in the oven and I start cleaning up. Flour and sugar coat the countertops like the snow on the ground in the town square. I swipe at it with a dishrag and watch it billow into the air.

My phone buzzes with a text from Jay: "Made it home safe. Where are you?"

I bite my lip. I type: "Glad you're safe. I should be home in half an hour."

He replies with a winking emoji, and I can almost see his smirk. A little flutter rises in my chest. It's like he knows exactly how to get past my defenses without even trying. I don't know whether to be comforted or terrified.

I'm having the best time faking this marriage. That's the problem. When it's time to call it quits, I'll be more than sad.

I'll be heartbroken.

When the éclairs are done baking, I stack the trays together on a rolling cart and let them cool. They should be ready for the morning. By the time I look out the window again, the weather has changed pretty drastically.

The storm outside has graduated from powdered sugar

to a full-on frosting frenzy, coating cars and sidewalks in thick, unmanageable drifts. I pull on my coat and grab my keys, then trudge to the back door. Am I going to be able to walk? Hopefully the sidewalks haven't gotten icy just yet.

The alley is a whiteout. It's the kind of scene that makes you want to curl up with hot cocoa and a sappy movie.

"Damn it," I mutter. There's no way I can walk anywhere. It's not like I have cold weather footwear just lying around. I'm frigging snowed in!

Disconsolate, I head back into the warmth and peel off my coat. I was really excited to see Jay when I got home. With a heavy sigh, I take the stairs up to my apartment. The building is old and full of character, with creaky floorboards and a clawfoot tub. My place is basically a studio apartment with a small divider wall to partially shield the bedroom. I love it, even if it's a bit drafty in the winter.

I turn up the thermostat and set my things on the kitchen counter. My phone buzzes in my pocket. It's Jay, responding to the text I'd just sent him about not being able to see him.

"Stuck?" he writes. "Are you sure? That sucks."

I miss him more than I should. This thing between us is getting dangerously real. "I'll just have to think dirty thoughts about you to keep warm," I reply, adding a selfie of me pouting while perched on my bed.

I wait for a reply, but there is none. Mr. Terminally Attached to His Phone has something better to do than respond to my vaguely horny texts? *We'll see about that.* I'm about to text him another, more risqué selfie, when the lights flicker and die.

Great.

I fumble in my kitchen drawer for matches and make my way to the living area, where an old, wood-burning stove sits in the corner. It was one of the reasons I rented this place. There's something romantic about a real fire. Well, that and the fact that it came free with the downstairs' rent.

I strike a match and coax the kindling to life, then hold my hands out to the growing flames.

Downstairs, I hear the pipes groan. Without electricity, the hot water won't last long. I dash to the bathroom and turn on the faucet, letting steam fill the room. A bath sounds perfect.

If I'm going to be stuck here in the dark, I might as well enjoy it. It's too bad that light creeping in through the windows is too dim for me to snap more pics to torture my husband with.

My husband. I need to remember the fakeness of this whole deal. I may have said I love you, but that doesn't make my situation less temporary.

The tub is nearly full, so I sink into the water with a sigh, letting the heat envelop me. I close my eyes and let my mind wander. It doesn't have far to go. Jay is there, waiting. I imagine his hands on me, his lips tracing the lines of my body. A soft moan escapes my mouth as I touch my own breasts, wishing my hands were his.

When I slide my hand between my thighs and find my clit, it feels good. I touch myself and think about Jay touching me, Jay sucking my clit.

My eyes flutter open. Though I'm loathe to admit it, Jay is better at touching my pussy than I am. I could probably grab a towel and get out to find a toy. But it wouldn't be the same.

I miss him.

Giving up, I submerge myself in the water until it cools and I start to shiver. Reluctantly, I pull myself from the tub and pat my skin with a towel.

The fire in the stove casts a warm glow through the apartment. *Damn.* I feel a pang of loneliness. This is the kind of night made for cuddling.

I wrap myself in a thick robe and pad to the living room. The flames dance in the stove, creating shadows that flicker and sway.

My phone is on the coffee table. I reach for it, then stop. If I call him, I'll just make things harder.

I take a deep breath and close my eyes.

A knock at the door downstairs jolts me from my hazy daydream. I rush downstairs and peer through the frosted glass. My heart does a ridiculous little flip. I fling the door open. "Are you crazy?"

Jay is bundled in a parka, his hair dusted with snowflakes, and he's shivering. He shrugs, a sheepish grin spreading across his face. "I missed you."

I throw my arms around him, squeezing tight. The cold from his body seeps through my robe, but I don't care.

He's here. He's really here.

"Come in, you're freezing," I say, pulling him inside. He stomps the snow from his boots. I grab his hand, tugging him toward the stairs. "Come on, let's get you warmed up."

"I didn't think the roads were that bad," he says, unzipping his parka as I lead him upstairs. "Then I walked here. It's only two blocks!"

"Jay, you didn't have to—"

"I wanted to."

That shuts me up. I take his coat and hang it on the rack at the top of the stairs before guiding him into the apartment and steering him straight to the wood-burning stove.

He holds his hands out to the flames. I stand behind him, unsure what to do with this rush of emotion. Gratitude? Affection? Something deeper?

I notice the quiet strength in his shoulders. The way he just does things that will make me happy without needing to make a production of it. My walls, the ones I've so carefully constructed, start to crumble.

I hug his back. "Thank you," I say softly.

He turns, and before I can react, he pulls me into an embrace. The robe slips from one of my shoulders, and his touch sends a shiver down my spine.

Not the cold kind of shiver, either.

"I'm warm now," he says. His breath tickles my ear.

I look up at him. Our faces are just inches apart. "Are you sure?"

He nods. "I've never been so sure of anything."

I stand on my tiptoes and kiss him. Slowly, letting it build. His hands explore my back, then shape my hips. I press into him, needing to feel his heat through the thin fabric of my robe.

"I touched myself," I whisper. "Thinking about you."

He lets out a low growl and lifts me. I wrap my legs around his waist and he carries me to the futon, where we collapse in a tangle of limbs and hurried kisses.

The robe falls away. His clothes follow. The urgency we both feel is almost overpowering.

The futon is too small for him. His legs dangle over the edge and we have to shift every few moments to keep from rolling off. It's awkward and hilarious. More than once, we burst into fits of giggles. But we don't care. We're in a blissful, happy bubble.

When it's over, we lie tangled together, his fingers tracing lazy patterns on my skin. "Hey Calla?"

"Shhhhh." I put a finger to his lips. "Let's enjoy the silence for a while."

"I just want to say one thing. Then I'll shut up."

My lips curl up. "Go ahead, husband."

He waits for several beats. I look up at his face.

"I feel something for you. I... have feelings. For you," he stammers. "God, I'm fucking this up."

I smooth my hand over his heart. My own is pounding out of control. "I feel the same." It's sort of lame, not really the declaration of love that I wanted. But it still feels good to say something.

Anything is better than the weirdness that we've been wading through for a week.

Jay pulls me close, kissing my head and pressing my face against his chest. I manage to grab the comforter and wrangle it over our bodies.

This is great. Too great. I wonder why we would even get the annulment.

Chapter Thirty

Jay

The set of the morning show hums with energy. Bright lights bounce off shiny surfaces, creating a kaleidoscope of colors that swirl together and send bright, rainbow-inflected glints all around us.

Calla and I are perched on a faux-leather couch. It squeaks when either of us shifts. Calla sits with perfect, almost painful, posture. Like a doll that's been propped up too rigidly.

Sliding a hand onto her knee, I give her a squeeze. Behind the camera, someone starts counting down. "We're live in five, four, three..."

The cameras roll and the host, a perky blonde with a megawatt smile, leans in from her swivel chair.

"Welcome back to Good Afternoon Atlanta. I'm your host, Brigitte Blanc. I'm here with Jay Rustin and Calla Nikolakis, the surprise couple of the season! You might have seen video footage of their impromptu wedding. Jay, Calla, thank you for joining us."

"Thanks for having us," I say, flashing my most disarming grin.

It's the kind of smile that usually melts any lingering resistance. But Calla's expression remains as firm as granite. This is not going particularly well and it's only ten seconds into the interview.

"You two have quite the story. An accidental marriage that took place the very same day as Jay was supposed to marry someone else! How did that even happen?"

I take a breath, ready to launch into the well-rehearsed spiel. But before I can get a word out, Calla speaks. "Tequila."

"Ahaha!" I laugh like she's just said something hilarious. "Calla isn't entirely wrong. We were slightly tipsy when we got married."

Calla shoots me a skeptical look but doesn't say anything.

Brigitte's eyes widen, her smile growing to cartoonish proportions. "That sounds like something out of a movie! Were you two... involved before this?"

I feel Calla bristle. She turns her head towards me, slowly, deliberately, as if to say, Well?

"We've been friends for a while," I say, trying to strike a balance between truth and the narrative we need to sell. "Calla was the pastry chef at my wedding, so we spent a decent amount of time together."

Brigitte's expression brightens like she's just uncovered a juicy secret. "Ah, so there was already a connection!"

I can feel the weight of Calla's glare without even looking at her. She hates this. She hates all of this. And part of me hates that I'm dragging her into my world, where smiles are currency, and every word is a transaction.

"Jay, your followers were devastated when your fiancée called it off. Do you think this unexpected twist with Calla is fate?"

Fate. The word hangs in the air like a balloon, waiting for someone to pop it. I know what my followers think. I know what the public wants. They all want a happy ending, tied up with a neat little bow. I need to walk the line between delivering that and choosing my words with care.

"I believe we make our own fate. Right now, Calla and I are just trying to navigate this situation as best we can. We know that we're in love. So, everything else is just getting comfortable, you know?"

Brigitte pivots her attention to Calla. "How has it been adjusting to life in the spotlight? Jay is a public figure. You're not. You're suddenly thrust into this world of social media and having every moment documented."

Calla hesitates. I can see her weighing her options, calculating the best way to answer without giving too much away.

"It's been... interesting," she says at last. Her words are careful, just like everything else about her.

I almost laugh at the understatement. *Interesting* is one way to put it. The truth is, she's handling it better than I expected. Better than I did when I first started out.

Brigitte glances at a stack of note cards, then back at us. "So, the big question. Are you going to stay married?"

"Absolutely," I say immediately. "We're committed to making it work."

Calla nods. She grabs my hand and smiles. "Definitely."

"Thank you both! When we come back, more with these two lovebirds."

"One minute!" someone shouts.

Brigitte turns her head, and a makeup artist scuttles over with powder. I exhale and lean back in my chair but have barely started to relax when a PA counts down again and the camera settles on us once more.

"We've talked about your adventures," Brigitte says. "But what do you think is the secret to making love last? Any tips you want to share?"

Calla straightens. This is a landmine of a question, the kind that can blow up a whole interview if not handled delicately. I expect her to defer to me, but she dives in.

"Love is like baking," she says, and I raise an eyebrow. Baking? "You need the right ingredients, and you have to follow the recipe. But even then, it takes time and patience. You can't rush it. You have to be willing to put in the effort, even when it's not turning out the way you hoped."

The crew nods, and I hear a few murmurs of approval.

I clear my throat and add, "And sometimes you have to be willing to throw the whole thing out and start over." All eyes turn to me, and I shrug. "Love is messy. It's not always going to follow a recipe. You have to be passionate and adaptable. Sometimes the best relationships come from the biggest mistakes. Without my first wedding falling apart, I wouldn't have married Calla."

Calla looks at me, her hazel eyes searching for something. Understanding, maybe?

Brigitte leans back in her chair, trying to smooth over the differing views. "It sounds like you both have a lot of experience. Jay, what makes this relationship different from your last one?"

The question hits me like a punch to the gut. I open my mouth, but nothing comes out. The cameras feel like they're closing in, their lenses shrinking the room to a pinpoint. This was supposed to be easy. Predictable. We had a script.

I take a breath, stalling for time. How do I explain that this marriage, fake as it is, already feels more real than the one I'd planned with Blake? That with Calla, every moment is charged with a tension that makes me feel alive, whereas with Blake it was just routine?

"Well," I start. I clear my throat again. "This time, I—"

"—have a partner who understands him," Calla interjects smoothly. "Someone who knows what it's like to balance work and personal life. We're both figuring it out as we go. But the important thing is that we're moving forward."

I look at her, grateful and confused. She's saved me, but why? Her answer is perfect. Almost *too* perfect. It's the kind of response Blake would have given, crafted to deflect and reassure without actually revealing anything.

Brigitte smiles widely. Clearly, she's pleased with Calla's diplomacy. "That makes a lot of sense. It's all about growth, isn't it?"

"Exactly," Calla says.

I let her words sink in. Growth. Moving forward. She makes it sound so simple, so attainable. But is it? Can we really grow from this, or are we just treading water, waiting for the inevitable sinking?

"It sounds like we should expect great things from you two. Jay, Calla, where can we find you both online?"

I give my handle and the one that I helped Calla start for her business. Brigitte gives the camera a strange, frozen smile and wraps up the segment. The cameras turn off, signaling the end of the interview and the usual post-segment chaos filling the studio.

Calla starts to gather her things with the precision of someone who knows exactly what comes next. I watch her, noting how composed she is, how seamlessly she handled the situation. I reach out to touch her arm, leaning my head close to whisper in her ear. "You did great. Thanks for agreeing to do it."

She smiles. "Of course. I'd do almost anything for you, Jay."

My mouth goes dry. I stare at Calla. "Do... do you really mean that? Or is it just a bluff?"

"Why would it be a bluff? It's just us two here." She smiles, crinkling her nose.

Before I can answer, I'm interrupted. The PA, sensing some weirdness, pops into view. "Excuse me, Calla? Would you mind giving us your website and social media info?"

"Of course." Calla heads off into the busy set.

I let her go, my mind a whirl of conflicting thoughts and emotions.

I think about what she said during the interview, about love being like baking. About following the recipe and putting in the effort. She wasn't wrong, but she wasn't right either.

Love isn't something you can measure out with cups and spoons. It's a force, a hurricane that sweeps you up, whether you're ready for it or not.

When you get down to it, we're on different wavelengths. She sees love as a calculated risk. Like it's something you can plan for and manage. I see it as a leap, a blind jump into the unknown.

What if she's as bad for me as Blake was? Calla might be nicer to look at and easier to laugh with, but I don't want to make the same mistake twice.

Blake had been safe. Predictable. We'd followed the script, played our parts. In the end, there was no passion, no fire. Just two people going through the motions. With Calla, there's a spark, an underlying tension that promises something more. But is that enough?

This was supposed to be easy. A few months of

pretending, a quick annulment, and we'd both be free from the media circus. But nothing about this is easy. The hardest part is knowing that, deep down, I don't want it to be over.

Not yet.

Chapter Thirty-One

Jay

Rubbing my eyes, I force myself to focus on the printouts that my agent Grady left for me. The stack of sponsorship proposals blurs together. Energy drinks, protein bars, outdoor gear, a line of performance T-shirts; the usual suspects. But there are some new things too. And those things make me pause.

A cookware line. A series of "Dad and Me" adventure books. A *love hotel* in Florida. What the hell is that, anyway?? All of them focus on one thing: playing up the angle of my brand-new *family life*.

Ick. I rub my eyes and lean back in my chair to stare at the ceiling.

The love hotel offer is cute, in a nauseating sort of way. "Bring your bride for a romantic weekend!" the brochure gushes. It's full of pictures of happy couples kissing in hot tubs and canoodling over desserts. It's very chintzy.

All right, I can totally see Calla and I enjoying the hell out of that place.

It's two months out, though. Way past the timeline

Calla and I agreed on. By then, we'll have the annulment. And I'll be... what?

Single again? Back to my old life?

What happens when I tell my followers that it was all a joke? That we were never really married, never really in love? I can only imagine that I'll lose some followers.

This whole set up was really short-sighted on my part. It would have been better to let sponsors down than to put this kind of pressure on our fledgling relationship.

I close my eyes. Maybe this whole thing was a terrible idea. Maybe I should have just faced the music after Blake left. But then I wouldn't have met Calla.

A future without her is a prospect too ugly to face.

The sound of Calla's voice pulls me from my sulk. She's in the kitchen, on speakerphone. I shuffle to the doorway and lean against the frame to listen.

"I just don't know if it's possible," I hear her say. "That's really soon. I don't even have any special cakes made!"

The woman's voice on the other end is tinny and desperate. "We're in a bind. The baker we hired flaked, and the wedding is *this afternoon*. You're our last hope."

I peek around to see Calla chewing her lip. I can almost see the gears in her head turning. "I have a lot on my plate right now...," she hedges.

"We'll take whatever you have on hand. Cupcakes, cookies, eclairs, donuts. We're not picky. Please?"

There's a pause. I hold my breath. Calla is the most capable person I've ever met, but she's also stretched thin. The last thing she needs is more stress.

"We saw you on Jay Rustin's Instagram," the bride adds. "You're basically famous now!"

Calla crosses her arms, one foot tapping the floor. She looks tired.

I can't help myself, and step all the way in the room to wave at Calla to get her attention. "Go for it!" I mouth, pointing to the phone.

Calla frowns at me and turns away. "Hey, Helen? Let me check some things. I'll let you know either way by the end of the day."

The bride sounds like she's going to cry. "Thank you. We really appreciate it."

Calla ends the call and turns to me, hands on her hips. "You're not my boss, you know."

"I know. But it's good exposure, right? Plus, you love a challenge."

She sighs and uncrosses her arms. "I'm not sure I can handle another 'opportunity' right now. I'm still catching up from last week."

I take the phone from her and set it on the counter, then take her hands in mine. "Calla, you've got this. They'll take donuts. You can make donuts in your sleep."

She softens just a little. "It's not just the baking, it's the delivery. The aquarium is all the way across town. I don't have a van—"

"But I do. I'll drive."

She looks at me as though I've spoken in an alien language. "You'll drive?"

"Yep. The whole point of you agreeing to stay married was for the exposure to help your business thrive. If you need a little help making it happen, then guess what? I'm your guy."

"Are you sure?"

I brush my lips against her knuckles. "Very."

She laughs. "Fine. I'll call her back and say yes."

Two hours later, I'm wheeling a bakery cart through the glass doors of the Georgia Aquarium. It's loaded with cupcakes, cookies, eclairs, and donuts; enough sugar to induce a city-wide coma. Calla walks behind me with her hands full of utensils. She juggles them while checking items off of a color-coded checklist.

"Thanks for encouraging me to take this," she says. "I was really unsure."

I glance back at her. "This is what you've been working toward, right? You should enjoy it. It's your first wedding."

"Well... technically it's my second." Calla gives me a teasing look. "The first one just got canceled."

"This one will go more smoothly."

"You're right." She exhales a big breath. "I'm just nervous."

We stop at an elevator. She leans in to kiss me on the cheek. It's quick, like a bird stealing a crumb, but it leaves warmth behind. "Thanks," she says, and my heart skips.

My dumb, traitorous heart.

The reception room is on the second floor. A huge Beluga whale tank fills one wall. The creatures glide through the water like fat, white angels. Calla's eyes widen when she sees them. "This place is amazing," she says, half to herself.

I start unloading the cart. "You've got this. Go set up."

She moves with purpose, talking to the wedding planner and caterers with the self-assured authority of a general. I watch her for a moment.

She really is a sweet person. She deserves to be taken care of, no matter what.

When I finish unloading everything, I join her in arranging the desserts on an exquisitely decorated table. She's meticulous, making sure each treat is perfectly aligned.

"Thanks for helping," she says while fiddling with the spacing between the eclairs. "I know this isn't your thing."

"Are you kidding? I'm learning so much. Like how to stack donuts without crushing them. It's a real skill."

She laughs, and I could get used to this sound. After this wedding is over, I should really talk to her about the feeling I'm having that annulling our marriage will shatter me.

The wedding party bursts into the room, loud and chaotic. Someone spots me and squeals. "Oh my god, it's Jay Rustin!"

Calla pauses with her hand in midair. I see the tension creep into her shoulders. I step away from the table and raise a hand, subtly redirecting the guests.

"Hey guys. Congratulations to the happy couple."

A groomsman, already half in the bag, stumbles over and claps me on the back. "Dude, can we get a picture?"

"Of course," I say. "But Calla's working right now, so—"

A purple clad bridesmaid cuts me off. "We want a picture of you two! Your Instagram is so cute. Are you really married?"

Calla is looking very pointedly at the eclairs. I need to defuse this, fast.

"Tell you what," I say. "Let Calla finish setting up, and I would be more than happy to shoot some video by the whale tank. I know all the best angles. You guys will never look better. Sound good?"

There is a chorus of agreement. I look to Calla. "I'll be back to help in a bit."

She doesn't say anything, just nods and goes back to her checklist.

I follow the wedding party to the tank and pull out my phone. "All right, let's get the Belugas in the background. Start by striking your sexiest pose."

They instantly suck in their cheeks and angle their bodies. It's more than a little funny because they're already four sheets to the wind. We do a few takes while I coach them through some shout-outs and goofy poses. It's actually kind of fun. Fans are the lifeblood of my brand, and moments like this remind me why I do what I do. They're good people. Plus, their drunk enthusiasm is infectious.

They take turns snapping selfies with me. I make sure to flash my best "Rustin Smile," the one that's equal parts genuine and camera-ready. The drunkest groomsman asks about taking photos with Calla, but I explain that she's working. They seem to understand, and I'm relieved.

I look over to the dessert table. Calla is talking to the wedding planner, her hands making small, precise gestures. She looks... happy. Like she's in her element.

I should go help her. I start to walk over, but someone grabs my arm. It's one of the other guests, an elderly woman holding a glass of champagne. "Thank you," she slurs, a little wobbly. "For everything. You're making this day so special."

I take the glass from her and clink it against the glass she's holding. "It's all her," I say, nodding toward Calla. "She's the real deal."

She follows my gaze. "You're lucky to have her."

"Yeah," I say, and it comes out softer than I mean. "I am."

She totters off and I turn back to Calla. She's alone now, tidying up the table. I walk over, slowly, thinking about what the older woman said.

I am lucky.

"Calla," I say when I'm close enough. She looks up, and I can't read her expression. Maybe she's wondering where

I've been and why I haven't helped more. "I'm sorry," I say. I jerk my thumb over my shoulder. "I got caught up."

"It's fine," she says. But it doesn't sound fine.

"I was trying to keep them off you. They just—"

Her lips thin. She glances behind her at the rest of the wedding guests filing in and nods towards the hallway. "Not here," she hisses as she tows me out of the room.

Uh oh. I can tell from the tightness in her lips that this isn't going to be a thank-you hug.

Once we're out of earshot, she rounds on me. "If you're not here to help, you should just go home. Today is about my business, not your social media audience."

I wince. "Calla, I'm sorry. I was just trying to take the pressure off you. I thought—"

"You thought what? That I couldn't handle it?"

"No, that... I don't know. That it would be easier for you if I kept them busy."

She crosses her arms and looks away. "I can handle a little attention, Jay. It's not like I'm a complete nobody."

"I know that. I'm sorry."

She lets out a long breath, then uncrosses her arms. "I appreciate you driving and helping with the setup. Really. But I need you to understand why I'm doing this."

"I do," I say, though I'm not sure I do. "I'm just trying to help."

She nods, but the gesture is half-hearted. "I forgive you. But I'm still mad."

"Fair enough."

We move back to the dessert table and start restocking the trays. The room is filled with the low hum of conversation, punctuated by the occasional clink of glasses. We're left alone until a man in a chef's coat walks up to Calla.

"These are fantastic," he says, holding a half-eaten

eclair. "Sorry. I snagged one off the tray of backups. Did you make these yourself?"

Calla wipes her hands on a towel and stands a little straighter. "Yes, I did. Thank you. I am trying to get my dessert shop off the ground."

"I have a question. How do you get the pastry cream so smooth?"

Her cheeks color. "Low and slow heat. Temper very gradually. I also pass it through two sieves to filter out any imperfections in the cream."

The chef looks genuinely impressed. "I'm a pastry chef in New Orleans. We are doing a home baking competition on WhiskTV soon. I'd love to talk to you about being a guest judge on the show. It would be amazing exposure for your business."

Calla's mouth opens, then closes. I can see a dozen emotions flicker across her face, but she's literally speechless.

She hands the card to me and I take the chef's card and pocket it. I nudge her, breaking her out of her awkwardness.

"It's so nice of you to think of me. I will really consider it."

The chef nods and walks away. Calla turns to me, her eyes wide. "Can you believe that?" she says. "A job offer on TV?"

"Yeah," I say. "That's huge. If you can manage it, I mean."

She frowns. "What?"

"Nothing. It's just... Your wedding cake business is just taking off. Can you really leave to do something else?"

She gives me a funny look, like I've said something in a language she almost understands. "It's just a meeting, Jay. I didn't offer to move to a new country or anything."

Why am I being such a dick about this? I can't seem to control the words coming out of my idiot mouth. "It's just a lot, that's all. You were so stressed on the phone earlier! You're already so busy."

She takes the card from my hand and studies it. "I can handle it."

"Of course you can."

She slips the card into her purse, then looks back at me. "Can you take some pictures of the display? I need them for my portfolio."

"Yeah, sure."

"And post them. Tag me."

I pull out my phone and start snapping shots from different angles. The desserts look like an enchanted sugary skyline. "You know, I can just send them to you. You don't need me to post them."

"It's better if it comes from you," she snaps. "Your followers are more engaged."

I finish taking the pictures and put my phone away. Now I've made her angry again. That's the last thing I wanted. "Calla, I'm really sorry about earlier. I didn't mean to—"

"Thank you for the pictures," she says without looking at me. "You know what? I can take it from here. If you want to go mingle with the guests, that's fine."

That's a dismissal if I've ever heard one.

I nod, not knowing what else to say. I walk out of the reception room, past the dessert table, and into the hallway. The sounds of the wedding fade. I'm left with the silence of my own thoughts.

What happens when I've given her all the exposure I can? When she doesn't need my platform or my followers?

When she's famous in her own right and doesn't need me at all?

I take out my phone and look at the pictures of the dessert display. They're perfect, just like everything Calla does. I start to post them, tagging her bakery and adding a few hashtags.

She deserves all of this, I tell myself. She deserves to be taken care of.

But when I close the app, I can't shake the feeling that I'm just a stepping stone for her. That when this is all over, the only thing I'll have left to offer is a fake marriage.

Chapter Thirty-Two

Jay

Calla. Sweet, caring, wonderful Calla.

The last two months since we got accidentally married have been a whirlwind. Now, though, I seem to be standing on the edge of something I can't quite see the bottom of. Basically, we've have had an amazing two and a half months together. But most of it was just for show. Is that really enough for a marriage?

I don't know. I need to talk to her, but these feelings are so foreign to me that I'm not even sure where to start.

I glance at my phone, hoping for a text from her, something to give me a clue about how she's feeling. Nothing. She's busy at the shop, as usual, leaving me alone with my thoughts. Well, that and the growing stack of work I've been avoiding.

It's just... what if we give it a real shot and it crashes and burns? Or worse, what if it works and I end up dragging her into this insane world of mine?

She deserves stability. She should end up with someone real. She shouldn't have to deal with the circus that comes with being linked to me.

The doorbell rings, yanking me from my thoughts and momentarily saving me from my own internal tug-of-war. I jog to the door, half-expecting Calla.

Frankly, I hope that she's as frustrated as I am and she's come to talk things out. Instead, I find Will and Lana standing side by side, a united front. Will's my publicist, Lana's my lawyer.

Seeing them together is never a good sign. The tight-lipped expressions they're sporting today? Especially ominous.

"Can we come in?" Will asks. His blunt impatience sets off alarm bells in my head.

I shrug and gesture them inside. "Did we have a meeting? I don't remember scheduling anything."

My mind races, trying to recall if I've missed an important note in my calendar. Not that it would be the first time, lately. My focus has been anywhere but on work.

"We need to talk," Will says, his tone cutting through the air like a cold front.

"That doesn't sound good." I steal a glance at Lana, hoping for some indication of what I'm in for. She's the more reserved of the two, so she just gives me a distant smile.

I close the door behind them. "Is this about the Q3 projections? I thought we were solid."

Will waves me off. "The projections are fine. This is... different." He looks around my house, taking in the decor like he's searching for something. "Did you redecorate?"

"Yep. New wife, new furniture. But I'm you're not here to discuss interior design." Will never stalls. He dives in headfirst, consequences be damned. So why the hesitation?

We move to the living room and that's when I notice that Lana is clutching a leather portfolio, the kind that usually holds contracts or court filings. My gut tightens. I've been doing this long enough to know when I'm about to get served something unpalatable.

"Well?" I say. I gesture to the couch. "Sit down and tell me whatever it is you're here to say."

"If you and Calla are sticking together," Will starts, his words slicing through the room, "we need her to sign a lot of post-nuptial agreements. This marriage has gone on longer than we expected, Jay. You have to protect your business assets. If something goes sideways, you could lose a small fortune." Lana slides a ream of papers out of the leather portfolio and I avert my eyes, because I know what one of the forms must be.

A surge of anger washes over me. "Will, you work for me, remember? Not the other way around."

He doesn't miss a beat. "Are you in love with her? Then get her to sign the post-nuptial papers. If not, you need to get an annulment, ASAP."

I'm supposed to tell him if I'm in love? If I can barely admit my feelings to myself, how am I supposed to reveal them to my publicist?

Will doesn't wait for me to respond. He launches into his agenda with a practiced smile, the kind that never reaches his eyes. My eyes drift to the annulment papers in Lana's hands. One signature and all this confusion goes away. One signature and I'm back on the path we set out, the path that's supposed to lead to success and happiness.

But whose success? Whose happiness?

Will is still talking. He paints a vivid picture of the potential scandal if we delay. The tabloids speculating about our relationship, fans questioning my integrity.

Is it bullshit? I can't tell.

"Will, it isn't your job to tell me to annul my quickie marriage," I blurt when he finally pauses for breath.

Will's lips press together for a brief moment, forming the kind of tight line you see on a kid who's just been told 'no' for the first time. "I have your best interests at heart, Jay. As always." His tone makes me wonder when he last believed in what he was saying.

I sit down in the armchair, crossing my arms, and study the two of them. Will and I have been through a lot. Crises, triumphs, more crises. His logic is usually airtight. I've come to rely on his ability to see around corners.

Lana, I don't know as well. I can't gauge whether or not to fully trust her.

Honestly, my gut is telling me that my best interests might not be the same as the PR machine's interests anymore.

"I'm just trying to protect you," Will continues after a beat. "To protect everything you've built."

He doesn't understand. Who could?

The pretending started to feel real. That's the crux of it. Calla isn't just some pawn in a game we're playing. She's a real person with real goals and feelings. And damn it, I've started to care for her.

Fuck. Straight up, I've fallen for Calla. Hard.

The way she lights up when she talks about her bakery, the soft determination in her eyes when she's telling a story, even the exasperated sighs she gives me when I tease her.

They're all lodged in my heart now.

"Look, I thought this was just an accidental thing," Will says, breaking the silence. "That you'd get it annulled quickly and move on. But this has dragged on, and the longer it goes, the messier it gets. I think it's high time that you proceed with the annulment."

I uncross my arms and lean forward. "Will…" I sigh, shaking my head. "I just need more time to figure this out. There's a lot at play here."

"Think of Alto & Ash. Slacking on signing the annulment papers for even another week can put the company at risk. Right now, with no prenup and no annulment, the company that you have worked so hard to build is in a very vulnerable position." Will studies me, his eyes narrowing ever so slightly.

"Vulnerable? To who? Surely you don't think Calla has any interest in hurting my business."

"I think that you can't risk it. You have to get her to sign a post-nuptial agreement or these annulment papers." He turns to Lana, giving her a small nod. "Lana can tell you more about it."

Lana slides the annulment papers toward me with a deliberate motion. "It's a straightforward process," she begins, her tone as measured as ever.

She goes on to outline the legalities, making it sound as routine as returning a defective product. I try to interject, to slow her down, but she bulldozes right over me. Every time I try to speak, she raises her voice slightly and talks louder until I go quiet.

This was Will's plan all along, I realize. He's stacking the deck against me, making sure I understand the ease and simplicity of the clean break they're proposing.

I take the papers in my hands, test their weight, then set them aside on the coffee table.

"I'm not ready to sign anything. I want to see what Calla and I might have beyond this arrangement. I love her." Saying it out loud to a third party makes it official. It's also a special kind of relief. The tension eases from my shoulders for the first time in a week.

"Oh." Lana's face shows a flicker of surprise. But it's Will I'm really watching. He's been with me for years, long enough to know when I'm bluffing and when I'm serious.

He also knows how to play the long game. I can *feel* him calculating his next move. "Jay," he starts.

"Will," I cut him off before he can launch into another lecture. "I'd rather you just leave the post-nup and then go. I have a lot going on at the moment."

Now that I've said that I love Calla out loud, I feel like I need to nurture it, approach it from the side like a frightened animal. I need them to leave before my fragile resolve shatters and I'm thrown back into the muddled confusion of the past two months.

Will gives me a tight, reluctant nod. Lana's expression is harder to read, a mix of concern and something else. I usher them out onto the porch and watch as they make their way down the steps. Will says something to Lana. She shrugs, then glances back at me. I hold her gaze for a moment before she turns away.

I close the door gently. Walking back to the coffee table, I eye the stack of papers with a mixture of dread and resignation. Annulment. Post-nuptial agreement.

It all feels so cold.

I sit down and run a hand through my hair. My thoughts are a tangled mess. This damn situation was supposed to be easy. A quick, clean arrangement that would tide me over until I could figure out what was next. But nothing about this situation is easy anymore.

I pick up the annulment papers and flip through them slowly. It's like a script for a play where I already know the ending and it bores me to tears.

One thing I for certain: I need to talk to Calla.

Chapter Thirty-Three

Calla

I can't believe I forgot my whole damn purse at the house. What was I thinking? I'm rushing up the front porch steps to retrieve it when I notice a strange sedan in the driveway.

Jay is probably working with some sponsors. Or something. It's no problem. I can be stealthy as a house cat. I know I left my purse in the kitchen, so I back carefully off the porch and sneak around the house to the kitchen door so as not to interrupt.

The door releases a slight groan as I open it. I slow down, moving as quietly as possible, and leave the door ajar as I pad into the room. My eyes land on my purse, left exactly where I pictured it.

I am just grabbing it when I hear voices drifting from the living room. They sound upset.

"—I thought this was just an accidental thing," a man says, sounding aggravated. Embarrassed to be overhearing something that is none of my business, I turn to creep away. But the next thing he says freezes me in my spot.

"That you'd get it annulled quickly and move on. But

this has dragged out, and the longer it goes, the messier it gets."

They're talking about the annulment? Wow. When did Jay decide to move forward with that? Anger fills me, overlaying a wall of solid sadness.

I squint and listen as the silence stretches for a few seconds.

Jay says, "I just need more time to figure this out. There's a lot at play here."

Ouch. My hand comes up to cover my heart. I feel wounded. Shouldn't I be involved in the conversation? At the very least, Jay could have told me so that I would be prepared.

Instead, he does this. And me? I'm *devastated.* I turn on silent feet and sneak out the back door again, feeling tears pressing at the corners of my eyes.

Jay's proposal to stay married for a few months, his assurances that it would help both our reputations, they were just what they seemed to be. A way to get what was most convenient for him. A way to buy time until he could figure out a plan B.

The air feels thick and unbreathable. Each footstep echoes with a thought as sharp as a shard of glass. *He never intended for this to be real. He's just using me.* He got what he needed, so he's going to just throw me out like a sack of hot garbage. I just feel... so stupid.

I know Jay didn't dupe me. I willingly went for this. Just like the other guys, he realized soon enough that he could do a million times better.

I smear the beginnings of tears away from my cheeks. No crying. I don't have time for crying. I have a career to salvage.

I have a life to rebuild. One where *I'm* in the driver's seat again.

* * *

I walk quickly across a busy Atlanta street, ducking behind a waiting car to get to the tall high-rise building. With tinted glass windows that reach into the sky and cool 90s chrome finishes everywhere that I look, Cora's law firm is a stark contrast to Jay's house. It's functional, unadorned, and brimming with the specific kind of purposeful energy that only an office full of high-priced attorneys can create.

Sniffling, I ask for my sister at the front desk. The young guy working Reception looks me over and makes a quiet phone call. A minute later, he is escorting me back to Cora's private office.

Cora is a serious rainmaker for her law firm and is a few steps away from being made an equity partner. So her office is the fifth nicest one. I helped her decorate it when she became a full-time associate and most of her stories are about the 'boneheads' that run her law firm.

"Calla," Cora greets me while dropping a stack of briefs onto her desk. She immediately strides over and closes the door. Then she turns and puts her hand to my shoulder. "Are you crying? What's wrong?"

I open my mouth to speak, but the words catch in my throat. Instead, I collapse into her arms, the tears I've been holding back since Jay's house now spilling over. Cora holds me tight.

"Shit," she murmurs. "Okay, come sit down. Tell me what's going on."

I sink onto the couch and wipe at my eyes with the back

of my hand. Cora picks up a box of tissues off a nearby table and pushes it into my hands.

"It's all such a mess," I start, my voice trembling. "We just wanted to help each other out. To make it look believable. But now..." I trail off, the enormity of it all crashing down on me. "I think I actually like him, Cora. And he doesn't feel the same. It's just business for him."

To Cora's credit, she doesn't interrupt. She merely sits down beside me and nudges at the box in my hands. Obeying her, I pull out another tissue and futilely blow my nose, then take a deep breath and continue. "I overheard him talking about the annulment. The way they were talking, it sounded like a forgone conclusion. I— I— I was so stupid to think that maybe we could make it work. I thought that our attraction was... *mutual*."

"Honey." Cora lets out a soft huff of air. "Calla, you knew this was a temporary arrangement. Why are you so upset?"

"Because I hoped!" I almost shout. "I hoped that we could turn this into something real. That he saw something in me beyond a convenient solution."

I start to sob. Cora takes my hands in hers. "Oh, sis. Don't cry! You are as real as it gets. The important thing to know is that you are safe and you are so very, very loved."

Her words are a balm. My wounds still bleed, but everything is better when Cora takes charge. I squeeze her hands, grateful for her steady presence. I sniffle and wheeze for a few more minutes before telling her my other bit of news."

"I got a job offer," I say after a moment. "In New Orleans. It's a big opportunity, and it would solve a lot of my problems. But if I take it, I'll be running away from everything here. From Jay."

"You know what they say. A bird in the hand is worth

two in the bush." Cora is always very practical in affairs of the heart.

I let her words sink in. The job in New Orleans is a sure thing. It would jumpstart my exposure and maybe even lead to more job offers. Jay is the bush. He's a huge gamble that I already took and lost.

Hell, I'm not even sure if he's going to be around for much longer. I need to commit myself to my new job.

But first, I need to sign those damned annulment papers... if I can bring myself to do it.

Chapter Thirty-Four

Calla

I stand in the kitchen, purposefully not looking at my husband, who clearly wants to talk.

My soon-to-be-ex-husband.

I'm currently following Cora's advice to get all my ducks in a row before making any moves. It feels sneaky and a little dishonest. But to put it in Cora's words, I have to be ready 'before I pull the plug.' It's the advice that she gives all of her divorcing clients.

She didn't give any advice on how to ignore someone who is trying to get your attention though, so after another moment of trying to look engrossed by the woodgrain in the table, I look up at him. "Hey. What's up?" I try to sound nonchalant. Like I'm not dying inside or anything.

"What happened to you last night? I was hoping that we could talk."

I fidget. "I slept at my apartment. I worked until really late and just crashed there."

A lie. I cried in Cora's office for two hours and then spent the rest of the day slumped in my bed.

"Ah." He rubs the back of his neck. "Well, I wanted to—"

Jay's phone buzzes on the kitchen counter. He walks over and glances at the screen. "Shit," he mutters.

"You wanted to—?" I prompt.

He runs a hand through his hair, mussing it further, and shakes his head. "I need to ask a favor."

I raise an eyebrow. Of *course* Jay needs a favor. The whole arrangement is one big favor, isn't it?

"I have a sponsor who's getting antsy," he says, holding up his phone as if it's Exhibit A in a court case. "I need to do a quick shoot at the Roadkill Café & Gift Emporium. They're a huge sponsor and willing to pay big time money. I promise, it won't take long. But I need you to come with me. They've seen our content and want us both there."

I stare at Jay. Over the past two months I've acted my heart out and, in the process, every touch, every kiss became real. Jay isn't held captive by the same feelings.

That's why I have to leave.

"I have a client meeting this afternoon. The Jensen-Barkley wedding. It's kind of important."

He's close enough now that I can see the stubble on his chin. It's the kind that grows in after a day of not caring. On anyone else it might look sloppy. But on him? It just adds to his annoyingly effortless charm.

He's so *hot* that I want to punch him.

"Calla, please?" There's a softness in his eyes that makes me look down at my Converse-clad feet. "I promise we'll be quick. This is important for me. For us."

I bite the inside of my cheek. I have no idea how things will be after we pull the trigger on our annulment. This could be one of our last days together. I love Jay and the thought of leaving him high and dry is shredding my stomach lining.

"Okay. Let's go."

He lights up like I've just given him a birthday gift. Another tiny piece of my soul flies away.

When we finally drive to the perimeter of Atlanta, The Roadkill Café & Gift Emporium is every bit as ridiculous as its name suggests. The exterior looks like a cross between a log cabin and a cartoon. There are oversized animal tracks painted on the walls and a giant, neon raccoon sign that flickers ominously.

Inside, the décor is a shrine to bad taste. It's filled with dusty taxidermied animals posed in absurd, anthropomorphic scenarios. In particular, I notice a poker-playing possum and a raccoon in a rocking chair. A peculiar smell wafts through the air, a mix of old wood and mystery meat.

Gross. I make a note that I don't want to try the cheeseburgers here.

I stand just inside the doo with my arms wrapped around myself in an attempt to ward off the 'ambiance'. Jay strides past me with the confidence of a man who's never met a themed restaurant he didn't like.

"Can you believe this place?" he says, grinning like a kid in a very morbid candy store. "'We scrape it, you eat it.' Classic."

I give him a tight, forced smile and an eye roll for good measure. The tagline makes me wonder if the health department has ever paid a visit. If so, how many violations did they find per square inch? I bet a lot.

He notices my lack of enthusiasm and his grin falters. "What's wrong?"

"Nothing," I say, too quickly. "Just having a bad day."

It's a lie, of course. It's this situation that's bad: the faux marriage, the playing pretend, the sinking feeling that I'm in way over my head.

But I'm not about to unload all that on him. We have a job to do.

"Calla," he starts, but I cut him off with a smile.

"Let's just get this over with. I really can't be late for my meeting."

Jay's eyes narrow ever so slightly on my face. Then he seems to make a decision and holds up his hands in surrender. "Okay, let's set up. How about over there?"

We move to a booth in the corner of the café where a display case full of souvenir T-shirts and keychains creates a gaudy backdrop. Jay pulls a small tripod and camera from his bag, then starts fiddling with the settings. I glance at the menu, which is printed on a piece of plywood. Items like "Smeared Deer Quesadilla" and "Flattened Feline Frittata" jump out at me. I suppress a shudder.

"Here," Jay says, tossing something at me. I catch it reflexively and find it's a T-shirt with the café's logo of a cartoon skunk with tire tracks across its back. "It'll make the video more fun."

I hesitate, then shrug and slip the shirt on over my top. It's scratchy and smells like a combination of gift shop and fryer grease. *Fun* is not the word I'd use.

Jay positions the camera and takes a test shot. "Ready?" he asks. I nod, though I'm anything but. "Hey everyone, it's Jay from Alto & Ash," he says. He slides into his spiel with the practiced ease of a news anchor. "I'm here at the Road-kill Café with my lovely wife, Calla. Say hi, honey!"

I flinch at the word "wife" but manage to wave at the camera. "Hi honey!"

Jay puts an arm around my shoulders. I go rigid as one of the taxidermied animals behind me.

"We're sampling some of the local cuisine and checking out the awesome gift shop. If you're ever in town, this place is a must-visit. Right, Calla?"

I press my lips together and then force a smile. Jay pulls me closer and I can't figure out where to put my hands. Simultaneously, I want to drag his mouth to mine and somehow not ever touch him again. It's perplexing.

My voice is stiff when I say, "It sure is unique. I can say with confidence that I've never been somewhere quite like this."

He pauses the recording and looks at me. "Calla, come on. You have to act a little. We have to make this road trip stop believable."

"Believable?" I snap. My frustration starts to bubble over. "Maybe it would be more believable if we weren't faking the whole thing."

"Faking?" He sounds genuinely hurt.

For a moment I feel bad. But only for a moment.

"This? The happy couple routine. The marriage. It's all just for show, Jay. Don't act like it's become real all of a sudden."

His calm facade cracks. "I know it's not real, Calla," he snaps. "But we agreed to this. I'm just trying to make it work."

"It feels like I'm the one making all the sacrifices here. It feels like I'm the one making all of the risks and saying all the I love yous."

He studies me for a moment. "I thought this was a partnership. I didn't realize you saw it as a one-sided deal."

A nearby customer gives us a curious glance while crunching down on what I hope is beef jerky and not raccoon. The absurdity of the situation hits me all at once. We're two supposed lovebirds having a meltdown in a restaurant dedicated to squashed animals. It's like a scene from a bad reality show. Half of me expects a crew to burst in and tell us we've been punked.

Or maybe flattened? Whatever the term would be at a place that worships roadkill.

I let out a short, bitter laugh. Jay looks at me, confused, then around the café as if searching for the punchline.

"This is so ridiculous." My anger can't stand up to the absurdity of this situation. I sigh. "Let's finish this. I'll try harder."

Jay nods, but there's a new wariness in his eyes, like a man who's just seen the fault lines beneath his feet. He turns back to the camera. I adjust the scratchy T-shirt, trying to smooth out the wrinkles.

"Ready?" he asks again.

"Yeah," I say, taking a deep breath. "Let's go."

He hits Record. We slip back into our roles as the kitchen delivers us several truly revolting food items fresh off the grill. Dutifully I cut, chew, and swallow, all while smiling at the camera instead of revealing how I really feel about this diner.

Once we're done filming, I am out of the booth and sprinting to the parking lot like a bullet from a handgun. Jay stays behind, presumably to shake hands with the owner. But he appears through the doorway soon after. "The owner offered me a gift certificate." He waves it in my direction. "Are you sure you don't want any taxidermied, square-dancing possums?"

I cross my arms, not just for warmth, and glance at Jay. His hands are in his pockets, his shoulders hunched. The tall, confident man has shrunk. I wonder if this is the real Jay, the one who lives beneath the surface of his public persona.

Or did I just make him smaller? That's entirely possible.

"I'm sorry," he says after a beat. "For pushing you. For everything."

I uncross my arms, then recross them, unsure what to do with my hands, my body, my words. "I'm sorry I snapped. That was completely uncool."

"Calla, I think we should have a serious talk about our expectations here."

"I'm trying!" I take a deep breath, the cold air stinging my lungs. "I've been in relationships where it was all one-sided before. Where I cared way, way more than the other person. It never ended well."

He stays silent, waiting. I appreciate that he's not rushing me, that he's letting me find my own pace.

"That's why I'm so cautious. It's not just about the time and effort I put in. It's about the emotional investment. I've thrown myself into things thinking they were real, only to find out I was just a convenience. Or worse, a joke."

Jay's expression shifts, the lines of his face rearranging into something more somber, more understanding. "Calla, you can't think that you're a joke to me."

"I'm saying that we don't really know each other. You don't know my past. I don't know yours. Everything was fine and easy until... you know, we start being real with each other."

"Let's focus on the positives," he says. "We're in this together, and we both have something to gain. Maybe we can even learn from each other."

God, that is exactly what I didn't want to hear from him.

"We'll make it work," he says. I want to believe him. I don't, but I want to.

"We'll see," I reply. That's all I can give him.

Chapter Thirty-Five

Calla

I lie awake, staring straight up at the ceiling. In the cool hush of the bedroom, the only sound is Jay softly breathing beside me. The room is bathed in the deep blue hues of early morning. No longer night, not quite morning. It's just some other, foreign thing.

I came to bed late. I thought about staying at my place... but I couldn't stay away from his house. I know this might be one of the last times I get to look at his face.

How stupid am I? Anyway, Jay was already asleep. I was hiding from him. Hiding from my feelings.

When I slip into his bed, Jay stirs and turns to me, eyes half-lidded with sleep. "Calla. You okay?"

No, not really. But I can't tell him that. I'm too much of a coward to risk making myself completely vulnerable to him. If I'm right, the outcome could shatter my heart. So instead, I lean in and kiss him. Gently at first, then insistently.

He pulls me closer, shaping my body with a quiet, sleepy touch. *What if this is the last time I get to feel his body pressed against mine?*

It's slow, drowsy dance. The kind of intimacy that speaks of something deeper than lust. I try to memorize the feel of him. The way his skin warms mine. The way he breathes my name.

"Right here, in your arms." His words are just a whisper against my bare, heated skin. He wipes the sheen of sweat from my forehead and gives me a husky laugh that I feel right down to my very core. "This is my favorite place to be, Lily."

But does he mean it? A man like Jay has everything going for him. He can have any girl he wants. Would he pick me if we hadn't accidentally gotten married? I don't know and the insecurity is eating me alive.

I don't know what to say, so I settle against his chest, as if that could keep the moment from slipping away.

He means it when he says he loves me. I can tell. But... is that enough to sustain us?

I already know the answer.

Jay's breathing slows and gradually becomes steady and deep. I lie against his chest, listening to the rise and fall, feeling the thud of his heart.

I love him. My feelings only make everything so much more complicated.

When I am certain he's asleep, I slide carefully out of bed, not wanting to wake him. I stand there for a moment and take in his sleeping form. He looks so peaceful, so content. A wave of longing crashes over me.

How can I ever tell him the truth? That I'm terrified of what loving him will cost me? That I don't know if I can handle the kind of like-but-not love that he's offering me.

I turn away, biting my lip, and tiptoe to the door. I allow myself one last look. He murmurs something in his sleep. My heart twists. For a moment, I think about crawling back into bed and dealing with this whole thing tomorrow.

But no. It's better to make the first cut as deep as is necessary to get this man out of my life.

I move through the house on silent feet. The warmth of Jay's touch is already fading and it invites a chill to creep up my spine.

Going downstairs, I find his office door ajar. I slip inside, closing it softly behind me. The room is neat and organized, the desk piled high with stacks of sponsorship offers, the back wall full of dusty old books. It's hard to imagine Jay in here flipping through one of the tomes. Maybe they're just for decoration.

I take a deep breath, steeling myself, then I rifle through the papers on top of his desk. Then I open the drawers one by one. Bills, receipts, a jumble of stationery.

Where are the papers? Did he hide them?

My eyes land on the trashcan beside the desk. Slowly, I peer inside. There, crumpled like yesterday's news, are the annulment papers.

I reach for them, my fingers hesitant, as if the papers might bite.

I stand, holding the papers like a fragile bird, and stare at the desk. The significance of the discarded documents sinks in.

Maybe Jay meant what he said when he told me he loved me. Maybe he really wants to give us a try.

But if I don't leave, I will always wonder *what if*.

What if he doesn't want to try? What if he doesn't want me forever? I can't take the risk. Not with something this big.

I have to leave. I need clarity, independence, time to sort

out what I really want. Staying would mean risking everything.

My heart, my career, my carefully constructed life.

With a deep breath, I remove the huge diamond ring from my finger. I sign the annulment papers that I found balled up in the trash. They take no time at all to sign my name to. I place the ring and the papers in the middle of the desk. Then I take a blank sheet of paper and scrawl a note.

The words are simple, but they carry the weight of all my conflicted feelings.

This was amazing. I'll never forget it. - love, me.

I leave my letter on top of the pile on the desk. After one last look at the ring, at the note, I turn away. My footsteps are heavy as I walk to the door, each step a tear in the fabric of what we could have been.

It takes a few minutes of sneaky stuff-gathering before I'm really ready to leave. Finally, I open the kitchen door and pause, listening to the silence of the house, before stepping out.

The door closes softly behind me as I step into the crisp morning air. It bites at my cheeks, a stark contrast to the warmth inside the house.

This already feels *terrible*.

I walk down the path, each step measured, purposeful.

At the curb, I pause and pull out my phone. The screen lights up, and I see a missed call from my mother the night before and a flurry of notifications from social media. I swipe them away and open my messages. My fingers hover for a moment, then type: *Hi, Chef. I will see you in New Orleans next week. Thanks again for the opportunity.*

I read the text three times, making sure it says what I want it to say. This is me moving forward, embracing new opportunities, and committing to a fresh start. This is me being brave.

It's not me running away from anything. Right?

Feeling my tattooed wrist, knowing that at least one Jay bird will be with me the rest of my life, I exhale a shaky breath. At least that will always be around to remind me of the best two months of my life.

So why am I crying?

Chapter Thirty-Six

Jay

A shaft of sunlight pierces through the gap in the curtains. I groan and stretch my long frame across the empty bed. I rub my eyes, yawn, and frown at the space beside me.

Calla is gone. She's been shifty for the last week. If I were feeling fancy, I would say she's been avoidant. That's a thing, right? She's probably already up and working at her bakery.

I roll out of bed, scratch my head, and shuffle downstairs in my plaid pajama pants. The sleek, modern lines of my kitchen blur as I rub my eyes again, still half-asleep. I open the fridge, stare blankly at its contents, then close it with a shrug.

It feels weird in here. Is it just the decided lack of Calla? Or is there bad energy? Hard to say. I put on the kettle to make a pour over coffee and then plod toward my office.

Something on my desk catches my eye. The fog in my brain lifts just enough for a spark of recognition.

The annulment paperwork. And Calla's ring, neatly placed on top.

A note in her tidy handwriting:

This was amazing. I'll never forget it. – love, me.

My mouth goes dry. I pick up the note and read it twice, three times. The words don't change, but my understanding of them shifts with each pass.

I crush the note in my hand, then smooth it out again, my fingers trembling. My thoughts race, struggling to grasp why Calla would leave like this.

We had a plan, didn't we? Sure, I needed to have the final "I love you and can't live without you" talk with her, but I was getting around to it!

Panic claws at the edges of my mind. Disbelief turns into a gnawing desperation to make sense of her decision. "Shit." I look at the ring, at the papers, at the note, and a knot tightens in my stomach.

This isn't how it was supposed to go.

I dash back upstairs, grab my phone from the night-stand, and tap the screen with a desperate urgency. It rings once, twice, then goes straight to voicemail.

"Calla, it's me. Jay. What are you doing? Can we talk? Just... call me back, okay?"

I rifle through a pile of clothes, pulling on a shirt, then yanking it off, then putting it back on again. I hop on one foot, trying to coax a stubborn sock over my heel, and nearly topple over.

"Come on, come on," I mutter, pacing the room. I grab the phone again, check the screen, and bite my lip.

No time to wait. I need to see her. I have to explain. I want to fix this.

I bolt downstairs, taking the steps two at a time, and snatch the car keys from the counter. I remember just in time to turn off the whistling kettle. My eyes flick to the desk, to the ring, and the note, and the cold, clinical papers.

Damn. How did she even know that they were here? I should have shredded them when I decided to throw them out. I hesitate, just for a moment, then rush out the door.

I sprint the short distance to Ryan's place and slam my fist against the door. The sound echoes through the sleepy neighborhood but I'm too panicked to care.

"Ryan! Open up!"

I bounce on the balls of my feet. My impatience is a physical thing, pacing like a caged lion. I am about to knock again, harder this time, when the door creaks open. Ryan stands there, bleary-eyed, clutching a mug that proclaims him the "World's Okayest Friend."

It's the thank you mug I got him for his last birthday. He takes a slow, disbelieving sip, clearly not comprehending me being here at this hour. "Jay? Dude, it's like, what, seven?"

I push past him. "She's going to leave, Ryan. No, she *left*. She left the annulment papers and the ring. I think she's serious."

Ryan shuts the door and shuffles after me as I pace the living room. "Who's leaving? What papers?"

"The annulment papers! Calla!" I throw my hands in the air. "She thinks she can just walk away and I won't even notice?"

Ryan sinks into a couch, his eyes still half-closed. He takes another sip from his mug, then sets it down on a cluttered coffee table. "Wait. Back up. What's going on?"

I stop pacing and look at my best friend. "Ah. Yeah."

"Seriously." He waves a hand. "You're going to have to graduate from monosyllables."

Briefly, I break down the pact between me and Calla. Three months, no real feelings, then I would announce that it was all a joke.

By the time I finish, his face is contorted with confusion. "Wait, wait. Why did you need to do this again?"

"Because my sponsors expected me and my new spouse to do the honeymoon road trip. But when I accidentally married Calla instead of Blake..."

He shakes his head and waves a hand. "What did Calla get out of it?"

"Just exposure." I can feel my cheeks heating. "Her bakery needed it."

"Uh huh. And while you were busy fooling all of us, you started to really like each other?"

"Yeah. But now she's gone. There is still another week to go in the three months we'd agreed on. She didn't wait around to talk it through with me." I suck in a deep breath. "Maybe she thinks it's not worth the trouble. Maybe she thinks *I'm* not worth the trouble."

Ryan rubs his face, the sleep slowly draining from his features. "Okay, so you're in deeper than you let on. Are you saying you actually have feelings for her now?"

"I don't know. Yes?"

"That's certainly very clear. I can see why she skedaddled," he snarks, arching a brow. "So, which is it? Do you love her or not?"

I rub the back of my neck. "Yes."

The last remnants of sleepiness in Ryan's expression are replaced by genuine concern. He leans forward, elbows on knees. "Jay, man. You know I'm here for you. But you've got to be honest with yourself. Do you really want to be with her? Or are you just scared of the fallout?"

"All I know is that I can't just let her walk away without trying to make it work. She's my wife, Ryan."

Ryan stands, stretches, and picks up his "World's Okayest Friend" mug, then starts heading into his kitchen.

"Look, from what I've seen, she's a smart and practical woman. She's not going to bail without a good reason. And the way you two have been... I mean, it looked pretty real to me."

I feel a tightness in my chest, a mix of hope and dread. "You think she'll change her mind?"

Ryan turns, leaning against the counter, mug in hand. "I think she's scared, just like you are. But yeah, I think she'll come around. The question is, will you?"

The weight of his words settle on me. I know he's right. This isn't just about convincing Calla. It's about convincing myself.

"I have to try," I say. "Calla's only been gone an hour and I already miss her worse than you could ever know."

Ryan walks back to the living room and puts a hand on my shoulder. "Then go. Talk to her. But remember, this isn't just a business arrangement anymore. If you're going to make a real go of it, you need to be all in. Don't make any bargains or haggle with her. Just tell her how you feel."

"Thanks, man," I say, turning to the door.

"Hey, that mug isn't a lie, you know!" he calls after me.

For the first time this morning, I smile. "I know. You're the best okayest friend a guy could have."

Chapter Thirty-Seven

Calla

Half a dozen A-line skirts lie in a colorful heap on my bed. They battle for supremacy with an army of Converse sneakers and a mountain of sleek tops. I'm in full triage mode, trying to salvage my wardrobe from the carnage of my last-minute packing. A half-eaten Danish teeters on the edge of my dresser. I shove it in my mouth, crumbs exploding like confetti, and chew furiously.

"Stupid, stupid, stupid," I mutter and fling a hairbrush into my suitcase. "Why did I ever think this was a good idea?"

The hairbrush bounces back out of the suitcase and lands on the floor, defeated. I know exactly why I thought it was a good idea. Jay's proposal had seemed so reasonable. So logical. A temporary arrangement with no emotions involved. Just a way to keep his brand intact.

If only I had managed to keep my heart intact.

The door to my apartment bursts open, and Cora sweeps in like a human hurricane, while somehow looking as neat as a pin. Her long brown hair is in its ever-present bun at the back of her head.

And people say *I'm* a control freak.

"Calla, you are not going to believe what—" She stops short, taking in the disaster zone that is my bedroom. "Jesus. Are you moving to New Orleans or fleeing the country?"

I collapse onto the bed, narrowly avoiding impalement by a stiletto heel. "I don't even know anymore."

Cora crosses her arms and leans against the doorframe. One foot taps out an impatient rhythm. "So? You've decided, then?"

I take a deep breath. "It's just... Jay and I are so different. He's Mr. Sparkling Water with a Twist of Organic Lime. I'm tap water with a slice of day-old pizza. How could I ever think that this would work? I mean, he likes pineapple on his pizza. Pineapple."

"Dear god, the horror." Cora's amusement plays at the corners of her mouth. "Next you'll tell me he prefers the Star Wars prequels."

I glare at her. "This is serious. We have zero compatibility. It's like trying to mix oil and vinegar and expecting mayonnaise."

Cora pushes off the doorframe. She walks over to me with her stride full of purpose. "You and Jay both have the emotional intelligence of a dense fruitcake. You know that, right?"

"We do not!"

"Okay." Cora puts her *I'm-Serious-Calla* face on. "Look. I am going to give you some advice that isn't law-based. You know you can get an annulment and make everything go back to the way it used to be. But... it kind of sounds like you don't want things to return to normal. Am I right?"

My hands slow. "No. I mean... I don't know."

"You know I'm the first one to yell 'divorce his ass, sister!'. But in this case, it seems like this is about you being scared of taking a risk."

I blow a raspberry. "Who says I'm scared?"

"Calla... Come on. It's *me*." Cora tilts her head. "You know, sometimes it's okay to take a risk. You and Jay are already married. The worst thing that happens is that you two talk it out and find out that you really aren't compatible."

I sniffle. "We did talk. It was horrible."

"Does Jay know that it was the last talk before you left for New Orleans? Because if not, you should give it another chance." She plucks the sock from my hand and tosses it into my suitcase. "You always find some ridiculous reason to sabotage things before they even start. This is a new one, I'll grant you. But it's the same thing."

I sit up straighter. "Maybe I do overthink things."

"The point," Cora sits on the bed next to me, "is that compatibility isn't as black-and-white as you make it out to be."

"I just... I want to end up as happy as Mom and Dad. And they got together when they were practically babies. How am I supposed to live up to that example? Should I go troll Facebook, searching for people that went to my kindergarten?"

By the last word, I have tears in my eyes. Cora puts her arm around me, rocking me. "Sis. Don't cry. You're breaking my fucking heart, hon."

For a moment, I think she's going to ruffle my hair like she did when we were kids. Instead, she purses her lips. "Calla, do you know how Mom and Dad got together?"

I frown. "They were childhood sweethearts. What does this have to do with—"

"Uh, okay. No." She shakes her head vehemently. "They made it all up."

"They did *not!*" I protest, flabbergasted. This is like telling me that Santa Claus has a sweatshop. I start ticking off the things I remember my dad telling me. "They met in kindergarten. He was the new kid in school. She asked him to share a desk. They kissed under the swing set. It's literally the picture-perfect romance."

"Nope!" She shakes her head. "They met in college. Mom was dating some other guy. Dad was her lab partner. It was a whirlwind thing. I found out a few years ago, but Mom leaned on me to stay quiet. I did because I figured that there's no harm done. But now that one of my sisters is going to make major life decisions based on her whopper? I can't just stay quiet. I'm not here to keep her secrets."

"What? I don't understand!" I pull my hand away, not sure I want to believe her. "Why would they lie about that?"

"Because it makes a cute story." Cora shrugs. "The truth is messier. They weren't instantly compatible. They had to work at it. It was all adorably 90s."

I sit there, stunned. My parents' neat little love story was the template I'd built my whole idea of romance on. If that was a fabrication, what else have I been wrong about?

"So you're saying I should just... what? Work at it with Jay? Make up a cute story and hope it turns real?"

Cora stands. "I'm saying that compatibility is a lot more flexible than you think. Sometimes the messier truth is better than a tidy lie. Maybe if you talk to him, you guys will break up. But maybe?" Her eyes soften. "Maybe you'll stay together. I can't predict the future or I would be in a very different job."

I sit quietly for the better part of a minute. Does this change anything? Does it give me enough courage to stay an extra day?

Cora reaches out. "You don't have to go, Calla. We can figure something out."

"You gave me a lot to think about." I bite my lip. The taste of pastry is long gone. Soon, I will be, too. "I think I need some alone time to figure things out. At the moment, my plan still involves leaving for New Orleans."

Cora lingers for a moment. She nods and leaves me to my chaos. I pick up the hairbrush from the floor, and stare at it, willing it to give me some kind of epiphany. Nothing.

I'm about to toss it back into the suitcase when Cora pokes her head around the corner. "I love you. Whatever you decide, just make sure it's actually a decision. Not an excuse."

"Love you too." I give her a crestfallen smile.

With that, she's gone. I'm left with the silence of my own thoughts. I brush my hair, slow and methodical. I imagine what it will be like in New Orleans.

The humidity frizzing my hair. The beignets expanding my waistline. The sound of jazz seeping through the walls of my tiny, temporary apartment.

I picture Jay. His easy smile and ridiculous dimples. The way he'd looked so earnest when he proposed our fake marriage. Could it ever be more than an arrangement? Could it be the romantic marriage that I'd always dreamed of?

I don't have the answers. I know I can't stay here, paralyzed by indecision. I stand. I zip up my suitcase. I wipe the streaked mascara from my cheeks.

I'm only planning to leave for a month. All this emotional baggage will still be here when I get back. I haul my suitcase to the door. I take one last look at my room, now stripped of its former chaos. Everything is in its place. Except for me.

With a deep breath, I step into the hallway and close the door behind me.

Chapter Thirty-Eight

Jay

I got one mysterious text message twenty minutes ago.

Calla will be on Delta flight 2224 to New Orleans tonight at 6:15.

I tried to text the number back a dozen times, to no avail. But its message zings through my blood.

One last chance. All I have to lose is my cab fare... and my heart.

Am I an idiot for buying the first ticket going anywhere just to get through security?

That remains to be seen.

Hartsfield-Jackson Atlanta International Airport isn't just a place where planes take off and land. *It's the busiest airport in the world.* It's a labyrinthine city unto itself. And it is always complete chaos.

My nerves have me unsure which is up and which is down as I exit the cab. With no other plan besides hurrying, I run toward the doors, hurdle a luggage trolly, sidestep a toddler wielding a juice box like a weapon, and almost trip over a wayward duffel bag.

But I keep going, because I'm a man on a mission. Every

fiber of my being screams with the urgency to reach Calla before it's too late.

"Excuse me! Sorry!" I call out. The knot in my stomach tightens with every step.

I've never been one to second-guess myself. This is different. This is crazy even for me. Yet the thought of her leaving and not having the chance to explain my side and plead my pathetic case propels me forward.

Do both airport employees and airline customers alike think I'm insane as I run past them like I'm being chased by vicious honey badgers? Certainly. But I don't care.

I round a corner. The security checkpoint comes into view like a gauntlet of metal detectors and impatient travelers. Security at the Atlanta airport is no minor matter. It takes up a huge hall that's at least two hundred feet long and has lines that stretch for miles.

I skid to a halt and my mind races. There's no way I'll make it through in time. I clench my fists, hesitate for the briefest moment, and then make my move.

First, I jump in the shortest line, the one reserved for the first-class passengers. I unbutton my jacket and yank off my belt in one fluid motion. The line is only four people long, but I muscle my way to the front anyway. "Emergency. Huge emergency. I'm so sorry," I plead. My usual charisma has been reduced to a raw, frantic edge.

Amazingly, people let me through. Maybe they're swayed by the sheer intensity of my panic.

I reach the metal detector and hesitate for a split second. The guards eye me warily with their hands inching toward their radios. In a burst of impulsive clarity, I kick off my shoes and make a dash through the checkpoint.

Alarms scream. Voices shout. I don't look back. I'm in a dead sprint now.

The hard linoleum bites at my sock-clad feet. I weave through terminals with the grace of a gazelle and the desperation of a man fleeing for his life. Security personnel give chase and their walkie-talkies bark orders.

I sprint through the terminal, my socks skidding on the polished floor. My heart pounds. It's not just from the exertion. I'm sure someone will stop me, question me, or drag me back to the security desk for some imagined infraction.

Or actual infraction. But there's no time for paranoia. I have to keep moving.

Then I see it. A boutique store with gaudy displays and overpriced trinkets. Without hesitating, I make a beeline for it. I nearly collide with a mannequin in the window. A sales clerk eyes me with suspicion and her gaze lingers on my disheveled appearance.

"Can I help you?" she asks. Her tone is as crisp as the folded T-shirts on the display table.

"Just looking!" I blurt. My voice cracks slightly. I dart past her, scanning the racks with laser focus. I need something, anything, to blend in. Or at least to look like someone who isn't currently fleeing an existential crisis.

Or the law, if you want to be precise.

My gaze lands on a rack of hats. I lunge for it and find a floppy sun hat that screams "Floridian retiree." Perfect. I jam it onto my head and catch my reflection in a nearby mirror. The hat sits lopsided and shades my face in a way that's more comical than mysterious. I grab a pair of oversized aviators from a nearby display and fumble them onto my face. The effect is ridiculous and I know it. I look like a budget version of a celebrity trying to dodge the paparazzi.

"That'll be—" the clerk starts. But I just throw a hundred dollars at her.

"Sorry! I have to go catch a girl!" I'm already halfway out the door. I duck low and move fast.

The terminal is a sea of faces. I feel each set of eyes like a spotlight trained on me. I tell myself to walk casually, to act normal, as I cut through the throngs and weave between luggage carts and distracted families. Every laugh and every glance in my direction feels like confirmation that I've been spotted. I duck my head and clutch the brim of the sun hat over my face.

As I round a corner, my heart skips a beat when I spot a cluster of security personnel. Their uniforms are stark against the neutral tones of the terminal. One of them points, and my mind explodes with a thousand escape routes. I'm ready to bolt when I realize they're pointing at a map, not at me.

I exhale shakily, my pulse still racing. I readjust the hat and sunglasses. I'm in too deep now to turn back. My stockinged feet pad against the tile floor as I dart through the terminal, scanning the crowd.

I'm three gates away from her, but that doesn't matter. I'd be able to pick out her beauty from cruising altitude. Her dark hair is pulled back in a no-nonsense ponytail and her overnight bag is slung over one shoulder.

Calla is on a moving sidewalk and she's headed away from me.

My heart skips a beat, then two. My feet are rooted to the cold, hard floor.

"Calla!" I shout and break into a run, parallel to the moving sidewalk.

In one desperate, clumsy motion, I try to leap the divider. My legs tangle and I go sprawling, skidding across the rubber surface like a human bowling ball. I hear Calla gasp, then laugh. It's a genuine sound that melts the tension in my chest.

I scramble to my feet and find myself directly in front of her. She's smiling and shaking her head in disbelief.

"Nice move. And nice glasses, I guess? What are you, some kind of terrible spy?" she asks. Her head tilts. "What the hell are you doing here, Jay Rustin?"

"Calla, please. Just listen." I'm breathless, both from the exertion and from the sheer weight of what I have to say. "I know you don't trust me. I know you think this is all just a convenient arrangement. But it's more than that for me. You're more than that."

Her expression hardens but she stays silent, waiting.

"I'm in love with you," I blurt out. I didn't know what I was going to say until this moment, but the second I tell her I love her, the tight fist of panic eases. I keep talking, word vomiting, "I'm in love with the way you have dessert for breakfast and how you always razz me for eating muesli. I'm in love with your family stories and the way you light up when you talk about them. I'm in love with your Converse sneakers, Calla. I'm in love with you."

She chews on her lip. There is a heaviness in her hazel eyes that I haven't seen before. Shit, is she about to tell me to leave? To go back to my high-profile, adventurous life and let her return to hers?

Then she lets out a shaky breath. "Do you really mean that? Because I'm not interested in being anyone's backup plan, Jay."

"You're not." I grab her hand. The words pour out of me, raw and unpolished. "You're not a backup plan or a last resort or anything less than everything. You're the only thing that makes sense to me right now."

"Jay..." Calla rubs her temple. "You can't love me. You

can't want me. It seems like you may just be repeating the same cycle with me as you did as with Blake. We had a good three months. All right, an amazing three months. But if we don't want the same thing, what are we even doing here?"

"We do want the same things!" I insist. "We both want to be happy. We want to be in love with our spouse. We want a big house jam-packed with kids. And we're already fucking married. There is literally nothing keeping us apart other than... us."

She quirks a brow. "You want an adventure partner. I'm looking for stability."

"I found the perfect person for adventures. She's right in front of me. And I want to be her rock, through thick and thin, for the rest of my damned life."

"Wha—" Her mouth falls open, but her protests don't have any real bite. "Jay, are you serious?"

"Serious as a graveyard." When I speak, it comes out as more of a growl. "You listen to me, Calla Nikolakis. I've never felt love before. You want to know how I know that for sure? Because I've never felt this kind of a connection with anybody else. I know I can seem like I just care about performing for the camera. But I want more. You make me care about having a life that's about more."

We come to the end of the moving sidewalk rather abruptly. I step off without a problem, but Calla nearly loses her footing. I grab her at the last second and pull her against my body. She looks up at me with a sheen of tears building in her eyes. An older couple huffs as they pass us and I draw Calla aside, out of the way of people hurrying to catch their flights.

This moment between us can't be rushed.

Calla wets her lips, her eyes fixed on me. "We barely know each other, Jay."

I clutch her hand to my chest. "I know you, Lily. I see you, inside and out. Even when you eavesdrop or maybe aren't your best self? I know you and I love you. I'm desperate to keep being married to you. It just took getting married by accident for me to figure it out."

"Oh god." She scans my face. "Jay, I love you too. When I thought that you just wanted to be... married with benefits... I couldn't handle it anymore. My heart broke and I had to leave."

I cup her jaw. "Stay with me."

She brushes away a tear before it can fall. "You mean it?"

"More than I've ever meant anything in my entire life."

Her eyes search mine, looking for cracks or insincerity. When she doesn't find any, her mouth wobbles. She's never cried in front of me before. But she's about to burst into tears here in the middle of the airport.

Calla pushes up onto her tiptoes, grips my shirt, and kisses me so passionately that my fucking toes curl. I thrust my fingers into her hair and kiss her back like this is our last moment on earth before the asteroid hits.

When she breaks the kiss and her cheeks are flushed, she has never been more beautiful to me. She shakes her head. "You're unbelievable. You know that?"

"Unbelievably in love with you," I say.

A laugh escapes her then, light and unexpected. "You're also a terrible runner."

I let out a breath I didn't realize I was holding. She's here. She's listening. And for the first time in what feels like forever, I can breathe again.

A heavy hand lands on my shoulder and yanks me. I stumble and spin, and that's when two police officers tackle me in a synchronized, NFL-worthy takedown. My cheek smashes against the cold floor.

"Oh shit."

"Hands behind your back!" one cop barks. The other wrestles with a set of handcuffs. I'm too stunned to resist. They've got me cuffed and utterly subdued before I fully realize it.

"Wait! Stop!" Calla's voice cuts through the commotion. She stands a few yards away. I turn my head and see her eyes are wide with shock and fear. "What did he do?"

The officers ignore her and haul me to my feet, my wrists bound and my hair a disheveled mess. I feel like a man who's just survived a kidnapping attempt only to be arrested for loitering.

"Calla," I warn her. She looks like she's prepared to take these cops on. "I deserve this!"

She rushes to me anyway. "This is all a misunderstanding. He was just trying to"

"Ma'am, step back," one cop interrupts. He holds up a hand to block her, then they start to drag me away.

"I love you," I shout over my shoulder to my wife. "Wait for me!"

"Where the heck are they taking him?" I hear her demanding of someone on the moving sidewalk.

"You can come get your boyfriend at the TSA offices," one of the cops yells over his shoulder, "They're right next to the baggage claim."

Calla runs after us. "He's actually my husband! Funny story... We had some tequila and got matching tattoos, right? Then we accidentally got married..."

Chapter Thirty-Nine

Calla

Six Months Later

Why am I so nervous? This is my second rodeo. Minus the tequila, of course. I'll be sober as a judge when I make my vows.

This time, Jay and I will both mean it. Till death do us part.

I stand in front of the mirror, fiddling with the neckline of my dress. It's a soft ivory, the exact color of a dollop of vanilla-infused whipped cream. It fits me better than I expected. Coupled with my shoulder-length veil and a bouquet of calla lilies, I look as graceful as a ballerina.

My hair, however, is doing that *thing* where it refuses to cooperate. It's a tangle of dark brown and its rebellion works against my usually meticulous style. I try to smooth it down. A curl pops up and I try for another full minute to get it to lay down. Then I give up and let it be.

My hair just refuses to be tamed, apparently.

I take a deep breath. Then I take another. It's not as if I'm talking myself into anything. Wild horses couldn't tear me away from meeting Jay at the altar. I'm not his ex-fiancée Blake and I'm determined to show up for him.

Plus, we're already married!

I pick up the small bouquet of white lilies and baby's breath. My hands are sweaty, ruining the delicate tissue paper wrapping. I set it down quickly.

God, is Jay this worried?

I open the door a crack and peek out. Jay is pacing the hallway, his brow furrowed. He looks tall and handsome in his charcoal suit. His movements betray a hint of nervousness.

So yes. We're both anxious.

He stops pacing. He checks his watch and runs a hand through his hair. There's a tension in his movements that I'm not used to seeing. My husband, and husband to be, is the epitome of laid-back. He is the kind of guy who can make eating a bowl of granola look like an adventure. This is endearing.

I retreat back into the room to grab two things. One, an expensive pocket square in a that I had specially made for today. It's in a brilliant shade of chartreuse. And two, a matching length of chartreuse ribbon that I wind around the base of my bouquet.

I take the bouquet again, more gently this time. Then I open the door.

Jay turns. For a moment, I think he's going to break into that easy, confident smile that disarms everyone in a ten-mile radius. But he doesn't. Instead, his blue eyes meet mine with an intensity that makes me want to look away because I couldn't believe a look like that would be directed at me. Now I can't stop looking back at him.

"Ready?" he asks softly.

"I have something for you." I beckon him closer and then tuck the pocket square in his suit pocket.

Jay breaks out into a grin. "You remembered my wedding colors."

"It's funny. I remember everything about that day except the actual marriage."

He stares at me for a second then shakes his head. "You're perfect. Do you know that? Absolutely meant for me. I feel really lucky."

"Not as lucky as I feel. Trust me." I wrinkle my nose and show him my bouquet. "We're a matching pair. In life, in everything. Chartreuse may not be a popular wedding color. But if we both wear it, nobody will say boo."

"I wouldn't worry about it. I'm pretty sure that every single person invited to this wedding is rooting for us." He helps me into a cream-colored overcoat to ward off the crisp autumn chill, then offers me his elbow. "Ready?"

"Beyond ready," I tell him. He shrugs on a dark overcoat and ushers me out of the building.

Leaving the house on Wildflower Lane, we walk side by side for the four blocks to the clerk's office. As we hit the tiled courthouse floors, I'm grateful for my Converse sneakers. Today's pair is cream, with little chartreuse hearts that match my bouquet.

The clerk, a no-nonsense older woman with glasses perched on the end of her nose, types something into her computer. She looks up and smiles. "May I help you?"

"We're here to file the paperwork to change my name to Calanthe Rustin." I make a face. "It's kind of a long story, but we actually already married. Today, we're having the official ceremony."

"Congratulations, you two. This is a big step."

"Thanks." Jay slides me a look and takes my hand. "It's been a long time coming."

The clerk accepts the paperwork that Jay hands her, then spends the next couple of minutes making sure everything is complete. Then she hands me a piece of paper and a pen. "Just need your signature, Mrs. Rustin."

Mrs. Rustin. I'm really, officially, going to be Mrs. Rustin. I squeeze Jay's hand. He bites his lip and gives me an encouraging nod.

I sign the paper with a flourish. It's funny. For the first time, I really wish that the Alto & Ash camera crew were on hand to film this moment. It feels like a scene directly ripped from a movie.

The clerk takes the paper back and stamps the form. "You're all set. Have a wonderful life together."

We step out into the open. It's blinding out here after the florescent dimness of the courthouse interior. I squint and shade my eyes with the bouquet.

"We did it, Mrs. Rustin." Jay's smile is as bright as the afternoon sun. "You're all mine now. No takebacks."

"Come here." I grip his collar and press a kiss to my new husband's lips. "It *feels* official."

"It's forever." He offers me his arm.

I don't hesitate before taking it and leaning against his body. I wasn't part of planning this part of the wedding, so I have only the faintest idea what I'm going to see.

We start walking toward the gazebo. Our footsteps are in sync, as if we've done this a thousand times before. Maybe we have, in other lifetimes or other timelines. I like to think that I'd find Jay, or he'd find me, no matter what.

As we draw closer, I see the gazebo is draped in white chiffon. Sunlight filters through the trees and casts soft shadows on the pathway. The whole scene feels delicate, like it might shatter if I breathe too hard.

"Oh Jay." I touch my heart, staring at the place we woke up as husband and wife. "It looks beautiful."

He leads me to the center of the gazebo, where a small crowd of friends and family has gathered. Phones are at the ready to capture every moment. I let go of his arm and circle one of the wooden pillars. The chiffon flutters in a gentle breeze.

This isn't the wedding I would have planned for myself. In fact, I doubt I would've insisted on a ceremony at all.

But Jay did this for us. And I absolutely adore it. I also hope that one of the Alto & Ash camera crew is capturing this moment from afar. It's something I want to remember and cherish over and over again.

It's odd. I never thought I'd be standing here as the bride. I mean, before I woke up here as the bride. But now that it's really happening, it seems sort of unreal.

The chaplain asks, "Do you, Jay, take this woman, to have and to hold from this day forward, for better, for worse, for richer, for poorer, in sickness and in health, so long as you both shall live?"

"I do." He looks into my eyes and smiles. "I promise to love you until my dying breath. It'll be my honor."

"And do you Calla, take this man, to have and to hold from this day forward, for better, for worse, for richer, for poorer, in sickness and in health, so long as you both shall live?"

"I do. I—" I choke up at this point. "I choose you, Jay. Today and always."

He squeezes my hands, then pulls me into his arms for a passionate kiss before the chaplain can say anything more. A cheer goes up from our gathered family and friends.

"—kiss the bride."

With the vows complete, the crowd erupts into applause. Jay pulls me into a spontaneous twirl. Our laughter mingles with the cheers. A brass band starts playing the familiar notes of "When the Saints Go Marching In" and several gold-suited dancers begin leading us in a procession arounds the town square. Jay hands me a white silk umbrella and I open it with a grin.

"Ready?" Jay looks at me mischievously. He opens his matching umbrella. All the guests walk behind us, waving white handkerchiefs. We bebop to the beat of the band.

I'm not familiar with the Louisiana-style second line tradition. But Jay is so joyful as we follow the procession that I can't help but enjoy myself. We are really celebrating getting married this time.

After making a couple of slow laps around the town square, we dance ourselves right into the Tin Shed Pub.

I can't stop grinning. Everyone in my family makes sure to hug and kiss both me and Jay. My mother manages to wrangle a kiss from Wren and welcome her to the family. Wren turns so red that I have to rescue her before she dies from embarrassment.

The celebration shifts to the cake cutting. My masterpiece takes center stage. I watch as Jay slices into the cake with exaggerated care. It's Gentilly Cream Cake, just like before. He feeds me a piece with a teasing smile that makes my cheeks flush.

There are a few toasts from my father and Ryan. But since we decided that this version of our reception would be dry, there isn't much weeping (only my dad violates this rule) and toasts only go on for a few minutes.

Bennett feeds everyone, while Wren and Jay's friend Gabe circle the room with bottles of non-alcoholic apple cider. And if anyone misses tequila, they are too smart to mention it.

As the night winds down, Jay and I share a quiet moment away from the crowd. He pulls me outside and we walk to the gazebo, both wrapped in his big overcoat. The fairy lights cast a soft glow on his face as he teases me.

"We've conquered the marriage thing. What's next?"

I tilt my head, considering. "Well." I draw out the word playfully. "I suppose we should start having kids."

His eyes light up. Before I can react, he kisses me. His lips are gentle but full of startling enthusiasm.

"I can't wait to start building our own family." His breath mingles with mine.

I blush. The heat rushing to my cheeks is almost unbearable.

"I can already imagine a little boy with your eyes." I surprise myself with the honesty of it.

The image is so clear in my mind. A tiny version of Jay, with the same blue eyes and disarming smile, runs around in a pair of miniature Converse sneakers. It's a vision that fills me with unexpected tenderness.

I hold up a finger. "But I want to wait a while before we start trying."

Jay's fingers trace the outline of my hand. His touch sends shivers up my arm. "Calla. I would wait for eternity if you asked me to."

There's a depth to his tone that makes my heart ache. I look up into his eyes.

"Ready to sleep over in the gazebo like the first night we got together?" I ask. I point to where Cora has tucked two rolled-up heavy duty sleeping bags on the ground.

His breath hitches and he smiles. "So ready."

I giggle and grab the sleeping bags, unfurling them both.

It takes a minute to zip the bags together to make them one big bag. As we untie our shoes and shimmy into the sleeping bags, I can't think of when I've ever been quite this happy. I have Jay by my side, now and forever.

We snuggle down in the cojoined sleeping bags. I fall asleep knowing I'll wake up in his arms tomorrow, and every damn day after that.

But hopefully never again on concrete.

Chapter Forty

Calla

The Epilogue

Has anywhere ever smelled as good as my mother's kitchen on a Sunday afternoon?

The aroma of freshly baked bread and roasted lamb wafts from the oven and radiates out, making hungry stomachs growl. My mother, still in a tizzy over me getting married again, insisted on throwing an impromptu *second* wedding feast.

Jay is in the other room with Wren. I can see them both on the couch; Jay is trying to shield his little sister from the persistent questioning of my nosy family. Questions about whether she is seeing someone, no doubt. I warned them both ahead of time to expect some Greek matchmaking for her. My family literally just loves love. And you know that, because they never shut up about it.

"Calla, chop the parsley." Mom thrusts a cutting board into my hands. I comply, though my mind is a thousand miles away. My eyes drift back to Jay. And I can't help but smile.

He's *mine.*

My father trundles in the kitchen, eyeing the food. "No lamb?"

"It's still in the oven," I reply.

"Calla mou." He comes over to where I'm standing and puts an arm around my shoulder. His eyes twinkle with mischief. "Now that you married him twice, you should know that we expect twice as many grandchildren. Your mother and I would've had seven or eight of you if God had willed it."

My mom makes a face and mouths, "absolutely not."

Typical Greek family. My parents are close as any two people could be. But they have some differing ideas about child rearing.

I flush, a mix of embarrassment and amusement heating my cheeks. "We'll have kids. *Someday.*"

He chuckles, patting my shoulder. "As long as you're happy, that's all that matters. Though I do wonder..."

Before he can finish, Jay strides into the kitchen, and all eyes shift to him. My sisters, who have been whispering in the corner of the living room all afternoon, catch up with their new brother-in-law.

"So, Jay," Iris asks. "How do you get started being an influencer? How many hours would you say you put in per week? Do you ever do conventions or anything?"

Cora flashes him a broad smile. "She's trying to fish out how much you make a year."

"Cora!" Iris turns red. "Jeez, have some class."

Jay handles their curiosity with the grace of a seasoned diplomat, weaving in just enough humor to keep things light.

"Well, ladies, the answer is a little complicated..." he starts.

I occupy myself with the parsley, stealing glances at Jay as he works his magic. It's like watching a master craftsman at work, someone who makes the impossible seem effortless. I didn't even realize that I needed a partner who could blend into my family in this way. Easy, gracious, even-keeled.

My family is a lot of things, but cool under pressure is not one of them. They all have hot Mediterranean blood and count squabbling as a past time.

But Jay? He knocks my family off their feet as easily as he did me. They're putty in his oversized hands.

"Calla, taste this," my mother says.

My reverie pops like a bubble. She holds out a spoonful of lemon rice. I take a bite, the familiar flavors grounding me. It's perfect, as always.

"You know that this rice is perfect." I give her a brief hug. "Come on. I'll help you carry dishes out to the table."

There are extra chairs and even a stool drawn up to fit eighteen people around the dining table. We all pack in, elbow to elbow. *Yiayia* sits at one end of the table, my great uncle Dimitri at the other.

I make sure to sit Wren between me and Jay hoping to give her a break from the onslaught of questions. Also, frankly, I have to make a special effort to make sure that her plate is full of slices of lamb, Greek salad, and lemon rice. Normally *Yiayia* would insist on doing it, but I begged her to let me take care of Jay's baby sister. Wren is pretty quiet and I'm afraid that she'll get lost under all these boisterous shouts.

"Got what you need?" I ask Wren.

She nods and gives me a quiet smile. "Thanks, Calla."

My mother, cheeks flushed from both the cooking and the emotional occasion, stands and raises her glass. The room falls silent. All eyes turn to her. When Mom talks, everybody listens like she's Moses handing down the Ten Commandments.

"To the newlyweds," she declares. She looks around the crowded table. "May your life together be as full and rich as this feast we've prepared for you. I love you so much."

"Yiamas!" my father cries. We all clink glasses.

I lean over to Wren. "He said cheers."

"I figured that." She grins and gives me a look. "But thanks for translating."

I take a small sip of wine, letting it wash over my palate, and try to absorb the reality of the situation. This is what I've always imagined for myself.

A loving family gathered to celebrate a milestone in my life. It's happening.

"So Calla, I heard you went to New Orleans to be a fricking TV chef!" my cousin Christopher asks. "How was it?"

"Absolutely amazing." I glance at Jay and he grins. "Jay came with me and we spent every minute I wasn't filming eating amazing food. The gumbo and trout almondine were *to die for.*"

Jay adds, "And the pastries. They made these fresh beignets that were so good. I definitely gained five pounds."

"That's not so bad. You're so skinny!" my aunt Chloe chimes in. "Somebody better pass the rice over here. Jay needs another helping."

"I'm still stuffed from the trip!" Jay catches my eye and gives me a small, reassuring smile. It's the kind of smile that says, "We've got this."

"Jay," my grandmother calls from the far end of the table. "When am I going to get great-grandchildren?"

The entire table falls silent, all eyes shifting to Jay. It's not the first time he's been asked about babies. In fact, I'm sure it's not the first time *today*. There are no boundaries in my family.

"Yiayia," I reply sweetly. "Please. Give us a few years before you start demanding children."

"What if I don't have a few years?" my grandmother asks archly.

Cora cuts in. "Are you kidding? The women in our family live to be well over a hundred. We have time."

Jay holds up a hand. "Actually..." He looks at me, raising a brow. I feel my cheeks heat. "We're planning to start trying sometime in the next six months."

The table erupts in joyful exclamations and congratulations. My mother clasps her hands to her chest. My father beams. Even my usually cynical older sister looks pleased.

"We haven't even talked about a timeline," I say to him, low enough so it seems private.

He leans back from the table, beckons to me behind Wren's back, and then whispers in my ear. "I'm not worried about it. I just wanted your family to know that I'm all in. As soon as you're ready, you can go off your birth control and we can start trying. In the meantime? Plenty of practice."

I blush, the heat rushing to my cheeks, and kiss him softly. The gesture feels more natural than I expect, like slipping into a familiar routine. My entire family catcalls us, which makes me blush even deeper.

I search his eyes for some indication of what he's really thinking. But all I see is the same calm confidence he always projects.

As the night wears on, the meal is cleared away. My father gets out the Tavli board and he and my uncle get a game going. While Wren and I wash dishes and joke about know-it-all men, my father starts a low conversation with my husband. I watch from my spot in the kitchen, my curiosity piqued as I wonder what advice or warnings Dad might be imparting. Is he telling Jay about the time he proposed to my mother? Or is he cautioning Jay about the challenges of being married to someone as stubborn as me?

Jay laughs, the sound rich and beautiful as the rosewood Tavli board.

It's amazing to me how seamlessly he has fit into my world. The way he interacts with my family, the stories he tells, even the affectionate touches. Now I'm actually Mrs. Rustin.

Don't tell my family that – they still believe in the woman's keeping her own surname. But I'm beyond excited. A new last name to go with my new life.

Chapter Forty-One

Calla

The town square is electric with excitement as we prepare for the pet adoption fair. The grassy center of the square is crowned by its iconic gazebo, aka our wedding site. It's already dotted with colorful tents and tables.

My husband and I are both in our element here. We work seamlessly together as we unload boxes from the back of his SUV. I steal a glance at him.

My husband. It still feels unreal. A giddy feeling rushes through me. Married life really does suit us. It always did.

"Don't squish the cupcakes," I remind him. "That's delicate cargo." I eye the box in his hands. Each cupcake is decorated with little fondant paw prints for the animal adoption event. A true labor of love from my bakery.

"Would I ever?" Jay feigns hurt. "These are practically your children."

"They are." I cross my arms and give him a playful glare. "You better handle them with the same care."

"Like I handle you?" He waggles his eyebrows.

"Are you kidding? You're forever trying to get me dirty."

I smirk. "Let's hope you're not going to do the same thing to the cupcakes."

Jay grins. His tall, dark, and gorgeous self towers over me. "When have I ever squished a cupcake?"

I raise an eyebrow. "Do you want the list alphabetically or chronologically?"

He laughs and sets the box down gently on the table. "Touché, Lily."

Ellie Haart, Ryan's younger sister and the event's organizer, waves at us from across the square. She is wearing her usual animal print scrubs. The bright pattern looks wild in the sea of casual jeans and T-shirts the volunteers wear.

"Calla, Jay!" she shouts, cupping her hands around her mouth. "Thanks for coming!"

"We wouldn't miss it." I wave back enthusiastically.

Ellie is a whirlwind of energy. She bustles from one table to the next. I have to say, I admire her commitment. As a veterinarian, she's already stretched thin. And yet, she still finds time to organize events like this. I don't know her that well yet, but I'm already in awe,

I glance over at Ryan. He's tying down a tent with Wren, or at least trying to. They seem to be having a serious disagreement over it. Frowning, I move closer.

"You're doing it wrong," I hear Ryan say. He looks at her with a taunting expression. "Do you need help? Just tell me you need me—"

Wren suddenly shoves the entire tent at Ryan and leaves him staggering, his arms full of poles and canvas. She stalks away and de notices my curious gaze. He smiles.

"She's so temperamental, you know."

I narrow my gaze. "Be nice to Wren. She's my family now. You? Not so much."

Ryan grins. "Aye aye, boss." He gives me a faux salute and returns to setting up the tent.

Jay lopes up to me, missing the entire interaction completely. "Ellie really outdid herself this time." He nods toward a table laden with animal-themed crafts and another with a towering stack of pet food donations.

"She did!" I glance at the table. "It's going to be a great turnout."

Jay pulls out his phone and starts a live stream. "Hey guys, we're here at the Greater Town Square Pet Adoption Fair. Come on down and meet some adorable animals. Calla and I will be here all day." He turns the camera toward me.

I give a little wave. "And we're giving away a free cupcake to everyone who visits." I smile, knowing that the lure of sweets will draw a crowd.

Jay ends the stream. He tucks his phone away. "Think we'll survive the sugar rush?"

"We can only try," I announce, faux-dramatically. Jay grins.

Ellie wheels over a large cart filled with animal enclosures. The sight of wiggling puppies, curious kittens, and a few more exotic creatures makes my heart melt on the spot. Jay makes sure they are safe in their enclosures and out of the sun.

"These are the stars of the show." Ellie's enthusiasm is infectious. "Take a look."

We crowd around the cart and peer in like kids on Christmas morning. Jay's face softens as he gazes at a tiny tabby kitten. Its big eyes and wobbly head are too much to resist.

I feel a pang of something maternal.

I turn my head and spot a three-legged Great Pyrenees

with a grumpy expression. It's like he's the canine version of a grumpy old man. "What's his story

Ellie sighs. Her usual upbeat demeanor dips for a moment. "That's Gonzo. He lost his leg in an accident and has been in and out of shelters. He's a sweetheart. Just needs the right home."

I kneel down to Gonzo's level and extend a hand slowly. He sniffs it cautiously. His big, soulful eyes take me in. Then he rests his heavy head on my palm. The warmth of his fur and the trust in his eyes are almost too much to bear. "He seems like a real sweetheart."

Jay leans in over my shoulder. His hand gently strokes my back. "What? Did you already fall in love?"

I look back at Gonzo. He has settled into a resigned, sleepy posture. It's like he knows his fate and has made peace with it. That just kills me.

"Maybe we could—" I start, but Jay cuts me off.

"Calla." His tone is cautious. "We have a lot on our plates right now."

I know he's right. The bakery, his brand, and our new marriage all take time and energy. But looking at Gonzo, I just can't shake the thought that we could make it work somehow.

"We could foster him." I try to keep my tone light. "Just until he finds a permanent home."

Jay rubs his chin. He considers it. He's never one to make a quick decision, especially when it involves a commitment like this. Except when he married me.

"Fostering is a big maybe. Let's see how today goes first."

I nod. I know this is the best compromise I'm going to get right now. "Okay, but just look at him. How could anyone resist that face?"

Jay bends down and studies Gonzo. I can see the

struggle in his eyes. He wants to say no. He knows that if we take Gonzo in, even as a foster, he'll become part of our family.

Ellie claps her hands together and brings us back to the present. "Whatever you decide, just let me know. I appreciate you even considering it."

We move away from the cart. I steal one last glance at Gonzo. The fair is in full swing now. Families and couples are moving from tent to tent. Children squeal with delight as they pet the animals.

Jay takes my hand. We walk back to the table where the cupcakes are stacked in colorful tiers. Each one is a miniature work of art, with fondant paw prints and bones. I'm proud of how far the bakery has come. It's become a staple in the community.

The fair kicks into high gear as more townspeople arrive. Kids rush to the animal enclosures. Adults peruse the tables filled with pet supplies. A line forms at our booth for cupcakes. The excitement is palpable. People eagerly pet and play with the animals. Many are already discussing adoptions. Jay and I take turns handing out cupcakes and making small talk with our neighbors.

"Calla, these are amazing." One woman licks frosting from her finger. "Are you going to start making pet-friendly treats?"

I laugh. "Maybe. We'll see how today goes."

Jay leans in close and whispers. "You should. They'd sell like hotcakes."

"Or cupcakes," I whisper back.

I see a few people lining up to pet Gonzo. One family, two moms and a little boy, seems particularly interested. My heart squeezes and when Ellie walks by, I snag her.

"What's going on with Gonzo?"

She turns and looks, then smiles. "I think they want to adopt him. They have a few acres on the other side of Greater. They already have a few rescues. A duck, a couple cats, and a blind Chihuahua. It would be a perfect environment for a big dog. But... They are talking about how expensive it would be to take Gonzo on."

My heart hurts. But even as I ache, I see Gonzo licking the little boy's hand. Out of nowhere, I blurt out, "What if I agreed to take care of his food and vet bills for a year?"

Ellie's eyes widen. "I thought you wanted to take him home!"

"I do. But... I mean, look at him. He's obviously meant to be their dog."

We look at Gonzo, who is standing up now and showcasing his missing front leg. He's leaning against one of the women. Ellie beams at the scene. "I think if I told them right now, they would say yes."

"Well, go! Get Gonzo a good home. Trust me, I will live to fight another day."

Ellie touches my hand briefly. "Thanks, Calla. Ryan said you were good people. It seems like he was right."

I work the cupcake stand for another hour, sometimes posing for photos. Inside, I'm still sad about Gonzo. When I see that his pen is empty, it hurts a tiny bit.

God, if I'm like this after just meeting a dog for twenty minutes, what will I be like as a mom? The dial on my mothering instincts is turned up to an eleven right now.

"Calla." Jay pulls me aside just as I'm about to hand out another cupcake. "I have a surprise for you."

"Oh?" I tilt my head, curious and slightly wary. With Jay, surprises can go in any direction.

After I hand off the cupcake I'm holding, he takes my hand and leads me to the back of Ellie's cart. He checks over his shoulder, then opens a small carrier carefully. Inside is a half-Siamese kitten with striking blue eyes and a delicate frame. Her tiny paws knead a soft blanket.

Oh. My. God. "It's so cute!!"

"Her name is Pocket." His voice is almost reverent. "I thought she'd be perfect for us. Lower maintenance than Gonzo, but still very much a pet we could take home."

The kitten is absolutely adorable. I can already picture her curled up in Jay's lap, purring contentedly while he works. My heart tugs at the vision.

"She's beautiful." I mean it, too. "About Gonzo... he's found his forever home on a farm with a great family. Aaaand I offered to pay for his expenses for a year."

"Oh god. That could be a lot of money." He smiles as he shakes his head.

I grab his hand and flutter my eyelashes. "It's a good thing the bakery is doing well."

"And your husband is a very successful businessman." He cups my cheek, kisses me gently, then draws my attention back to the kitten. "So? What do you say?"

"I say YES!" I announce. I squeal and throw my arms around his neck. "Let's do it, Bird."

"You got it, Lily." He picks me up and twirls me around.

"Gah, get a room, you two," Wren mutters as she walks by. "You're embarrassing the family."

I crack up as Jay picks up the carrier with sweet, baby Pocket. We walk over to Ellie, announcing our new family member.

"Look who's coming home with us!" Jay says.

Pocket stretches her paw out, batting at my hand through the carrier door. I open the door and pull her out, laying her against my chest. She looks at me with eyes that are so big they should be illegal.

"Miaow?" she trills.

"I can see who has all the power in this relationship from the start," I coo. "Isn't that right, my little Hot Pocket?"

Pocket settles against me and starts purring. Jay puts his arm around my waist and nuzzles my cheek. I realize that I've never felt quite so content as I do in this moment, right here on the sidewalk in the middle of the town square.

Chapter Forty-Two

Wren

"Okay, everyone. These are all good ideas for the shoot next month." Marcus White, the director of the new reality show, Heartbreak Island, sits back in his chair and peers down the long conference table. "Mostly, I just wanted everyone to meet and mingle. Get to know each other before we fly to a tiny island and film for six weeks. We'll all be on top of each other there. To avoid tension, I'd like you to pair off into same sex room assignments. This is not summer camp, so you can pick whoever you'd like. Anyone who doesn't pick will get randomly assigned a roommate."

"Elena?" He looks to his left at Elena Pérez, the show's head executive producer. "Is there anything you'd like to add?"

"No. You have done a wonderful job of that, Marcus." Elena speaks with a strong Spanish accent, so when she says his name it sounds like Marc-yus. She stands up, her bright yellow power suit doing all the talking for her, and spreads her hands wide. "I really look forward to working with you all. Make sure you get some rest so that you can be at the top of your game when we touch down in the Bahamas."

She's so confident and cool. She announces what she thinks. The best part? She is very powerful, so when she talks, people *listen.*

God, I so want to be her when I grow up. I look down at my baggy, retro Killers T-shirt and worn-out checkered Vans. I have a long way to go.

The meeting breaks up, everyone talking amongst themselves. There are a handful of young producers like myself, both guys and girls, that seem to be deciding who will sleep where. A lot of the older producers, sound engineers, and camera crew are walking out of the conference room already.

They have been on a set before. Likely, they're working with the same people as they have on previous shoots. Rooming with one of them is... unlikely. I swallow.

A little bit of my brother Jay's gregariousness would go a long way about now. But he got all the charm and outgoingness. I'm much shyer and more introverted. One of my friends described me once as "looking like I'm perpetually on the way to the library". I feel like that's apt.

The library is, in fact, one of my favorite places to be. What's not my favorite? Being here, right now, staring awkwardly at the young producers as they chat.

Say something. Anything.

Yeah, no. I pick up the packet of paper that was distributed during the meeting and flee the room.

As I'm leaving, a young woman with fiery orange hair, black leggings, and an oversized Echo and the Bunnymen T-shirt raises a pierced eyebrow at me.

"...bye?"

I stop at the door, flushing, and give her an awkward wave. "Uh, bye."

She stares at me for a few more seconds then turns back to her conversation. "What was I saying?"

Another successful conversation with a coworker! I groan to myself. Loping down the hallway, I collapse into the worn swivel chair in the production room and rub my temples.

I take a deep breath. It's the kind that fills your lungs with hope. Despite the embarrassment and exhaustion, I'm thrilled. My first day as a producer is in the can. I didn't totally screw it up.

Thank God Jay recommended me for this gig. It's a breath of fresh air after two years working as a PA for his company and waitressing on the side. Even if it's left me feeling like a wrung-out dishrag, I'm a slightly more independent dishrag. That's what matters.

I worked my butt off to get here. Now that I can actually sink my teeth into the job, there's no way I'm letting it go without a fight. I pull out my phone to text Jay a quick thank you.

The door swings open with a thud and Elena strides in. Her black hair is a so shiny that I'm momentarily enraptured. Behind her trails Marcus, looking like a puppy who just got scolded. I sit up straighter. Elena is the kind of woman who commands a room with just a glance. I've admired her from afar for years.

I look around the room. Clearly, I'm in here. They can see me... right?

"One of the bachelorettes has backed out." Elena's Spanish accent slices through the air like a hot knife through butter. She pinches her fingers together as she gestures. "She was a real character. A proven drama starter."

My heart skips a beat. This is big. I try to make myself as small as possible. It's like a mouse hiding from a cat. Still, I'm dying to hear what they say next. For the next few months, this show is my whole life. If it tanks, so does my shot at a real career in production.

"We could bring in a ringer." Mark scratches his head. "Someone with the same... qualities."

Elena crosses her arms. She looks unconvinced. "Do you have any idea how hard it is to find another perfect specimen? Melanie was *perfect*. Perfect hair. Perfect teeth. Perfect *tetas*. She was a power yoga instructor. Have you ever tried to touch your heel to the back of your head? Because Melanie could. She was the whole package."

I wonder what Elena would say about me right now. My long, mousy brown hair is a frizzy mess. My comically large glasses are smudged. My oversized T-shirt looks like something a toddler would swim in. I've never been hip or magnetic like Jay. He's the guy with the perfect Instagram life. I'm the girl in the background, hiding behind a camera.

Basically, I'm none of the things that made Melanie perfect. What does that leave for the rest of us? Not much.

Feeling low, I start to slink out of the room. Then I trip over ... well, I'm not sure. The floor, maybe?

Classic Wren. I brace for impact.

A strong hand catches me and turns me around. It's Elena. "Are you all right?" She sounds more curious than concerned as she helps me stand.

"Fine!" I insist, brushing my knees off. "See, no harm done. I'll just get out of your way."

Elena doesn't turn me loose. "Who are you?"

"Me?" I am sure I turn red as a tomato. "I'm Wren Rustin. You hired me as a producer."

Her eyes narrow in contemplation. Marcus comes to my

rescue. "Wren is Jay Rustin's little sister. You know, that guy whose face you see everywhere?"

"I don't know him," Elena answers in a flat tone. "But you have pretty eyes, carina." She smooths back my hair. "So blue! You should wear your hair up more, let them do some of the talking for you."

I'm entranced by her touch. Gulping, I nod. Then Elena gives me a once-over. I can almost see the gears in her head turning.

"What about a ringer?" she asks. "If we used someone from the crew, we could control the storyline. It would be *excelente*."

Mark's eyes light up. "That would be a lot cheaper than hiring someone new. We could script the drama. Make it more believable."

I scrunch my face. Why is he acting like this wasn't his idea?

My stomach does a somersault. My very first thought is *no*. Absolutely not. This is the worst idea in the history of bad ideas.

Elena tilts her head. She's still staring at me. "You would have to 'win' the show. Make the bachelor choose you. We need the drama." She pauses. She considers her next words. "We need you to fill in for Melanie. Just temporarily. We'll glam you up. Make sure you 'win.'"

I can't think of a bigger nightmare.

"I'm really more comfortable behind the scenes." My voice is shaky. "I'm a shy girl. Uncomfortable on camera. I don't even like having my picture taken."

Elena isn't listening. Or maybe she's ignoring me. "Would you like a hundred thousand dollars? I could arrange that to be your bonus if you played along. Plus, a promotion. We're counting on you, Wren. Remember, you must win the show."

A hundred grand? My mind races. The promotion would mean job security. My first venture outside of working for Jay would be a success. God, I really want that.

I make a face. "I'm not even the type of girl usually featured on these shows. They're poised and polished. I'm... something else."

"We could fix that for you." Marcus sizes me up. "A haircut, a new wardrobe. Maybe we'd whiten your teeth so they pop on camera..."

My hand flies up to my mouth. What's wrong with my teeth?

Elena grabs my hand. "You are the perfect ringer. You are the right age, the right height, the right..." Her eyes travel to my waist. "Well, I can't see what kind of body you have. But it doesn't matter. In a month, you could be ready. And I could be writing you the biggest check you could imagine."

The money is pretty damn tantalizing. I'm trapped. They know it. "I... Okay." My voice is barely a whisper.

"*Excellente.*" Elena's tone is firm. "This will do wonders for your career."

They leave the conference room. I follow on unsteady legs, wondering what I have just agreed to. I'm not cut out for this kind of attention. I can't even handle a staff meeting without breaking into a cold sweat.

As we step outside, I suddenly stop, doing a double take. "What is *he* doing here?"

By him, I mean Ryan fucking Haart. He's leaning against a wall, all casual arrogance. My heart does that stupid flutter thing it's been doing since I was twelve. He's a perfect specimen. Even more so in person. Tall. Blond. The kind of blue eyes that make you believe in clichés. His abs have abs.

He's also fucking *awful* to me. Literally the meanest boy I've ever met.

Elena waves. "Ryan, we should talk about your agent."

But Ryan's eyes are on me. He looks shocked. No, wait. More like horrified.

Great. I feel my face go hot.

"Wren?" He looks like he can't believe I exist. "What are you doing here?"

"Why are you on my set?" I blurt out. "Seems like we all have questions."

"Ryan, Wren. Please. We're introducing Wren as the new bachelorette." Elena's tone is calm. "Don't worry. We'll take care of her. She's in good hands."

Ryan laughs, but he looks so dismayed that it's hard not to take it personally.

Elena gets a call. "Oh, let me take this, Wren. I'll be right back."

And then she leaves us alone in the hallway together. An awkward silence settles in. Ryan scratches the back of his neck. It's a gesture I've come to recognize as his tell. He's uncomfortable. That makes two of us.

"So." He drags out the word. "You're really doing this?"

I shrug. "I don't have a choice. They're making me."

He laughs. It sounds forced. "This is going to be interesting."

"Why are you here, Ryan?" I already know the answer. I just want to hear him say it.

"Jay didn't tell you?" He sounds surprised. "I'm the next bachelor."

My jaw clenches. "He might have mentioned something about it. I try to tune Jay out when he gives me updates on your life."

A part of me in the back of my head says, *Yeah. Of course Ryan is the bachelor that you're supposed to lust after. You didn't think getting that $100k was going to be easy, did you?*

"You're a contestant now?" Ryan folds his arms across his chest and smirks. "You're never going to win. You realize that, right?"

My hands ball into fists. His constant leer makes me feel *violent*.

"And *you're* the worst human being ever. It's hard to choose between Scylla and Charybdis."

Ryan blinks. "I don't even know what that means. No one does."

"Charybdis was a sea monster who could become a giant whirlpool. Scylla was a monster who was part human, part fish, with three dog heads—"

"Jesus, Chirp." He uses the cruel childhood nickname that he tormented me with. "Are you kidding with that story? Get to the point already."

"Fine." I glare at him. "Idiot."

He studies me for a moment. I can't read his expression. "Good luck, Wren. You're going to need it."

I turn to stomp down the hallway, but Ryan stops me with his question. "Hey, Wren. Remember that time we played truth or dare in your basement?"

I freeze. How could I forget? It was the night I thought my heart would explode from sheer joy. Then shatter from crushing disappointment. All at Ryan's hands.

"I remember." My voice is tight. "What about it?"

He pauses. For a moment I think he's going to apologize. Instead, he says, "I dared you to kiss me. You chickened out. You realize that you're going to have to do a lot more than kiss me while the world watches?"

"In your dreams, jerkoff." I wince. It sounded cooler in my head. As I walk away, he calls after me.

"Bye, Chirp. I'll be seeing you real soon."

I walk away. My heart pounds in my ears. This is going to be a disaster.

As I'm opening the door to the parking lot, Elena catches up with me. "Don't worry about Ryan." She sounds so calm. "He'll play along."

I bolt toward my car, desperate to escape. "Why didn't you tell him I'm just filling in? That I'm still part of the crew?"

Elena smiles. It's the kind of smile that holds *secrets*. "Because the audience isn't the only one we need to convince."

I'm speechless. This woman is a genius. A manipulative, brilliant genius. Or a psycho. I'm not sure which.

"Trust me, Wren." Her tone is confident. "This will be good for you."

"Thanks," I mumble. She squeezes my shoulder and then turns away, back toward the building.

I slide into my seat. I close the door but I don't start the engine. I just sit and stare at the steering wheel. I try to process everything.

See, Ryan is my tormentor. My *almost* bully. He's also the guy I've never gotten over. Thanks to Ryan being best friends with my brother, he's been a fixture in my life since I was still in braces and pigtails.

Ryan picks on me *relentlessly*. I've always suspected it's because he knows how I feel. But if that's true, his reaction to my never said out loud feelings is inappropriate. And *mean.*

I thought I was getting out in the world. I thought I was stretching my wings. Now I'm not so sure.

One thing is certain. I'm in *way* over my head.

Chapter Forty-Three

Thank you for reading The Accidental Honeymoon. If you loved this book, please consider leaving a review. It's the best way to let me know that you want me to write more books like this one!

I'm so excited for what's next. I know that if you liked this, you'll love Say Yes to the Nemesis... It's Ryan and Wren's story.

Forbidden love is very close to my heart... and I am very excited to be able to present this combination of some my favorite tropes: enemies to lovers, sports romance, brother's best friend, forced proximity, spicy romance, hockey player hero, sarcastic nerdy heroine, unrequited pining, reality TV romance, island destination, fiery banter, makeover transformation, workplace drama, and childhood rivals.

Their rivalry was legendary. Could one reality show rewrite their ending?

Ryan is a hotshot hockey player and Wren's big brother's best friend. He has always tormented her mercilessly, making shy, geeky Wren feel like she could never measure up to his effortless cool. She's loathed him for it... even while secretly nursing a pesky crush on him for years.

When Wren lands her dream job as an executive producer on a dating reality show, she's thrilled. But then disaster strikes. First, she's forced to fill in as one of the bachelorettes on the show. Second, the bachelor they're all competing for? None other than sexy, villainous Ryan.

The producers, delighted by their antagonistic chemistry, sweeten the deal with a big promotion if Wren plays their vapid TV game to win. Forced into close quarters and increasingly ridiculous dates, Wren grits her teeth and pretends to be in love with her worst enemy.

But no one warned her about the dates. The hand-holding. The roses. The hot and heavy make outs. The sneaking around to avoid cameras when the teasing becomes too much. Or the way Ryan looked at her like she was the most breathtaking woman he'd ever seen.

He's leaning into their fiery banter with what feels like genuine heat. But is it all for the cameras? Or could their adversarial relationship finally ignite into something real?

* * *

Here's a list of all the couples in this series!

The Accidental Honeymoon - Jay & Calla - Woke up married
Say Yes to the Nemesis - Ryan & Wren - Enemies to lovers, brother's best friend

About Vivian Wood

Vivian likes to write about troubled, deeply flawed alpha males and the fiery, kick-ass women who bring them to their knees.

Vivian's lasting motto in romance is a quote from a favorite song: "Soulmates never die."

Be sure to join her email list to keep up with all the awesome giveaways, author videos, ARC opportunities, and more!

Vivian's Works

Wildflower Lane
Small Town Rom Com
The Accidental Honeymoon
Say Yes to the Nemesis

Cape Simon
Small Town Romance
The Grumpy Boss Agreement
The Fake Fiancée Proposition
The Playboy Rival Arrangement

Sinfully Rich
Steamy Billionaire Romance
Sinful Fling
Sinful Enemy
Sinful Boss
Sinful Chance
Sinful Teacher

Billionaires Ever After
Steamy Bad Boy Romance
His Best Friend's Little Sister
Claiming Her Innocence
His Fiancé To Keep
His Lovely Virgin

Hush Hush Club
Forbidden Billionaire Romantic Suspense
Such A Good Girl
Such A Spoiled Brat

Married At Midnight
Forbidden Billionaire Romance
Deal With The Devil
Wed to the Devil
Vow to the Devil

Ruined Castle Trilogy
Forbidden Billionaire Romance
The Single Dad
The Nanny
The Caress

Broken Slipper Trilogy
Forbidden Billionaire Romance
The Patron
The Dancer
The Embrace
Possessive

Fifth Avenue Villains
Fifth Avenue Devil

Dirty Royals
Forbidden Royal Romance
Cruel Heir
Sinful Princess
Pretend Princess

King's Capture Duet
Dark Billionaire Romance
King's Capture
Queen's Sacrifice

Addiction Duet
Angsty Dark Romance
Addiction
Obsession

Other books
Wild Hearts

For more information....
vivian-wood.com
info@vivian-wood.com